ROYAL TEA SERVICE
TEA PRINCESS CHRONICLES BOOK 3
CASEY BLAIR

ROYAL TEA SERVICE
Tea Princess Chronicles: Book 3

Copyright © 2022 Casey Blair,
All rights reserved.

No part of this edition may be reproduced, distributed, transmitted, or used in any manner whatsoever without permission in writing from the author, except in the case of brief quotations in a book review. For permission requests, email Casey.L.Blair@gmail.com.

This book is a work of fiction. Names, characters, places, and events are either the product of the author's imagination or are used fictitiously. Any resemblance to actual persons, living or dead, events, or locales is entirely coincidental.

Cover design by Hampton Lamoureux of TS95 Studios, 2021.
Author photograph by Mariah Bush, 2013.

Ebook ISBN: 9798985110142.
Paperback ISBN: 9798985110159.

www.caseyblair.com

CHAPTER 1

I TRY NOT TO collapse onto the couch, exhausted to my core. I ignore my awareness that this is a losing battle: Deniel hasn't collapsed, and since I'm responsible for this, I don't get to either.

I drag myself towards his—our—kitchen. "I'm going to make some tea."

"That's the same tone you used reading the story to Yorani with the warrior charging grimly into battle," Deniel says, amusement in his tone, but not so much that it disguises his own weariness.

He follows me into the kitchen, and I stop and watch him in confusion.

"The neighbors brought us a pot of pre-cooked dinner to welcome you, remember?" Deniel asks. "And there's my mother's cake. I think we could both use some food before we run out of energy to eat it."

I had forgotten, but now I glance around the kitchen hopelessly. "Where?"

Moving into Risteri's grandmother's cottage had been easy: I'd had no possessions, so Risteri had set me up with the essentials until I had time to acquire more gradually on my own.

Moving in with Risteri had been a production, but I'd expected that: neither of us had any furniture or supplies to our names, so we'd had to effectively start over. With the political circumstances mandating our move, our community had turned out to help.

Today came as a surprise. Deniel's home was already set up, after all. But I was barely involved in helping Lorwyn move in, as preoccupied as I was with moving out, or in, myself.

In retrospect, perhaps I should have expected this, or forgive myself for not expecting it, because I've never moved in where another person already lived. I hadn't had to make the choices of who kept what, or how to make a space designed for one hold two instead, and make that space feel like it belonged to both of them. Us. It had felt like home before, but it had also felt like his, not mine, or ours.

We both agree that's what we want, but it's difficult to tell, in the mess of rearranging, if we are succeeding in any meaningful way.

"How is there still this much stuff everywhere?" I wonder. "We've been at this all day."

"It's a sign that you're settling in here, I think," Deniel answers. "You've begun to accumulate objects that reflect your priorities and that you're thus attached to."

"But so much? I haven't been here that long."

Deniel smiles faintly. "You're making up for lost time. Though if you continue to acquire things at this rate, we may have to move elsewhere."

I wince. "No. Perish the thought. I'm never moving again."

"Not even to the couch?"

Deniel reaches onto the top of cooler, back past where I can see, and pulls down a bag.

His smile grows at my perplexed expression.

"It's not my first time helping with a move," Deniel says. "I figured we wouldn't store anything there, since you're not tall enough to reach. So our dinner is safely findable."

"You are a perfect person," I say fervently, and he laughs.

In short order, we have cleared space on the low table in front of the couch by expediently setting more things that will need sorting on the ground. I know better than to relax into the couch, but before I can take a sip of tea Deniel plucks the cup out of my hand and replaces it with a soup spoon.

"Please eat first," he says. "You look like you're about to keel over."

I sigh. My body may need food, but my spirit needs tea. Still, I don't argue. At least not about the eating.

"You shouldn't have to be taking care of me right now," I say. "You've worked just as hard as I have."

Deniel pauses in reaching for his own food. "Amazing. Those are both completely nonsensical statements."

"Are they?" I don't mean it as a challenge—he appears to have made some connection I've completely missed.

I am too tired for this conversation, but that won't stop us from having it.

Deniel prudently eats a few spoonfuls of soup before answering. "Firstly, no one is making me take care of you. I am helping you because I want to and because I can, and you would do the same for me, so let's not backtrack into a conversation about obligation. We are partners. We help each other when we can. Right?"

I wince, nodding. He's right, and I am falling back on bad mental habits.

"Secondly, we are not in competition. The same work doesn't have to take the same amount out of each of us. We can have different levels of energy. It's silly to compare in that way, but since you've started, please allow me to note that your exhaustion is probably not only due to physical work, but also mental."

"Because of all the decisions," I murmur.

"Right. These kinds of everyday life decisions—they're things I've been doing for longer than you. It makes sense that they would be easier for me. And before you worry that will be an imbalance forever—"

"I'm already much further on this path than I was weeks ago, I know," I interrupt. "Thank you."

"You're welcome," Deniel says, bumping his leg into mine. I smile faintly at him, and we both settle into silence but for the slurping.

I bolt upright. "Where's Yorani?"

"Last I saw, investigating the pile of boxes outside with Talsu," Deniel says. "Cats and boxes are natural friends. Or enemies, I suppose, but they go together one way or another. I should warn you, we won't be able to get rid of all the boxes at once because Talsion will keep sitting in them."

"But they're not soft."

"I don't think that's the appeal. Though I do wonder how Yorani will react to them. She seems to find teapots comfortable enough."

I stop inhaling my soup and settle back with the cup of tea, gazing at the wreckage around us. "Maybe Lorwyn could make me into a cat. Then I'd be comfortable sitting anywhere here without having to do anything about the situation."

"She did permanently turn your hair green," Deniel says. "I'm sure cat is the next logical step. You and Talsu will look very cute sharing a box together."

"Apparently Talmeri hasn't ordered new Cataclysm ingredients for Lorwyn to experiment with since the tournament started, so Lorwyn's taking the opportunity to focus on magecraft, and body changes in particular. She says she'll get in touch with Ari once she's confident in what she can offer them."

"I don't mean to question her abilities," Deniel says gravely, "but I fear I must point out that body changes are not the same as species transformations."

"Sad but true." I sigh. "A life full of naps remains regrettably out of reach for me."

Deniel smiles, leaning back now with his cup of tea so our shoulders touch. "You'd be bored."

I shift so I can tuck myself more fluidly against his side, curving into him. Deniel obligingly slides an arm around me, and this time when I sip my tea, I can feel the warmth spreading through me.

The real perfection of a cup of tea is about feelings, after all. I should know that better than anyone.

Except perhaps another tea master.

Like the one I still need to arrange lessons with, because apparently I will never be done.

"At this point, I wonder if I could do with a little more boredom," I admit. "I was in such a rush to figure out how I can serve, and now... I'm being ungrateful. I have a path that matters and that I believe in."

"You've also been going nonstop, and you need to live, too," Deniel says.

I glance sideways at him, not turning completely. "Serving people will always be the most important thing I do with my life."

It's something we haven't talked about, that I simply took as self-evident, and now I wonder if it's a problem. I love Deniel, but if being with him kept me from being able to serve people, I wouldn't be able to do it. The very thought of having to choose—

Fortunately, I have no cause for concern on that front, as Deniel responds, "I'm aware, but I think it's also important to remember it's not the only thing in your life, nor should it be."

Ah. I close my eyes, relaxing again. "Yes. I can't serve well if I don't remember what it's like to live."

"That's true, but you also to deserve to live for your own sake, not just to make sure you're fit to serve others."

That makes me blink and sit up. Spirits, I have so much work to do—on myself, first and always.

I believe everyone is inherently valuable beyond their utility, but if I don't also believe the same of myself, how can I model that so others will believe it for themselves?

"Miyara?"

I set my cup down, brushing my bracelets for reassurance. "I'll be right back. I'm going to check on Yorani."

"Miyara."

"I don't disagree, Deniel. Just give me a minute?"

Deniel subsides, watching me carefully, as I step out into the front.

Yorani is toddling around, pushing a small box into position against a stack of boxes.

Once she's finished, she chirps, and Talsion regally climbs the staircase Yorani has created to sit on the top of the boxes.

Yorani crows and flaps up to join him there, and then they both stare at me expectantly.

My eyes blur a bit as I go to pet them both.

Deniel was right, as usual.

Especially after the events surrounding the tournament, if I don't want people to see Yorani as a tool to be used, but an autonomous being inherently deserving of respect, she has to have the freedom to build box forts with her feline best friend if she wants to.

Yorani is herself, but she is also my familiar, and this is not so different from what I need, too.

Which, I smile to myself, is not Talsion's need to imperiously look down on his work from above but Yorani's desire to build together with her friend.

"Here," Deniel says, coming up behind me. "Yorani, flap up for a moment?"

To my surprise, Yorani complies, as Deniel lifts Talsu with one hand and places a small woven blanket on top of the box with the other.

Cat and baby tea spirit settle back down together, looking somehow smugger.

"Where did that blanket come from?" I ask.

"I have no idea," Deniel says. "Or rather, I don't know where it was stored, but all the reorganization produced it somehow. I made that ages ago."

"You can weave, too? Oh, what am I saying, of course you can weave."

Deniel laughs, hugging me from behind. "I've always liked working with my hands. Before I settled into pottery, I tried all kinds of crafts. That was supposed to be a gift when my father's friend was having a baby, but I wasn't happy with how it turned out and begged Glynis' mom for scraps to try making a baby quilt instead." He settles his chin on top of my head.

"Always the perfectionist," I tease. "I bet it was your first quilt, too, and nevertheless worked fabulously."

I can feel him shrug. "I don't remember what it looked like now, but I must have been happier with it since I was willing to give it as a gift. And you're hardly one to talk."

"I am not the one who's an expert at anything involving their hands."

"What a thing to say, now of all times when I can't prove it," Deniel says softly into my ear.

I smile, suppressing a shiver. "Why, because we're both too tired for more physical activity?"

Then Deniel's hands slowly begin sliding up my sides, and I catch my breath.

I may be feeling a boost of vim.

"Because we're both outside, in full view—of neighbors and companions," he murmurs.

I am abruptly aware that Yorani and Talsion are both staring directly at us, and I turn in Deniel's arms, laughing into his shoulder.

"It would be wrong to scandalize an impressionable young tea spirit," Deniel manages with some solemnity. "Talsion, I'm afraid, is a hopeless case. Are you satisfied?"

That Yorani is safe and happy for the time being and I don't need to hover? Yes.

"Never, I fear," I say, but I tug him back into the house by the hand regardless. "And you agreed to give me a minute."

"I did," Deniel says. "One minute exactly."

I can't help but laugh. "I'm going to regret getting the best lawyer I know to tutor you, aren't I?"

"I hope not," he answers more seriously.

"I was kidding."

"I wasn't," he says. "I think this is a perfectionism thing again."

I should sit back down and take a break, but seeing the physical mess of our lives surrounding us is making me feel like a mess, so instead I start tidying again as we talk.

I'm tired, but I don't misunderstand him. "I don't think it's unreasonable for me to expect to have internalized more by now," I say. "Of course you're right. How long until I stop thinking of my own life as transactional, when I don't for anyone else?"

"Miyara, you haven't had time," Deniel says, joining me in the work. "How long have you thought of your purpose in life as existing to serve others?"

"As long as I can remember," I say, surprised. "That service to our fellow humans is service to the spirits is the foundation of our spiritual labor."

"And how long have you been preparing yourself to serve, and searching for the form that would take?"

Ah, that's where he's going with this. "And I've only been on this specific path for weeks, so it's natural that I haven't worked it out? That doesn't mean I shouldn't expect myself to figure it out."

"No," Deniel says gently, "but it does mean you have time. You don't have to do everything perfectly right away."

I carry a load to our rapidly filling trash box. "That, I'm not sure I agree with," I admit. "It still feels... precarious. Like I can't really settle, like it's only my constant movement that's holding this place together. First I thought my family would find me, and then there was Kustio's threat, and needing to become a tea master right away. And then of course my family did find me and try to take me back, and the tea mastery alone wasn't enough to protect me or anyone else. Saiyana has backed down, but what's next? What now? I somehow both can't believe there can be anything more and yet can't not believe it, either."

"You have time," Deniel repeats, and this his hands are steering me toward the pedestal.

The pedestal Thiano procured for me for an altar. It's one of the few pieces of furniture I moved in here. It's been updated since, combined with pieces from Deniel's prior altar. But it's mine: a physical space for me in our life together.

"I'm not saying what you've done up to now didn't matter—the opposite, actually," Deniel says. "I think you've won yourself a grace period to re-center and decide where you want to go. Take a breath."

I do.

Breath, for air.

Air that fills me inside; air that can blow in so many directions.

I want everything, and I want to be able to do it all at once. I want to serve people, I want to have friends and family, I want to be my whole self—

"I want to be with you," I say, turning to face Deniel.

He gestures around wryly. "We are making good progress on that being an always thing."

I grip his hands, silently, and his expression turns soft.

Our relationship, and exploring it, together, is a priority, and Deniel is right.

I have time. We have time. And I know what I want to do with it first.

I lean forward and kiss him.

His fingers tighten on mine, and I smile against his mouth.

"About those hands," I say, before I can over-think it.

Deniel laughs quietly—

And then there's a knock on the door.

We both freeze, staring at each other.

"It's probably a neighbor," Deniel says. "We don't have to answer if you don't want to set that expectation, but you might want to make a nice impression in case we need to borrow flour or something from next door."

He's talking about setting boundaries, and this makes sense, or it ought to.

Except it's like he's talking about another world when somehow I know, I know, that's not what's waiting outside.

"It's not a neighbor," I say lowly.

Deniel frowns, his head turning back toward the door.

As if in a trance, I am already gliding toward it, and Deniel follows at my back.

We have time, ha. I knew it, and I of all people should also know by now to trust my instincts. It's not habit telling me I can't rest, or at least not just that.

Still, when I open the door, I cannot quite believe what I'm seeing.

Two women stand there, conspicuously nondescript cloaks hiding their features and forms from view.

It is their relative height and positions, I think, that makes me sure of who has somehow come to be at my doorstep. I am so used to seeing them together from a distance, one falling into step just behind the other.

The porch is eerily silent.

"Yorani, Talsion, this is not a good time for pouncing," I say.

Yorani huffs a whorl of smoke in annoyance, shattering the stillness, and the figure in the back turns just slightly, her movement utterly controlled even in surprise, to glance at the baby dragon behind her.

"She was so still," the one in front says as Yorani alights on my shoulder. "I didn't realize. The spirit we've been hearing about? What a wonder."

That voice, so rarely addressed right at me, still dispels any doubts I didn't have.

"Crown Princess Iryasa; Princess Reyata." I bow to my two oldest sisters, almost angling how I've always bowed to them out of habit rather than as a tea master, and hear the barest sound of Deniel sucking in a breath behind me at my words. "What brings you to my home?"

CHAPTER 2

REYATA SHOULDERS FORWARD UNTIL Yorani puffs out another whorl of smoke. My second oldest sister halts, recognizing it for the warning my tea spirit intends.

Reyata is the general among the princesses, the one who excels in both combat and military strategy: sensitivity to threats is, I imagine, a necessary part of that.

"I don't want her out in the open," Reyata says. "Let's take this inside."

I grit my teeth against my instinctual twitch into motion, into doing whatever Istalam demands.

"The last sister who found me here also disrespected common courtesy and did her very best to remove me from my chosen path," I say evenly. "That you are uncomfortable having brought yourselves uninvited to my door is not my responsibility, your Highness."

Reyata stiffens, her piercing gaze fastening on me in an entirely different way. Now, for the first time in my life, she studies me as a threat.

I am happily surprised I feel no urge to squirm under her regard, though there is a degree of petty vindication. I am not sure she has ever truly noticed me before.

Iryasa holds up a hand, and we both focus on her.

"My apologies," she says in her lyrical voice as she bows slightly to me, causing Reyata to narrow her eyes. "I understand this is sudden, as circumstances prevented any warning. But I assure you removing you from your path is the last thing I want. In fact, it's the reason I'm here. May we come in, sister?"

I blink and almost laugh. I've spent so little time with these sisters and do not know them, but hearing Iryasa speak is like listening to my echo. What she is careful to say and how, what she takes responsibility for and what she does not, calling me sister when she wants something from me.

We grew up steeped in court manipulation.

"I must apologize in turn, as we are not prepared to receive you in any considerate fashion," I say, holding up a hand of my own before either can stop me. "To be blunt, I have spent the day moving furniture and possessions, the house is still a mess, and I am tired. If you are not able to contain your judgment on my current living situation, I will ask you to return another time."

Iryasa nods easily. "I can't say I'm not curious, but I will take that under advisement. I, too, am tired: it is a long journey from Miteran, as you must know. But this cannot wait."

I glance back at Deniel, only to find he has vanished. I extend my awareness past the immediate situation in front of me and realize he has been rapidly tidying while I delayed them at the front. I take that to mean he does not intend to object.

"Then please be welcome in my home."

They follow me inside, through the pottery shopfront.

"Saiyana didn't exaggerate your Deniel's talents," Iryasa observes. "This is stunning work."

Of course she's been in touch with Saiyana. How else would she have known where to find me?

Our grandmother's spies. But I am not sure what access a crown princess has to that network.

"Is that how Saiyana termed him, too?" I ask, not sure if, while I am pleased she recognizes Deniel's skill at pottery, I should be grateful or annoyed. My Deniel. On one hand, it indicates acknowledgement and acceptance of our understanding. But nor does he belong to me.

"No," Iryasa says. "That I inferred. Does it bother you?"

"That depends entirely on how you mean it," I say, glancing back at her as we enter the living room.

And then I blink.

"Your hair," I say inanely.

Iryasa has flicked back the hood of her cloak, and now she smiles. "It's amazing, how such a simple change affects how people see you. I'm sure you understand," she says, gesturing at my own emerald-colored hair.

"I thought being unrecognized would help me sneak out of the palace without fanfare, and this was enough."

"That's not what I mean," I say, and she nods.

Iryasa has, my entire life, looked like the model of Istal beauty, elegant with long, sleek hair.

Today, her hair is wavy.

Exactly like mine.

"We all bear some physical marker of our father's heritage, don't we? Reyata, his stocky build; Saiyana, the blue eyes that crop up in Velasar; Karisa, the height. And you and I both inherited his curls. I wonder what else we have in common?"

I wish we were only sisters, and I could take a question like that at face value as an attempt to connect. I wish I could talk to her about the fact that she has apparently disguised who she is even physically her entire life in order to fill a role: Istal's future, independent of influence.

But I recognize a starting negotiation tactic of finding common ground when I see one.

"A talent for secrecy and surprise, evidently," I say.

Her eyes brighten. "Did you hear that, Reyata?"

"Your talent is aspirational," Reyata says flatly. "You weren't kidding about the mess."

"I also wasn't kidding about the judgment and the leaving." Yorani's claws tighten in my shoulder.

"Peace, sister, I mean no offense. Do you have any idea how many tents I've slept in?"

"No," I say, "though I suppose the number is likely higher than I'd imagine."

Reyata snorts. "Indeed. It's a nice place. I take it you're Deniel?"

He's finished shoving some trash out of view and crossed the room to bow. "I am, your Highness. It is my honor to make your acquaintance."

"It's my honor to make the acquaintance of one of whom two of my sisters think so highly," Reyata says, bowing in turn. "Thank you for making a home for Miyara."

Reyata is not the diplomat among us, but I should never forget how sharp she is, even if she prefers to wield her words bluntly.

Deniel blinks and relaxes minutely. "That is both my honor and my pleasure, your Highness."

Reyata nods as if they've settled something. "While I'd value the opportunity to get to know you better, I will take this opportunity to see about arranging appropriate accommodations for us while you conduct your business."

This last is said with faint accusation that I think is directed at Iryasa—so Reyata doesn't entirely approve of whatever Iryasa's up to, but approves at least enough to help her sneak out rather than ensuring she's caught. Interesting.

Yorani watches them both carefully, silently.

"Forgive me, but I'm not sure anywhere in Sayorsen is currently prepared to host a guest of your statures," Deniel says. "Sayorsen has experienced some upheaval of late."

"The main concern is the magecraft protections," I say for Deniel's benefit. "That's why Reyata isn't worried about leaving Iryasa here."

"Saiyana did good work on your house," Reyata agrees. "If she hadn't told me about them here I wouldn't have known."

Deniel looks at me, startled. "Did you know?"

"I can't see their details—I'm nowhere near her level of magecraft—but I confess I assumed, once she came to town and knew I spent time here," I admit. "Do you mind?"

"I wish she had asked," Deniel says, "but otherwise, no."

"She probably set them up while she was still having her people spy on you, before you were introduced, and when she could count on me fighting her about everything," I explain.

Deniel rolls his eyes. "That doesn't actually change my position in the slightest."

Fair enough. "I'm surprised Saiyana doesn't have something set up for you, though?" I ask Iryasa.

Her expression doesn't flicker, which is a giveaway on its own.

Saiyana doesn't know Iryasa is here—or that she was planning on coming.

What is the crown princess here for?

"I see," I say smoothly, before anyone has a chance to fill the silence. "For tonight, you can probably stay where I used to: there's a private cottage on the Taresim estate that should suit, if Risteri's grandmother hasn't returned to town."

"Thanks for the tip," Reyata says, bowing. To Iryasa she says, "Don't make her feel forced to throw you out before I get back."

"Your faith in me is astounding," Iryasa says solemnly, and my heart aches to see these two pinnacles of my childhood, the sisters I never could reach, behaving like real sisters in truth, and letting me witness it.

Reyata adds to me, "Please try not to throw her out."

"I believe I can handle a princess for at least a little while," I say just as gravely.

Reyata smiles then, and it occurs to me I'm not sure I've ever seen an expression on her face that wasn't stoicism. "You really have come into your own, haven't you? I'm glad to see you well, sister. The hair's a nice touch."

I am not prepared for the flood of emotion that fills me there. Her approval, which I never would have expected, her easy use of the word 'sister', despite my choices—

But I don't have the opportunity, as Reyata wastes no more time, leaving the way she came.

Iryasa breaks the silence. "She always thinks I'm joking when I call her a breath of fresh air."

I shake my head slowly as if to clear it. "She is so very much herself, isn't she? I never knew."

At that, my sister sighs. "Yes. You know what the palace is like. I wonder sometimes if I'm the only one in Istalam who knows. But now I know you do, too."

"And that's only Istalam," I point out.

Iryasa looks at me sharply. "That is common knowledge?"

"Not as far as I'm aware. But if I figured it out, I assumed you must know."

"Loath as I am to interrupt Miyara when she's being mysterious," Deniel says, "your Highness, may I take your cloak?"

Iryasa and I both blink. But then as I duck my head in embarrassment, murmuring an apology, Iryasa's expression habitually defaults to smooth, calm, and collected.

It's the mask I learned to take off, that she probably never can. We glance at each other as Deniel hangs her cloak, and I know we're both noting it.

"Let me make some tea," I say. Yorani flaps off to the kitchen ahead of me, though rather than heading for the kettle she begins poking her head into boxes. "It is a long journey from Miteran, though I slept most of it. Backlash of a magecraft anchor. It looks like Deniel has managed to clear the table, if you'd like to sit."

Iryasa looks at me sidelong. "Will you perform the tea ceremony for me tonight?"

I smile and shake my head, already busying myself with the kettle. "I see you're related to Saiyana, too. Not tonight, no. It's not time for it."

"Am I not a sufficient judge of my own needs?" she asks.

"You of all people may well be," I allow. "But I am the best judge of my own services, and tonight there is too much in flux for you to receive what you need from me. It would be my honor—another time."

"Hmm." She doesn't sound offended, only contemplative. "May I ask what the story is behind this?"

She has, of course, singled out the altar.

"It's the result of an elaborate exchange of favors with a Nakrabi spy during the Kustio investigation," I say.

"It's more than that, I think."

"Yes," I agree. "It's my story. This is the one space in our new home that unequivocally comes from me."

"Ah. Stories, narratives. That is my work."

Yorani's head snaps up out of the box she was investigating, staring at Iryasa.

Yes, little one, I felt it too.

Whatever is coming, Iryasa will try to control the narrative. Although I don't know what she needs yet, one thing is certain:

I can't let her.

"Deniel, will you join us for tea?" Iryasa asks as she slides gracefully into one of the well-worn chairs.

Deniel glances at me. "Would you two prefer to speak privately?"

"No," I say. "I think whatever Iryasa is here for will involve you somehow, so I'd like you to listen so I don't end up repeating everything." I gauge my sister. "I believe Saiyana has told both her and Reyata that attempting to break us apart is a losing strategy."

At this, Iryasa relaxes utterly. "Oh, thank the spirits."

I tense in response. Making people aware of the extent of my ability to listen does not usually make them glad, let alone relieved.

She needs that ability for something.

"I see," Deniel says. "Who did Saiyana tell this to, exactly? I only wonder if I should prepare myself for less welcoming receptions with other members of Miyara's family who theoretically have no reason to visit her yet nevertheless appear suddenly."

"They do keep turning up, don't they?" I ask. "First Saiyana, now Reyata and Iryasa. Who's next?"

"Karisa, I hope," Iryasa says. "Though don't tell Reyata I told you that, please. She isn't aware of that part of the plan."

I go still, watching her.

All four—five, if I count myself—princesses of Istalam in one place, outside the protections of the palace?

"You are planning something, and you have a role in mind for me," I say matter-of-factly, bringing over the tea. Yorani hops up on the table but only curls up, watching all the while, like she knows something is up but is willing to let me handle it—for now. "You must know I have spent the last few weeks working to establish my independence."

"That's actually the main reason I'm here," Iryasa says. "I knew I could trust you wouldn't be working on behalf of anyone else."

Deniel had approached the table, but at this he pauses. "This does sound like a conversation for just you two," he says. "I don't want to be a distraction. If you don't mind, I'll continue working in the background."

"Here. Take this first." I hand him a cup of tea, grateful beyond words for his unspoken understanding of what I need: space and support, all at once.

Yorani, I realize, is doing the same, in her way. All of us are learning each other.

I kiss Deniel softly and smile. His cheeks are tinted pink, probably due to my sister's presence, but for once mine are not.

"You are only ever the best kind of distraction," I say. "Please feel free to chime in. You know I value your insight."

He smiles his perfect, crooked smile. "I do. And I appreciate your saying so in front of the crown princess, but I don't think you need to prove anything to her, at least where I'm concerned."

I look back at my sister just in time to see her studying us with a soft gaze.

Now I feel my cheeks turning pink. Deniel laughs gently, kisses me on the cheek, and then backs into the kitchen.

I sit slowly, my heart pounding with a sudden suspicion as I face my sister, and decide to try directness. "You told me the main reason you're here. What's the rest?"

Iryasa takes a sip of tea, a steadying gesture.

And a reminder for me that she in fact needs steadying: whatever she is here for, she is unsure. She has taken a number of risks to get here and whether they will be worthwhile depends on me.

"I have been thinking for some time about how to begin this, but I find I cannot gain the distance necessary to frame this dispassionately. How can I? But you are my audience, and given the background we share, and the actions you've taken, I hope I can count on you to understand when I say the role of a princess is not without unique struggles."

I sip my tea as well. "If you don't mind my saying, that is actually a remarkably dispassionate way to put it, but also so broad it's difficult to know to which aspect you refer. Perhaps a smidge of passion might not be amiss, considering your audience."

Iryasa studies the tea cup, rotating it in her hand. "I knew you would ask that, but it's harder than I thought to counteract years of habits, isn't it? It's incredible to me that you have been able to fit in here with no one realizing who you are."

I lean back in my seat. "I wouldn't say I have managed to fit in, precisely," I say. "I walk around in formal robes and speak in too high a register out of habit. I don't abide by the same hierarchies that go unspoken for anyone else. But I have managed to make people see this is as a consequence of who I am, rather than a signal. Or, to put it another way: they see these as not as general characteristics of a princess, but as unique characteristics of Miyara, which is, in fact, who I am. I have made a role that I am able to fit into."

"Whereas my role was made for me," Iryasa says. "There are expectations of a crown princess. I always knew where my path leads. But there are different ways to be a princess, and there are different ways to be queen. I fear the path I am on is one I fell into rather than one I shaped, and that it is not the correct path at all. It did not occur to me soon enough that perhaps there are different ways to be crown princess, too."

I swirl my tea, mulling that over, trying not to let this series of revelations from the sister who always seemed a perfect and untouchable rock me. But that's it: she thought this was the best way to serve, and so she filled that role.

"There are two key differences between a princess' path and that of the crown princess," I say. "The expectation of a future as a ruler, and responsibility for the succession." I meet her gaze directly. "Are we talking about only the former here?"

Iryasa's fingers tighten on her cup, just for an instant, but that's enough to make her wince. "No."

The sounds of cleanup in the background pause for a moment as Deniel takes that in with me.

"I admit I always assumed you and the queen had a plan," I say.

"I'm glad to hear that, but nothing could be further from the truth," Iryasa says, and it's like piercing this façade causes a dam to burst. "Our mother does not wish for me the situation that was done to her, but nor does she have a viable alternative. I think she would like to leave this choice in my hands, as there are, in many ways, so few choices I can make. But I have lived my life as her echo: I am the blank page for our people to project their hopes and fears onto, a representative of stability but not a person with desires."

Few choices. Hmm.

But I summarize, "If you can't be honest about who you are and what you want, how can you find someone to match you—or how will they know to find you."

She sighs, deflating. "Yes. That's it."

"Do you know who you are, beyond the role?"

"Beyond the influence of what others want for and from me, and how I've shaped and hidden parts of myself to fit?" Iryasa asks, a hint of tartness in her tone at my bold question; she is still crown princess, and I am still her little sister.

"To fit, and to survive," I agree softly, which appears to mollify her.

"Yes," she says. "I know who I am. Whether I can be that person in action as well as theory is less clear."

"It's also the only question that matters, in this case," I say. "If you can be open with your whole self with someone, I don't think you will be able to be the same kind of queen our mother has been. The two go hand in hand."

Iryasa swallows more tea. "I hope you are right," she says. "I hope there is a way forward through a seemingly impossible choice with no clear path for me to be both myself and serve meaningfully and that may require dramatic action. And so I came to the one person in my life who's faced something similar and come out the other side."

I blink, an array of emotions coursing through me.

That is one way to look at what I have done.

"I am honored and somewhat aghast by your faith in me," I finally manage.

In the background, Deniel muffles a laugh.

Iryasa's lips quirk. "It is enough to be able to speak about this openly with someone who can understand why I feel conflicted on this. I wish I could have been someone you could come to for counsel, before. I would like to become that person in the future."

"I would like that too," I say softly. "But we're not really speaking openly yet, are we? We are only beginning to know each other here. And there is a reason you are here now, suddenly, with no warning."

Iryasa's posture shifts—not less relaxed, in fact perhaps more relaxed, but into a mode familiar to me having watched her from afar. We are moving away from the personal, it seems.

Still, I am not prepared for what she says next.

"In looking into the barrier breaches that occurred during the tea tournament, Mage Ostario discovered that the barrier—or, more precisely, the Cataclysm—is expanding," Iryasa says.

My breath rushes out of me, and I can only stare until a whap from Yorani's tail brings me back to myself.

The barrier is all that defends Istalam from the chaos of the Cataclysm enveloping us all. It's all that defends the world. There's so little continent left already compared to what there once was. For it to be expanding further, again—I can scarcely compass the depth of disaster such news heralds.

If the Cataclysm continues expanding indefinitely, it will mean, in no uncertain terms, the end of the world.

"Indeed," Iryasa says, "you see why there is cause for concern."

"Obviously," I say, attempting to wrench my mind back away from the horror, to a conversation where the crown princess of a nation next in line to be devoured by chaos magic can sit here detached, and I realize that of course she has had time to process this information where I haven't. That pricks enough at my newfound independence I'm able to find my focus again. "In fact this is such catastrophic news I am confused as to why I wasn't told?"

I thought Saiyana and Ostario trusted me. No; I still believe they do. So why—?

"I am telling you now," Iryasa says, utterly unruffled.

"I am Sayorsen's tea master," I say. "Nowhere is more directly affected by the Cataclysm than this city. This is clearly information I must have in order to fulfill my role."

"And Sayorsen is part of Istalam," Iryasa says, tone deceptively mild. "Mage Ostario works for the crown, Miyara, which you know, and it is our purview to dispense knowledge or not when the time is right. That is now, as fast as I could travel here. Ostario reported through the appropriate channels."

Now I see. It's not that Ostario and Saiyana personally don't respect my position, but that Saiyana understands the crown's expectations and is defending Ostario from ending up on the wrong side of them. This is, in fact, Saiyana trusting that I can handle myself and my own business and leaving it to me to work this out for myself.

"You are treating me as though I am an agent or a governor serving Istalam," I say. "I am a tea master, Iryasa. The dynamic is not the same."

"Indeed not," she agrees readily. "The dynamic is, in fact, unprecedented. But you have carved a space here, on the border of the Cataclysm where so much centers, that is both unique and yet still Istalam. Now, when we have discovered treachery inside our borders from forces within and without, exacerbating the greatest threat our world has ever known, do you think this is the time to quibble over jurisdiction?"

"It clearly is," I say. "I discovered that treachery. The crown did not stop Kustio's machinations or uncover Velasar's plot. So it is baffling and outrageous that you will now step in to limit the scope of my ability to deal, in truth, with this space where so much centers, when Istalam has failed it. It is about responsibility, Iryasa. You are undermining a mantle I have taken on the burden of."

"I'm undermining your responsibility?" Iryasa sets her cup down firmly. "Hardly. But let's talk about responsibility, sister. You unilaterally negotiated a treaty with a sovereign people and relied on our relations to make it stick when you need it. Actions have consequences, Miyara. You cannot have Sayorsen be both part of Istalam yet independent when it's convenient for you. You can't assume we will sign your treaties and deal with the political fallout if we cannot also rely on you to hold your end."

"My end of bringing a traitorous plot to light and rescuing an entire sovereign people from it?" I ask pointedly.

"Do you think the Cataclysm was expanding before you arrived? No. The mages have careful records of these things. I am not innocent enough to believe recent events have no bearing on our current plight, and nor are you. You brought a terrible plot out into the open, and now I expect you to use your power here to resolve it."

Expect? I narrow my eyes. "I assume you have a specific role for me in mind?"

Iryasa leans forward. "I want you to serve in your chosen, made role as tea master of Sayorsen. Host a summit where we bring all the parties here, from Velasar to the Isle of Nakrab, and put an end to this."

I lean back in my chair.

That... is a lot to take in.

She's attempting to make me her instrument in saving the world. Because one thing is clear: Istalam's advising council would never have approved this idea. This is Iryasa, trying to strike out and shape her—our—future.

Together with her sisters.

"You brought Reyata here as your guard to meet me privately," I say. "Karisa?"

"I am relying on her character to find her own way out here," Iryasa says.

Karisa hates any appearance of being passed over and is not shy about making a scene. She'll follow, one way or another.

"So all the princesses will be in the same place at the same time," I say. "You think the opportunity that presents will goad whoever is moving against Istalam into revealing themselves."

"That is my theory, yes," Iryasa says. "It will be hard to draw the necessary players all the way out here, quickly, and we must. We don't know whether the Cataclysm's expansion will accelerate. If it does, all of us are doomed. If not tomorrow, then a hundred years from now. One way or another, we must settle this."

She is not wrong.

I'm also fairly sure she isn't intentionally working against me, which makes this more complicated and impossibly necessary.

"Speaking of responsibility," I say, "without the council's approval, are you certain Queen Ilmari will stand by your actions?"

Iryasa's gaze is clear. "Our mother has never been content, and her way did not prevent this," she says quietly. "She will let me choose the future."

I lay a hand on Yorani, and Iryasa tracks the motion. "Then it's important you understand, sister, that it's not just you. It's us."

"You will do it, then?" Iryasa asks, in the tone of one who never doubted—and does not acknowledge what I've just said.

So be it.

"I will host the summit, but I will do so on my own terms," I say. "The first of those is that any information pertaining to the Cataclysm comes to me without the crown as intermediary."

Iryasa narrows her eyes. "You have misunderstood the nature of this arrangement."

"Not in the slightest. You think it will be difficult to bring all the necessary players here? I disagree. But if they arrive and you have not met my terms, I promise you I have the ability to send them all out of Sayorsen and out of the sphere of your influence forever."

"You are threatening me?" Iryasa asks incredulously. "At a time this serious?"

"You threatened me first," I say calmly, as my heart threatens to pound out of my chest. "But I will also promise you that I can make this work. I will bring these people together and find the answers we all need to create a solution we can live with, and not just be content. That is what I do. You just have to trust me to do it my way. I will not bend on this point."

Because she's right: this is my responsibility, the Cataclysm's expansion and whether it can be stopped. Yet it must be stoppable, not just because it has re-started after decades of stasis, but because anything else means our doom.

All these years later, we don't know what happened to cause the Cataclysm. But it's past time we learn enough to keep it from happening again, and I will see it done.

Iryasa stares at me, her hand clenched on the cup of tea in front of us, as Yorani crawls up my arm to twine herself around my neck and return her gaze; a deliberate reminder of what I can do: the impossible.

"After all," I say, "isn't that why you're here?"

Iryasa closes her eyes and drinks the remainder of the tea in one gulp.

CHAPTER 3

AT A LOUD THUD from behind me, I turn past the altar and its flickering fire that indicates a change in the air to meet Deniel's gaze, and my chest constricts.

Air, that knows no boundaries, as I have plunged myself headlong into another world-shattering plot. And this time, on purpose.

A familiar knock shatters our reverie.

"That's Reyata," Iryasa and I both say at once before exchanging a glance. There are patterns we were trained to use as children, but it is also the particular weight, speed, and rhythm Reyata uses. I am not close to my eldest sisters, but as I could recognize them from just their stances at the door, I can recognize them in this, too.

My eyes narrow on Iryasa as it occurs to me she didn't apply one of those knocks when she arrived: intending to surprise me, and see how I took it.

A test. Court is always tests, and while in a way, that is familiar for me and easy to navigate, I am also newly grateful those sorts of tests need not intrude on every aspect of my life anymore. I have not incontrovertibly internalized them the way Iryasa evidently has—or has had to, as crown princess.

"I'll get it, then," Deniel says, leaving the room quickly. To get away from me and what I've just done, or to not keep a princess waiting? I hate that I'm even wondering.

"I've caused you trouble, haven't I?" Iryasa asks softly. "I'm sorry for it."

I nod. "You have, but not in the way I think you intended. I am not upset that you came to me."

Her eyes narrow slightly at that, the implication that she does not understand what she's done or why I've made the choices I have. "But you are upset," Iryasa says.

"And you did intend to cause me trouble," I say. "So."

She sighs. "So."

Reyata strides into the room, flicking back her hood. "So?"

"We have much to do all at once," I say. "We'd best begin tomorrow morning. You arranged lodging?"

"The cottage," Reyata confirms. "Saiyana will have something longer term for us tomorrow night, now that she's temporarily done swearing at me. I assume we will be taking her up on that?"

"We will," Iryasa confirms, rising. "Miyara has agreed to host the summit."

"With some specific terms," I say. "Namely, that any information regarding the state of the Cataclysm will come to me directly."

With only Deniel as witness to our agreement and Iryasa not overly pleased about those terms, it is worth being blunt to make my stance explicitly, abundantly clear.

"Oh?" Reyata asks slowly.

Iryasa's face tightens, but she nods in assent, a bare dip of her head.

Reyata's eyes narrow in turn, weighing me with her gaze. Reyata may not always agree with Iryasa, but she *will* always back her unquestioningly. The implication that I am not her partner in this will not speak well to her.

And now we are all watching each other carefully, which is a dreadful way to begin the task ahead.

Abruptly, I take a step toward Iryasa and as she freezes, unsure what I'm about, she allows me to take her hands in mine.

She somehow stills further.

Not just anyone is permitted to touch a princess. That she allows it, not knowing what I intend, means the world to me.

And that I would reach out to her on purpose—I know how that feels from the other side. I know how I react every time Deniel touches me with consideration, even when there is no romance involved, and so I know what that means for her.

I bow over our combined hands.

"We will be very busy, but it is my hope we will also be able to take this opportunity to talk as sisters," I say. "It would be my pleasure to invite you over, once our home is in considerably less disarray. Though you may have to risk my cooking."

"You cook?" Iryasa manages. Her tone is polite, but I feel the warmth in her hands.

"In a limited fashion," I demur. "If Deniel's schedule allows, he can supervise to make sure we don't burn the kitchen down. And also put my meager skills to shame."

"Miyara exaggerates the danger," Deniel puts in dryly. "But if my—I would be happy to speak with you more over less fraught conversation."

He aborts, but not fast enough I don't know what he was about to say: *If my presence wouldn't interfere.*

He did change direction midway, but I have made him doubt his place with me, on the day I've moved into his home.

Our home.

Spirits, what a mess.

I gently release Iryasa's hands and bow in turn to Reyata. "I would welcome the opportunity to speak more with you as well, sister. I'm not sure we've ever spent time together unsupervised, and I would know you better, if you would know me."

"You do know me," Reyata says simply. "And you know exactly how much time we've spent together unsupervised."

"Only after the age of three," I say with a smile. To Deniel I explain, "I once slipped my security bracers off and hid in a cupboard for some peace and quiet and then couldn't get out. Reyata's the one who found me."

How I got them off is a mystery no one was ever able to explain; at that age, I shouldn't have been able to remove them on purpose, and after that incident I never did again.

"I should have suspected you of quiet trouble as a child," Deniel says lightly. "I assume you chose your cupboards with more care after that?"

"In a way," I say, relieved he's at least willing to tease me for the moment. "Reyata practiced with me how to work the latch from the inside and also showed me some... less dramatic hiding places for more frequent use, so people would have fewer opportunities to search for the truly hidden ones."

She also made a fuss and got my entire bodyguard staff changed, which I didn't figure out until later. To her mind, if the way they were doing their jobs made me feel so uncomfortable I had to hide from them, they weren't the right guards for me.

Remembering that—that Reyata understood enough right away to know I was ill-suited to court and make accommodations to help me survive it—I realize meeting her eyes now that she already knows me, too.

"And now I've found you," Reyata says.

I nod. "And I'm not hiding."

Her expression relaxes, and she nods in return, now with the understanding that my earlier clarification wasn't a challenge, but a statement of intent. At court that kind of bluntness is uncommon, but I will deal with her honestly.

"Come, let's stop intruding and get you situated," Reyata says to Iryasa.

"I'll meet you at the cottage tomorrow morning," I say as I walk them to the door. "Sleep well."

Iryasa dons her cloak; we bow; they take their leave with little further ado. They are all at once gone as suddenly as they arrived.

The silence rings.

"Well," I say, resisting the urge to clench my hands into fists to have something to do with my hands.

"Well indeed," Deniel says next to me.

"Are you mad at me?" I blurt, turning to him quickly.

Deniel sighs, rubbing a hand through his hair. "Maybe a little."

My chest tightens. I was afraid of that.

Maybe I'm not so far from the court games I was raised to after all, if I can fall into them so easily and out of sync with the person who should be my partner.

"Should I go?" I ask, my voice coming out somewhere between a squeak and a whisper.

"What?" Deniel glances up at me, startled. "Miyara. Of course not."

"But—"

"Miyara."

"Why are you saying this like it's so obvious and I'm silly for not understanding?" I flail my hands as if to encompass the mess I've made of his home. "I don't know what I'm doing!"

Deniel catches my hands in his, and I go just as still as Iryasa did.

"Yes, you do," Deniel says calmly, a hint of exasperation in his tone. "And give me some credit for knowing you. You're thinking you need to do this in your capacity as tea master of Sayorsen to establish both a relationship and clear boundaries with the crown princess from the outset of your position, right? Then she'll know what you're capable of and what she can expect from you, so in the future—once this danger has passed, and for tonight let's assume it can because I think we're both too tired to process the alternative—you'll be free to live your life on terms you're comfortable with. Or am I wrong?"

Oh.

I shake my head mutely. He has it exactly.

Including that I am not currently capable of processing that it is possible the world will end if I can't stop it.

Deniel sighs. "I think we need to sit down again."

I feel too jittery to sit again, like the aftermath of navigating the sudden demands of my sisters and this news is just now landing. But then all at once I remember how tired I was before they even arrived and realize the adrenaline is likely crashing. I'm shaking because my knees are, in fairly short order, not going to hold me.

"I should make more tea," I say as Deniel leads me to the sofa holding one hand.

"I think you have done more than enough with tea tonight," he says. "Don't forget I just watched you manage the crown princess."

"That's only because it was opening moves with her," I say wearily, sinking down into the sofa, drawing my knees up and tucking my feet under me so I can curl into a ball resting my head on my knees. "That's why I had to talk to Reyata, so Iryasa would know I was serious. But she's going to think she can maneuver me into a place more advantageous to her."

"Not realizing that the most advantageous place is where you are." Deniel nods, sitting next to me and facing me. "I get it, Miyara. I don't think I even disagree with your decision, but I don't have to like how that played out, either. She waltzed in and demanded your time, and you let her."

"What else should I have done?" I ask, squeezing my eyes shut like I am squeezed between impossible choices, again and always.

"I don't know," Deniel says. "And what I think doesn't matter—"

My head snaps up. "Of course it does."

"No, it doesn't, because you have to decide how you want to move forward," Deniel says. "I was in the room. You knew I was listening. And you didn't stop at any point to ask me whether I thought this was a good idea, did you? Even once you realized I wasn't happy?"

Horror dawns as I stare at him. I had told him to feel free to chime in, but that isn't the same as actively making space for his opinion or soliciting it.

"Exactly," Deniel says. "You're going to make your own choices without me. So you have to decide what you can live with."

And what he can live with. What *we* can live with. Because it isn't fair for me to continually careen into disastrous situations that will cascade onto him, as he helps care for me or helps me with my work at the cost of his own. Part of being a partner means I have to look out for myself.

"I'm sorry," I say quietly.

He leans forward, bumping his forehead against mine. "I know. I still love you, Miyara."

I inhale sharply, then tumble forward into him, wrapping my arms around him.

"It's my own fault," Deniel says, his voice muffled against my hair. "Your propensity for taking on the entire world at once is part of you. I just wish you could ever rest."

I will have to find a way. I'm not sure I can stop taking on the world, as he puts it, because I don't truly want to. But I need to find a way to not burn myself, and him, up in the process.

Something bangs into my back.

And her.

Another bang.

"Evidently a certain baby dragon of our acquaintance believes it's time for bed," Deniel says.

"She can go on without us," I mumble into his chest.

Deniel laughs, brushing a kiss against my temple, and I am all at once very nearly enraged that I have once again been confronted with a situation I can't possibly avoid that will draw me away from his arms. But only nearly, because I can't quite work up the energy for a proper rage. It's all nebulous and distant now that Iryasa and Reyata are not standing in my home.

My home.

My first night with Deniel.

Interrupted; aborted; made fraught between us.

Another bump.

"Miyara," Deniel says, and I disentangle myself. I don't want to chain him to me. He deserves so much better than I can give him in my current state.

Deniel starts to lead me upstairs, but I shake my head and gesture for him to precede me.

Once he's gone up, I drag myself to my feet to clean up after the tea I made for Iryasa. Even crossing the space, it's clear what kind of minor miracle Deniel worked tidying—making our home into more of a home while still listening and paying attention to support me, bringing order into our lives while I brought more chaos.

I dump the remaining tea; wash the cups. Deniel wouldn't object to doing these dishes too, I know. But I have to do my part, and it starts here.

Yorani lands on my shoulder, nuzzling my neck as I somehow manage to finish this one thing.

This *one*. I am in so much trouble.

On my way out of the kitchen, Yorani still with me, I bow at the altar, staring at the flickering flame there.

Air may know no boundaries on its own, but I can create them for myself. Without the containment becoming so stifling I can't breathe.

I have no idea how, only that I must.

Yorani bumps my neck again, and I pet her absently, tearing myself away from the altar.

Given that I can barely stand of my own accord, it's not the time for spiritual reflection. The spirits deserve my best effort, and I don't have it in me now.

I'd better have it in me tomorrow.

I had worried—and, in a way, hoped—that our first night in our home, officially living together, would be awkward. Bumping into each other as we bustle around, figuring out where to focus our attention while changing clothes; the moments that make me turn red and smile to think on them later.

But not this kind of awkward.

My shoulders tense as I put Yorani's bedtime socks on, while Deniel moves carefully around me like he doesn't know which way I will turn. I could blame tiredness for how stilted my movements are, but the truth is I just don't know what's safe to do—where are the boundaries with us, now? What have I taken too much for granted? If I am too careful, will I fall back into hiding who I am from him, and will I then lose myself?

Then warmth envelops me from behind.

Deniel has covered me with both a blanket and his arms, hugging me fiercely.

"I'm sorry," I whisper. "I'm too tired to think."

"I think you're too tired *not* to think," Deniel murmurs into my ear, which is the spirits' own truth. "I love you, Miyara. We'll figure it out."

For once, those three words don't fill me to bursting with feeling. I feel shriveled. "You mean me."

"No—"

"No, you were right," I interrupt him.

He spins me to face him, interrupting me in turn. "No, you've misunderstood me."

That shocks me quiet.

"We're partners, right?" Deniel asks. "This is your work, but that doesn't mean I'm not here for you. I meant I don't get to decide what your boundaries are—how you approach your work or what you're okay with. I may not agree with every choice you make, but I will always support *you*."

My eyes are burning. I spend so much time crying around this perfect man.

"Am I distinct from my choices, though?" I ask. "Actions define who we are."

"And were you worthless before you left the palace?" Deniel asks me.

I'm silent once again, reeling at that.

I stand there in his arms for a long time while Deniel waits for me.

The answer, I think, is both yes and no.

After a while, I finally squeeze out, "Nothing important is ever easy, is it?"

"I'm not sure about that," Deniel says, walking me back with him, still wrapped in his arms, all the way to the bed. "My feelings for you have always been perfectly clear."

We bump into the side and fall over, and he gently rolls me, still cocooned in the blanket, over to my side of the bed while I laugh.

"Smooth *and* wise," I murmur as Yorani lands on my feet and plants there, forcing me to hold still for her comfort.

"There's one thing earlier that I don't think I understood," Deniel says, getting into the bed himself.

"Oh?"

"The worry about the succession," Deniel says. "Surely that's been a concern before, right? I see that her Highness intends to use the immediate political situation to establish the kind of ruler she means to be, but why has who she marries suddenly become so urgent, too? I know she's older than you, but not so much she can't still have children for more years—"

"Oh." I yawn. Despite everything, somehow I am already slipping into sleep.

I am, after all, at home with Deniel.

"It's Reyata," I explain.

Deniel pauses. "Come again?"

I try to dredge up coherence. "The Velasari have been working against Istalam inside our own borders."

"I'm aware."

"And our father, Cordán the Consort, is Velasari," I say. "My parents' respective political aims have always taken precedence over their personal relationship; they do not have trust between them. So at this rate relations between Istalam and Velasar are likely to collapse badly."

"I'm missing where Reyata fits into this."

"It's my understanding that she and General Braisa of Velasar are in love," I say, "which is information that obviously doesn't leave this room."

"Oh," Deniel says, as surprised as I've ever heard him. "*Oh*. Obviously. None of you ever do anything the easy way, do you?"

"Told you," I mumble, relaxing.

"But—they've waited a long time to do anything about it, haven't they? So why—"

"Because Iryasa's marriage is more politically important, so it has to be sorted out first," I say. "If Iryasa has to marry a Velasari to try to restore relations between our kingdoms, Reyata might not be able to also, lest Velasar be seen to have too much influence. And Iryasa doesn't want a marriage like our parents'. So: she has to find a match that will be more advantageous politically *and* suit her personally, and she has to do it before relations with Velasar fall apart completely and become the priority, which they are currently rushing toward. That's the sudden urgency."

Deniel is silent for a minute, processing. I've almost fallen asleep when he says, "You don't sound troubled about this at all, which I'm guessing means you already have an idea of who to introduce the crown princess to. Who do you have in mind?"

I smile, slipping into sleep. "It's a surprise."

CHAPTER 4

WHEN I AWAKE THE next morning, Deniel is already gone.

Disappointment fills me. It's not as though we had anything particular planned, and yet I realize now I hoped we would both be here upon waking, jointly starting our first day of living together. While I didn't think he had any reason to be up so early today, it's also true we did not have much opportunity to discuss it yesterday—and yet he was rightfully unhappy when I didn't consider him in making my plans.

There will be other mornings to wake up together. We have all of them, don't we?

Except this one, which is lost to us.

I press my hands to my eyes for a long moment and then heave myself out of bed, Yorani squawking at the sudden movement.

No sense lingering when Deniel isn't here, and I have work to be about elsewhere.

How well we are able to respond to challenges that arise during the summit will depend on the quality and thoroughness of the preparation I do in advance. The delegates may not be here yet, but the real work at the heart of my task begins now.

It's time to save the world. I will try not to think I'm making an inauspicious beginning of it.

I arrive at the old cottage with Yorani curled around my neck, napping. She wasn't ready to begin our task, either; I couldn't convince her we should take off her sleeping socks to go out.

It's odd to be here. In a way it still feels like mine, even though it never really was at all. But it's a place that was a welcome and a refuge, for a little while. Until everything went sideways.

I'm beginning to wonder if everything is always going sideways; if that isn't simply life. Or at least mine.

When I knock, it's Iryasa who opens the door, a cautiously hopeful glint in her eye.

I smile. "How does it feel to open a door for yourself?"

"Strangely unnerving and empowering both," she says, stepping back to welcome me inside. "I'm not entirely sure what I'd have done if it wasn't you on the other side of the door."

I wish I could say, *open it*, as if the only people she could expect are messengers and people without ulterior motives. But that will never be her reality.

"I hope I am not too much a letdown from the potential for excitement," I say instead, and then pause. "Do I smell—?"

"Gaellani sweet bean pastries," Iryasa confirms with a small smile of her own. "I see this was just from him, then."

I understand her meaning instantly. "Deniel sent you breakfast?"

"Us, rather," Iryasa says. "Reyata has already had hers and gone, but there's one for you, too. I'll send him a gratitude message later—it would be tempting fate for Reyata and me to go visibly among the public, but our cloaks are anything but subtle. I wasn't sure how we were going to get food today."

My chest tightens. Deniel did think about me this morning at all, then. That's something, though it's still not thinking of me specially or talking to me about what I want from him.

Because now I realize I had also hoped to take my sisters to the Gaellani courtyard for the first time while they were anonymous, and that was a foolish notion. Of course the crown princess of Istalam will be recognized where I, who spent my adolescence in the shadows, would not. Until Saiyana and Reyata have arranged protection for Iryasa to their satisfaction, she cannot be publicly visible.

Perhaps it's for the best. It would be cruel to offer Iryasa a taste of anonymity she could never again experience. We cannot ever simply be two sisters; she, at least, must always be a princess, too.

Not that, currently, the demands on me are so substantially different.

"Saiyana would have taken pity on you eventually, but I have a plan for lunch," I say, taking my own pastry. "In the meantime, grab your cloak. We have meetings to be about."

Iryasa arches her brows but complies. "This won't be too conspicuous for clandestine meetings?"

"It will be perfect," I say with a smile. "Though I can't imagine it will matter."

Iryasa considers that but ultimately doesn't ask, content for the moment to let me guide her into a new act, and we head out into the morning light.

~

The streets are bustling, and Iryasa watches it all with avid curiosity. Not wide-eyed, though, like I had at first—and still do, sometimes.

"You've snuck into town in Miteran?" I surmise.

"Some," she agrees easily. "Though it's not as though I can interact with people. There have been plenty of official visits, of course. But you must have had an interesting time when you first arrived."

"My first attempt to bathe was an exercise in confusion," I say, and Iryasa laughs. "My first attempt to do my hair was worse."

"And yet instead of making it easier, you made it different," she says.

The green. "I had help," I say. "I needed... different. How long have you been straightening your hair?"

"As long as I can remember," Iryasa says, her smile fading. "Our father was never to know."

That the crown princess bore any part of him. I hate what politics has done to our parents, and to us.

"You can't straighten it yourself?" I ask.

"I have a spell for it now, of course," Iryasa says. "I will use it again when I am publicly supposed to be here. But for now..."

For now, she will seize this small measure of anonymity. My chest tightens, and I abruptly tow her over to a stall.

"Miyara—" she hisses, and I ignore her, tugging her along behind me.

"Somehow I've never tried a tea egg before," I say to the surprised vendor, who clearly recognizes me. "That seems unnatural, doesn't it?"

"Extremely, tea master," the vendor says, relaxing with a smile. Nearby others have started whispering as they watch. "Happy to help correct that. How about two for each of you?"

"An extra for the tea spirit too please," I say, passing my purse to my sister, who has frozen, her head ducked to keep her face invisible.

"How much are they?"

He names the sum, and I ask Iryasa to count out the money and hand it to him.

"These are boiled in a few different kinds of tea today," the vendor tells me. "What's your fancy?"

I look at Iryasa. "How about you choose?"

She pauses in her careful consideration of coins she's rarely had occasion to hold. "I'm sure I'll like whatever he recommends," she says quietly.

I narrow my eyes. "I'm sure you will. Why don't you choose anyway?"

Iryasa's gaze flicks to mine, some combination of fear and annoyance there.

I know I've pressed her. But I also remember not knowing what my preferences are—and if she's going to be the kind of queen I think she means to be, it's not enough to be polite and know her own mind privately. She has to be willing to act on it.

"This one," Iryasa says, pointing at the egg nearest her.

The vendor clearly realizes something is going on, but he covers. "An excellent choice! Those are my favorite as well. A nice mild flavor to ease you into the day."

"Do you have anything with a little more spice to it?" I ask. "I fear I may have the sort of day ahead of me that could benefit from a kick to get me started."

"How much of a kick?"

"A strong black tea sort of kick rather than a Nakrabi death pepper sort."

He laughs. "I should hope the day isn't dire enough for that! How about some cinnamon and clove?"

"Perfect. Let's do that one for Yorani to try, too."

In due course, we're on our way with a small bag of eggs.

"That was reckless and unnecessary," Iryasa says.

"It was a calculated risk and completely innocuous," I counter. "You confirmed yourself you've been out among Miteran without being recognized. And now you've ordered and paid for food from a street vendor in an unfamiliar city. Though you have bad habits to break."

She doesn't pretend not to understand. "Diplomacy combined with decisiveness is extremely useful."

"I'm a tea master, and I'm aware of that," I say. "But you don't always have to make decisions without gathering information. And you're allowed to want things for yourself."

Her mouth twists. "Am I?"

"If you're not, you're not going to be able to have a satisfying romance," I tell her seriously. "Here. Trade eggs with me."

"What if I don't want to?" she asks archly.

"Then you don't have to," I say. "But if it turns out you're more prideful than curious, I'm going to actually worry about our chances."

Iryasa glares at me for a moment before abruptly laughing and trading our second eggs. "This is truly going to be an adventure with you, isn't it? I wish we could have been like this at the palace together."

"So do I," I say honestly, relieved I've read her correctly, before trying her egg. As I expected I prefer the milder green tea flavor she chose, and as she takes a bite of the spicier one her eyes light up. "Maybe someday we can be."

Yorani abruptly snaps her neck out and gobbles the remaining egg in one gulp, then hisses out smoke in satisfaction.

"I'll think on it," Iryasa tells me, which is as much as I can hope for—for now. "Now, will you tell me where we are headed?"

We're already midway through the Central Market, so I'm not at all surprised to hear a sharp voice say, "Right this way."

"He's literally correct," I confirm, in case she thought that voice belonged to just any vendor prepared to hawk their wares and not a crafty old Nakrabi spy.

Yorani zips off my shoulder to fly circles around Thiano's head.

"That must have been some egg," he says to her gruffly, valiantly keeping his amusement off his face. "I guess you are powered by tea after all."

"She's powered by her connections to other people, too, and she's happy to see you," I say. "Clearly."

Thiano snorts. "Flattery will get you nowhere with me."

"Which is why I save it all for Talmeri," I say smoothly, and Thiano lets out a crack of laughter at last.

"A much better use of your time," he agrees. "I'm glad to see time has agreed with this one, too."

My smile this time is earnest, as I ignore the weight of Iryasa's focus behind me. "Thank you. So am I. May I steal a few minutes of your time this morning?"

"Here we are," Thiano says, leaning back and not moving.

I roll my eyes. "Yorani, have we talked about blowing smoke at people who pretend to be dense?"

"She likes me too much," Thiano says smugly. "You think you have anything to say to me that can't be said outside?"

"Certainly not," I say, "but I have information I can only show you inside."

"Miyara. You know I know—"

"*Do* you, though?" I interrupt pointedly, and his eyes narrow.

This is the man who set up elaborate tests for me to demonstrate who I was to him. He can't possibly know who Iryasa is from only careful words.

"Fine," Thiano says abruptly. "Yorani, you breathe fire at anyone who comes near my table while I'm gone, you hear?"

The tea spirit chirps agreeably, to my surprise. I pause.

"Can you be separated from her, for this?" Thiano asks me. Challenges me, because of course he does.

Yorani's not worried, but I am. Things are afoot, and so much could go wrong at any moment. But when will that not be true?

Yorani, too, is waiting, watching me.

"Smoke only please," I say to her. "Unless you're in danger, in which case fire. And yell to let me know, please?"

Yorani huffs out a plume of smoke and squawks quietly, which I take as agreement. Then she plants her sleeping socks in the middle of Thiano's table, facing out at the street.

"What are you going to do if she decides those are her wares?" I ask Thiano.

"I'm sure we can work something out." He smiles tightly at me. "Follow me."

And I do, against my better judgment, leaving Yorani behind me, and Iryasa trails us inside.

When the door has closed behind her, I whirl on Thiano. "What was that for?"

"I see your renounced family is more important to you than your found one," he says.

That hit lands, and I glare at him. "You think I'm not giving her enough credit."

"Not enough, too much..." Thiano waves his hand this way and that, the latter clearly indicating not Yorani, but Iryasa. "Who can say?"

"You must be Thiano." Iryasa steps out from behind me. "Your reputation precedes you."

"Does it?" Thiano asks. "And what reputation is that?"

"That you knowing everything but help no one without a price," Iryasa answers coolly, lowering her hood.

Thiano smiles sardonically. "Then you have heard correctly, your Highness."

I snort. "And you say flattery goes nowhere with you."

"Certainly not from you," Thiano says, "though perhaps I'll make an exception for the crown princess."

"Don't," I say seriously. "Please."

They both frown at me. Iryasa, presumably wondering why I'm undercutting her to attempt to deal with him on her terms, and Thiano why I believe he should treat her differently than another politician.

"We are about to make things around here even more exciting," I tell Thiano, "and before we move further, I wish for your counsel."

"Oh?" he asks.

With one last look at me, Iryasa seizes the reins of her story again with a different approach. "You know what has been going on in Sayorsen with the Cataclysm."

"Hard to miss, your Highness," Thiano says, which I assume is at least in part to annoy me, since I clearly did miss pieces.

"And you know the princesses of Istalam are here in Sayorsen."

"Are they?" Thiano asks, which tells me he knows perfectly well we still haven't met up with Karisa. She may be here, but if so she's saving up for a dramatic presentation.

"Then I assume you can figure out for yourself why."

"I surely can, your Highness," Thiano agrees. "Though of course you're not confident the presence of all the princesses will be enough to lure Nakrab into your scheme, even if it brings Velasar. You want me to send a message to help tempt them."

That gives Iryasa pause, because she's not stupid, and she recognizes the trap.

"Not exactly," I cover.

"Oh no?" Thiano challenges.

Iryasa narrows her eyes and then abruptly says, "Yes, exactly. If not the message itself, then confirmation that it is valid. Do you think I can't afford your price?"

Thiano chuckles. "You can't even conceive of it, princess. Why are you here?"

"Because my sister believes you can be useful in saving us all," Iryasa says. "Is she wrong?"

"Yes," Thiano says frankly.

"Let me rephrase," I say, irritated with them both. "Iryasa is here because she trusted me enough to follow my lead, and this is where I brought her. And I brought her here because the details of our plan are still not finalized, and it would be stupid in the extreme not to solicit opinions from the one person in this city who knows the Isle of Nakrab better than any of us and whose opinions on every subject abound."

"And if I don't choose to offer them?" Thiano asks.

"Then we proceed less informed," I say. "Obviously. But we do proceed with or without your opinions."

Thiano looks at Iryasa. "Well, princess? Is she right? Will you act on no information, to push other people into whatever plans you desire?"

Iryasa regards him for a long moment while I hold my breath, not knowing how, in fact, she will play this—but however she does will change everything. I wonder if she recognizes the moment this is.

"My preferred plan is already moot," Iryasa says finally. "Miyara will not let herself be easily led, so I must work with her or against her. I don't wish for the latter, and so I am here, attempting the former. Without sufficient information, acting." She grimaces. "I suppose I must hope I improve with practice."

Thiano regards her keenly. "If I could give you any information, what would you have it be?"

Iryasa's chin comes up, insulted by the suggestion she should just lay her plans on the table for him. "You disrespect me."

"You're not my princess." *And I'm not your spy*, he doesn't need to add.

"What do *you* want from *me*?" Iryasa demands.

"Miyara thinks you have hidden depths I'm unaware of," Thiano says immediately. "I want to know if she's deluding herself."

Iryasa freezes.

Then lets out a slow breath.

"Ah," she says quietly. "Now I see."

"And will you now show me a different side you think I wish to see, your Highness?" Thiano asks sarcastically.

"No," Iryasa says. "I will show you the side of myself I don't wish to display. Which is that I am out of my depth and untried, when the fate of the world may depend on how I choose to move, and I can't even get you to take me seriously." She glances at me. "You think I am too much a princess and too little a person, when the fact is I can't separate the one from the other. I do not have that luxury."

"No," I say softly. "I think you don't know how to integrate them together, by design. But I think you must. The people who can't or won't respect your title must nevertheless take you seriously if we are to succeed."

She stares. "This is what you brought me to learn in front of a spy?"

"I brought you to ask him pointed questions so we could plan our strategy," I say.

"Don't believe her, your Highness," Thiano tells Iryasa. "Miyara can't ever do only one thing at a time."

"Oh, well if *that* isn't a teapot calling a kettle—"

"What does Nakrab want?" Iryasa interrupts. "What will tempt them to the summit we mean to hold?"

"Wrong question," Thiano grunts.

Iryasa narrows her eyes, then relaxes. "Ah. I see. Thank you. What does Nakrab *need*?"

"Magic," I murmur.

Thiano considers me. "You answered the first question, not the second."

Nakrab wants our magic. I know that, even if I don't know why; I know they're stealing it. But if that's not what they need, then—

"*Our* magic?" I blurt. "This, from the people who maintain they don't need anything from us?"

"They must maintain that," Thiano says. "To do otherwise would acknowledge what they cannot and still be who they are." He glances at Iryasa. "That was for you."

"Thank you," she says dryly. "I caught it. But to the matter at hand, that sounds like it will be less useful to tempt than to threaten."

"Aggressive trade sanctions," I agree.

"No magical items leave our borders, and foreign travel inside Istalam will be suspended outside the summit." Iryasa tests the idea out loud. "If Nakrab wants access to the magic of the Cataclysm, they will be forced to come to negotiate. Will that be sufficient?"

"Can you make it happen, your Highness?" Thiano asks. "You are, after all, untried. There will be objections. Will you evict the Nakrabi already here? Do you have the power to declare war if a Nakrabi ship sails into your harbor?"

"I can do whatever I must," Iryasa says coolly. "If you understand only one piece about what it means to be crown princess, let it be that. Nothing else is an option."

"Your mother the queen would not make this choice," Thiano notes.

"I will make my own choices," Iryasa says.

"Right, sure, I understand the point of this exercise, but how do you expect others to follow you?"

"Happily, a tea master will call this summit to order," I say. "I will handle any evictions necessary, too."

"A clearly partial tea master, if you're planning to summon everyone to the farthest and most dangerous spot in Istalam and expect them to travel here," Thiano points out. "It's a power move in Istalam's favor."

"And Sayorsen is where the transgressions have taken place," I say. "The choice is valid, and the tea masters will back me if it comes to that. Nakrab may not come to avoid being cut off from the biggest source of magic in the world, but they will to make sure they have agents in place if we demonstrate we might actually make good on that threat in the future. Iryasa's authority doesn't need to be unassailable before they get here."

"The act of their coming will help build it," Iryasa says. "Clever."

"You can still undercut it," Thiano warns. "If you're going to do this, princesses, you need to understand that the leadership of the Isle of Nakrab has no interest in you."

To Iryasa I explain, lest she get the wrong idea, "He calls me 'tea princess'."

"I wasn't going to question the title," Iryasa says, and my gaze snaps up to her face—and so does Thiano's. "You mean we cannot induce them to see us as fellow people."

"Exactly so," Thiano says. "That's where your authority will have to come in, princess, to back up Miyara's. Make sure you're prepared to exercise it."

He's so sure we can't find common ground with them, even after knowing what I can do? *That* is interesting.

Troubling, too, and I think I begin to see the shape of why Thiano is here, and not in Nakrab. But clearly there is a large gap I do not yet understand.

Iryasa looks thoughtful. "I'll think on that. Thank you."

"Don't mention it, your Highness. Under any circumstances." Thiano looks at me. "Was there anything else?"

"The price," Iryasa says.

"You paid it," I say before Thiano can speak, and he grins lazily at me.

"You think you can speak for me?" he asks. "Miyara, Miyara."

"I trust you to look out for yourself, Thiano," I say. "You wouldn't have answered if you didn't wish to."

"But you, of course, have a question for me too," he drawls.

"Velasar knows something about the power of my bracelets," I say without any ado. "What will it mean when an emissary from Nakrab sees them?"

Some emotion flashes through his expression too quickly for me to read, so I know he has understood my question to refer not just to what it will mean for me, but for him.

"They will not know what to make of them," Thiano says finally. "I have no intention of changing that understanding at this time. I will be vague, and I recommend you should be, too."

Has Thiano ever recommended a course of action to me before that wasn't a test? I think not.

I bow and say with utmost seriousness, "Thank you for your counsel."

"Oh, get out already," he snaps. "And you can have the pleasure of extracting your tea spirit from the ring she's attempting to fit onto her tail."

"After she's spent so much time trying to impress you? Perish the thought," I say, but motion Iryasa to the door. "If you want the ring back, come remove it yourself."

"You'll regret that when you find out about the curse on that ring," Thiano says smugly.

"I'm sure it will be educational for her then, before she neutralizes it. By which I mean destroys it utterly."

"You just can't let an old man have his fun, can you?" Thiano complains, stomping after me.

"I already did, and you know perfectly well I'm going to pay for it," I say.

The look he fixes me with then isn't even slightly amused. "Get your house in order, Miyara," Thiano says, "while you can."

My house and my home; my relationships and my boundaries. I don't question how Thiano always knows more than anyone should be able to, only stare numbly while he and Yorani tussle. But when he delivers a mock-irritated but secretly delighted Yorani back to me along with a bundle of her sleeping socks removed at last, I bow my head before turning away.

Iryasa follows me in silence until we've left the street. She continues to be silent as Yorani hops around, and flutters, and eventually settles in my shoulder, looking for all the world like she's a captain directing a ship, and me her chosen vessel, as she avidly surveys our surroundings perched on her hind legs—almost like Iryasa's expression earlier, I realize.

Finally the crown princess says, her tone deceptively even, "Do you want to tell me what that was about?"

Iryasa works in narratives. She began with one, inside, and was forced to change course, again and again, refocusing until she landed on the required approach. Frustrating, necessary work, and I am glad to know she's capable of it; and I hope she understands she'll have to be ready to dive straight to the heart of things, again and again, if we are to succeed. The world is at stake.

"Thiano doesn't trust easily," I say.

"I gathered. You two have a strange relationship."

"I may be the only person in Sayorsen he has a relationship with at all," I say. "At least anything approaching an honest one. And he has been here a long time."

"You have a theory," she says.

"I think he saw right away that fundamentally, I want to help people," I say. "He's tested my commitment to that in various ways, but he saw that, and that people will listen to me. I think he wishes he were that kind of person—or perhaps wishes that he could have been. So he tries to help me. Haltingly, bitterly, because he has clearly been hurt badly by this world and can't quite believe it can work out, but I believe both that he knows much more than he has ever let on, and that he wants to make something right. And I can't believe this current business with the Cataclysm is unrelated to whatever that is."

Iryasa considers that. "You want him clearly on our side," she says, "and you thought an honest demonstration of my own commitment to helping people would be necessary to make that happen, which is why you didn't warn me."

"Yes. I'm sure he doesn't need a warning from me about what's to come, but I also want him to know that I see him, too. I think it will matter. I'm sorry I couldn't prepare you."

"Did you get everything you needed?" Iryasa asks.

I wince, remembering Thiano's parting words. "It's enough."

"Will you tell me what that was about?" she asks directly.

I sigh. What I intended primarily as a task for Iryasa, Thiano has turned into a pointed lesson for me. Pots and kettles. "In short, I need to immediately be much better about communicating who I am clearly and without compromise to both myself and the world at large. I'm working on it. In a way, your presence is helping."

"By pressuring you into a situation you didn't want," Iryasa says, looking away.

"Oh, no," I say. "That I chose. And we are both going to have to become more ourselves very quickly to pull this off. The summit is the end of our task; what we manage before it begins is just as important, if not more so."

Iryasa nods slowly. "The groundwork we build defines our later arsenal. Yes. I'm beginning to understand that may be a bigger task than I anticipated, along with everything else. But after how that meeting went, I hope you don't think I'll go into a second one unawares without a strong reason."

"No, that's the only surprise," I say. "Thank you for trusting me enough to go along with it."

"I will try to work with you, Miyara," Iryasa says. "But understand it does not come naturally to me, and I am on edge."

I wince. "With regret, I fear you may expect to remain there yet for some time. Too much has to happen too quickly for us to be able to ease into anything. Though in a way, that's what our next meeting is about: moving to a place of ease as quickly as we can."

Iryasa pauses; looks at me. "Where, precisely, are we headed?"

"To meet the Te Muraka," I say. "Before anything else, we need to introduce you to dragons."

CHAPTER 5

IRYASA RESUMES WALKING with me, but more slowly. Yorani takes the moment to scurry to my other shoulder for a different vantage point. "I always intended to meet the Te Muraka, of course," she says. "They were another sovereign people we have only begun integrating into our own. But I admit I thought it would be with Saiyana at least with me, and probably more advisors and mages besides. Why is it important for me to meet them alone with you, and right away?"

"Several reasons," I say. "First, we know Kustio was smuggling magical items the Te Muraka created to Velasari agents working against Istalam and in league with Nakrab."

"'Know' is a strong word," Iryasa murmurs, but doesn't gainsay me.

"We may not know in the way of an airtight case in a court of law, but that doesn't mean it isn't truth, and it doesn't mean we shouldn't incorporate that understanding into our decision-making process," I counter.

"I don't disagree," Iryasa says. "Just—"

"I do remember how to speak at court," I say. "It has not been so long, and I promise I am able to code-switch. May I continue to dispense with those necessary formalities when our words are not being recorded for future examination? Yorani's attention excepted."

Yorani doesn't turn away from her study of our surroundings but does flap a wing into my face.

Iryasa takes a moment to look around, absorbing that thought. "I can scarcely believe the truth of that—not being recorded. What a wonder. Yes, you may continue, though do remember I will not always respond with equal candor, even if I might wish to."

The responsibilities of a crown princess cannot be so easily cast aside. "Of course." I hesitate, and then add, "I can't promise I won't push, but it is something I am working on, and I do expect you to push back."

Iryasa's eyes glint at that—not offended, but perhaps—challenged?

She is likely not used to being able to push back in any meaningful way, where it concerns the personal or political, that goes against the official grain of our mother's decisions. Probably she has not been able to, let alone expected to.

For Iryasa, weighed down with so many expectations, an expectation like this is more freeing than choosing preferred flavors.

"I will." Her eyes blaze with resolve. "I merely wished to determine your facility with the language of court politics, as you were not an active player in them before your dedication ceremony."

Oh. "I know we do not in many ways know each other that well, but I assumed you would take that ability as read," I explain. "My apologies. Careful speech is perhaps the only quality I was positively known for within the palace."

"No, I did know that," Iryasa says, not denying my estimation of my former esteem in our peers' eyes. "I wasn't sure, given our conversations up to now, if it was a mode you had entirely rejected on principle."

Oh. "Not as such," I say. "This is more in the interest of habit-forming. I need you to understand that my role is not as a princess, and I will behave accordingly. I am attempting to set expectations, so you are not later betrayed by a false impression of who I am."

"You are a princess, Miyara," Iryasa says. "I will not forget it."

A wonder to hear those words from my eldest sister, given what I have done. After the events of the tournament, it no longer feels like a trap, as when Saiyana claimed it; only a gift of my sister's blessing, that to her I will always be her sister, too.

"Nor have I," I say. "But it's not all I am, now."

She smiles. "So I see. And I did notice you did not say your actions won't surprise me, no matter the expectations set."

I purse my lips, wondering how far to tip my hand. "It does seem likely. I appear to have a latent talent for surprising people, even when I don't mean to."

Iryasa laughs. "I can't help taking that as a challenge—if nothing else, to hope we discover a similar talent in me. But first, there are the Te Muraka, and we have gotten somewhat afield from the particulars."

"My point was only that it is impossible the Nakrabi do not know something of the Te Muraka," I explain. "Their strategy has incorporated them—or more accurately, utilized their existence—down to using them to fuel rumors making them responsible for the barrier's destabilization."

"So any strategy we employ must accordingly work with the Te Muraka, to effectively counter the Nakrabi, or else we will be divided by default," Iryasa finishes, looking thoughtful. "An excellent point. And that means to incorporate the Te Muraka thoroughly, we must begin with them from the ground up in our strategy building. And the rest?"

How to put this? "There has been much cause for distrust," I say, "on many sides. You and me. Our people of the Te Muraka. And the Te Muraka have more cause to distrust than anyone, given their experiences with the former lord Kustio and then how they were blamed—anyone except perhaps the Gaellani and the witches, who have been systematically taught not to trust. I don't think we should go into an undertaking with the kinds of stakes we are dealing with without a measure of trust between us, and given our time constraints, that can best be achieved without the barriers a formal meeting will necessitate. I do realize the formalities exist for a reason, to take care in the differing ways of showing respecting, in learning our boundaries in a safe and managed way, as a form of protection we can use to ease in or out of negotiations. But we simply don't have time."

Iryasa takes that in, processing, and I notice Yorani staring intently at me, too. How many human nuances does my tea spirit understand, and in what ways does her perspective differ from mine? Our bond is clearly stronger now, but there's still so much I don't know. Perhaps someday she will be able to tell me.

Or I will be able to hear her truly.

Finally Iryasa says, "You would have me expose more of myself in a single morning than I have done in almost all the years of my life. I cannot be who you are, Miyara. A crown princess can't be as honest with the world and still succeed."

"I know," I say softly, turning back to my sister and feeling the weight of Yorani's gaze lighten, too. "I do not envy you. But we are dealing with the fate of the world, Iryasa. We have to be able to risk ourselves. Without understanding that and believing it, the Te Muraka can't afford us the fundamental trust for a working relationship we will need, for them to be allies in truth. Nor would they be wrong to hold back, given their experiences of Istalam to date. I'm not suggesting you pour your secrets out on your first meeting. Just, talk to them. Like the people they, and you, are."

If anything, this makes her look more uncomfortable. "You do realize nothing in my life has prepared me to be able to do that. I craft narratives in advance and guide those I face into them, however I must. This is improvisation without a script."

"I realize that well. But remember, the Te Muraka don't know what a casual Istal conversation looks like, either. And they need you as an ally as much as we need them."

"Not you, though," Iryasa says, missing nothing. "You, they already hold in esteem, because you brought them out of the Cataclysm."

"If I'd had any doubts of them, they would have been banished when Sa Rangim freely gave his personal magic to save Yorani's life," I say. "But during the summit we will not have time for me to be negotiating between you as I did for them when Saiyana arrived. I will not have time to continually convince you that they are not working against Istalam intentionally or accidentally, or them that Istalam will not reject them due to fearmongering or institutional biases. It will be best for you to have your own relationship with them."

"Which is why you, with whom they do already have trust, are introducing me," Iryasa says, working through the implications. Her shoulders relax, making her every jot the picture of princessly elegance, and I know this pose does not indicate relaxation, but that she has accepted the challenge ahead.

That's good, I decide. Let us see how Sa Rangim handles her in full-force, if well-meaning, princess-mode.

Our conversation subsides as Iryasa withdraws inside her head, mentally preparing alone. I will be present to help guide conversation with the Te Muraka, but she understands it must be her that makes a connection with them, and I will leave her to do it her own way, writing her own story as she wishes to live it. Perhaps not dissimilar to how Yorani has been interjecting only intermittently, to break tension or give me pause to consider other angles.

And that very thought does give me pause: Yorani learns from me, but a relationship with a familiar must work two ways, surely? I would do better to pay attention to her cues in terms of what I can learn from her, too.

As we get closer, Iryasa's distraction by the area we pass through draws my attention. She steals a glance at me but doesn't ask, and I can practically see her putting pieces of information together and drawing her own conclusions.

The unofficial Te Muraka headquarters are in an immensely poorly maintained area of town; it's why there was so little objection in ceding such a large building to them. Iryasa will understand that—perhaps knew it already on paper—but now she is seeing its reality. Not just what this means for the Te Muraka's current challenge, but for Sayorsen's and how we arrived here.

I say nothing at all, but nor do I need to. It is not an accident I chose to walk her through this area with no one else to filter her sight, and she knows it.

However she came by the respect for me that allows her to let me lead her, at least for now, I will use it ruthlessly.

The building itself has changed even more since my last visit—even on the outside it looks less ramshackle, if not precisely spruced. Like it was cracked clay whose edges have been smoothed but is still in need of a coat of paint.

I knock outside, and to my surprise it is Tamak who answers.

"Well met, Tamak." I bow, and Yorani curls her tail around my neck to hold on so she can join me in it. Tamak returns the gesture but more deeply, one for me and one for Yorani both. He's already learned so much, in such a short time. "I apologize for visiting without notice. I was hoping I might find Sa Rangim here, and that he might be available to meet?"

"He's in the middle of something," Tamak says, "but he won't mind being interrupted for you. Who is this?"

I snort a laugh. "You started so well there, too."

He almost smiles, a glint in his eye that reminds me he works at the tea shop because among the Te Muraka, he's considered rebellious. "I have so much more to learn—maybe I can't be trusted with a responsibility like this one," he says.

"As boring as that?" I tease.

Tamak considers. "Worse. I thought..." He trails off, but I don't need him to finish: that Sa Rangim believed he was capable of more.

My eyes narrow suddenly. "Is it Sa Rangim who put you on door duty?"

Tamak's golden gaze focuses on me, then on Iryasa's cloaked figure beside me. "This is a place of Te Murak," he says more formally, slowly testing out the possibility I've implied. "We would know who it is we welcome within our walls. Will you name yourself?"

Iryasa tilts her head to one side, considering. "By name, not outside your walls, I regret," she finally says. "But I am here as ally and, I hope, growing friend to Miyara. I know her to be ally and friend to you. Will that do to enter?"

Tamak's expression has shut down as he processes that: what it means that she won't name herself but is here with me; what it means that Sa Rangim somehow knew someone of import would be coming, and chose Tamak to greet them—to choose how to greet them.

His gaze flicks to me. "She talks like you."

"In some ways," I agree equably.

He sucks in a breath and bows to Iryasa—the same degree he extended to me.

Which tells me he has realized she must be a relation of mine, for a formal bow—not just to a stranger, but deeper, as one that should be respected—yet not lower than he has bowed to me, because she has indicated she does not wish her identity public until we have entered the walls.

"This is a place of Te Murak," Tamak says again. "Enter and find welcome."

We follow him inside, and he shuts the door behind us stiffly, probably both embarrassed by his error in judgment and not actually sure how to handle Iryasa's presence.

But that is, in fact, why I am here.

Tea mastery is art; it's a fundamentally creative endeavor in building connections. But there is more than one way to create, and here, my role is less to forge than to shape: to make the space for Iryasa to create her own story and future in her own way, and to help smooth its rough edges and meanderings so the truth of who she is and wants to be shines through.

"Tamak works with me at Talmeri's," I say to Iryasa, guiding us over this gap, and gesture Tamak to lead on.

He ducks his head, a silent acknowledgment, and does; we follow.

"He's one of the youngest Te Muraka, and the first to apprentice with an Istal. As perceptive as he is, I hope he will not be the last."

Tamak casts me a look at that, probably thinking I'm poking fun at him for his treatment at the door, but I bow seriously in response. He glances away quickly, disconcerted.

"He must be," Iryasa says, "to learn to navigate so many worlds so quickly. It's my honor to make your acquaintance, Tamak. Perhaps one day I will become as unimpressed by opening doors as you."

He jerks to a halt.

"That was teasing wry humor, not scolding," I gloss for him.

"No, I got that," Tamak says, moving again. "It's just exactly what I expected Sa Rangim to tell me, except with him it would have been a scold too. Anyway. Here you are. I'd be happy to give you a more verbal tour later, if you're interested in the work we have undertaken here."

The bare, scrubbed rooms we've passed through. I'm surprised Iryasa hasn't asked about such a dubiously welcoming entryway yet.

"Thank you," Iryasa says. "I hope I can take you up on that."

Tamak nods and raps sharply on the door before him. I wonder if this is always how he behaves in the Te Murak headquarters, adopting Istal etiquette norms, or if this is a special show he—or Sa Rangim—have chosen to deal with Istal visitors.

"Miyara and a princess to see you," Tamak announces.

The door latch clicks, and Tamak steps back to allow us to enter.

Iryasa looks at him. "I didn't have to be a princess," she says softly.

He stares at her like she's just told him he's stupid. "Of course you did, your Highness."

Before she can respond to that, I push open the door and gesture for her to precede me. She cuts me a look that tells me she's not impressed with being managed but is also grateful for it, and does.

I step in after her, and Sa Rangim and I exchange warm smiles.

Then Iryasa flicks her hood back, and Sa Rangim's eyes focus on her at once.

But it's not surprise, or not just that. That change I can now identify in Te Muraka eyes. This is a look I've never seen from him.

I have seen it, though.

Yorani nips my ear, as if to tell me to keep my smugness to myself, and flies off to bump noses with Sa Rangim, forcing him to focus on her.

"Welcome, little one," he laughs. "You know you are always welcome."

Yorani chirps and settles down—right on top of his head.

Sa Rangim closes his eyes in amused resignation, and I burst into helpless laughter. I cannot imagine this is the figure he hoped to impress Iryasa with at this moment.

"Iryasa, this is Sa Rangim, leader of the Te Muraka and Yorani's personal hero," I say. "Sa Rangim, my eldest sister and the crown princess of Istalam, Iryasa."

Sa Rangim bends gracefully in a bow, and Yorani flaps up off his head rather than fall only to land on it again as he rises. "It is my honor to welcome you, your Highness."

Iryasa bows in turn, but not before I catch a kind of wistful note in her expression.

I rethink my earlier estimation: a leader who is not threatened by appearing to another leader as a baby dragon's seat of choice is perhaps exactly what Iryasa needs to see. Impossible to know if that was Yorani's intention or simply a happy side effect.

"Please, call me Iryasa," my sister says in her lyrical voice. "The honor is mine, but I believe Miyara has brought us together like this to circumvent time-consuming formalities."

"As you say," Sa Rangim says, inclining his head. "But time can be made for whatever formalities will make you feel more welcome here, Iryasa."

Her eyes widen at the end—at her name. She truly isn't used to people calling her by it.

Now she will always know what it sounds like in his voice.

"Shall I set a kettle?" Sa Rangim asks me.

Yorani chirps and bonks his head happily with hers, then zooms off to the back room.

"If it's not too much trouble, please," I say. "I'll see if I can capture Yorani before she gets into too much trouble."

Sa Rangim waves this off. "She's never a problem here. She'll be distracted exploring all the new changes for some time. I'm glad your familiar is so comfortable in our place."

With that, we begin our work here in earnest.

I incline my head with a smile. It's only an implication that, by extension, I must be comfortable here as well, and what that means, but it's one Iryasa can infer; and one that Sa Rangim clearly expects her to.

Sa Rangim lifts a kettle from a table behind him; a tray of tea accoutrements is already laid out for us. "What sort of tea may I offer you, princesses?"

Iryasa looks at me, then winces. "Oh, no. I think I will not let the tea master choose for me after all; I mistrust that smile."

Sa Rangim's lips quirk. "Perhaps you've been spending too much time with a certain tea spirit," he says to me. "I think you may be beginning to acquire her expressions."

"Surely it's supposed to be the other way around," I say.

"Caring for others is never a one-way path," Sa Rangim says, "which you know." He looks expectantly at Iryasa.

"A white tea, if you have one, please," Iryasa says.

"At your service," Sa Rangim murmurs.

I look away to contain my own smile. She does know what she wants, after all.

But I look back at Iryasa's intake of breath as Sa Rangim heats the kettle with a touch of his hand and passes it to me.

Their eyes meet. Iryasa holds his gaze but says nothing, and Sa Rangim bows his head.

A test cleared. I should have thought more—in my copious spare time—about what it would mean that both of them are like this, with tests. We will never get as far as we need to today if they are allowed to fall into this habit, so it's time for me to take a more active step, refocusing.

The tea tray is laid before me, and I begin to work my own magic.

I don't perform a true tea ceremony, but it is still a social ritual with a kind of magic to it: it is bringing people together, finding connections and building bridges. It is finding the air current common to both of them and swirling it together.

"I have been spending a great deal of time with Yorani," I say, keeping my movements both casual and deliberate, easing and calming. "Enough that I believe she's beginning to be annoyed about it. But it hasn't been that long since she nearly died, and I'm nervous to let her go too far."

"Natural, but unavoidable," Sa Rangim says. "She's young, growing and resilient. She's not unaware of what happened or what it means—she's become more watchful. She knows as well as you that you can't keep her safe by keeping her at your side."

I sigh. "I know that in my head. It's still hard not to panic a bit when she flies out of sight, though. Stifling her won't help, I realize, and coddling my fears now will probably only make them harder to manage later, but I worry it's too soon."

"I suspect, if you let her, Yorani will demonstrate her judgment has grown faster than her body," Sa Rangim says. "But not if you bind her wings. Trust goes two ways."

Iryasa speaks at last. "I see you really do know each other well." When I just glance up, she flicks a glance at Sa Rangim and continues, "You're open with him with yourself. And he seems to intuitively know exactly the root of your concern."

That conversation was about Yorani—but it could just as easily have been about me.

Or her.

"It's true," I agree, pouring the tea. "In some ways I know Sa Rangim better than you. It has been an eventful few weeks, and I know we can count on each other when it matters. But in this case it does help also that he has counseled me more than once at the shrine."

Sa Rangim inclines his head. "The reverse is also true. Miyara's insights are a gift I do not take lightly. But I am surprised you would think to know me better than your family."

"Ah," I say, lifting my cup. "That's because the first sister you've seen me with is Saiyana, who is closer to me in age."

"Karisa is also close to your age, and you are not notably close to her," Iryasa points out.

"And," Sa Rangim adds, "I have not observed you to relate substantially better to one age group than another."

"Both true, but while it was not always so, the current conditions of our court have made for some unusual divisions," I explain. "Iryasa and Reyata, as the eldest, naturally found their paths crossing most. Saiyana was next, and with our two eldest sisters' dynamic already well-established, she looked to me for more equal companionship. And in Karisa's case... let's say circumstances made it difficult for any of us to get close to her. It's not the age gap precisely that has intervened in our relationships, though those matter more when we're young, as our sharing stages of life experiences. Iryasa had already assumed official crown princess duties before I was born."

"Only just," Iryasa concedes after a sip of her tea, "but true nonetheless. I am grateful for this opportunity to learn more of who my sister is now that we are both acting in the world. Is it different for the Te Muraka?"

Sa Rangim considers as he drinks. "In some ways," he finally says. "Some of those I hope will change, when our common experience need not be focused on survival. When we have the space to flourish instead. I am gathering that your childhoods at the palace were their own sort of trial to survive—not physically, perhaps, but spiritually." He meets Iryasa's gaze directly. "You will forgive me, but I can't say I don't find that troubling."

Iryasa's eyes widen at the audacity, then narrow again as she considers his words carefully before responding.

I take another sip of tea, and she mimics me.

"I can't fault you for that, nor can I truly disagree," Iryasa says. "Our generation's experience has been... perhaps unique for royals, but raising children to the level of responsibility and capability required to serve Istalam is never an ordinary task."

"Such destined children must learn to look at the world differently," Sa Rangim says. "But I have helped raise many, and in my experience feelings of isolation produce perspectives more warped than considered. I wonder if it is so different in your culture."

I ask, "Are these children you have raised in your capacity as leader of the Te Muraka, or of your own body?"

"The former," Sa Rangim says. "Te Muraka bond for life, and my status among our people has made finding that sort of partnership... complicated."

"As well as your role," I murmur. "To maintain the fierce discipline required to survive the Cataclysm..."

"Just so," Sa Rangim says simply.

I feel the sudden weight of Iryasa's stare on me and return it with a deliberately even expression.

I didn't really expect her not to realize what I was up to, but I had hoped to give them a chance for as normal of a first meeting as either could ever expect.

Iryasa's eyes communicate the rapid fire of her thoughts even without words, and after too long a silence Sa Rangim asks softly, "Is there something I should be aware of here, Miyara?"

It is not an accident that he has asked me, who he knows will not betray his trust.

I meet his gaze fully. "Yes, but it must be secret for now. I can only promise you those secrets will not endanger you or yours, and I do."

Sa Rangim studies me for a long moment, "Then I will take you at your word, tea master. And as I fear whatever spell you have wrought to help bring us together in ease has been broken, perhaps we should discuss the secrets between us that can hurt all of our people." He looks at Iryasa, his vast knowledge reflected in his gaze. "For the crown princess herself to be here, I am sure you must know of the situation with the Cataclysm."

Iryasa meets his gaze head-on; she may be new to running her own plots, but politics is a world she understands in her spirit. "The barrier is expanding as the Cataclysm pushes slowly outward. We will be calling a summit of representatives from our remaining neighbors to discuss the cause and what is to be done."

"And by 'we', you mean—"

"It is Iryasa's idea, but I will be leading its execution," I say. "The summons will come from me in my role as Sayorsen's tea master, to negotiate on behalf of Istalam."

Sa Rangim sets down his cup. "Interesting. And you have a role in mind for the Te Muraka?"

"No," Iryasa says, surprising me, "but I would like to, if you are amenable."

Sa Rangim's eyes glint with interest, and he motions for her to continue.

"As I was reminded on the way over, the Te Muraka have already been badly abused in whatever power struggle we're currently caught in," Iryasa says. "I think the best way to prevent that from continuing is to make you an active player in the plots afoot—or rather, to make it clear that you should be treated as such. I would like to be your partner in this, in crafting a strategy that includes all of Istalam, so none of us are forgotten. But I don't presume to know you, and or what you need. So I am here, Sa Rangim, to ask if you will work with me."

Sa Rangim studies her. "You do have an idea though, I think. Will you share it with me?"

Iryasa purses her lips, and I am once again startled by how similar our expressions are. "I will if you insist, but it is a flawed one. I had thought, if you were positioned visibly with Istal royalty as guards, it would indicate both our value and trust in the Te Muraka and your abilities. But it seems to me that's a different kind of trap for you, where all Te Muraka would be valued for only one type of service, and that to the crown. I would hate for any person to find their only path to equal consideration thusly constrained, let alone someone like Tamak, who might prefer other outlets for their skills."

She looks at me as she says this, and this time it's me who looks away.

Iryasa of all people knows what it is for your future to be inescapable.

"Yes," Sa Rangim agrees softly. "That is not a path to freedom for us—at least not alone. But if that is truly your goal, then perhaps together we may come up with a plan that will suit all our people's."

"That is my hope," Iryasa says. "While time is of the essence, you have had time, if under dire circumstances, to learn of Istalam and our ways, and I cannot say the same. I know this building belongs to the Te Muraka to restore, and Tamak gave me to understand that there have been many changes of late. Will you show me how you are making your space, that I might know you better?"

Sa Rangim nods, his expression unreadable, but the pleased gold of his eyes tells me while he may be wary of her intentions, he is thus far impressed by her.

"It would be my pleasure," Sa Rangim says. "It is my hope that you will feel as welcome here as we have been in your native land."

Iryasa smiles so brilliantly even I am almost dazzled as she rises. "I think we can do better than that, on both counts, Sa Rangim."

"A challenge for us both, then," Sa Rangim says, and his hint of smile combined with the gold in his eyes is equally devastating.

I finish my tea all at once, and its light flavor no longer buoys me but rather makes me feel untethered. Even with both of them careful, this has gone so easily I fear the expected complications haven't been avoided, merely pushed to the future when we can ill afford them.

This meeting has also slipped so easily out of my conscious control, as powerful art can when the players involved express their previously hidden goals. And while they've talked, I've had time to reflect how much worse breached trust can fail us than a lack of trust at all.

Thiano advised me to get my house in order, and I meant to. But as Sa Rangim and Iryasa walk out of the room together, I look toward the active fireplace, the physical representation of air, and offer a prayer to the spirits that I can be light enough in my touch not to blow us all too far, too fast, spinning this disaster situation even further outside of anyone's control.

CHAPTER 6

FOR LUNCH I SEND a courier to bring us back plates of Gaellani sweet soy noodles to eat at the Te Murak headquarters. No one will think anything of it, since many Te Muraka aren't comfortable outside among people yet, and it allows Iryasa and Sa Rangim to eat together unobserved.

Even a dish as simple as this is an opportunity for cultural exchange, the foundation we need to have firmly established before any delegation arrives. The Gaellani, from whom Sa Rangim observed etiquette for eating this dish, slurp their noodles to indicate enjoyment; among Istals, the sound is considered crass, but to be silent among the Gaellani is to be rude.

The use of utensils, too, differs: there is more oil in this street food than the fare Iryasa is typically served at the palace, and so she is careful, slow and intentional, at lifting each noodle to avoid splattering. Sa Rangim, by contrast, is further along, though we learn that in the Cataclysm the Te Muraka didn't use eating sticks at all, deftly twining foods like this around a single thin blade.

Or, as he demonstrates after a moment of consideration, a tightly wielded knife of magical flame.

Iryasa and I both go still at the sight, in awe not just of the casual power, but the extreme control displayed so effortlessly.

"Is such skillfulness standard among the Te Muraka?" Iryasa asks.

I hold my breath. This is why I brought her alone, to circumvent the formalities, so they would not be trapped in the kind of tests they started with when he first heated the kettle. Still, it's a direct and bold question that leaves little room for Sa Rangim to maneuver gracefully.

He considers her question carefully before ultimately answering, "No. I am attempting to impress you."

That surprises her into a laugh, and me into taking in air again. "You have succeeded. But control *is* standard among your people. Does it manifest in other ways?"

"It does," Sa Rangim says carefully. "This is the ultimate result of such fine control."

"And a partial step?" Iryasa asks shrewdly.

Spirits, I breathed too soon. I tried to ease Iryasa out of her assumptions of constraints, but to blow past them entirely—

Sa Rangim sets down his utensil and holds out a hand, not breaking eye contact with the crown princess.

Slowly, one of his fingers transforms into a massive, dangerous claw.

I am tense and unmoving, waiting for Iryasa's reaction. Of course I know that Te Muraka transform into dragons; I have seen it. In theory so does my sister, but there is a great difference between seeing and truly grasping.

But I understand Sa Rangim's dilemma. On one hand, any rationale that could encourage people to think of the Te Muraka as beasts, as less than human, is a step toward disaster. But on the other, Istalam must be able to accept the Te Muraka fully for who they are, or their betrayal will only be slow, but still inevitable.

"Fascinating," Iryasa breathes, and her gaze flicks up to Sa Rangim's. "May I—touch? Is that rude?"

Spirits. She can't stop pushing any more than I can. Are all of us like this?

"You may," Sa Rangim says after a moment. "It is not rude with permission."

Iryasa extends her hand carefully, fingers gently tracing along the edge of Sa Rangim's claw, while he holds shock-still.

I carefully nudge my sister. He may have consented, but this is clearly uncomfortable for him.

She glances between me and him, then leans back into her chair. "You are remarkable," Iryasa says simply. "Though I imagine eating noodles cooked in oil might create complications in cleaning your claws."

"So we have found," Sa Rangim agrees. "It has helped motivate some among us to improve with eating sticks."

"And some to try other foods," Iryasa murmurs.

"Just so. Are noodles a favorite of yours, princess?"

Iryasa narrows her eyes and glances at me. "What *is* it with this question?"

"It is a way people learn to know each other," I say. "What you choose, why and how. It is also a way, as you know, to indicate care—by how far you attempt to cater to a person's preferences or disregard them. It is both consequential and inconsequential small talk, and you will have to grow accustomed to answering it."

Iryasa deflates. "So that's why you didn't accept my deflection earlier. If I always deflect out here, people will begin to notice. You know I have spent a lifetime learning not to allow personal preferences to matter."

"To yourself," Sa Rangim asks, "or to your people?"

She knows this question is a trap, and yet she answers him honestly, if tensely. "Both. My preferences carry weight and can be used against me. So I have learned to guard them."

"I see," he says. "A useful way to remain aloof from people, but not to form a connection. Yet you are here to do the latter as efficiently as possible, are you not?"

"What are you proposing?" Iryasa asks warily.

"An exchange over food," Sa Rangim explains. "I will promise not to be offended by your opinions of Te Murak cuisine if you will also promise the reverse. I think we might learn a great deal about each other, and our peoples, with such a trade."

And themselves. It is a boon Sa Rangim is giving her, the opportunity to develop preferences that can't be used against her. But again I wonder at the fairness of it: if she will treasure the opportunity, or resent it for the knowledge of what she must leave.

Though as I observe Sa Rangim's banked intensity, I wonder if that is, perhaps, his true gift and challenge for her: that perhaps she need not leave it.

Easier said than done. For me to escape that fate, I turned my back on my future. Iryasa is crown princess; that path is not open to her.

"An interesting proposal," Iryasa says finally, and her long silence tells me she understands at least a great deal of what he has implied in the asking. "I have one for you to consider, too."

The gold in Sa Rangim's eyes shimmers. "I am listening."

The afternoon passes not in a rush, but a painstaking abundance of nuance and care. We are all so intent on our words and their effects, how many ways they can be interpreted, what to imply or infer, that I am both exhilarated and ragged by the time we part ways.

I am also cautiously optimistic and irrepressibly terrified. I never expected their first meeting to last so long, to cover so much ground. But they are both leaders of their people, and they have committed themselves to forging foundations for the work ahead.

We must begin the summit as soon as possible, but there is so much to prepare first. This was an afternoon critically spent, but I am thrumming with the weariness of work done and the work still to do.

In touring the Te Murak headquarters, Iryasa advised Sa Rangim on spaces intended to cater towards people who aren't Te Muraka, as well as the sorts of effects the Te Muraka might wish to become accustomed to in the sphere of politics, the nuances of décor and symbolism. Involving herself in the Te Murak project in a way they can collude together, where it still clearly remains Sa Rangim's jurisdiction but with her expertise, is masterfully done; a way to give them a project to work on together and mutual respect for the opposite roles they will likely fill in our strategy. Iryasa may not have been running her own plans alone these past years at the palace, but she has been crafting them her whole life.

It gives me hope that we will be able to prepare what we must in time, but I know something about quiet plans, too. Iryasa is working with me now as I help set her on the path, but I will have to make sure she doesn't try to run ahead with her own plans prepared without me.

Although we did not leave with a full strategy hashed out, our work, though more nebulous, was more important: the solid beginnings of trust, mutual respect, and common ground.

And, for all that we exhausted ourselves with our care, it was easy. This is what concerns me more than anything.

It's always been easy for me with Deniel, too, but that doesn't mean we haven't had our share of deeply hurtful miscommunications. Iryasa and Sa Rangim don't have time for them.

We need for them to get as close as possible, fast, and yet that may also have been a severe tactical error. They are the leaders of their peoples, from vastly different backgrounds. There is so much to bridge, and so many ramifications if it goes badly.

When Saiyana shows up without warning to escort Iryasa to her knew lodging, I am cowardly glad that she has given me a way to not have to explain myself to either Iryasa or Sa Rangim alone just now.

I acknowledge Saiyana's weighted stare with a nod—we *do* need to talk, desperately—but tomorrow.

Tonight, I need to grapple with my fear that I lied to Sa Rangim after all: that my secrets may, in fact, cause harm to him and his, and to make sure I am prepared to defend them from fallout in that event.

※

Deniel's storefront is still open when I arrive home, which marks the first time this has happened. My sudden appearance causes a stir among his customers—it is not a secret that we decided to move in together, but it's not as though informative pamphlets were issued; and even so, for Istals to come upon a tea master in her own home, let alone one she shares with a Gaellani, is cause for remark. So I spend a few minutes applying my flagging energy to set everyone at ease as if I were hosting tea at the store before retreating.

I had Meristo call Taseino in to cover for me at the store today with him and Lorwyn, but our business has remained busy since the tournament. If I try that two days in a row without explanation Lorwyn will find me and murder me, and rightfully so. The summit is more important than anything, but that doesn't mean life stops.

As tea master of Sayorsen I am responsible for looking out for both Iryasa's and Lorwyn's interests in the matter at hand. At least I have Deniel with whom to share my secrets without fear.

In whatever way I do, in fact, have Deniel.

Yorani nips my ear.

"You're right, that was unnecessarily morose," I say. "Shall we prepare dinner, then?"

But it turns out Deniel, even though he's still working, has procured dinner. He's already eaten his, apparently intending to work late, so we won't eat dinner together our first full day in our new home, either.

My eyes fill with tears, which is probably unreasonable, but I can't even do this for or with him.

I pour Yorani's portion into a bowl, and as she eats I survey the room with a vengeance.

I can do *something*. This is my home, too, and I should be able to set it to rights just as well as he can. I'm already mentally exhausted, and every choice of where to put one of the many items cluttering up the room, even if it's into the trash, is still a choice that drains me further.

But every decision Deniel makes when crafting a piece of pottery is a choice, too, and even if he has more practice making them continually, I will do my part.

After a little while I fall into the rhythm of it, the edge of anger and desperation ebbing. Yorani and Talsu's antics sitting on boxes I've packed to move, weaving dangerously among delicate objects, and hiding exactly where I'm going to step make the task feel less daunting. Not easier, but a fact of life rather than a symbol of my failures.

It's later still when I hear Deniel lock the shop at last. Yorani blows fire on the kettle, and I take her unsubtle hint and quickly grab for a cup and tea.

Deniel enters the back. "Sorry that took so long," he says. "I—"

He stares around. Our common area isn't totally clean, but it's close. "Have you been working this whole time?" he asks, aghast.

I hand him the tea. "You brought dinner. I had to do *something*."

Deniel stares at the teacup and doesn't drink. He looks—frustrated?

"Was I not supposed to help set up my own home?" I ask slowly as my chest tightens.

He looks at me. "I hoped you would take an opportunity to actually relax. To take care of yourself."

The knowledge that he arranged this—dinner, his absence—with me in mind doesn't stop my anger from rising, especially as he didn't consult my actual mind. "Being involved in creating my home *is* caring for myself."

"You didn't have to do all this yourself," Deniel says. "It's my home too."

"And you worked on it last night while I committed to even more work. And you keep feeding me—"

Now *he* goes still. "Since when is it a problem when I make dinner? Are you going to insist on doing that yourself now, too?"

"No! I just—"

I stop, breathing hard. After all my care negotiating Sa Rangim and Iryasa's relationship, why can't I do it in mine?

I turn away from him, and it feels like giving up. Thiano told me to get my house in order, and I know he's right, and yet—

Why is nothing ever easy, with me? My relationship with Deniel had been going smoothly enough it seems impossible the problem isn't just my propensity for difficulty cascading down, for pushing as relentlessly as Iryasa. I'm going to break my own life trying to save everyone else's.

But when I turn, Yorani is flying right in front of my face. I see sympathy in her eyes, but also strength.

And then she glares behind me at Deniel and huffs a whorl of smoke.

Deniel catches his breath at this reproach, and my shoulders tighten. It's not his job to manage our relationship more than it is mine. I take a breath and turn back—

And he is sipping the tea.

I swallow.

Yorani nips my ear and then settles on the kitchen counter, hunched and staring at us through narrowed eyes, as if ready to pounce if we don't work this out.

"What have you been teaching her about how diplomacy works, exactly?" Deniel asks lightly.

"Evidently that there are times when a third party's perspective is necessary," I answer.

He smiles, just barely, and everything in me coils tighter—because he is worth everything I can give him, and if I can't make everything with him work I don't know what I'll do.

"I think you need a sip of this too," Deniel says, stepping up to me and lifting the cup.

I take it and drink deeply, centering myself.

"I don't mind your providing food to me," I say. "But I want to be your partner, not just someone who drags your life down."

Deniel's eyes widen. "What?"

"I know we didn't talk about this, but I—we just moved in. And I feel like we're not doing it together; it's all separate. Everything we do is alone, and it's our first day and we haven't even *eaten* together, let alone talked, or I don't know, discussed where anything in our home should go? Made a meal together and served it to each other? I don't want to live with you if it doesn't mean living *with* you, Deniel."

Deniel looks stricken. He takes the cup out of my hand, but before he puts it anywhere Yorani launches into his face, plucks it out of his fingers, and flies off again.

Without missing a beat, Deniel takes my hands in his. "I'm sorry," he says. "That's what I want, too. We don't get this day back, but we get every other day for the rest of our lives to make how we choose. But after what last night set into motion we had a limited window of time."

I frown, noting he's not laying responsibility for last night at my feet, even though he should. "What do you mean?"

"I worked late hours to account for the fact that I spent the morning meeting with Saiyana about *my* role," Deniel explains, holding my gaze. "Not just as your partner. I'm putting myself forward as the official spokesperson for the city council and liaison to the crown princess. I know this summit is important on a grand scale, and for your role and relationship with your family, but it's also an opportunity for Sayorsen as a community. You'll be managing so much on the international scale; this is a way for once that I can help you."

I choke. "For *once*?!"

"I gather that is not how it seems to you, if you can even consider yourself to be dragging me down," Deniel says, smiling wryly. "But you got me the position on the council, to do the kind of work for our people I hardly dared to dream of. Then you got me a princess as a personal tutor, to help me be able to do it. Believing in me and supporting me the whole way. You've used your tea mastery to support my work, and now I have a chance to use my position to support yours. Ours."

I am staring at him in wonder. "How is it that we understand each other both so well and sometimes also so poorly?"

"You don't mind, then?"

"*Mind?*" I echo. "Deniel, I hardly know where to start. This is sudden, but while I'm supposed to be the tea master of Sayorsen now this is not an angle that had even occurred to me. I'm embarrassed. I'm ashamed you're going to work harder because of what I started—"

"*That's* what I was afraid of," Deniel says, his hands tightening on mine. "You do not have to do everything yourself. Part of being tea master is lifting us all up to work together so our lives don't hinge on one person, right? Sayorsen is my responsibility, too. You're going to have to share."

"You make it sound like I hoard responsibility," I say, halfway joking. "I did pass on the council seat."

"So you did," Deniel says, his grip easing. "And you know what I'm going to do with it? This summit is going to involve a lot of work—finding suitably comfortable and formal places for international guests and caring for them during their stay. Creating meeting spaces. Entertaining them and watching them and processing information.

"It's not just going to be Istals involved in the effort: I'm going to make sure it's Gaellani, too. That we favor any bids where Gaellani and Istals work together, especially if Gaellani lead the teams. We'll pitch it as a joint effort between a Gaellani city council member and an Istal princess—Saiyana, I mean. Iryasa we have to convince to pay for it, and to favor the joint bids."

The city council will likely let him take the lead without too much trouble to avoid any fallout, like they were unwilling to confront the difficulty Kustio presented them. But pitching this as a joint effort also means that if something falters with Gaellani leadership, the brunt of criticism can fall to Saiyana, who is more than able to bear it.

I squeeze his hands back. "You're amazing. I love you."

They are words I've said before. Somehow, with every repetition, rather than gaining familiarity, they've begun to feel like a prayer, or perhaps a promise. A layering of my commitment to him with every utterance.

Deniel eyes me carefully, though there's a twinkle in his eye. "You're not just saying that so we'll stop fighting and we can have sex?"

"I—*what*? Of course not!"

Only after my flabbergasted response is out of my mouth do I realize Deniel was trying to pierce the tension between us, as he is now doubled over laughing.

I smack him on the shoulder, and he collapses to the floor, still laughing. A smile tugging at my lips, I crouch down to join him, and he pulls me into his lap like it's the most natural place for us in the world.

"Next time I'm not going to miss a beat," I grump. "I'm going to say, 'yes Deniel, you're on to me, that's exactly my nefarious plan to have my way with you', and then it will be me on the floor unable to breathe at your expression."

"Not now that you've warned me," he says, then reconsiders. "No, you're probably right."

That gives *me* pause. "Is it so unbelievable that I want to have sex with you?"

Deniel shakes his head, smiling. "I hope not. It's only unbelievable that you would go into sex without all of your spirit focused the same direction."

Ah. That's true: I've read enough of the novels Risteri's lent me now to understand there are many reasons people choose to have sex, and what I consider obvious isn't necessarily the most common.

"And I'm not that amazing," Deniel says, bending down so his forehead rests on mine, his lips tantalizingly close. "I haven't talked to Iryasa about this yet. I still have to get her to agree, and I'm the weak link: she already respects Saiyana. I'm meeting her alone tomorrow morning."

I close my eyes to help me focus. "That," I say, "is perfect. Give her a tour to help get her situated—details of Gaellani craftsmanship in the courtyard she might not otherwise notice. Tell her what they did for me with the pop-up shop in the tournament. And in particular, help her sample food without having to choose what kind."

I open my eyes when Deniel closes the distance between us to kiss me softly, and I wrap my arms around him.

"See, this is what I mean," Deniel says. "You have no doubts at all in the ability of a Gaellani potter to arrange a deal with the crown princess of Istalam. You're just giving me tips to make it easier."

"I'm taking advantage of you," I admit. "While you're keeping her busy, I'll have the opportunity to meet with Saiyana and find out what Iryasa isn't telling me."

But instead of being bothered by my manipulation, Deniel smiles. "You are shameless." He kisses me. "And relentless." Another kiss. "I love you too."

I would sit just like that forever, but a soft pawing noise draws my gaze. Talsion is trying to get Yorani's attention, but my poor familiar is so exhausted by a day of exploration and looking out for me she just curls around the cat and tries to go to sleep. Talsion, apparently in a rare mood where he's not immediately ready for naps, stalks off, batting at the air as if to defend Yorani from spirits.

"Well, if Yorani is willing to let us out of her sight, I assume we're going to manage somehow," I murmur, resting my chin on Deniel's shoulder. "I probably shouldn't let her push herself so hard."

"I hear where you're coming from, but if she's anything like you—and she is—I'm not sure how you intend to stop her without breaking her spirit," Deniel says.

"I am nowhere near as mischievous," I counter lightly.

"You cause infinitely more trouble," he teases back. "And you know she learns from what you model, Miyara. If you want her not to push herself to exhaustion—"

I sigh, and Deniel breaks off, rubbing my back. He's made his point.

My voice muffled into his shoulder, I say, "I want to wake up with you tomorrow."

The movement of his hand pauses; tightens. "What about tonight?" he asks.

I look up. "I'm already awake."

He smiles, his perfect crooked Deniel smile. "Then how about we make something? I hear it's our first full day together, and we have a remade kitchen to explore now that it's both of ours. There's also a small matter of cake."

I stare.

And then my own smile blooms impossibly wide, and I take his face in my hands and kiss him with enough force that I unbalance him, and we land in a laughing heap together.

CHAPTER 7

WHEN I ARRIVE AT the barrier to the Cataclysm the next morning, Saiyana is engaged in a meticulous spell setup. After a careful look at the boundaries, I negotiate my way inside and hold out a thermos.

"I'm not thirsty," my sister says.

"Your fingers are turning purple. It's soup. Warm and nutritious, the better for continuing to push yourself harder than your body can take."

Saiyana pauses long enough to glare at me, but she does take the thermos and drinks deeply.

After a quick hello chirp, Yorani flies off toward the barrier.

"My body will cope," Saiyana says. "The stakes are too high for anything else."

I understood that already, but hearing it from her still makes my stomach drop even while watching Yorani flutter around as if playing with invisible spirits. "You have no idea what's causing the expansion?"

"Oh, I have ideas," Saiyana says. "Ideas on how to stop it are a different matter. Does Iryasa know you're here?"

"No," I say. "But she agreed to the condition that any news about the Cataclysm goes directly to me without needing to be filtered through her first. On the chance she might have forgotten to mention that to you, I thought I'd stop by in person."

"I can't help you," Saiyana warns. "Not with this."

"I gathered, and I appreciate your concern, but you also know I don't need you to," I answer. "I will handle Iryasa. But I do need to know what's going on."

She looks at me hard. "Don't underestimate her, Miyara. Iryasa is very practiced at people trying to handle her."

"And I am very practiced at being thought useless," I say. "Nevertheless."

Saiyana sighs. "It's not going to be that easy."

"I never said it was. That doesn't change that it's necessary, so I will accomplish it. Just like you will learn more about the Cataclysm all at once than mages have managed in decades. Tell me."

Saiyana wastes no more time. "Look at this." She completes her spell diagram with a deliberately placed rock and triggers it with a snap.

It's like she has layered a lens between where we stand and the barrier: I can see whirling magical currents in colorful shades as well as faint lines leading toward dark spots.

"Incredible," I murmur. "You can isolate the weak spots in the barrier?"

"To a point," Saiyana says grumpily. "The barrier is like a dome, as far as we know, though I think it's more likely a sphere that extends underground. This won't show me any weaknesses outside of my field of vision. That's our next step, to get a complete picture of the problem before we can confirm any theories."

Completely dismissing the depth of her achievement when it doesn't fully solve a problem is extremely like her. I've never even heard of magic like this, and I haven't been gone from mage training that long. She and Ostario invented this within the last month. For any other mage it would be a pinnacle achievement of their career.

Since she's not going to accept any more of my praise, I stay on target. "The Te Muraka might be able to get you eyes on the top of the barrier for more immediate, if not entirely complete, data."

She looks wistful. "I thought of that, but I think for now we're better off close to the ground. I don't want to be caught in the middle of the sky when a breach happens. There's too much we don't know. But from what we do, I have suspicions."

"Which are?"

"Politically fraught," Ostario says, coming up behind us. He takes the soup thermos from Saiyana and replaces it with another. "Tea."

Saiyana pulls a face. "Oh good, both of you are mothering me. Just what I need."

"Evidently," I murmur, and she glares at me.

Ostario sips his own tea and points at the dark spots. "Saiyana's working on getting a complete data set of the spread of magic throughout the barrier. My focus is on mapping those dark spots to vectors within the Cataclysm."

"Inasmuch as we can," Saiyana adds. "The Cataclysm being constantly in motion and all."

"I've been relying on the guides, but I think I'll work more closely with Risteri from now on," Ostario says. "The information I need and what it means is... politically sensitive, which she can be trusted to know how to handle. I suspect I will be able to definitively determine these weaknesses in the barrier are a direct result of the foreign technology released within the Cataclysm of late."

I was afraid of that, but I'm also not surprised. I watch the colors of the barrier fluctuate where Yorani darts in and out of the barrier, wondering if it's her magic making the difference or something else.

"That's not all you have to tell me," I say, "is it."

Saiyana says, "Magecraft, witchcraft, and Te Muraka magic have all been practiced inside the Cataclysm for years with no notable effect. All of a sudden Nakrabi magic is used, and the Cataclysm is erupting? Yeah, of course I have suspicions. Not enough evidence for a legal case yet, but we think the Cataclysm is reacting against the Nakrabi magic. Every usage of their tech inside roiled the Cataclysm magic strongly enough that the barrier is expanding. And it's not slowing, just building momentum in increments. If we don't stop it—"

"But why?" I ask. "Is Nakrabi magic truly so different for not being from the continent?"

Saiyana and Ostario exchange glances. "Yes and no," my sister hedges.

Ostario picks up the explanation. "We have two theories, and both of them are troubling. The first is that the Cataclysm recognizes the feeling of Nakrabi magic and is attempting to purge it."

I suck in a breath, this thought having never crossed my imagination in all the years of people blaming one group or another and usually witches. "You mean you think the *Nakrabi* are responsible for the Cataclysm?"

"Not sufficient evidence," Saiyana warns again. "But it's a theory."

A terrifying, horrifying, galling theory.

If all this time the devastation on our continent is the fault of outsiders who then refused to help—

"What we do have evidence of is bad enough," Ostario says. "Which is that Nakrabi magic is immune to magecraft."

I stare, thinking furiously. "You're sure? But at the final tournament match, Ari destroyed the weapon—"

"By applying force to the physical structures, not by unraveling or overpowering the magical ones," Ostario says. "Believe me, we've discussed it at length via remote message."

"It must be killing them to not be here," I murmur.

Ostario sighs. "It was. I'm having them do a lot of supplemental work independently on our current projects, as they're the closest mage to an expert besides the two of us, even with their unorthodox training. It's an unfair burden for them to bear while trying to acclimate to their studies."

"The relevant point," Saiyana says, probably unhappy with being forced to rely on anyone else for magework, "is that this is remarkably bad news in light of the fact that the Nakrabi will be en route imminently, if you and Iryasa have your way."

"We will," I confirm.

"Magecraft defenses will be able to cope with any workings from Taresal and Velasar, though," Ostario points out. "The latter is not insignificant, all things considered. There is also witchcraft, and it may be time for the crown to employ it openly."

"I don't want to just use Lorwyn," I say. "Being seen primarily as a weapon is not going to help witches in the long term."

"If we don't deal with this short-term emergency there won't be a long-term," Saiyana says grimly.

"Don't discount the Te Muraka as well," Ostario adds, "though that carries something of the same problem."

"It does," I agree, "but Sa Rangim and Iryasa are working together on that already."

Saiyana looks at me sharply. "You're up to something, aren't you?"

"Always, it seems," I say. "How do you handle it?"

"Don't ask her that," Ostario says. "The answer is poorly."

Saiyana glares at him, and to my surprise, Ostario glares back.

Aha. I take that to mean their mutual romantic inclinations toward each other are definitely not resolved, but nor are they vanished.

Yorani chooses that moment to fly through the magecraft lens, shattering it utterly.

Saiyana swears as she doubles over at the sudden backlash. "What in the name of the spirits was *that* for? If your spirit can't tell a magecraft working on her own, keep her in line, Miyara!"

"Or perhaps," I say, holding a hand out to the hissing tea spirit, "the problem is that in all our discussion we failed to consider a present source of alternative magical assistance. Is that it, Yorani?"

She huffs a whorl of smoke and settles grumpily onto my shoulder, tail lashing.

"Well aside from breaking my mageworks, what does she have in mind?" Saiyana asks sarcastically. "If only I trusted all my plans to magic I don't understand and that can't communicate with me. What a fantastic way to plan for us to depend the future of the world on."

As wary as I am of involving Yorani again in political dangers that can get her hurt, I can't help defending her. "You're learning more about the Cataclysm. We'll learn more about what Yorani can contribute, too. Don't count her out just because you don't understand her." Turning to Ostario, I say, "And as Lorwyn's mentor, you may be in the best position to guide Lorwyn and Iryasa in coming to likewise mutually beneficial terms for witches as are currently underway with the Te Muraka."

"No," Saiyana snaps. "Miyara, don't be stupid. You know what position that would put Ostario in."

Ostario eyes her narrowly. "I am not ashamed of how I was born, princess."

Saiyana waves that off like it doesn't bear considering. "I didn't say you were or should be. That's not the same as how the mage council will see it and you know it. Publicly tying yourself to witches at that level—"

"Won't hurt me if witches are publicly accepted."

"You know bigotry doesn't get rooted out that fast."

"I also know it's not your job to manage my career," Ostario says with an uncharacteristic edge in his voice. "Which I have told you before."

Saiyana clenches her jaw and turns away. She can't argue with that without undermining Ostario's autonomy, but I know she doesn't believe it, either—and nor is she entirely wrong.

Over the years she has made more than one problem borne out of bigotry against him vanish. I'm not sure how much of that Ostario has inferred.

"It is the responsibility of those with greater ability to leverage that power to the benefit of those who can't," I say softly. "Saiyana's political power is greater than yours, Ostario, though yours can grow—and in some ways, you have more freedom than a princess. Perhaps you might consider how else you can use it."

This time they both look at me sharply, aware but unwilling to say what we all understand: that while Saiyana feels she has to protect Ostario's life and hide behind that role, the dynamic between them will never support an equal relationship.

I smile and pass Ostario the other bag I'm holding. "In the meantime, please use your powers of actually being invested in survival to see that Saiyana eats more this afternoon."

Ostario's face freezes just for a moment, and I almost lose control of my own expression.

Does he truly think Saiyana is actively that self-destructive?

Is he right?

"What's for lunch?" he asks.

But he holds my gaze evenly, and I understand what this time it's he who isn't saying.

That he will handle her.

It will be no easier than my handling Iryasa, and just the same I will have to trust him.

And I do.

"Fermented beans in egg rolls," I answer lightly. "Full of energy to keep her going. Absolutely nothing objectionable to her."

"Fermented beans smell awful," Saiyana says neutrally.

"And yet you love them," I counter serenely, as Ostario takes the bag. "If she doesn't remember to eat them, please push them into her face."

"Miyara," Saiyana says in a warning tone.

"If only the Seneschal of Istalam could be trusted to manage something as basic as remembering on her own to eat," I say solemnly. "I'm grateful there to be able to put my faith in you, Mage Ostario."

"You wretch," Saiyana snarls.

Because of course if the alternative is allowing Ostario to feed her, I am confident Saiyana will find she is able to remember.

Ostario's eyes dance with renewed humor as he bows over the bag. "You have my solemn vow I will see it done."

Saiyana says to me, "You have ten seconds to leave before I murder you."

I smile as I turn on my heel, taking her at her word and leaving before I can push her too far. The remaining familiarity and tension between them, though utterly unlike my relationship with Deniel, for them I think bodes well. They will work through their problems by challenging each other, as they always have.

But my smile fades as I consider the meaning of what I've learned from her.

What they theorize is concerning enough.

What they're sure of is worse.

Yet before I can begin to work through the implications, Entero is suddenly in front of me, looking grim.

"I need you to come with me," he says tightly. "Right now."

Despite that, I pause. "Lorwyn is waiting," I test.

His jaw is clenched so hard I can see lines of strain on his face. "Even so."

"Will you tell me why?" I ask calmly, as if this hasn't sent my heart rate accelerating like a dance.

"Oh, I'll tell you everything," Entero says grimly. "But you may not want to bring Yorani."

Danger. Wherever he's taking me, he doesn't trust Yorani to be safe there.

But Yorani immediately digs her claws into my shoulder and hisses in his face, a touch of flame escaping her mouth—not enough to burn him, but like a candle flickering against his face, a clear threat of her own.

I regard her where she sits on my shoulder, and she glares back at me. So be it.

"At the first hint of threat to you, you will fly directly to Saiyana," I say. "Is that understood?"

She hisses at *me* this time, though without the flame.

"I know you're angry at her, but she can be relied on to immediately understand a threat to you is a threat to me and do something about it without causing a political incident. Otherwise, believe me, I'd send you to Sa Rangim or Lorwyn instead. We're not there yet."

"Yet?" Entero asks me.

I ignore him in favor of holding Yorani's gaze until finally she turns away, hunching tensely on my shoulder.

"She's coming," I tell Entero. "Where are we going?"

He starts walking, and I fall into step. "The cottage you used to live in on Taresim grounds."

I frown at him. "Iryasa and Reyata stayed there last night, but Saiyana's settled them in a different location now."

"Yes," Entero says tightly, "because Risteri's grandmother is now in residence."

Whatever I could have expected, it wasn't that. "Risteri's *grandmother* is the danger? Or do you mean—"

"Yes," Entero grits out. "Lady Kireva, Risteri's grandmother and current de facto head of House Taresim, who is also one of *your* grandmother's most trusted and most dangerous assets. Now will you stop talking and let me brief you?"

Risteri's grandmother is a spy. Reeling from all the surprises the morning has brought already, I nod, keeping my mouth tightly shut.

※

By the time the cottage comes into view, much has become clearer.

The reason Entero had been sent so quickly as an operative for Sayorsen, despite not having completed law enforcement interfacing training, was because my grandmother's first choice of operative who already had a network in place on the ground, Lady Kireva, had taken sick and been unable to travel.

I posited that the stress of Kustio's scandal combined with her age might have made anyone susceptible to illness; Entero's scorn for the possibility in her case was sufficient to communicate that whatever face the Lady Kireva is prepared to show me, I should operate on the assumption that her claws are always prepared to strike.

"Anything else I need to know before we go in?" I murmur as we approach the door.

Entero's expression is like an angry rock. "Not that you haven't already gleaned."

I nod. It has not escaped my notice that Entero doesn't want to be bringing me to meet Lady Kireva, yet is nevertheless. I'll sort out the rest as it comes.

The cottage door, which seemed so familiar only yesterday, has taken on a sinister cant. She didn't have the cottage set up for any emotional need for space, but for secrecy in her dealings on behalf of Istalam's spy network and associated assignations. It was never intended to be a welcoming place, but a front to hide true purposes behind.

Well. I had been in hiding myself when I arrived. But it is all to the good that I found a purpose to be open about and left it behind me.

Before I've had a chance to wipe my shoes off, the door opens.

"Do come in already," Lady Kireva says brusquely, turning her back on us and heading into the living area.

A show of power: that she already knew we were here, that we are not worth niceties, and that we are already inconveniencing her with that expectation, putting the burden of niceties on us.

So I stop exactly where I am and don't move a step further.

After a moment, Lady Kireva makes a sound of disgust. "*Really?* You think your ego is more important than my intelligence? Grow up, child. I am too old to be impressed by you."

"I think you will treat me with basic respect, or I will manage without your vaunted intelligence one way or another, Lady Kireva," I say.

"I am here at the personal request of the dowager queen, and the end of the world is at stake," she snaps.

"And isn't it a pity that even in such circumstances you can't cease playing petty games."

I wait, the two of us eyeing each other across the room.

"Shall we begin again, lady?" I ask softly.

Lady Kireva chuckles roughly. "Hardly. You don't forget any more easily than I do, I daresay. Come in and let me tell you what you need to know."

That will do.

Beside me, Entero lets out a breath as I cross the threshold.

"Your shadow there could benefit from lessons in managing social power plays," Lady Kireva remarks, laying out a prepared tray of tea.

Fully prepared to offer us courtesy, but only after I passed a test. I can't say I'm surprised.

"Yorani isn't a shadow of anyone," I say. "She's a familiar and a being in her own right."

"Don't be dense, dear," Lady Kireva says.

"Really, I don't think that was too subtle for you." I lean back easily in one of the chairs I used to live with, that probably had hidden magecraft workings the whole time. "Don't be rude. If you have something to say to Entero, say it to Entero. Who has a name, and isn't my shadow, which you know perfectly well."

"I know nothing of the kind," Lady Kireva says, but she does look at him. "You think you're an agent without a handler, but you don't have the faintest idea how to operate in this role."

"I'm finding my own way," Entero says tightly, and the fact that he has spoken at all in his own defense makes me want to burst with pride.

"You're not finding it fast enough. I can help." She glances at me as she pours the tea. "And so can you."

She waits for me to take a cup.

It's unlikely she's slipped anything into the tea, given the three cups present, and even if she treated a cup in advance to counteract it, leaving me to choose is a show of openness—and a challenge. Because of course this is another test, to see how I react.

The end of the world is at stake. Trusted by my grandmother as she may be, I have no patience for such blatant wastes of my time.

I turn to Yorani. "Do you think we should have some of this tea?"

Like she's been waiting for the chance, Yorani breathes flame over all the cups. The tea in each sparkles briefly before settling into a perfectly innocuous-appearing liquid.

As I pick a cup and sip easily, Lady Kireva's expression is calculating. But she sits very, very still.

I have reminded her very blatantly that I have no need to play by her rules.

"I understand my grandmother may have once had aspirations that I might succeed her in her work," I say. "It is not to be. I am a tea master, and I am specifically Sayorsen's tea master. With a tea spirit at my side I am uniquely suited to dealing with the problem at hand. If you are here to distract me from my course, Lady Kireva, say so now and we can be done."

The old woman taps her fingers on the arm of her chair.

"You are bold," Lady Kireva says after a minute. "I can see why my granddaughter likes you."

"And you clearly like to live as dangerously as she does with a penchant for secret-keeping, but if there is other familial resemblance between you I have yet to witness it," I say.

Her eyes flash with something I'm not sure what to make of. "Very well. If you're not willing to train to manage a spy network, then *he* must," she says, nodding to Entero. "You're both relying overly on foreign intelligence you don't control."

"You mean Thiano."

"Oh, I certainly mean the Nakrabi, but not just him," Lady Kireva tuts. "A teenage Taresal mage-farmer. Dragons. Witches—"

Entero and I both rise as one.

"Oh sit down, I have nothing against the girl or her ilk," Lady Kireva says.

"Then 'ilk' is quite the choice of word," I say softly, "and you should be very careful what you say next."

She rolls her eyes. "My point is that all your intelligence is coming from outside the systems you have to understand to change them effectively. Or do you mean to suggest that witches are thoroughly integrated into our political systems?"

"In that they're systemically marginalized, certainly," I say.

"Quite. So." As if we're in agreement, she turns her attention to Entero. "You don't have the luxury of time, child. If you want this role to become your reality instead of another ephemeral assignment, you need different skills, and I can teach them to you."

"Why," Entero asks flatly.

Her eyes narrow. "I am aware that the witch is my granddaughter's closest friend, and that without all three of you she would probably be dead by now by my own son's hand," Lady Kireva says softly. "Do not presume I do not understand all of what that means."

Spirits, understanding even half of the implications would be a minor miracle.

At Entero's silence, Lady Kireva nods and continues, "I am also, of course, here for you, Tea Master of Sayorsen. Queen Ilmari is content to let her daughters take the lead, but never think she is disinterested in how you fare."

That generic 'you'—neither explicitly singular nor plural—can only have been deliberate, from someone who claims to understand fraught family complexity.

"Are you to be a source watching us or helping us?" I ask.

"Both, of course," she says. "Your recent triumphs along with Princess Iryasa's initiative are promising, but neither of you has years of experience behind you. The situation is too dire to trust that you will simply manage."

"Do they trust us or don't they," I murmur. "Do you think they know, whatever they say?"

"I think," Entero says suddenly, "what she means is that Lady Kireva's oversight is the price of letting you lead."

Lady Kireva smiles at him. "Just so, dear. Perhaps we'll do well together after all."

"I will of course welcome your counsel," I say, "but I will not accept your oversight. And I imagine you will likewise have your work cut out for you with your ostensible reason for being in Sayorsen: putting your own House in order."

"Ah, you judge me for my son's actions, of course. You are young. Do you imagine it is so easy to keep a House in order, child?"

"I do not," I say seriously, and this time she seems to understand I mean it.

"Well, then," Lady Kireva says. "Now that we all understand each other, we have business to be about. You." She points a finger at Entero. "Visit me tonight, and we'll get started."

Entero's expression is unreadable as he bows without a word of protest—or agreement.

We take our leave.

Only once we are outside Taresim's premises do I ask softly, "Yorani?"

The tea spirit twitches her tail and curls up, which I take to be a negative on whether we are being magically observed.

"Somehow," I say to Entero, "I am both envious and appalled for you." When he glances down at me, I explain, "I have wished for so long for someone to guide me, to teach me how to navigate the role I would fulfill and where its boundaries lie. Yet it is difficult for me to imagine wishing for such a teacher as she."

I thought that might elicit at least a note of humor from him, but Entero's shoulders tense—as close to hunching as he gets.

"We do understand each other well enough," I say quietly. "She is going to continue to test my boundaries. It is who she is. But you're going to have to be prepared to negotiate boundaries with her, too."

Entero laughs darkly. "Oh, I'm aware. I know better than you what it means for her to have summoned me to do her bidding. But the boundaries are different among spies."

"Are they?" I ask neutrally.

"I'll handle it, Miyara," Entero growls.

I'm not sure he knows how, but I am confident he will fight. That's all any of us can do. "Good," I say, and turn in the direction of Talmeri's—and Lorwyn. "Then let's see about getting *our* house in order."

CHAPTER 8

"GOOD OF YOU TO stop by and visit us peons," Lorwyn snipes as soon as we enter the back of Talmeri's. Elowyn shoots us a troubled glance before quickly turning back to the leaves she's helping Lorwyn prepare.

Yorani flaps off to go hover around Elowyn, poking a scaly nose into her business.

"No Tamak?" I ask.

"On his way," Lorwyn answers. "But if you think his presence makes up for your silence—"

"I'm sorry," I say. "I have a lot to update you on."

She chops a little harder. "At least one of you will."

I raise my eyebrows at Entero.

"I work for the crown, Miyara, even if you don't," Entero grits out.

It didn't occur to me before that perhaps as Tea Master of Sayorsen I might need staff, and now I wonder if I should have made an effort to bring Entero with me into this role—further out of the shadows for his own happiness, and more to the point, to a place where necessary lies would not have to exist and be a barrier between him and Lorwyn. "Perhaps that's worth renegotiating, too," I tell him.

He nods shortly. "I'm working on it."

There's a lot he has to work on, I think to myself, interrupted as Lorwyn snorts.

"What he's working on is becoming a cop," she says.

I frown. "That's hardly news. Interfacing with the police is his job. What am I missing?"

Lorwyn and Elowyn exchange glances.

It's Entero who answers me. "You're missing that the police exist to enforce the law of the systems as they currently exist, not as you would wish them to be."

Oh. Stupid of me not to see immediately. Of course the police, as enforcement representatives of a system that has oppressed the Gaellani for years, are not officers Lorwyn or Elowyn can look to for fairness. Even a police officer who earnestly wanted to help them would be steeped in bias and constrained by the oppressive system it is their job to uphold.

"But you have to be able to work with them," I say. "How is that going?"

To my surprise, he actually winces. "Not particularly well."

"Well enough," Lorwyn says, "that he moved into one of their spirits-cursed neighborhoods."

"To help integrate socially?" I surmise.

Lorwyn slams down the knife in her hands so hard it digs into the wood. "He shouldn't integrate with them. He shouldn't be trying to be one of them."

"I'm not trying to be one of them, I'm trying to get them to be comfortable with me," Entero growls with the air of someone who's had this argument before.

"And are you going to get them to be comfortable with me?" Lorwyn challenges. "Because the reverse sure isn't going to happen."

"It's not like I'm comfortable with them either," Entero snaps. "Or have you forgotten who I am?"

"I think you can't bury who you are," Lorwyn says, staring him dead in the eye. "And sooner or later the cops will realize why they're not comfortable around you."

Entero has no response to that, and after the morning he's had I decide to rescue him.

"Is your house very far from the apartment?" I ask him, thinking that will be safe enough, but Lorwyn makes a sound of disgust and turns around.

"It's only an apartment," Entero says. "And yes, fairly."

His eyes flick toward Lorwyn and back to me, and I realize that this effect, at least, is intentional on his part: some physical distance between them to help them ease into the idea of commitment.

I raise my eyebrows at him, as if to say, You may want to reconsider that, too.

And he rolls his eyes back, clearly meaning, Not all of us are like you.

Which is true enough, but before I can say any more on the matter one way or another, the door to the front opens, and Taseino steps in, a cleaning rag in his hands.

"Taseino, thank you for putting in extra time while I've been out so suddenly," I say.

He shrugs. "It's no trouble. Tea Master Karekin is out front, though, and I don't have a key on me. I assume he's here for you."

The shop isn't open for the day yet, but he must have known we'd be here preparing. Or, more troubling, it's not the first time he's tried to reach me here.

And of course what I'm truly preparing for isn't serving customers at all, but all of Istalam and beyond.

Don't think that way, Miyara, you'll scare yourself.

"I'll see to him," I say, grateful for this intervention to prevent me from meddling between Lorwyn and Entero. They're both talking—or yelling, or knifing—about their concerns to each other, which surely is the most important part of developing trust in what they have. They'll work it out on their own, and if they need me to mediate I'll be here.

Yorani flutters back to my shoulder to join me as I move through the front, and I silently pray my thanks for Taseino to the spirits. Everything is clean and orderly, except for one area behind the counter that Taseino has clearly noticed and begun remedying on his own. He has stepped in to fill out my role here unflappably. He's always been calm and with an eye for detail, but he's grown, too: not just his knowledge of tea, but his ability to manage under pressure and the insight to know how to deal with different people at a glance. He won't ever be a tea master, but soon I think there will be little left for him to learn here.

It's a challenge to myself, to not let myself be so overrun that I don't continue to grow, too, to make sure I can do right by my people and help facilitate their growth. But it's... both reassuring and oddly sad to realize that it won't be too long before he won't need me, as he flies to other directions.

I unlock the front door and find Karekin studying the wearing sign above Talmeri's Teas and Tisanes.

"I'm surprised you haven't replaced that," he notes. "It doesn't reflect what you want to signal."

I sigh. "For now, at least, it signals continuity."

"But not change," the tea master points out. "And not any sort of rebirth, or new direction, to indicate there is any difference between things as they were before and the new era out from under the thumb of Kustio. As the employees of Talmeri's were instrumental in bringing about his fall, don't you think the rest of Sayorsen will look to you to lead them in this?"

I sigh, leaning back against the door with the relief that I can perhaps talk to him of all people about this openly but also unutterable weariness that I can't hide even this.

"I haven't had time," I say simply. "I don't disagree. But there isn't time."

"Priorities," Tea Master Karekin muses, running a gentle hand along the worn doorframe. "You've had to take on more than most, and much faster. But some things cannot, or should not, be put off."

"When I have too many of those things, inevitably some must be," I say. "Unless you have some secret trick to extend time?"

Karekin meets my eyes. "There is no such knowledge among the tea masters, but there is much else, and I believe you will need it sooner than you know."

"I needed it before Yorani nearly died," I say.

He nods, bowing to Yorani. "Indeed. I know you are busy, Miyara. But I have not heard from you in days, and if I do not miss my guess it's more important than ever for you to not tarry any longer in beginning the training that should have been yours already."

"Then tell me how to balance doing all of this," I say, somewhat desperately. "I would be delighted to train with you. Tell me how."

"An air of mystery helps," Karekin drawls.

I blink, completely startled by what I think is a joke.

"What I think perhaps you may need to remind yourself," Karekin says after I've only managed to gape at for a moment, "is that you do not have to do everything, personally, yourself. Learning the secrets of the tea guild you do; perhaps responsibility for this sign need not be yours alone."

"It sounds very easy when you say it that way," I say, "but then I will only be tracking other people doing my tasks, or teaching them how."

The tea master looks from me to Yorani and back again. "Do you believe in other people or don't you?" Karekin asks. "Do you believe in your judgment of them or don't you?"

I blow out a breath, and beside me Yorani puffs out a whorl of smoke in solidarity. "Well. When you put it like that."

"Quite," he says, smiling slightly. "I thought that might get your attention."

"I wonder, then, if it's important for me to be here at all," I admit, staring back toward the tidy front room. "Perhaps they can manage everything without me."

"Ah," Karekin says. "And what do you believe makes them able to live up to your trust?"

I glance at Yorani, and she meets my gaze steadily.

This is my first lesson, perhaps: that even tea masters sometimes need to be checked—and who better to do so than another tea master?

As I did for the entire guild, only weeks past.

What matters is that I lead by example: when I demonstrate my commitment, and my faith, people rise up to meet me.

My attention is drawn at the same moment as Yorani's toward the back door, where my people are, and my heart beats slightly faster.

"Thank you for your counsel, Tea Master," I say with a bow. "I will message you presently to schedule."

"It is my honor." Karekin bows in return. "I see your presence is required. Spirits be with you both."

Unsure exactly what we've picked up on, I rush back into the shop, into the back—and stop dead.

Tamak has arrived, but he's not the only one. Everyone but Taseino, who has occupied himself with a teapot at Lorwyn's work station—which she has shockingly allowed—is staring tensely at the newcomer.

"Your Highness," I say, bowing low. "What an honor and surprise to find you here."

My younger sister Karisa flashes a pleased grin at me. "Miyara," she says slowly, as if savoring the syllables of my first name rather than my title. "It is an honor, isn't it?"

I can't say I have much missed this sister, but I've had a lifetime to learn to ignore her barbs.

To my further surprise, though, Elowyn takes a step forward.

Yorani launches off my shoulder and flies to Elowyn, snuggling up to her neck and cooing, as if to reassure her.

Karisa's eyes narrow. "Was there something?"

Although she's older than Elowyn, they're of a height: the physical characteristic of our father that Karisa inherited is the shorter Velasari stature, and I have wondered if she always assumes the rest of us figuratively look down on her or overlook her for that.

Petting Yorani, Elowyn returns her gaze with a measure of steel. "Yes. Her proper title is tea master, your Highness."

"Well," Karisa says, "it's a good thing Istalam has such devoted servants as you to tell your betters what they already know and have chosen to deliberately disregard. Unless you're an expert at politics? Rhetoric? No? I thought not."

Barbs at me are one thing; bigoted insults at my people are quite another.

"She recognized perfectly well what you were doing and countered beautifully, as someone of your education ought to know," I say sharply. "Whatever welcome you were given on entry, Karisa, I withdraw it."

Karisa draws herself up to her full height, which, though smaller than anyone in the room but Yorani, she manages to make loom. "You have no right—"

"I do, but even if I didn't I don't care," I say. "Princess or spirit, no person who would treat another so callously is welcome here. Leave."

"You would throw your sister out on the streets," Karisa sneers. "So this is the true self you've been hiding all these years, is it? So be it."

She whirls, and as she does I take note for the first time that she's dressed not dissimilarly to Lorwyn, but more expensively—hyper-fashionable in a way that will blend in utterly here. How did she manage it?

Entero is already at the door, holding it open for her, and Karisa tosses her hair at his face so he has to jerk back away, and she slams the door behind her.

As suddenly as that, scarce sentences exchanged between us, and she's gone.

Silence rings, and I let out a breath.

"Well," I say. "I see you've all met my younger sister. My apologies."

After a moment, Lorwyn drawls, "Okay, I'm impressed. I have never seen a single person get under so many people's skin so fast. That is quite a talent. You're sure you're related?"

I sigh. "Regrettably. How do you think she always knows exactly where to poke?"

"More like stab," Lorwyn says.

Elowyn wipes the tea leaves off her hands and turns. "I think someone should let Princess Saiyana know she's here, since I gather this wasn't planned? I'll follow her in the meantime."

I glance at Elowyn, startled. Messaging Saiyana should have been my first thought, and Elowyn, the one Karisa has just slighted, should not have to take on the burden of keeping an eye on her.

"You don't have to put yourself in a position to be hurt," I tell Elowyn seriously.

She regards me calmly. "I'm not going to talk to her, Miyara. And you would do the same if you could."

If I could follow, she means. I can certainly hide in plain sight well enough, though Elowyn's skills at shadowing eclipse mine to the point hers seem almost magical in nature.

But what arrests me is that, although I should follow Karisa, at this moment I have absolutely no personal desire to. Yet Elowyn does.

Are years of enduring Karisa informing my judgment, or are they affecting my character?

"Besides, it looks like Yorani will be going with me," Elowyn says, "since she's resisting my attempts to dislodge her. Is that okay?"

I hold Yorani's firm gaze, wondering what she thinks of Karisa. The tea spirit doesn't seem to be in one of her vengeful moods.

Maybe she wants to form an opinion of my sister without my judgment influencing hers, and maybe I need that.

I bow my assent, and Elowyn flits out into the shadows.

Lorwyn eyes me thoughtfully. "I don't think I've ever seen you be that short with someone, that fast," she notes. "I'm surprised. Surely being around people who are so spoiled they don't have to know any better was normal for you before. She fits that type exactly."

I shake my head. "No, she absolutely does know what she's doing and that's it awful," I say. "That's the entire point. But I have never understood why."

Taseino gives me a profoundly skeptical look.

"Please, if you think I am missing something obvious, by all means tell me," I say.

"This doesn't seem complicated, Miyara," Taseino says, looking for all the world like he doesn't understand why he's having to explain this to me. "She just watched you treat Elowyn like your little sister instead of her."

I blink at him, replaying that interaction. How my familiar, flew immediately to Elowyn, and what Karisa would have understood that to mean; how I immediately stood up for Elowyn and did not make the slightest effort to make Karisa welcome in my life here.

Saiyana pointed out that Karisa and I were not that different in age, and I told Sa Rangim that circumstances prevented us from being close. But how much of that distance was due to my unwillingness to try?

Oh, certainly, the circumstances existed; trying to be closer to her would have caused scenes and political ripples, and in hiding my true self as I was I never tried, nor cared to.

But if Karisa cared to, only to be met with what must have looked like aloofness—if the only way she could ever get anyone to care about her was to make scenes, and she came here to me first to see if that had changed—

"Miyara?" Lorwyn asks, poking me. "You look like you've seen a spirit. And not the small winged kind."

In a way, I have. The wrongness between Karisa and me isn't news, but my awareness of it, my perception of it, is fundamentally realtering, casting our past in a different light. I've arrived at a critical turning point without even noticing, and if I miss it, something important will be lost forever.

I don't know how I know. Perhaps my instincts are something the tea guild can help me understand. But in this moment, I can perceive just enough to know that my relationship with Karisa will determine our course, even if I don't understand why.

Or perhaps it is only that my sudden guilt and anger at myself will be debilitating unresolved, and this is at its core a selfish impulse. Even so, I am decided: I am going.

But Elowyn, not me, followed Karisa, and I can't even guess where my sister might have gone. How alone must Karisa feel, if even I, with my vaunted powers of perception, have failed to notice her?

I stare at Lorwyn. "Can you track Karisa? She wears magecraft security bracelets."

Her eyebrows shoot up. "I have no idea. Can you give me a hint about how to set up the spell?"

I'm already moving to her bag of sticks. "Taseino, my apologies, but can you stay a little longer? I'll be back as soon as possible."

"I can do that," Taseino says.

I look at him seriously. "Thank you."

He nods quickly—embarrassed by me or by my thanks, I'm not sure—and heads back to the front without another word.

Lorwyn has grasped the shape I'm working at and finished without me, but after a moment she shakes her head. "Sorry. Nothing. Did I miss part of the structure?"

"Not as far as I can tell, but this is somewhat beyond me," I say, frowning down at it. I don't see any reason why it shouldn't work, given that I know the particular dimensions of how the bracelets work, but perhaps there's a further layer of complexity that neither I nor Lorwyn, new as she is to magecraft, have grasped. Maybe Glynis could—

I round on Tamak. "Can you find her?"

Tamak's expression shuts down immediately, and I'm seized by a sudden intuition.

"Or Yorani," I say, watching him intently.

Tamak nods. "I can locate the tea spirit."

Part of me is relieved, but—spirits, I can't pretend I didn't notice without doing a different disservice. We'll have to talk about it on the way.

"Then let's go," I say. "Entero, can you get Lorwyn up to speed and then have Glynis get a message to Saiyana?"

Entero's gaze flicks to Lorwyn and back. "You don't think the princesses should know their sister is here right away?"

"I'm her sister too," I say firmly. "I will take care of her."

CHAPTER 9

TAMAK LEADS US SWIFTLY and silently away from Talmeri's.

"Do you know where we're going?" I ask.

He shrugs. "They haven't stopped yet. But we can catch up. They're not moving that fast." He cocks his head to the side. "No, they're slowing down. I think it's the bookshop."

The bookshop? Karisa has never been known to be studious.

Then again, maybe that's what she wants everyone to think—or maybe there's something specific she needs there, and maybe it isn't even a book. It's shameful that I can't guess which.

"Then we have a moment," I say, putting on some extra speed so that I'm in front of him, facing him, so he can't pull away from me.

Tamak's expression is totally blank, and I know it for a mask.

"I am not going to ask whether you have a way to track Elowyn," I say. "But I am going to tell you that it would be unethical to do so without her awareness and consent."

Tamak looks away. *Spirits*, I knew it. "Hypothetically, it can't hurt her."

"Ah, yes, keeping secrets from the people they're about certainly never ends badly for anyone," I say.

"You don't understand."

"You are correct. What makes you think Elowyn will, if I don't? Or do you truly believe she'll never find out, and that she won't take it as a betrayal of her trust?"

Tamak hisses out a breath. "It's not a thing I can help, and the reason for that she'll take just as badly."

Well, *that's* interesting. "As I don't know the reason, I can't say. But consider that you are relying on Elowyn to trust your good intentions without trusting hers. Hypothetically."

Tamak balls his hands into fists. "This is so stupid. There's no way to handle this that doesn't involve me losing my only friend."

I place my hands over his fists and stare steadily at him until he meets my eyes. "If you hold her in such high esteem, then give her some credit," I say. "Trust that she will also extend it to you. Unless you've demonstrated to her that you don't deserve it which, to be clear, hypothetically you would be on your way toward doing, if you don't reevaluate your course."

Tamak drops his head and mutters something I don't catch.

"I assume," I say, "this is something you cannot speak to Sa Rangim about?"

Tamak shakes his head violently. "No. Definitely not. Please don't tell him. I'll... handle this."

I consider that and nod slowly. I have many questions to ask Sa Rangim. "Then I will leave it to you. Are they still at the bookshop?"

"Yes."

"Then I can find my way. Thank you. No one is expecting you for a bit, are they? Take some time to think."

He scowls. "I don't need to brood."

I laugh, releasing his hands. "Tamak, you are a champion level brooder. But use the time however you think best. I trust you."

I leave him staring after me as I make my own way toward correcting a grievous mistake.

When I arrive at the bookshop, I consider ruefully that perhaps I too could have dealt with more thinking, and should have kept Tamak with me a few minutes longer until I had in fact located Karisa. The thing about a room full of bookcases is it's hard to locate people, on account of you can't see over the full shelves. They are ideal for hiding.

Which is probably why Karisa made her way here. She's too Istal not to be noticed in the Gaellani courtyards, and even outside formal robes, it's too likely any Istal might recognize her for her to linger in their quarters. But a quiet bookshop is ideal, to discover, and in fact simply as a place to exist peacefully without needing to act.

Perhaps Karisa, who has always seemed to excel at scenes, plans them carefully, and needs time either to plot them or to take a break from the emotional toll enacting them exacts.

I, however, have spent a lifetime not acting. It is how I have failed her for years, and I won't continue now.

I explore the bookshop, eyes sharp for potential hiding places, so I find Elowyn first even though she's blended in like an innocuous customer. I touch her gently on the shoulder without saying a word, and she melts away, Yorani's eyes meeting mine just for an instant as she goes. They won't be far.

Karisa is sitting on the floor, back pressed against a bookcase in a secluded nook surrounded by tall shelves with only one entrance. Not what I would have chosen: I have always considered escape routes, at least since the time Reyata rescued me. But Karisa will know who approaches her and will be prepared to face them head-on.

She looks up from the book she's reading—a Sayorsen history, though the pages when she lays it down are substantially smaller than the cover: another book sitting inside it. Even alone she's prepared to show people what they expect to see and keep her true aims hidden.

I sit down in front of her, a small distance between us in case she decides to throw the history of Sayorsen at me. "What's the smaller book?" I ask her.

Karisa's expression flickers. "That's what you want to know?"

"Among other things, but yes, that is one reason I ask questions."

"No greetings for your discarded sister? No apologies for your rudeness? No—"

"Oh, come off it, you were unconscionably rude and you know it," I say. "You wanted a reaction and you got one. There are many things I'm sorry for in our relationship, but that's not one of them."

"Oh? Then what *are* you sorry for?"

"The fact that we don't really have a relationship," I say.

Karisa scowls. "Who says I want a relationship with you?"

"Indeed, imagine my surprise and dismay to consider that the sister who as far as I could tell has had no interest in me other than as a target to safely take out frustrations on when I couldn't hit back might actually have an ulterior motive that isn't entirely awful, and that I failed spectacularly by not making any overtures of my own accord," I say.

There has been so much unsaid between us. If I am ever to repair what is broken, or to build something new, I must begin explicitly with truth. Perhaps especially truths that are uncomfortable to one or both of us.

"Your... " She can't manage to say *friends*. "They told you that?"

"Not in so many words," I admit. "I filled in the gaps. So. What are you reading?"

"Ah," Karisa says. "A safe, innocuous question that sets up the potential for conversation that isn't entirely fraught while implying interest in my choices. But of course I should just answer you at face value or *I'm* the problem."

"The fact that you can't take my greetings at face value without interpreting them as a personal attack and lashing out at someone innocent is *not* my fault, Karisa."

"That's *your Highness*," she says flintily. "And I do hope you're not going to try to convince me of the innocence of a person willing to talk back to a princess?"

"I wasn't, because you picked on her precisely because you thought she couldn't strike back," I say. "But since you've mentioned it, it was only weeks ago that girl barely uttered a word neither to strangers nor to people she'd known her whole life. The fact that she was willing to even speak at all in your presence is nothing short of a heroic change."

"Well, there's no way I could have known that—"

"Clearly not, since you came in snipes blazing first and foremost," I say. "If I can apologize, so can you, *your Highness*."

Karisa closes the books. "It's hardly the same. An apology costs you nothing."

I laugh in utter disbelief. "Oh, no, only my entire sense of self, on which I base literally everything I am attempting to accomplish, which currently includes saving the world. No, no cost at all. Karisa."

"'Saving the world'?" she echoes. "Well that's pompous."

I roll my eyes. "'Wow, Miyara, that sounds very unexpected, would you tell me why you would say something like that?' Do you see how I did that?"

Karisa narrows her eyes. "Do you think I'm stupid?"

"No, I think you're so in the habit of obnoxiousness you're no longer deploying it as a tool and can't tell when it's not a useful tactic," I say.

"So let me be clear. I have no reason to ignore your behavior anymore. If you treat me or anyone else badly without provocation, I will call you to task. If you want more from me than that, I would honestly be delighted, but I'm not going to put up with being your pincushion ever again. Do you have any questions?"

"Sure," Karisa says. "Why do you think I'm going to take you at your word now, when I've never been able to before?"

That lands, when her other sallies haven't.

In the space between us, I set down my tea kit.

"You expressed some interest before, even if it was rhetorical, in knowing who I am now that I can be honest with myself and the world," I say, laying out the tray. "Let me show you."

Karisa watches me for a moment, then finally says, "Doesn't look like you have water or a heating spell in there."

This is entirely true and a weakness in my plan.

Fortunately, I have help. Yorani flutters in, holding a cup of water between her front feet in the cutest tableau I've ever seen.

"You are the best tea spirit in the world," I tell her, plucking the cup of water out of her claws as it sloshes over the edge when she slows. "Thank you."

"You're telepathic?" Karisa asks incredulously.

"No," I say. "Not exactly. But we're very in tune with each other emotionally. At least, when I'm not making a mess of things."

Karisa's eyes are still narrowed as I pour the water into the pot. "And your tea spirit just materialized from where, exactly?"

"Presumably from where she's been spying on you, having followed you from the tea shop out of concern and curiosity when I was too angry to do so myself," I say easily. "Which is how I found you."

"Oh, well that's not creepy."

I look up at her. "Are you ready?"

"For you to demonstrate your vaunted skills that I should be falling over myself to praise?" Karisa waves a hand. "Pass."

"For me to show you who I am, if you're willing to see," I say. "To decide if you're willing to cut a measure of the nonsense between us for us to try to have an actual relationship, or not, because it has to come from both of us. Right now."

Karisa shifts in her seat, watching me, and I wait, poised on this moment.

Her choice, the first of which will decide us.

"Fine," she says, making a magnanimous gesture. "Let's see what you've got."

The second choice is mine.

I have multiple traditional teas in my kit. There's a water blend, which I could choose for change; the dark earth, for roots entwining us. Either of them feels comfortable, after my spiritual contemplation of water and earth these past weeks.

Instead I choose air, because I need a different path, a path that can go anywhere. A path that *won't* feel familiar, because with us what has become familiar is a symptom of our problem.

Yorani blows fire on the teapot and settles between us; a judge, perhaps, of my performance, or a referee—or a witness to us both as we are.

With a spirit as my witness, I begin the tea ceremony.

It has not escaped me that when Iryasa requested a tea ceremony from me, I told her she wasn't ready to hear what I can communicate to her. Karisa, though, who for all her protestations of scorn, desperately needs it; she has wanted forever, and as I have made her wait so long for me to be ready I cannot let her wait a single moment more.

To me Karisa has always seemed dramatic, hot-headed. While I tried to slink through life escaping anyone's notice, as though that would prevent them from realizing how unsuitable I was, Karisa has relished throwing herself in everyone's faces and forcing them to confront what their expectations mean.

But it's not just that I falsely perceived her as my opposite in behavior, but that it was not in fact herself that she presented for the world's consumption.

That self she has hidden as deeply as I hid mine; just with a different outward cover on the book, a different way of coping.

All her older sisters share an experience of neglect from our parents: until our dedications our father could spend no time with us if our mother did not, and so to prevent Velasari influence we were raised effectively without either of them.

But with Karisa, that changed. Perhaps our mother decided she wanted at least one chance to do the work of mothering; perhaps she decided after four other daughters that surely one potentially influenced by Velasar could be borne. But whatever the reason, she chose to spend time with Karisa, and thus so could our father.

So unlike the rest of us, she has had them for parents. Which means she has been caught more directly between them.

Iryasa's path was set, but the rest of us had the semblance of choice, to decide for ourselves how we could best serve. Our parents had little opportunity to influence us in those choices, but with Karisa—she has been told all her life what she should think and why. The very choice to raise her meant she could be considered both a spare and a pawn. She has been the one our parents had the opportunity to shape, and under that pressure what could she do?

She could be molded, of course; or she could merely appear to be. And she could appear to be so un-moldable that the efforts were abandoned, leaving her with... what?

Not common experience with her sisters. Not any better idea of what her path should be, certainly.

But anger? Well. I can hardly blame her for that.

I have spent so much of my life hiding from who I am, knowing that self could not survive the only world it had, that I have only recently begun to appreciate how angry I should be for what has been done to us. Karisa has never had that luxury.

She has also never had anyone look at her and see her for more than a bargaining piece between two existing powers, never a power in her own right. So she has taken that role and fed into it, forced people to treat her as though she *can't* be used as a bargaining chip, twisting that into its own kind of power that she clings to, because she has to—because what else does she have?

She has sisters.

She has a chance to take a different path, the sky limitless, if she will choose to.

If we will help her.

I am in my place of power, now. I have decided on my path and learned what I am capable of and lived it. I am a person who will not hesitate to challenge awfulness from villain or princess and can make it stick.

But I am also a person who lives for lifting people up into the sky, and I am a person who can see her; and who wishes to.

This is what I tell her, with every deliberate movement. *I see who you are, because I see where you came from, and I will do whatever is in my considerable power to see what you can be, when you get to choose.*

And I will make sure you get to choose.

It's how I should have thought to shield her years ago. She found her own way, then. I will be here for whatever way she finds now.

Karisa's hands do not tremble as she takes a sip any more than mine do; we are both too well-trained for that.

But as we drink, our eyes are both wet, and my chest is tight with emotion.

I did what I could; the next choice must be hers, and it will determine how we go from here, together or separate.

"I've never seen you cry," Karisa finally says.

I consider, glancing at Yorani, who remains sitting utterly still, unblinking. "I didn't at the palace, in general. Odd that I am significantly happier with my life now but cry more. I suppose because it's safe to."

"Do you cry every time you perform the tea ceremony?" she asks.

I huff. "No. The tea master who administered my exam just advised me to effect more of a guise of mystery, though."

"He thinks you need to be *more* mysterious?" Karisa asks incredulously.

I laugh outright at that. "More mysterious than bluntly telling everyone in the world I will be personally responsible for calling out their bad behavior."

"How's that working for you?" Karisa asks, a hint of snideness in her tone I think she means to be at once teasing and challenging.

"Eh." I lean back on my hands. "Fairly well in the long view, I think? Exhausting in the short."

Karisa eyes me carefully. "I assume the exhaustion is related to your saving the world bit. And to do with why you decided to address our relationship all at once instead of patiently."

It's almost a question, and I answer it bluntly. "The Cataclysm has started expanding again. If we don't figure out how to stop or reverse it—"

"We're all going to die," Karisa finishes, silent for a moment. She glances at Yorani too, and for her benefit my tea pet moves, blinking at her once before returning to her previous impassive pose. A confirmation, of a sort.

"Well," Karisa says. "I knew something catastrophic must have happened to get Iryasa to do something so out of character, but that's outside what I was imagining."

Curiously I ask, "What were you imagining?"

Karisa shrugs and tosses the small book inside the history of Sayorsen my way.

I burst out laughing when I see the cover, recognizing the series as an espionage romance Risteri gave me. Karisa can't decide whether to turn defensive or share a joke with me, and I quickly add, "I read the earlier books in this series. I didn't realize there was a new one."

Karisa's eyes bug. "*You*? Read *these*? No."

"My former roommate decided I needed to expand my education," I explain wryly.

"You had a roommate," Karisa says wonderingly. "What was *that* like?"

"Strange," I say. "Interesting. How did *you* get into these books?" She definitely didn't find them in the palace library; its contents run to the academic, and the vast majority of the novels are books there are academic papers written about.

Karisa tosses her hair. "I have my sources. But since you don't seem to think the world ending is inevitable, will you tell me what Iryasa is planning?"

"Yes," I say. "Though I do want to add that she's been counting on your arrival, too."

Her eyes narrow. "Really."

"You are sometimes predictable." I shrug.

Karisa looks affronted for a minute, and then laughs. "Well. I suppose I earned that."

I am entirely startled by how well she takes that. "For someone who looks for the maximum ways to interpret an action, you really do appreciate bluntness, don't you?"

"Honesty isn't exactly a trait I've had much cause to witness," Karisa says easily, and the tragic truth of that isn't surprising and doesn't deserve to feel like such a stab right at my heart. "This is terribly refreshing. However: do you want to call your protégé over?"

She noticed *Elowyn*?

"I admit I'm not entirely sure where she is," I say. "Only that she's nearby, and probably the one who filled the cup for Yorani. When did you see her?"

"I didn't," Karisa says.

That can mean one of several things: 1) She's lying. 2) It was a guess, fishing for information, which I've confirmed. Or 3) She knew without seeing her.

I suspect it is the last, though I can't guess how, and Karisa isn't forthcoming.

"Do you want to tell me how?" I try.

She smiles, and there's an edge to it. "No."

I nod, because for me, that settles this. "Elowyn, if you're listening, please join us."

Karisa's still smiling, though it's a little tighter as she says, "So there's no difference in what you'll tell me and her?"

"There's some," I say. "But Elowyn is the younger sister of my—" I break off. "Spirits, I've forgotten the common term. Pass me that book?"

Karisa stares at me. "The spy book?"

As soon as I sense Elowyn behind me I turn and ask, "What is the term I should be using for Deniel?"

She blinks. "A potter? A councilor?"

"As regards his relationship to me, I mean," I say. "Like a suitor, or a spouse, or a lov—" I go red and wave my hands. "*You* know."

"Oh," Elowyn says, also going red. "A romantic partner, or partner, I think is what you want."

Karisa stares between us. "You're dating a Gaellani potter?"

Elowyn bristles. "Is that a problem?"

"Yes I am dating a Gaellani potter, and I had just moved in with him when Iryasa arrived at our home with her grand plan that I am taking over," I say. "And no, it is not a problem."

Both of them look at me. So does Yorani.

"That," Karisa says, "sounds like a problem. You're *what*?"

Tea Master Karekin advised me to delegate, to have faith in people and let them rise.

"In my capacity as Tea Master of Sayorsen, I am calling a summit of world leaders to resolve the matter of the Cataclysm once and for all," I explain. "We're going to get to the root of the bad actors working against us, and the plot goes all the way back to the Isle of Nakrab."

Karisa looks between me and Elowyn and back again. "You don't sound like you're taking this all that seriously. This is what you're claiming to be planning, and you're off serving tea in a bookstore?"

"I am preparing for the summit right now," I say. "This *is* the work. The summit is the performance, which matters, but what we do now, the relationships we build and their strength, determines whether it succeeds or fails."

"Oh, I see," Karisa says. "So you're inspired to talk to me so you can use me, like everyone else."

I open my mouth and close it again; take a moment while Yorani curls up and stops staring, which I decide to take as a vote of confidence. "You're not wrong that I rarely take an action for only one reason. I am having a lot of epiphanies in short succession, and I may be overly conflating the solutions to them in my mind. Because on top of saving the world I want this summit to be a resounding victory for all of our sisters, a statement of who we are and what that means for our future. I want you to be part of us, and this. I have an idea in mind for you, and it only works if we actually trust each other. But there is definitely also some insecurity on my part in that I'm worried if I've messed up our relationship so badly and can't fix it, I can't be trusted to save the world."

Karisa stares at me for a moment and then just says, "By talking."

Being this openly vulnerable and not knowing whether it will be thrown in my face, or if she's even intending to throw it, is fraying my nerves. "Yes, by talking. And listening. Relationship building is what I do, and it's how I intend to win. I'm sorry if that isn't flashy enough for you. I'm fairly sure it's not the path you want for yourself. If you're not interested in putting in the necessary work without an attentive audience, then we will do it without you. But I will ask that if you don't decide to actively help, at least please help by staying out of our way."

"Well if that's how it is, should you be telling me all your grand political plans with her listening?" Karisa demands, jerking her head toward Elowyn.

"If you're implying I'm not being honest with you because Elowyn is here—"

"I was in the middle of the Velasari agents' attack using Nakrabi technology," Elowyn tells her, lifting her chin. "A little late for that."

Karisa's baiting is bringing out the spine in Elowyn, which is both delightful and troubling.

"I can tell whatever I want to whomever I want, which I am happy to remind our sisters if they forget," I say. "But in this case, your presence together will save me time. Because it isn't going to be enough for me to just negotiate with the foreign dignitaries."

"You need information," they say together, and exchange a glance.

I let out a breath. "I need information," I agree. "And here is Elowyn, who can hide in plain sight better than assassins I know."

"You know so many?"

"And here is Karisa, who is better at provoking unplanned reactions from people than any courtier in Istalam," I continue.

"You want us to work together," Karisa says, her expression considering but not happy.

"Iryasa thinks having all the princesses and heirs of Istalam in one place will provoke those working against us into rash action," I say. "But I think there is another way to go about this, more tactically. Iryasa will naturally represent Istalam in negotiations, and Reyata will guard her. Saiyana will hold down the mage side of affairs, and I'm out of the line of succession."

"So I'm the best target," Karisa says, her voice odd. "You want to use me as bait."

"I want you to bait the Nakrabi for all you're worth," I say, looking at her intently. "I want you to play the spoiled princess to have an excuse to establish a connection, and I want you to make them think you're harmless but valuable and destroy them with it."

"There will come a point in these negotiations when we will not give the Nakrabi what they want, and they will decide they have to take it. They will seize whatever they can that they think will force us to accede or that they can steal. It's how they operated in the immediate aftermath of the Cataclysm, and it's how they operated over the past weeks. So since we know that's coming, I propose we prepare to trap them with it. Can you do it?"

Karisa's eyes begin to gleam. "You would trust me to smuggle intelligence from foreign spies?"

"If you're committed," I say, "I think you can do whatever you want."

I look between them. "This is something I can't do, and it is delicate work, even if it's not as bodily dangerous as infiltrating like a spy. You will be talking, but I think you both know how much someone can do with words alone. Elowyn's role isn't a bodyguard's; it's to keep watch invisibly and get you out if everything goes sideways. If Iryasa knew I was even thinking about this, let alone talking, she'd wrest back control of this so fast I wouldn't see the doors of my cell closing."

"Then why are you asking?" Elowyn asks.

"Because I believe in you both, and part of that is because I trust both of you to tell me if you think I've crossed a line."

"And because," Karisa says, "we're facing the end of the world, and you don't just need information, you need people you trust to get it—and to you specifically."

I close my eyes, remembering how sure I had been in the face of Risteri's grandmother earlier today, and that I am now asking two teenagers to be spies. My stomach twists.

Elowyn says softly, "You didn't want anyone to know."

I know what she means: her skill at fading into the shadows is something she takes joy in, and something I've cautioned her against revealing to anyone, Saiyana in particular, lest they use it against her. And now I've let Karisa, another princess, know.

"It is not Karisa's job to exploit potential assets," I say. "Which is also why I am not going to tell Saiyana or Iryasa. But this is something you want to explore, in addition to tea mastery, right?"

Elowyn nods. Part of me is sad, that she isn't wholly committed to tea mastery as a possible path for her, but I am also glad she is comfortable enough with me to be honest.

"I can't promise the job will be safe. But if you change your mind, it will be safer for me to be the one who knows than anyone else." I look at Karisa. "And Karisa will keep her mouth shut, or I will make her."

Karisa's eyebrows shoot up at that, and then she grins. "Harsh bluntness. I do like the new you. And this..." She looks at Elowyn. "I'm sorry about earlier. I know this is messed up, but this is also the most excited I've been about anything in my future for a long time. I want to do this."

I'm glad she seems to understand that my willingness to allow it—and that my willingness matters—depends on Elowyn's willingness to have her back.

Elowyn folds her arms. "Accepted. We're going to need to figure out a silent method of communication."

I close my eyes, and when I open them again, all three of us are matched in resolve, the paths between us beginning to take shape in the air.

This is yet another task to add to my list, the systems that must be put into place to make sure they are, in fact, safe. But it is also a necessary role that I can't manage myself, and they can and, I have no doubt, will. I look between them and know I have set a critical piece into motion—of the plan at large, and all our paths.

This will work. Yorani's ears are perked up, listening, but she remains curled in a napping pose, leaving us to work.

"Then let's talk about what you need to know."

CHAPTER 10

I HAVE ELOWYN LEAD Karisa to Saiyana's headquarters in Sayorsen as an opportunity for them to work out amongst themselves how they're going to work together. I make a mental note to check in with each separately later to make sure they are able to work unsupervised without harming each other.

Saiyana can arrange Karisa's lodging, and I can set more plans in motion.

At this rate, I'll need Glynis to recommend me another messenger or to get her seconded to this effort from the guild. But she's waiting for me at Talmeri's when I arrive, having anticipated me, and I waste no time.

A good thing, too, since when we have only half an hour before the tea shop has to open in earnest, a frighteningly tense Lorwyn escorts none other than Iryasa into the front where I'm preparing.

I control my expression as I put down the drying towel I'd been using to clean a cup and emerge from behind the counter to bow slightly to my sister. "Iryasa, I see you've met my friend Lorwyn. To what do I owe the pleasure?"

Iryasa turns and bows more deeply to Lorwyn. "An honor to make your acquaintance, Grace Lorwyn. Thank you for showing me to my sister."

Lorwyn scowls, a sure sign that she's unnerved. "Your Highness. Should I expect any more princesses?"

Iryasa's eyebrows lift, perhaps at Lorwyn's preemptory phrasing. Or perhaps she recognizes well enough someone who is totally out of their etiquette depth and scrambling.

"Not to my knowledge," Iryasa says, looking at me. "Unless there are things afoot you know and I don't, Miyara?"

Ah, she's here because she's unhappy with me. "Lorwyn, I'm sorry to steal all your helpers, but could you have Taseino take over up front again please? I think my sister and I should speak undisturbed in Talmeri's office."

Lorwyn's gaze searches mine, probably wondering when the disruption of her life at my instigation will end. But she nods abruptly, turns away—turns back when she remembers she didn't bow—and after that heads off.

I lead Iryasa to the office and shut the door behind us.

"This is..." Iryasa frowns, looking around. "I was going to say an uncharacteristic mess, but it's that you're slowly establishing order amid the chaos, isn't it? That's why everything here is so disjointed. Why not do it and be done?"

I let out a breath. "Spirits, you don't waste any time when you're angry, do you?"

"I'm sure I don't know what you mean," the crown princess says evenly.

"Because while I am gradually taking over many of Talmeri's responsibilities, I am not aiming to displace her, any more than you are looking to oust our mother by handling this diplomatic enterprise," I say. "But the summit, while your idea, is mine to run."

"So for all your talk of working together and trust, you see no hypocrisy with setting plans into motion without consulting me," Iryasa says. "I see."

So that's what this is about. I worried she would attempt to edge me out, and instead in her eyes I have done the same to her. Yet I am also doing precisely what she came to me for, even if she didn't realize fully what it would mean for her.

But I am glad she is here and bringing this to me so I can nip her feelings of betrayal before they fester, lest she decide to run ahead with her own plans prepared without me. We must reach an understanding on what our roles in this endeavor are, if not the particulars on how we will each play our parts.

"I am not going to consult you on every decision that needs to be made," I say. "In part because we simply don't have time for that duplication of effort. But also because I don't answer to you, Iryasa.

I'm a tea master. You asked me to run the summit. You trusted me to do so my own way."

"On your terms doesn't mean cutting me out entirely," Iryasa says sharply. "You may be a tea master, but do not forget I have a great deal more experience in diplomatic meetings than you do, sister."

"I have not forgotten, and I am counting on it," I say. "But I am also not going to run these negotiations in a typical way, because what we need is a completely atypical result. I'm not choosing a neutral spot, Iryasa. I'm choosing one that's mine." I wave my hand around. "The negotiations will be held here, at Talmeri's Teas and Tisanes. I have a lot to do to get it ready."

Iryasa's eyes narrow. "So you will reject any assistance I offer in the setup, then."

I sigh. "Probably, because the changes need to come from me and my community to adequately reflect it as my space. And, frankly, also because you seem to be more interested in having a say than in whether I need your assistance in this. There are other ways you can be spending your time, and one doesn't decorate their own ball, Iryasa."

Iryasa scowls, and it's so reminiscent of Lorwyn's expression I realize she too is deeply uncomfortable.

Before I can address that, I hear a commotion from the front—suddenly raised voices, one of which includes Talmeri herself.

I open the door to find that Yorani, who had been napping peacefully in a tea kettle when we went in, has begun flying around the room knocking tea canisters off shelves as Talmeri yells after her but is unable to catch her.

"Sorry," Taseino says beside me. "I tried keeping Talmeri out of the office, but since it's hers and I couldn't tell her why, that... didn't go well. I think Yorani started a distraction to help."

Across the room, Yorani pauses mid-flap, and I swear by the spirits she winks at me.

Helping.

"Thank you for your service," I say to Taseino dryly. He bows, to me and to Iryasa, who has followed me out, and Talmeri finally takes note of our presence.

She freezes, eyes widening, and drops into a startled, deep bow. For a person as conscious of status and connections as she, she cannot fail to recognize Iryasa, even with my sister's hair in its natural form.

(Yorani thankfully subsides, settling onto a table to watch the show, as there is no further need for dramatic distraction. Taseino begins tidying up after her.)

But as Talmeri straightens, she is staring between Iryasa and me, and I can practically see her mind whirring.

"You're sisters," Talmeri breathes, flabbergasted. "You're that Miyara."

Oh, no. I thought I was past worrying about being found out, and yet—

"Oh, I'm so flattered you think I look like the crown princess," I start, but trail off when Talmeri glares accusingly at me.

Spirits. Talmeri saw me with Saiyana, too, but Saiyana and I are more different in appearance and manner. With Iryasa's hair wavy, and both of us holding ourselves so formally—I have only begun to notice our strong resemblance, but to the outside sharp observer it must be uncanny.

Iryasa says smoothly, "You have found us out, Grace Talmeri. I would so hate for word to get out and cause my dear sister any trouble."

Well, nothing for it then. In the same smooth tone weighted with double meaning and unsubtle threat, I say, "You don't have to worry about Grace Talmeri; she has always been respectful of my boundaries."

Talmeri's jaw drops, unable to miss all the evidence laid out like this at once. "Spirits, you really are related."

Unaccountably, my throat tightens, and I bow. "I truly hope you won't treat me any differently, Grace."

Her gaze flicks uncomfortably—but shrewdly—from me to the crown princess. "I'm not sure I can help it, princess—but you're not, are you? Spirits, I can't believe I didn't put this together before now. How can I be of service to the crown?"

Ah, there she is.

I almost laugh. I should have known even revelations about my identity wouldn't throw Talmeri for long, not when there's business afoot.

A reminder to myself, to trust people to be who I know they are.

And that the real reason my house is out of order is because I am; my ability to believe in people will make or break this whole endeavor.

But I know how to bargain with Talmeri, and I explain to her how I plan to temporarily take over the shop and make it the location for the most important political summit of our lives and lives beyond us.

When she is skeptical about how this will affect her currently booming business in the aftermath of my tournament performance, I look her in the eye and say, "You have worried about what will happen to Talmeri's if I am one day forced to leave, and the service of a tea master goes with me. With this, Talmeri's will forever be known as the place where this historical summit was held."

"Tourist revenue," Talmeri muses, eyes narrowed. She doesn't hate the idea, but she isn't sold; she has always focused on short-term planning, and in that sense this doesn't look good.

Before I can argue my case further, Iryasa adds, "And the crown of Istalam will reimburse any loss of revenue—using the average of the last full week Miyara worked as a baseline—not immediately made up in the month following the summit."

Clever, to set those numerical limits, and yet—

"A very generous offer, your Highness. But a boom in business like we have right now could carry us through another year, and we won't get its like again," Talmeri says.

Iryasa's expression goes blank—I think with shock that even with such overt generosity Talmeri is still trying to negotiate with her, and I step in. "And yet, Grace Talmeri, the designation of this shop as a historical landmark will be a gift that continues to give, over and over forever. You will come out ahead and you know it."

Talmeri purses her lips, but I can see the amused glint in her eye. She wanted to see how far she could push a princess—and how far I would let her. "I am, of course, honored to be of service to the crown. Miyara, you'll message me the particulars of how you intend to alter my shop?"

I bow, glad she's planning to leave me to it even if she'll want more oversight than I'd prefer—it isn't unreasonable, given that it is, in fact, her shop, though I assume she knows if she creates a fuss Saiyana is likely to try to buy it out from under her. And this way, of course, Talmeri can leave to tell her friends she met the crown princess and gain one last day of overwhelming profits. "If it's not too much trouble. Thank you."

Once Talmeri has taken her leave—and Taseino too, leaving us with the façade of privacy once more—I say to Iryasa, "How exactly are you intending to get the funds to pay her?"

Iryasa shrugs. "You'll be negotiating, won't you? I'm sure you'll figure it out." As I stare, she snickers.

Snickers!

"I'm kidding," she says. "Mostly. I think you'll make back more in the month following, actually, given the rise in profile this will bring your shop. And if not—it will probably be because we all have bigger concerns."

I let out a breath. Indeed. If we're facing the end of the world, one small shop's profit margins won't even register.

"In the future, would it be better," Iryasa asks slowly, "if we aren't seen together in public?"

I look at her sharply. "Better in what way?"

"I don't want to limit your freedom," my sister says softly. "Our resemblance—"

I cut her off. "My freedom is meaningless if I can't take a walk with my sister. People can recognize who I was or not. It doesn't matter."

"Doesn't it?" she asks pointedly.

I sigh. "It shouldn't. I am too in the habit of hiding, and perhaps it's time I'm forced to break it. No one is threatening my place here anymore. And after all, if our opponents realize all the once-princesses of Istalam are here, that only furthers your plan. But speaking of plans, I'm surprised there is one of mine you have yet to bring up."

Iryasa's expression flickers. "Sa Rangim."

"Sa Rangim," I confirm, watching her carefully. "So?"

She sighs, exasperated. "You know what I think."

"I am entirely certain I do not."

"I know why you arranged things this way," Iryasa says. "I can't even truly be angry about it. And you must at least know that he—has my attention."

"I had an inkling," I say.

"I confess I did not truly expect you to introduce a possible solution to that particular problem at all, let alone so quickly, nor one that changes all the variables." Iryasa glares mildly. "I suppose I should have, given what I am learning of you."

"Which variables?" I ask.

"Miyara." Iryasa waves a hand. "An entire other just-discovered race? Spirits, we don't even know if the Te Muraka can produce heirs with other peoples!"

"I imagine something could be arranged with magic if it turned out to be an issue," I say, making another mental note. "The Te Muraka are people first."

"I know. I simply—" She breaks off, laughing with an edge. "Simply wanted something in my life to be simple for once, I suppose, and this is anything but."

"Your life isn't simple," I say. "It seems only fair that you match with someone capable of handling that complexity."

"By coming from an even more complicated background? Are you and Deniel so matched, then? I admit he's played his part in your plans beautifully—I'd have believed it came from him."

I tilt my head. "Which part?"

"We met this morning," Iryasa explains. "He and Saiyana briefed me about what they're setting up with local workers."

"Oh! That wasn't me at all, actually," I say. "He came up with that on his own and broached it with Saiyana before I had any idea."

She blinks. "Truly?"

I nod.

Iryasa is silent for a moment, processing that. "You trust him enough to let him work his own angles on this project you're in charge of, knowing what's at stake."

"I do," I say. "I didn't elevate him to the council seat out of fondness, and Saiyana didn't agree to tutor him out of pity or as a favor."

"I didn't say—"

"I know you didn't," I say. "I'm trying to be clear. Creating an initiative that will lift up the Gaellani and benefit the community as a whole is exactly why he is on the council. Deniel and I do not share all the same strengths—as I said, this idea was his, and I feel guilty it didn't occur to me right away—but it would be foolish of me to not trust him to do his work just because it overlaps with mine. We do not often work on the same initiatives, but I respect him and his work.

"We are well matched. I suppose it looks surprising from the outside, but from where we sit it seems... obvious, perhaps? Our backgrounds are both complicated in mostly different ways, but we are nevertheless compatible, in our values and our drive. There's no reason you can't find that with someone, too—unless what you mean is that you don't want that. But given what you've said to me, I think it is." I watch her, and she watches me, but her focus isn't on me, now. "Or do you disagree?"

Iryasa's gaze distances as she considers her next words, and when she speaks again she speaks slowly, tentatively. "I always imagined," she says, "I would find someone who would be... simple is the wrong word, I don't mean stupid, but... outside politics. An oasis, where I could let go of the barriers court trains into us.

"I can't have our parents' relationship, Miyara. I won't do it. This break with Velasari relations has given our mother the freedom to crack down aggressively for the first time, and she's allowing me to be her instrument in the most important turning point in her lifetime. I don't know how much of that is because this habit of maintaining an appearance of removal from situations is so ingrained in her and how she's handled politics for decades, and that she wants to hold that removal in reserve in case. But I know she is also aware of how circumscribed she has been, by the political situation her mother left her with, and saddled with a political enemy. She's letting me do this because she doesn't want to inflict that again on Istalam or me, and she's desperately hoping I will find another way.

"And I don't know how.

"I have all the responsibility in the world, and none of the knowledge of how to make it happen without becoming as caught in the only habits I've witnessed as she was. The enemies I know how to fight are the ones she would prevent me from ever having to face.

"Sa Rangim... Miyara, I have no idea what to do with a man like him."

Impulsively, I hug her, and after a startled moment, she returns it.

When I pull back, I say, "I hear you and sympathize. The first thing I'm going to say is that already you aren't repeating our mother's tactics, precisely because you're in the thick of building relationships personally, rather than staying at a remove."

"At your instigation," Iryasa points out. "And I hate it."

I huff a laugh. "No one told you to seek me out. No one told you to bring all of your sisters together, or to bring all of the political players together. You started this without me. But the way you finish it differently than our mother is by building relationships you want to keep, so that not everyone around you is only a potential enemy. That's the most important work you can be doing right now, and while advising my decorating choices would I'm sure be a welcome distraction, it helps you not at all. Not being involved in this one aspect doesn't mean you're not driving the plot: it means the work you're doing is less visible, not that it matters less."

Iryasa considers that, and then asks, "Is the second thing you're going to tell me a conversation starter for Sa Rangim?"

I smile. "No, because you demonstrably don't need any help there."

She makes a face. "For a tea master, you are fantastically unhelpful."

"I am as helpful as every little sister should be," I say serenely. "Saiyana will confirm."

Iryasa huffs.

"The second thing," I say, "is that someone complicated enough to understand the full depth of you may be a more effective oasis for you. It may be harder at first to get there, but you will be able to decide for yourself if the potential of what could be between you is worth it."

When she meets my eyes again, I know she already has.

Believe in people, Miyara. Iryasa said she knew herself, and she does.

"It is worth it," she says softly. "Is it wrong that I'm terrified by the possibility?"

I take her hands in mine again, stepping in close and resting my forehead against hers. My oldest, unshatterable sister breathes deeply.

"On the contrary," I say. "It's the opposite. It means you appreciate the potential consequences to actual people, and you appreciate the value of what you might find together. Believe in yourself, Iryasa. I do."

CHAPTER II

THE REST OF THE day at the tea shop feels even busier than it is, which is quite, because my mind is trying to hold too many plans at once. I believe myself to be a fairly capable manager, but trying to do so much at once is taxing my ability to serve well all the people I need to.

I do my best, and then sit and exhaustedly, numbly supervise as a crowd of some of the most inspired magic workers in Istalam argue about the best way to set up mixed magical protections on Talmeri's.

Lorwyn for witchcraft, Sa Nikuran for Te Muraka magic, and Saiyana for magecraft. Unfortunately Ostario, with the most experience of the overlap in witchcraft in magecraft, was in the middle of an experiment at the barrier and couldn't be interrupted.

In a moment of inspiration, I asked Glynis to join us instead. Ostario arguably has more experience keeping magecraft and witchcraft separate, whereas Glynis and Lorwyn have figured out how to combine them more than once together.

"We set it up with a magecraft framework," Saiyana says. "That gives us the structure to work everything else into."

"Only if everyone's magic works with structure, your Highness," Lorwyn points out. "Let's not forget magecraft is the one we know isn't effective against Nakrabi magic."

"Nor do we know that witchcraft is, unless you've been holding out on me? Or are willing to come in for testing?"

"Like you have time for testing," Lorwyn says. "But thanks for the threat. That's real classy, princess."

Saiyana makes a rude gesture, and Lorwyn laughs.

Histories are rarely honest about how much bickering goes into new discoveries. No magical shields like this have been attempted, which ought to be momentous. I am torn between amusement and wanting to bang my head against the tea counter.

But mostly, aside from weariness, what I feel is relief, to see the effect of my work in action: that I do not have to step in to negotiate for them now, nor is this my problem to solve. Tea Master Karekin was right.

Glynis puts in, "Of course we know witchcraft works against Nakrabi magic. Lorwyn's power met it head-on in the final tournament match. We may not know why or how, but we know the what."

Lorwyn tilts her head to one side, frowning. "If you knew why and how, could you figure out how to adapt magecraft to counter it?"

"I shouldn't promise anything, but—yes, I'm confident I could figure something out," Saiyana said. "You have an answer?"

"Not right this second, but I'll think about it and let you know," Lorwyn says.

"Do," Saiyana says seriously, and I hold in a fierce smile that the two of them have come to respect each other after all.

"I know less of your magic, but I will also think on this," Sa Nikuran says.

"Right," Glynis says. "You can both counter and sense it, can't you?"

Sa Nikuran wrinkles her nose as if at the memory of a disgusting stench. "Yes."

"This is all well and good," Saiyana says patiently, "but we know magecraft will defend against workings from Velasari and Taresal representatives, and magecraft requires structures in its setup."

"Sure," Glynis says, "but we don't need to start there. Here, if you move this—"

"Don't touch that; that's the anchor for the entire—"

"Breathe, princess, I wasn't done."

Saiyana scowls, but her heart isn't in it. She's developed enough of a rapport with this young Gaellani messenger to accept her criticism, and that makes me glad, too.

People can change. People from different backgrounds and experiences can come together to create incredible changes. I can see it in action, and I have to hold it in my heart that it is possible and worth striving for.

It is worth striving to create the conditions that make it possible: the connections, the boundaries, the advocacy, the consequences.

Amid it all, Yorani flutters around them, watching. But not always watching what they do: rather, she's watching the currents in the air, movement I can't see. Sometimes she swats her tail or takes a playful swipe, and I remember how she was at the barrier with Saiyana and Ostario so much earlier this morning.

I am increasingly convinced she can see spirits the rest of us cannot. I'm not sure what to do with that knowledge.

That also reminds me that Talsion was playing with invisible foes in our house, too, and I am not sure if that should concern me more or less.

Yorani turns to stare at me, as if sensing my thoughts, and I lift a teacup as if toasting her. So far she and Talsu have handled their own affairs; it is probably in all our best interests if I leave interacting with invisible spirits to them unless they solicit my intervention.

That is a hypothetical problem for future-Miyara, who will doubtless thank me for this moment of passing responsibility off to her.

Then I notice all of my magic-working friends are looking at me, and I blink. How long did I drift in my thoughts? "I'm sorry. Did I miss something?"

"We're going to put these protections on your house too," Saiyana says.

Lorwyn glares. "No, in point of fact, we were *asking* if that's acceptable to you."

"That's a good idea," I say. "Let's minimize the chance of retaliation against me outside official circles. I'm so glad you asked."

"Don't be obnoxious," Saiyana says. "I'm not going to run every necessary security measure by you, and you and I both know this is advisable and not intrusive."

Here we go, then. It was a nice vision of harmony while it lasted, but the whole reason I need to be here is because the work isn't done.

"If you're not going to ask my permission, then you can detail every single measure you take in writing and deliver an edict to my home so all inhabitants are transparently informed about what to expect and can register complaints as needed."

"In what spirits-cursed world do you think this is a reasonable application of my energy? Miyara, we do not have time for this."

"To treat me and Deniel as people and not assets, we certainly do. If you don't want to file a mountain of paperwork, ask me questions like a person who is conscious of boundaries and risk analysis and can make informed, intelligent decisions, rather than issuing condescending pronouncements like a tyrant. I won't support the latter in anyone, Saiyana."

"You are a sanctimonious piece of shit," Saiyana tells me.

That stings a bit, which means she probably isn't entirely wrong, but I stand by my point. "Did Deniel not mention how pleased he was to learn you'd worked magic on his home without even informing him, which is in fact illegal considering at the time you had no documented cause?"

My sister's expression shutters, because she knows full well that was out of line. The fact that I'd assumed she'd done it and hadn't protested made her think it was okay; I'm correcting that now. "I was protecting you," she growls.

"I know," I say. "And I appreciate it. Just put question marks on the ends of your sentences and we're fine. Is that really so hard?"

Saiyana scowls, because of course it's not just about punctuation: it's about intent. It's about deliberately allowing someone the opportunity to refuse the care she considers mandatory. It's about giving up control, which she hates, and she hates how obvious her antipathy makes her care.

"I'm going back to work," Saiyana says abruptly. "I'll adjust my part of the shields on Miyara's house once you're all done."

She stalks out, slamming the door behind her.

"Wow," Lorwyn says. "We were getting along so well, too. Didn't escape my notice she didn't agree to ask instead of demand, though."

"She'll come around," I say, surprising myself in how sure I am, how much more confident I am in her and our future relationship now than I was weeks ago. "I've pushed her pretty far lately, in more ways than I can tell you. She's already come further than I ever expected. She's working on it."

"If you say so," Lorwyn murmurs.

Still, her departure leaves me feeling... raw, in a way I didn't expect. Like she's revealed a vulnerability I didn't know I had, and it only takes me a moment more to identify what's ultimately quite simple.

My friends, my people, are here with me, and I don't want them to leave.

In the long term, I obviously knew that. I hadn't realized how much I was missing their physical presence in my life *right now*. Although I know duty and sleep call us all and we must go our separate ways, I find myself wistful, not wanting this evening of listening to my friends gently bicker with each other to end.

I blurt, "Do you want to get dinner?"

Everyone stares at me, Yorani included, and I feel myself reddening.

Was that too sudden, or strange? Perhaps they don't want to spend any more time with me. Truly, given how much I ask of them I can't blame them—

"Yes, that is an activity that groups of close acquaintances in Istalam engage in, isn't it?" Sa Nikuran nods like I've proposed a satisfactory answer to a philosophical proposition. "I would like to partake in it."

"I mean," Lorwyn says, "yes, friends going out to dinner is a thing that normal people—okay how in the world have we gotten to a situation where I am the person explaining normal behavior? Miyara, I am absolutely sure this is your fault."

Their tentative acceptance—or at least lack of rejection—of my overture fills me with a sudden fervor. *Friends go out to dinner.* "We should invite Risteri."

Sa Nikuran chimes in, "As well as your Entero and Deniel!"

"He is *not* my Entero," Lorwyn says.

"Of course he is," Sa Nikuran says, looking at Lorwyn like she's stupid.

"Is seven too many for dinner?" I ask Lorwyn.

"What? No—I don't think so? It's not like I go out to eat with people!"

Glynis cuts in, "You are the most socially confused adult friends. It's adorable."

I look back at Lorwyn. "Is this what's known as 'trash talking'?"

Dryly, Lorwyn answers, "Yes, but only if it takes."

"Like I can't tell by now when Miyara is playing innocent," Glynis says. "Go to the Luck Dragon restaurant in the central district. You'll all do great."

I hadn't even thought about how we'd pick a restaurant. But my relief is short-lived as I ask, "You're not coming?"

"As a seventh wheel? Hard pass," Glynis says. "Also I still have messages to run, but I'll catch Risteri on my way back from your house, Miyara, and Entero will meet you there."

"How do you know where they are or where they'll be?"

Glynis shrugs. "It's my job. Come on, let's go see what Saiyana did to your house."

My house. My friends.

A bubble of nervousness and hope floats in my chest, and I hold it there carefully.

To my surprise Yorani opts to stay at home with Talsu. I thought she would want to experience this first of Istal culture with me, and it makes me wonder what she is plotting with the cat. But maybe she, too, wants time with her friend.

Or doesn't want to be a seventh wheel.

The six of us—me and Deniel, Lorwyn and Entero, and Risteri and Sa Nikuran—sit around a circular table covered in a patterned blue cloth in a brightly lit space, and I think Glynis chose well: people here are dressed in a variety of styles, the atmosphere is relaxed, and the staff are friendly and efficient. There are a few double-takes when we walk in, but after the initial whispers I am delighted to find no one pays us much mind.

Of course, this leaves us to navigate ourselves, and although I am almost giddy to be here I have no idea what to do. I look around the table and then settle hopefully on Entero.

He blinks, doing his own scan of the table, and makes a face as he comes to the same conclusion: that given his past as a spy, he probably has the most experience of any of our mixed group with restaurant customs.

Entero haltingly starts explaining how the menu works, picking up confidence as he answers questions mainly from me and Sa Nikuran, who have no shame about our ignorance about what to expect: when the waiter will arrive for what, what to say and how. Occasionally Risteri chimes in for my benefit on how customs differ from formal dinners—she has apparently eaten out with other guides occasionally and picked up some norms that way—or from what I'm accustomed to at the tea shop, and Lorwyn with acerbic notes about the ridiculousness of the customs and what it says about the people who partake in them.

Deniel is mostly quiet, but when I look at him, he is relaxed and smiling. He considers, then puts an arm around my back, and I lean into him contentedly, and content to let him be how he is.

"You two are cloying," Lorwyn says, throwing a snack bean at me.

I don't have to dodge, because Entero catches it midair and informs her patronizingly, "It's impolite to throw food."

"Why do you think I did it?"

"Because you're a rude person," he says matter-of-factly. "Much superior to all the other peons here who convince themselves to follow the rules."

Lorwyn's eyes flash with humor even as her face shows annoyance, like she can't decide whether to respond to his teasing as a compliment or an insult.

"That reminds me, Sa Nikuran," I say. "Are there courting rituals among the Te Muraka involving food?"

Her eyebrows lift. "Why do you ask?"

"I don't think anything is going on," I say carefully, "but it occurred to me that if Tamak and Elowyn's relationship were to evolve from friendship, I might want to be prepared with some answers."

This is nearly a lie. I suspect something would absolutely be going on if Tamak were willing to admit it, and I don't know why he won't. And while I consider myself responsible for them both, I am arguably both more and less responsible for what may happen between Iryasa and Sa Rangim.

At this table, only Deniel is aware of the latter, and I feel his gaze on me as he understands the former for the first time.

My chest tightens. Spirits, I should have talked to him about this first—

"Do you think I should I expect to be an uncle of dragonets?" Deniel asks lightly.

And then I thank the spirits again for this man. For trusting me, even with matters concerning his sister; for not letting the focus shift even hypothetically to Iryasa and Sa Rangim; for not making an issue of this right in this moment when he realizes there's an important piece I need.

"That, we are actually not sure about," Sa Nikuran says. "We have not had the opportunity to test. I can tell you anatomically we are human in the ways that matter for reproduction, but as for what sort of magic offspring between Te Muraka and Istals might manifest?" She shrugs. "Impossible to predict with certainty."

I blink. "Well that's exciting." It certainly speaks of adventure in Iryasa's future if her relationship with Sa Rangim progresses, if not the kind any of us had envisioned.

"We do have customs involving exchange of food, though," Sa Nikuran continues, as if this isn't a huge revelation. Though I suppose given our collective knowledge, there's not much more she can usefully add on the subject. "If a Te Muraka wishes to seriously pursue another, though, they'll know to make it explicit. Courtship involves a... I suppose you'd call it a bond, among us."

"Not something that ties two people together," Risteri clarifies. "It's an individual thing you feel, like a commitment. Like, Sa Nikuran feels it, but I don't—at least that we've noticed so far. So it's not something that can be imposed on you. But there are... boundary issues to negotiate."

"Courtship brings out our possessive natures," Sa Nikuran explains. "It heightens instincts in us applied to the person we would mate with that we typically only feel in our dragon shapes. So it cannot be done without consent."

"*Can*not, not *should* not?" I clarify.

"Yes," Sa Nikuran says. "Sa Rangim's law is clear."

That is not exactly the same, though perhaps effectively so, for the Te Muraka. Still, now I am thinking of Tamak with more unease. "What kind of consent is required, exactly? How much would another person have to understand?"

Deniel's hand squeezes my arm. "I don't think you have to worry Elowyn would agree to something without understanding the implications."

That gives me a breath; he's right. Tamak cannot go outside Sa Rangim's laws, and Elowyn has too much facility with words.

But that makes me wonder if Tamak asked for her consent accidentally. If he asked her, as a friend, if she would let him protect her during one of the recent attacks by Velasari agents, and she agreed, and he didn't realize his magic could take that as permission to begin forming a different kind of bond...

I definitely can't ask more questions on this now without giving him away, but I believe I have some idea now why he is so panicked about Sa Rangim finding out why he has the ability to know where Elowyn specifically is. Tamak may be trying to protect Elowyn from feeling pressured into a different kind of relationship with him by his mistake.

"Consent can always be revoked," Sa Nikuran says seriously. "But a bond is not a light thing for us. Courtship and sex and bonds are all related but separate. I can have sex with Risteri and court her without magically bonding with her.

"But to the best of our knowledge over these last decades, once a bond is solidified, those Te Muraka never experience a bond with another. Perhaps someday we will learn differently—remember we do not have so many generations of knowledge or such a great population, and not all of us bond at all—but as we understand it now, Te Muraka bond for life."

Risteri puts her hand on Sa Nikuran's shoulder as she looks at me. "Sa Rangim oversees developing bonds," she says. "Apparently a bond can be severed entirely, but if so it can't regrow with the same person ever again. But he also has the power to basically freeze a bond in its stage of development, if people need more time to work things out once the process has begun. That's what I meant about boundaries. We're just starting to try this, and he enables us to set the pace."

There are so many pieces of this to unpack. There's what this means for Tamak's feelings for Elowyn, and why he's so uncomfortable about being forced to acknowledge the situation to her or to Sa Rangim. I always intended to follow up with Tamak, but now I realize I will have to—for his sake and Elowyn's, on multiple axes.

There's what that could mean for Iryasa and Sa Rangim, and how I have inadvertently pushed my oldest, emotionally vulnerable sister into a situation potentially even more completely outside any of our knowledge of how to handle than I intended. I may have to reveal what I started to Risteri and Sa Nikuran just to get more information—but not yet.

But there's also that Risteri has been learning about this and making these decisions about her life and future and once again I have not been part of them. Even if I'd wanted to, I haven't been around.

I also can't help thinking my own relationship with Deniel seems fantastically less complicated now by comparison of having a third party have to monitor the state of a magical bond between us.

Though I suppose Yorani's observation and interference was to our benefit, so perhaps it's not as awkward as all that. A little mutually solicited help and counseling can go a long way.

"So how is it going?" I ask. "Can I ask that? I mean, is it hard since you don't live together, or—"

"I think it helps, actually?" Risteri poses this as a question to Sa Nikuran, who nods firmly.

"Physical boundary," she agrees.

"You basically do live together though," Lorwyn points out. "You're both always in the apartment."

"Physical boundary between Risteri's room and communal space," Sa Nikuran amends with a glint in her eye.

Lorwyn snorts.

"You knew about this already?" I ask Lorwyn, careful to keep my tone surmising and without the pang of hurt I feel at being left out. They have been friends so much longer than I have known them, and I have been busy, and yet.

"Since we live together, it was possibly going to affect me," Lorwyn says with a shrug.

Risteri rolls her eyes as if she can't believe Lorwyn can't understand Risteri just wanted to talk to someone about this, except of course she can, and I almost smile. Their friendship is better now, but they are still so bad at saying what they mean to each other.

"It hasn't actually changed much, though," Lorwyn notes. "We all still fit together easily."

Then she clams up, as if realizing a moment too late her comment about the fact that she and Risteri actually make good roommates could be interpreted as a broader comment on all their relationships.

Entero can't resist baiting her, despite the apparent touchiness of the matter of his living situation, and the moment is lost in a tussle between the two of them as our conversation moves on to the exhaustions of moving and fitting everything into limited time and generally catching up.

I walk home with Deniel, catching each other up on our days and observations—not least of all what I suspect is going on with Elowyn and Tamak, which I am comforted to find him less worried about on account of his trust in Elowyn and favorable opinion of Tamak's character. He concurs it's worth checking on with them, but not an urgent disaster. They are young, but extremely mature for all that.

We walk quietly for a bit until Deniel says, "You had fun at dinner, but there's something bothering you."

"I wasn't ever fully happy living with Risteri," I admit, "but I both feel like I should have been and am envious of them now. I don't want to move back but still miss them. It seems unfair to want it both ways."

"They're your friends," Deniel says simply. "You'll find a way to make a different space for them in your life, even if it's not that one."

"But I'm missing things now."

"You always will," he says. "But you worried about not being there before when Risteri was making huge choices about her future with Sa Nikuran, too, and she's gone ahead and done it again. She doesn't always need you to weigh in on everything, so you don't need to beat yourself up about not doing something she doesn't want. She knows where you live if she needs you."

True, and important for me to remember—provided she does in fact understand I will always make time for her when she needs me. That, at least, is on me to demonstrate.

"Part of me is also comforted that at least I'm not the only one who doesn't have everything figured out," I admit.

Deniel smiles. "But you also think you should."

"Am I really so predictable?" I complain.

Deniel laughs. "A little. I've been wondering about something for both of us."

"Oh?"

"Do you ever think we spend so much time planning and worrying about what we could or should be doing, we don't ever just—" he waves his hand around us "—be?"

"Yes," I say instantly. "But I am also not sure I know how to not."

Deniel stops in front of me. "You just dined out at a restaurant with your friends for the first time. A triple date, in fact."

I blink, and smile delightedly. "It was, wasn't it?"

Me, going on a triple date with friends. I can hardly compass what my life has become.

"And here we are," Deniel says. "Two people among many others walking down these streets to our home, together. Talking about our days—"

"The events of our days may differ somewhat in content," I murmur.

"Talking about the events of our days that are important to us and our lives," Deniel says with eyebrows raised, challenging me to contradict this isn't what anyone else would discuss.

I huff with a smile and he continues, a sly smile tugging at his own lips.

"We're part of the everyday movements and rhythms of this city, but right here we're also alone, together, under a beautiful sky full of stars," Deniel says, stepping close to me.

His eyes still stare a challenge into mine, a grin playing on his lips, and I close my eyes, listening to the sounds of people and rustling leaves and the feeling of the city around us and us alone in this moment in it.

And he kisses me.

CHAPTER 12

MY WORLD DEVOLVES into moments. I attempt to float through it all being present and accessible, at the expense of floating above and seeing how all the pieces fit into the whole of what I'm trying to accomplish.

There are moments of renovations at Talmeri's Tea and Tisanes. The old, worn sign is replaced with a lovely wooden one, text and decorations painted on in the same shade of green as my hair.

It's the emerald color Thiano showed me when we first met, and it's fitting he insisted on being the one to provide this anchor in my space.

"I want it commissioned from Gaellani craftsperson," I told him.

"It will be."

"Then why should I pay the additional fees you'll charge rather than going straight to them?"

"Do you know who to talk to? Do you know how to make sure you're getting a high-quality product that won't crumble into bark a year from now, the paint washing away? Do you have time? Miyara, really."

I'd eyed him for a moment and finally said, "It will have to sync with any wards the shop already has without negating them."

Thiano's eyes had glittered, but he'd said only, "I'll make sure it doesn't."

From the man who still has not told me what magic resides in the bracelets he procured for me, this guarantee is one another person might question. But not me; not now.

So then there's the moment when I meet with my four sisters, all of us alone together for the first time in Sayorsen.

At House Taresim, which Saiyana has requisitioned on my sisters' behalf.

Despite living on the grounds, I don't know the interior of the mansion, or even my way around the grounds. Even if I had, it wouldn't resemble its prior state now that Ostario first and then Saiyana have been through with teams of mages to strip any suspicious secrets out of its foundations.

The five of us meet in Kustio's library which, while the shelves are missing entire sections of confiscated books, nevertheless possesses sufficient seating for us all, large leather armchairs around a table.

The chairs are not plush. Kustio wished to appear cultured and knowledgeable, not to actually make visitors comfortable. Combined with the effect of the raided bookshelves, the effect of the space oddly mimics us: pretending on the surface that everything is in order, that we are comfortable in our roles as sisters to each other, but the gaps and cracks and stiffness are visible for anyone who but looks.

I'm the last to arrive. Karisa is huddled in a chair, arms crossed and glaring across the room ignored as Saiyana goes over some report with Iryasa. Reyata appears to be surveying the shelves, but the angle of her body tells me her attention is nevertheless turned toward Iryasa.

"Good of you to join us," Saiyana says, glancing up.

"It's your own fault," I say. "I assume you sent me the address to locate on a map rather than just telling me the destination because you knew I'd object and didn't want to deal with it? The library is not exactly easy to find in here regardless."

"Designed so guests will have to wander through a whole bunch of intimidating aristocratic splendor, yes," Saiyana agrees. "But in terms of seating, it was this or that gigantic dining table, which is not only excessive in a place this remote but also has way more holes in the walls to plug. So the library, such as it now is, will do."

"I have concerns about the optics of this move," I say, since someone needs to, "not to mention the holes that need filling."

"You mean that our power base has moved in right into the location of Sayorsen and the Te Muraka's previous oppressor?" Iryasa answers me. "We're presenting this as the crown acknowledging its mistakes and taking an active hand in remedying the problem. The narrative works."

"Only if you don't mess up," Karisa remarks.

Iryasa arches an eyebrow at me. "'We'," she corrects.

Perhaps I should be glad that she's internalized that part of her role, but I can't help noticing she didn't even look at Karisa when she said it.

"Let me rephrase," Saiyana says. "It will have to do, because we're not going to find another place set up more suitably with protections than here."

Reyata finally turns around, taking a seat on the other side of Iryasa. "I thought all spells had been stripped from the foundations?"

"Not all of them," Saiyana said. "We did do a full sweep, but not everything is harmful. Nothing wrong with spells to heat bathwater."

"You can't trust where he could have snuck something in," Reyata warns.

"We did a full sweep," Saiyana repeats with more patience than she has with me; I imagine Reyata benefits from being an elder sister. "Anything we didn't find in this case is only going to work to our advantage. If Kustio didn't think he had protections against Nakrab, what stopped them from taking over his supply chain instead of continuing to fund his operation? Because one thing we can be sure of is that the Nakrabi didn't consider him an equal partner, or they would have provided him the means to keep him out of prison—and more to the point, kept his operation intact."

"Unless he didn't think that was a possibility," Reyata points out.

"Kustio, say no to power?" Saiyana snorts. "No. I'm sure."

"You'd better be," Reyata says, "as you're betting the safety of the crown princess on it."

Karisa mutters, "The rest of our safety being inconsequential, naturally."

Saiyana rolls her eyes. "I'm sure. You approved the additional security measures, too. If you're all quite finished questioning my ability to do a job I've been unprecedentedly successful at for years and which most of you don't even understand, let's move on."

"One last thing on this," I say.

Saiyana sighs. "Yes, Lady Taresim graciously offered us the use of her home, and yes, I'm aware that she intends to watch us for information and have already taken steps. Anything else?"

"You're also aware she's a spy for our grandmother?" I ask.

Saiyana scowls, while Iryasa and Reyata's expressions turn bland. "Miyara."

Their politics-faces are trained as well as mine, and I'm not entirely sure whether this means they already knew or if she's simply reproaching me for speaking it aloud. "Just wanted to make sure we were all on the same page. Although she is ostensibly here to support our cause, I am not convinced her methods will serve our means."

"A resource to be wary of," Reyata summarizes. "Noted."

"We should be wary of all resources," Saiyana says dryly. But her I know well enough to recognize another note in her tone, and my eyes narrow slightly. Her trust issues go deep.

An awkward silence falls over us, all five sisters in one room together—and not with anyone else. Not a servant, official, delegate, or tutor.

I try to remember the last time this happened and realize it may have never happened.

Iryasa draws herself up, and I recognize the posture—our mother begins official speeches the same way.

I almost wince. Part of me knew I would have to manage this interaction among the sisters, but I am also the fourth youngest, and to some part of me that seems unnatural. Nevertheless, what Iryasa is about to do is not appropriate for what we need to become, so I intercept.

My work—even, or perhaps especially, among my sisters—here begins. As long as I'm already wincing, I decide to get the big fight out of the way.

"One last thing about magical protections, before we begin in truth," I say. "You should be aware that Thiano may be introducing unknown magical elements to the wards at Talmeri's—"

"What?" Saiyana explodes.

"—which I absolutely insist be allowed to stand if they cannot be conclusively proven detrimental," I finish, eyebrows raised.

Karisa cackles. "Harmless like bathwater."

Saiyana spares a glare for her before launching into a tirade.

It's Reyata who overrides her objections. But then, Reyata's a strategist, and she recognizes the utility of allowing this and testing what it means. Just like with the house—which she points out to Saiyana, who would have been mostly taken aback by the introduction of a variable she doesn't control into her plan without her approval.

So Reyata, Saiyana, and I can all be open with each other, even if we're still learning each other and who we've become separated: that's something.

From there we begin in earnest, if perhaps with more conversation. Iryasa doesn't try to take back launching the meeting; she lets it flow around her and then redirects its course gently.

All my sisters defer to Iryasa whenever she deigns to speak, with gestures, with looks in her direction for approval. Iryasa catches me watching it happen and shakes her head with a smile: we don't have time to re-work years' worth of familiar relationships before the summit for the sake of her loneliness. She's as comfortable as she can be in this situation, bringing us all here without the defense of formality to hide behind.

We're together: that's how we start to shift the narrative.

I am less surprised by how they all mostly ignore Karisa, but more, initially, by how she allows it. Yet I realize Karisa truly is perfect for the role I've devised for her, and already she's playing it. Let even our sisters think her harmless and predictable, and they'll worry less—about her, and about the part we've planned for her that we're not sharing.

We argue. We plan. We don't do it as equals, but we do it together. As a beginning, it's not what I would want, but I think—I hope—it will serve, as long as it's not the end, too.

That's on me. Because even if I'm the fourth youngest, I'm the tea master.

Then there's the moment I have to withdraw from a dinner Deniel has set up on my behalf with his contacts in the Gaellani community, on the council, and with merchants he's dealt with over his years of running a successful pottery shop. Deniel assures me they can review how each will contribute to the summit without my presence, and that managing this is his role: my time will be occupied with the actual negotiations and can't also include these logistics.

Still, while I know I am the only one who can have this meeting with Tea Master Karekin and that I've been unable to prioritize this for days, I go in feeling like I am being blown by the wind in different directions, tossed and turned rather than flowing easily on a current.

I meet him at the tea shop, and without ado he points at the sign that now graces Talmeri's door: a statement of who we are, and a welcome.

"It is well done," he says simply, and a note of my tension eases.

Tea masters can see the pieces and the whole, and his words mean I'm doing something right, at least.

Once we're inside, Tea Master Karekin gestures at the tea counter and asks, "May I?"

I blink, realizing that never once has he served me tea, and motion for him to help himself, as I bemusedly take a seat in my own shop.

"We have much to cover," Karekin says, "but yours is an unusual situation. Before we begin, let's not repeat past mistakes."

It takes me a moment to catch up. "You want to know the details of my current situation?"

Karekin bows. "So I can prioritize your curriculum only, Miyara. There was information you needed that I could have provided before it became a problem, before. Let me do so now."

I am silent, weighing. There are so many secrets I now carry; which are safe for me to reveal?

On intuition I look up to see Karekin's gaze resting seriously on mine. "I promise to keep all your secrets," he says. "Every one."

"Because I'm a tea master now?"

"Because it is what you need," he says, "to give me what I need to be able to help you. And that is why I'm here."

His gaze drifts to Yorani, where she is playing a game among the shelves I don't understand.

I stop delaying. The decision is made; I am uncomfortable with the position the tea guild has put me in, but not with Karekin himself. I cannot afford for Yorani to be put in danger again because I have learned they don't deserve my full trust as an organization.

I summarize while Karekin moves through my space. A gentle smile blooms on his face as he begins evaluating the various canisters of tea, occasionally replaced with surprise or amusement as he investigates their contents.

"So I suspect the Isle of Nakrab is in need of some magic to do with the Cataclysm," I conclude. "Since we don't know how their magic works, nor how to counter it, Yorani may yet be in danger again."

"Then it is for the best that you're deeply involved in this," Tea Master Karekin says, "since if anyone can assess magic these days when there are no arcanists, it must be a tea master."

I pause. "When there are no what?"

Karekin looks at me. "Arcanists—aha." He abruptly picks another canister of tea. "That is where we'll begin, then."

"You're telling me arcanists are real." It's an inane thing to say: I have an arcane teapot. But I've never heard anyone talk about them as casual fact, like they might have been colleagues in another industry a few years back.

"Were," Karekin corrects. "My apologies; I assumed you knew."

"I know legends, of course," I say. "They exist in countless myths, as wandering individuals with incomprehensible power that show up and vanish without explanation as stories require."

Karekin's hands are busy with the business of tea. "They exist in history, too, but older histories."

"Ancient histories of debatable historical integrity, which are not unlike myths."

"A fair point," he concedes. "Arcanists had removed themselves from worldly affairs so thoroughly by the time of the Cataclysm that few people know anymore they were, in fact, real, and not gone from this world for so long as that."

"Then why would you assume I knew?"

Karekin looks up. "It was a tea master who, once people became aware of a magical disturbance in the east, persuaded an arcanist to come down from seclusion, who then brought others. After the Cataclysm occurred and the arcanists were all destroyed, the tea masters were part of negotiations between the remaining nations in the aftermath. Forgive me; I thought it would have been part of your political education, especially since you have never doubted the trustworthiness of witches."

Whatever Karekin sees in my expression makes him sigh with sympathy.

"Do you mean to imply," I say, "that my grandmother in fact knew for certain that witches weren't responsible for the Cataclysm, but allowed them to be punished anyway?"

"Your grandmother fought many battles in the wake of the Cataclysm," Karekin says. "This is one she lost. You know politics are never simple, always a matter of priorities and impossible choices. My understanding is she considers it her greatest failure."

"That's not good enough," I say in a low voice.

"It is not," Karekin agrees. "The tea guild does not lack culpability here, either. But understand that people were terrified, and they wouldn't believe the truth—especially since the arcanists left no evidence. The tea guild knows they were involved at the end, but we cannot prove it. And there are circumstances when no amount of proof can combat fear. I know you know this, Miyara, or your campaign to rehabilitate the reputation of witches would have proceeded very differently."

It's not whether he's right or wrong that gets to me. But there is no cure for feeling aimless quite like sudden rage.

I have a moment of crystal clarity, which is that I hate secrets. Ironic for someone keeping so many, but perhaps also why I cannot let them alone.

It must both be why my grandmother thought I would make an excellent spymaster, and why I will never do it.

Because I am so angry that all this has been kept not just from me, but from everyone.

People may not have been willing to accept the truth then—though even this I doubt. But why did we not keep saying it as the initial panic about the Cataclysm faded, over and over and endlessly? Why was this piece of history allowed to be forgotten?

How could my grandmother, the woman who believed in me and the power of listening, personally, specifically have allowed it?

"I think," I say evenly, "we need to speak more of the history of tea masters."

Karekin carries a tray of tea over to where I'm seated and sets it down. It is perfectly, simply arranged, which of course I had assumed: he is a tea master.

But it is not a scent I have smelled in this shop before, and I know every tea on those shelves. Which means he's combined at least two different teas to make something new, effortlessly.

While I am teasing out the notes in the scent, Karekin says, "I agree, but allow me to suggest what may be more urgent: which is, the history of tea mastery itself, and what it has to do with both arcanism and your familiar."

That gets my attention away from studying the tea. Karekin takes advantage of this to pour, and I realize he has also very efficiently brought me out of an anger spiral and to the point at hand.

He will be an excellent teacher if I allow him to be, and I clearly still have a lot to learn.

"We expect delegates from the Isle of Nakrab to arrive the day after tomorrow," I say. "Can you summarize?"

The corners of Karekin's eyes crease in amusement. "Yes. But take a sip first."

I sigh. That's my own tactic turned back on me, but I drink anyway: preparing to take this new information into myself and incorporate it into my understanding along with this new taste of tea, accepting this directive with this tea not without question, but accepting nonetheless like I will this lesson.

"To the best of our knowledge, which may be imperfect given its bias, tea mastery actually predates arcanism," Karekin explains as I sip. "Although our modern magic—magecraft, witchcraft—derives from arcanism, arcanism itself derives from tea mastery."

I have so many questions all at once, but one is clearly the most pertinent. "But tea mastery isn't magic."

Karekin smiles. "Isn't it?"

I sigh. "You know what I mean."

"I do, and may I remind you that you created a living spirit through performing a tea ceremony?"

He has me there.

Rather than pursue the point, Karekin says, "The critical significance when it comes to magic is that it comes down to perception and patterns. As tea masters, we learn to look at people and discern what drives them, what it means, what they need, how to supply it. Magic workers look at the world. I admit my knowledge of witchcraft is weaker, but it is not an accident that magecraft is baked into physical structures, and the people with a talent for it are those who can look at the world in a certain way."

I think of Glynis, how sure I was quickly that she could be an excellent mage—and that Lorwyn, brilliant but accustomed to witchcraft, struggles to wrap her brain around magecraft, accustomed as she is to different paths to magic.

And I think of me, and Saiyana's endless frustration that I wasn't the mage she thought I should be. Perhaps I found a different form of magic for myself, after all.

"But that difference," Karekin says, "is why I am glad beyond measure you are pushing the tea masters back into the realm of human affairs. Into working with people, rather than above them. Because separatism, ultimately, is why I believe the arcanists fell. In focusing their study on the world without people, they weren't prepared for what people could do. And if you're correct in your suspicions about Nakrab, it is critical that you are positioned as you are on this path: to bring us all together."

As his new tea vanishes between us, Karekin tells me what he knows.

CHAPTER 13

MY MIND WHIRLS FROM revelations of what Karekin has revealed to me, upending foundations of my understanding of the world. I don't know what to do with this new knowledge, but I know what I'm going to do next.

It's what I should have done long before now.

Yorani is excited at first—this is one of her favorite places—but as I stare distractedly ahead, she gives me a long look before flying off on her own without so much as a chirp.

I let her. She's not the one struggling with this, or indeed anything of late: she may be my familiar, but it's only me who's been out of sorts. Maybe with distance from me at least one of us can stay clear-sighted.

With shifts of this magnitude in my life, the best place for me to think and reflect is the shrine, in contemplation of the spirits.

As I walk, even this now gives me further conflicts to consider. One of the purposes of a public shrine outside of the home is as a separate location, removed from your typical surroundings, from which to benefit from the perspective that comes with difference.

But that also in a way separates the practice of contemplating the spirits from daily life, when the spirits should be with us always. That's why we have altars in our homes, too, and perhaps that simply means both are important, the distance and the presence where we live.

Because a shrine is also about focusing on the spirits specifically. But it may now more than ever be important to remember that the concentration that comes from removing the distractions of daily life is not superior: the revelations we have under the pressures and comforts of our daily lives are not just equally valid, but equally necessary.

It's not enough to contemplate: we also have to live. Epiphanies that are separate from lived experience must be able to bear up under the reality of living, or they're too flimsy to be revelatory. Part of a tea master's strength is perspective: too close or too distant, and we can't do our work effectively.

My thoughts are still swimming as I nevertheless enter the shrine.

I will take advantage of the perspective its distance and focus can aid in me, but I am not sequestering myself from the world just by visiting here. I will take whatever insight I gain, and return, and put it to the test.

The way that, eventually, the arcanists apparently didn't.

I make my way through the altars, beginning with water. I can understand the allure of separating from worldly concerns, perhaps now more than ever. My time is always taken over by plots and plans, by the minutiae of working and eating and dealing with humans. The currents of different concerns pull me one way and another until I feel drained, worn by a thousand inevitable, unavoidable tracks, emotionally battered against rocks.

I continue to the altar of earth. That remove is exactly what I left the palace to leave behind, to find the place where I can feel rooted; like there is solid foundation beneath my feet rather than being adrift. That remove is also what I took the entire tea guild to task on: the failure to be entwined with people and their lives has caused the tea guild—them or us, now?—to fail. The ties between us are critical to lift us up.

I move to the altar of air, staring at its flickering flame.

Then I take my place at the side of Sa Rangim, whom I somehow am unsurprised to find here with me at this moment.

Air floats above the flow of water; it fills the spaces between our roots. It's the space above and between, and somehow I must find a way to be both, too, to fly as gracefully and surely as Yorani.

I demanded both the royal family and the tea guild do better at this and set myself up as a lead to follow. But this is not a balance I'm confident I can navigate.

I don't know how to be everything people need from me, to keep the perspective of both distance and closeness and not lose myself. Air has no boundaries.

But it's also uncontainable.

It's a force we move through with ease, not noting its presence until a wind whips up. We breathe it into our beings without a second thought. It bides its time until it's ready to strike—

My lips twist wryly. What a convenient answer, that supports my not having to take action right this second.

Then my amusement fades, as I wonder how many arcanists thought they would somehow know when the world really needed them, until the world surprised them. Until, unprepared, it was too late for even their collective number to stop what had already begun.

No. Air is here, now, always. Decisions are not for later.

Somehow, I must learn to float both above and between at once.

I wonder which the harder way to begin is, and decide to go with the one that may be easier for Sa Rangim.

"Tamak has been surer of himself lately," I remark. "I think his time—not just at the tea shop specifically, but as a trusted party among recent events—has done well for him. And us, too."

Out of the corner of my eye, Sa Rangim's lips quirk into a smile. "That was well done."

I raise my eyebrows.

"Establishing your trust in him and his growth as a starting point to test my position on the matter, and to have already set that parameter in case what you have to tell me would cause me to lose faith in him."

"You did set him at the door when you knew Iryasa was coming," I say blandly, blatantly continuing in the vein I've begun. "I can only assume you hold a measure of respect for his growth."

Sa Rangim laughs outright. "You wish to look out for both Tamak and Elowyn without betraying a trust," he says. "I commend you."

"I have been thinking a great deal about boundaries," I say with a nod toward the flame. "I don't suppose you could also answer some questions?"

"Ah, boundaries. An important consideration, given your power."

He doesn't elaborate, and I raise my eyebrows a bit higher in mute encouragement to give me something that will set my mind at ease.

Though he could as easily confound it utterly. Perhaps I should have been more specific.

Sa Rangim inclines his head, still smiling. "You are right and wrong to worry for Tamak," he says. "I was aware the moment Tamak's magic changed."

And he hadn't said anything. Not to me, but then, while I have been his confidante in many ways, serving his own people is not a new charge for him, nor one necessarily within my scope to assist at.

But he also hadn't said anything to Tamak, clearly, or Tamak would not have been so worried about Sa Rangim learning about it.

"I didn't realize a bond was a shift in magic," I say. "Unless I have misapprehended the nature of the situation?"

"You have not," Sa Rangim confirms, his gaze sliding away from me—less worried now that I have not challenged his handling outright, I realize. "As you say, Tamak has grown, so I watched to see how he would handle it."

I purse my lips. "And he didn't tell you."

"Not at first," Sa Rangim says, surprising me—because that means Tamak has, now. Before I can feel relief at that, that at least now his accidental magic is being monitored by someone I trust, Sa Rangim continues, "Before he did, I confess I was shocked at what he did do: years before a Te Muraka his age should have such facility, he figured out how to freeze the bond on his own."

"That's rare," I surmise.

Sa Rangim meets my eyes again more seriously. "I don't know how to fully express to you how rare that is. To form a bond at all at his age is uncommon, but not unprecedented. Among other things, it's indicative of the profound connection he's found with Elowyn, which I cannot regret."

Nor can I. They were both effectively alone and friendless. That they may not know how to navigate such a remarkable friendship is a concern, but that each of them has found such a match in each other is remarkable.

"But freezing a bond," Sa Rangim continues. "That requires a tremendous amount of fortitude, and I don't mean only magically. To freeze a bond at all requires strength, yes, but to freeze your own? It's not simply self-awareness; it would go against every instinct he possesses."

"It's empathy," I murmur.

He nods. "Profoundly so. I am ashamed that someone so young, that we thought lost and undisciplined, possesses it in such abundance. I am humbled, and I remind myself that given opportunities, people can rise in ways you don't expect. I hope I would possess comparable fortitude in his place."

I study him at that. Sa Rangim's discipline and empathy were easily known to me the first time I met him. I'm not sure if this is humility, or if he truly doesn't know.

Or if, with his strength of magic, the strength of his draconic instincts is comparably large.

Sa Rangim already sat in contemplation of air before I arrived. Perhaps I'm not the only one with work to do on the subject of boundaries.

"You said Tamak has come to you now, though," I say.

"He asked me if he should sever the bond," Sa Rangim says.

I start, surprised. "If he should sever the bond? Not you?"

"Indeed," he says.

"And?"

Sa Rangim glances toward me, and I can make out the mischief in his gaze. "And I asked him what Elowyn thought."

My eyebrows shoot up before I can stop them. Sa Rangim smiles gently. "They may still be children now, but not for much longer," he says. "They are not as young as that. As with your tea spirit, we have to not just prepare them to fly alone: they must have the chance to make choices on their own, or how else will they learn?"

I remember the assessing look Yorani gave me before flying off on her own tonight, already able to soar easily through the air. More than anything, I think this is her natural element.

I wonder which of us is really being given the autonomy to work through issues on our own and learn, and which of us needs a guide.

The answer is both. The answer is I'm fortunate as an adult to have a being who knows me well enough to nudge me in the direction I need to go or stay out of the way when I need to find it myself. I hope I can be equally as mindful of her.

Sa Rangim is watching me, and I realize I've gone silent and internally contemplative. I wave a hand toward the flame. "Don't mind me, just reflecting on how much I have to learn from the children."

"May we always remember," he agrees as the colors in his eyes swirl.

"So? Did Tamak speak to Elowyn after that?"

"As you might expect, he was... discomfited by the question, but he was at that point already able to answer: which is that she is fine with keeping it."

"Really." Elowyn, who loves to be able to vanish—

But perhaps, she also likes knowing someone will always be able to see her. I wonder if she'd have ever listened to me if I hadn't spotted her that time in the market.

"I tell you this in confidence," Sa Rangim continues, "because while Tamak, I hope, will believe now he can always come to me, it is possible he may come to you instead. And Elowyn, likewise."

"You're not going to monitor them, like Sa Nikuran and Risteri?" I ask.

"Sa Nikuran requested my guidance and counsel," Sa Rangim says. "Tamak has not—I believe because at the moment he does not wish to take things any further. But given what he has demonstrated, I also do not believe he needs it.

"I can still sense the changes in his magic, if that is your concern. I told Tamak if he wants to keep his fledgling bond, then it is on him to never cross Elowyn's boundaries of consent, which requires being sure he has clearly communicated to her what a shift would entail in advance. And if he's not sure a step further will cross, and he's not comfortable talking to her about it, he will not take it. That rule is my condition for operating without my oversight at each potential step."

"Good."

Good for Tamak, for proving he has the character to be trusted to handle this on his own. Good for Sa Rangim, for trusting him—and for making it explicitly clear what constitutes a violation of that trust.

"Ah, you think I'm done," Sa Rangim says. "But Tamak came up with another idea that has been fascinating to pursue with him. We have been designing a new kind of Te Muraka device together."

I think through the implications there: this Sa Rangim is overseeing personally, because any Te Muraka device would have political ramifications given how their trafficking was abused by Kustio in the past—and to make sure he is keeping a watchful eye on how his people use their magic to interact with the non-Te Muraka population.

And that while Sa Rangim has the expertise when it comes to designing magical devices, Tamak shares the aptitude to the degree that Sa Rangim can train him personally.

"What does the device do?" I ask.

"It allows Tamak to track Elowyn," Sa Rangim says. "Speaking broadly, it externalizes the bond."

I blink, and then I realize: "So she can choose when he can find her."

"Just so. He abused her consent before, even if he didn't mean to. So since she did not want him to sever the bond entirely, this is how he has chosen to demonstrate that he will be careful about respecting her boundaries going forward."

There's more to it than that. It's also a self-imposed punishment, because Tamak thinks he deserves one and both Sa Rangim and Elowyn declined to do it for him.

But he may have underestimated Elowyn. She would accept his punishing himself for something that didn't upset her if she thought it would help him trust himself—and maybe trust her, both to know her own mind and to be able to take care of herself without his protection, too.

And I thought Sa Nikuran and Risteri had a more complicated relationship than Deniel and me. The teens have outdone us all.

With one noteworthy exception. I take a breath.

"Sa Nikuran mentioned there are food customs involved in courting, among the Te Muraka, though she did not go into any specifics," I say. "I can't help but remember the exchange you proposed with my sister involved sharing food."

Sa Rangim doesn't move; I'm certain of it. Yet it's as though his entire being has sharpened, somehow, in a way I can't place.

"Would that be an error?" he asks softly.

Politically, personally; so many ways to mean that question or answer it. Will she be offended by pursuit? Will I feel betrayed? Will he be betraying his people in the attempt? Did I not know what he was about?

The latter, at least, I owe an answer to, as it was absolutely my intent.

And I can't deny satisfaction at this confirmation that it is not only Iryasa who is interested, even though I knew.

"It is my fondest hope that it is not," I say. "But you should understand that Iryasa cannot, and will not, be as flexible about boundaries as Elowyn."

"You speak of her position, as crown princess," Sa Rangim says. "Please believe that I have given thought to the repercussions given our statuses as heads of state."

"I don't mean that, actually," I say. "I know you are perfectly aware of understanding what this would mean for your people, and all our people; better, I imagine, than I can. I'm speaking of Iryasa, and how we were raised, and what that will mean for her more than anyone."

His eyes glow brighter than before as he looks at me.

I have Sa Rangim's full attention.

"Our mother, Queen Ilmari, is married to Cordán of Velasar," I begin. It's odd to speak of my family impersonally, but there are few other ways I can speak of them.

"Cordán the Consort, as he is called," he says. "I'm aware."

"Do you understand that it was not by either of their choice?"

Sa Rangim's eyes narrow. "Your people mate for political reasons. It is a thing I can understand intellectually only; viscerally, I do not."

"Good," I say firmly. "With Iryasa, that will help."

It's his turn to raise his eyebrows.

"Forgive me; I must give you some historical context for this to make sense. In the aftermath of the Cataclysm, there was incredible instability. My grandmother, when she was queen, had always been bold. She'd been the queen of an enormous, wealthy, powerful empire, with few who would dare challenge her throwing of her political weight around.

"The Cataclysm changed all that. It also meant, in her wake, that the resentment she'd built up doing whatever she felt necessary to enact her policies demanded a rebalance of power. Taresan was hurt by the Cataclysm, too, but our presence east of Velasar's borders protected Velasar from a comparable collapse of infrastructure. They were whole when Istalam was broken and traumatized.

"Velasar is no longer a miniscule nation to the west, overwhelmed by its eastern neighbor: we're of a size. As Istalam needed their stability to help regain ours, one of the concessions was for the then-crown princess of Istalam, my mother, to marry a Velasar consort.

"From the start it was understood that my father would never be an equal co-ruler of Istalam; even then, that was a bridge too far. But Velasar has long dreamed of overthrowing Istal power and instating its own in that place, and they thought with this move, they had: by the terms of the marriage contract, any child of Ilmari and Cordán would be raised equally by both of them, which meant that each child would, through our father, learn to know and love Velasar. From there, Velasar believed that, even once Istalam stabilized, the eventual weakening of the Istal royal family's power in Velasar's favor was inevitable."

Sa Rangim studies me. "Queen Ilmari is famous as a diplomat. Could they not find common ground?"

"Knowing what I do of my mother's tactics, I suspect they may have at first," I say. "She would have needed him to go along with her. With the Cataclysm's upheaval, it was important—I wish I thought my grandmother hadn't pressured her, but I don't believe it—to demonstrate a stable line of governing continuity to the population even before my mother ascended the throne. So very quickly, my parents had their first child, Iryasa. And this is when Cordán would have become aware of my mother's plan.

"My mother," I explain, "was responsible for ensuring a stable line of Istal rulership. Velasar's interests ran counter to that goal, attempting to destabilize from within. So since, contractually, my father was owed as much time with their children as my mother, my mother's plan was simple: she spent no time with us at all."

Whatever Sa Rangim had surmised, it was not this: he cannot keep the astonishment from even his schooled face. "She what," he breathes.

"'At all' is an exaggeration, but not by much. Tutors and servants had the raising of us, because whatever time my mother couldn't spend with us, neither could my father. You may rightly imagine the wording of their contract has been pored over since. And so in this way, my mother attempted to ensure the Istal line would not be corrupted by Velasari influence despite her husband."

Sa Rangim stares.

"It's not impossible it was also out of spite," I admit. "My mother did spend time with Karisa, after the elder four of us grew up 'safely' without our father's potentially corrupting influence, so I don't think it was an aversion to mothering in general.

"I don't know if my mother hated our father from the beginning. And I suppose it is possible that he knew all along what she was planning, and simply didn't believe she could or would manage it. Not for multiple children; not for more than a decade. My mother is famous for diplomacy in part because she is a master at sticking to the letter of an agreement but never letting anyone close enough to hurt her and never, ever letting down her guard."

"Oh, she was hurt," Sa Rangim says, a wealth of emotion in his voice.

I incline my head. "I imagine so. But Sa Rangim, understand: I can only imagine so. I left the palace the day I dedicated to my path, which means I left the day my mother—or my father—could have been free to try to know me. My relationship with my mother is not personal; it could not be.

"But for Iryasa, who has trained with our mother closely for years since her dedication, it is personal. She will know exactly how lacking in not just love, but trust, our parents' relationship is; she will know how two people bound together can trap each other and tear at each other. She will know what a fight looks like when two people don't understand each other, but nowhere in the model indicates it may be possible to bridge that gap. But she knows too well what it can look like when two politicians with agendas of their own are married."

"Against their wills," Sa Rangim says.

"Certainly, but they both went through with it, and they are still married today."

"I understand the complications of consent, and freedom, and choice, Miyara," Sa Rangim says.

"I know you do." And because I'm not sure if it was truly humility earlier, I say explicitly, "I knew that the first time I met you, Sa Rangim. In a single conversation, you proved to me how fiercely protective you are and also the depth of your control."

I wait, meeting his gaze, until I see the colors in his eyes swirl. He bows his head; an acknowledgment of what I've said, and that I believe it.

Only then do I continue. "Believe that not just as a royal princess, but as my mother's daughter specifically, contractual language was greatly emphasized in my education. I didn't set up the treaty the way I did by accident any more than I introduced my sister to you the way I did by accident. I believe you two will suit, and I am trusting you with her. But to do right by you both, you don't need to just understand the state pressures she faces as the future leader of her people."

"What do I need to know then, tea master," he says, "to court the crown princess?"

I am almost startled that he would address me so in this moment, rather than as a princess, given the subject of our discussion. But given the subject of our discussion, he is also not wrong. It is a tea master's role to see to the core and bring disparate threads to light and together.

"You need to know that the model Iryasa knows best for a combination of political and romantic relationship is our parents'," I say frankly. "And she knows it is deeply unhealthy, and she wants nothing less than to be trapped in such a cold affair."

"I would not offer her one," Sa Rangim says.

"And she will crave that," I say, "but she will also be completely unprepared for it, Sa Rangim. Nothing in her life will have prepared her to know what to do with devotion and intensity in a partner, or possessiveness that isn't chains. She may want it, but with everything expected of her—"

"She won't know how to accept it," Sa Rangim says, turning to stare hard at the fire again. "She won't know what it means, or what a healthy boundary is—possibly on either side of one."

"Yes. That's it exactly. Then when you add in the matter of a magical bond, that involves partners negotiating toward being more open to each other, rather than on the defensive—"

He raises a hand. "Enough. I take the point, Miyara."

I exhale sharply, not belaboring it further. "I wish I knew how to advise you to proceed."

"That," Sa Rangim says, flashing me a sharp smile, "is not your place, tea master. That work is mine."

All at once I can breathe easier again. I can trust Sa Rangim—with my people, and Iryasa specifically. Now he knows all of what's at stake.

"I did hear possessiveness is part of Te Muraka courtship," I remark, flicking his shoulder lightly.

Sa Rangim's grin widens. "So it is. But I think the boundaries you have to consider are, while perhaps related, somewhat different than mine. Have you found what you need here with air?"

I think about our conversation, and what I've learned. These are not the boundaries I was considering when I arrived at the shrine tonight, but they're what I should have focused on all along: the people.

Elowyn and Tamak both are looking out for their own and each other's boundaries, just like I am. I tried to shield Tamak and poke my nose into his affairs without also treading on his agency, and it has turned out he didn't need it—but that someday he or Elowyn might, and I will be prepared. Not to solve their problems, but to help them solve them on their own.

I do not know Iryasa's boundaries, and only she can decide them; but I can give Sa Rangim context to understand what they may mean for her, to smooth the establishment and negotiation of them. I can help two people who mean each other well to take care with each other—not doing the work for them, but since I am in a position to, making it easier for them to do it for themselves.

My familiar can feel my emotions and fly at my face to hiss or to fly away and give me space as appropriate. She can fly with me throughout my life, interspersed but separate.

We're all in this together, all these pieces of the same struggle, like air is everywhere, but all each dealing with this our own way; still distinct. But what lets us be both separate and everywhere simultaneously like air is trust, and care. Believing in the people we care about to be who they are.

That includes, perhaps especially, ourselves.

"I think," I say slowly, "I have one further revelation I should share with you now."

His eyebrows lift. "Because we won't have another chance to speak privately before the summit begins?"

"Because I have no idea what to do with this information," I say. "I'm not sure there is an answer. But it feels right that you should know."

At this, the expression in Sa Rangim's eyes changes once more, as he understands more than what I say.

That this is something momentous; this is something that, as a tea master and a princess, I consider outside my scope; and it is something I will trust to him, and to him first, before anyone else—my family included.

Because I do already consider him family, and mine. Our future as a family will not be like our past. We will make our future together, and it begins with trust.

Sa Rangim bows his head. "I will hear you," he says, and there's ritual in this: a promise to do more than listen to my words.

So as the flame flickers, always changing its shape before us, I share with him my story.

CHAPTER 14

SAIYANA HAS CONFIRMED: only one day remains before the delegates for the summit will have all arrived, and I'll meet everyone together for the first time.

One day remains, and I'm already exhausted before the summit has even begun. I told Karisa that this *was* the work, that even if it's not dramatic it's harder, and I feel that weariness in my bones in a way I only intellectually knew before. Still I wonder if I've done enough.

One day remains, but with the revelations from Tea Master Karekin about the arcanists, I fear that if I've missed a piece of history so critical to our present, I may have missed more. If the foundations of my approach aren't built on truth, how will they hold up when tested?

Early in the morning, while I can be moderately certain where to find her since Karisa will still be asleep, I knock on the door of Deniel's parents house, Yorani perched on my shoulder.

I can almost feel Elowyn's suspicion in the silence that follows. Despite the run-down construction, I don't hear her coming before she opens the door.

Yorani chirps a happy greeting.

Elowyn blinks at her, then me. "My parents are already out."

"I know." Her mother's a baker's assistant and would have been off hours ago, and with Deniel and Saiyana's initiative favoring Gaellani craftspeople in preparations for the summit, Deniel's father has a job using his engineering training rather than working as a manual laborer for the first time since they arrived in Istalam. "I'm here for you."

Elowyn's head tilts in query. "What couldn't wait until the tea shop this afternoon?"

It will be my final day working a regular shift at Talmeri's until the summit is resolved, so we have a staff meeting today to make sure everyone knows their roles. As the most experienced tea worker, Meristo will be the point person at the shop—the less said about how I arranged for it not to be Talmeri the better—but everyone will be helping fill in different roles at different times. In fact even today my shift won't be regular, since it's more like a final check to reassure all of us we're prepared for this.

Perhaps it is mostly to reassure me.

So the crux of Elowyn's question is, what has changed since I last saw her? Or: what didn't I want the rest of our team to know about?

"I need to speak with Thiano," I say, "and I think you should come."

Elowyn's eyes narrow thoughtfully. "You didn't want me anywhere near him before."

Because an operator as canny as Thiano will recognize that there's more to Elowyn than meets the eye immediately. If she ever wants to have a future outside a spy's life, then the people who could lure her into it in a way she couldn't escape should never be allowed the opportunity.

"Thiano's situation has changed," I say. "It's not that he isn't dangerous, but whatever crack exists between him and the Nakrabi government is widening."

Elowyn considers that. "You don't think he'll try to take advantage of the chance to use me in the conflict?"

I'm not sure she would have thought that way before she spent so much time with Karisa—or with me—or if she's simply now more comfortable voicing impressions she always had. I hope it's for the best, and I haven't twisted who she is.

"I think it's worth the risk to know if the Nakrabi will be able to sense the magic on the device Tamak and Sa Rangim designed," I say. Her eyes widen as she realizes I must know about the bond. "But the risk is yours, so—"

Elowyn closes the door behind her and locks it. "I'm coming."

Guilt twists in my gut. She's mature and competent but still in her teens. What am I doing?

Elowyn frowns at me until she appears to sort out the source of my unease—namely, that it's not related to the bond. "Disappearing into the shadows and listening in on conversations I shouldn't be hearing is what I always do, Miyara. It's not like you asked me to talk to anyone."

This is perhaps not as reassuring as she means it to be.

It's true, I'm not asking her to do anything outside of her skillset or comfort zone. Karisa will be not just talking, but lying, and that is also fully in her comfort zone.

But.

"I am still asking it of you," I say, "after warning you that people would try to use you for this skill. What does that make me?"

Her expression hardens into a glare. I should be glad she's comfortable sharing this expression with me, challenging me, but I'm caught off guard by its intensity. "Do you trust me or don't you?"

I wince. There are her tea master instincts, going straight to the heart. "I fear it's me who shouldn't be trusted," I say softly.

She watches me quietly. "I have watched a lot of people from the shadows. I don't think I've seen anyone who has never made a big mistake, or a choice they regret. Most people are just doing their best, right? You're... a role model for me, but I don't expect you to make only decisions that no one will ever be able to argue with. That *I* should never argue with."

"*I* expect that," I say. It wasn't so long ago that Elowyn considered me perfect, which makes me feel surer that I've failed her.

"And *I* chose to do this. I'm not too stupid to understand what you asked, and I'm not too young to make the choice, or I wouldn't be capable of bringing you the information you asked for at all, right?"

I open my mouth and Yorani takes that moment to nip my ear, which, fair enough. I didn't have anything cogent to add.

Elowyn isn't done.

"I trust your best," she says, her glare morphed into something a little less angry but no less intense. "And part of your best has always been trusting me, and doing what you can to prepare me for the life I'm going to find, even though you know other people will judge you for it. For treating me like the person I am rather than what you think is best for me, and helping me learn how to choose as safely as you can. So I will go with you to Thiano so you can help me learn, and I won't try the same thing on my own because I trust you when you tell me it's too dangerous or I'm not ready. Okay?"

I stare. That is possibly the most words I have ever heard from Elowyn at once.

I'm having *an* effect on her, all right.

While parenting was probably anathema to arcanists who removed themselves from human societies to contemplate alone, I can't help but think in this moment that perhaps the greatest temptation of the time and distance they sought would be to think through all the possible consequences when our choices can affect the well-being of other beings, to be sure we're not doing harm.

But that degree of extreme separation means separating from people, and so separating from the possibility that actions can have effects on people at all, and that is why a tea master had to bring them back.

Or perhaps thorough awareness of all the consequences was what paralyzed them into inaction, and that is how they failed.

I can't afford that.

"Okay," I say, and that is that.

Yorani transfers herself to Elowyn's shoulder as we make our way to Thiano's market stall, and Elowyn tells me more of the personal side of the challenges she's been facing. Some of those have been learning to work with Karisa, since her primary task during the summit is to shadow her: the difficulty is not, apparently, because my sister is inherently infuriating, or not just that.

Elowyn is used to working alone and making her own way. Accounting for Karisa, and in some sense being circumscribed in her options by Karisa's choices, has added a layer of difficulty. But she's satisfied with the method they've worked out to communicate silently, and that's all I need to know about that.

What Elowyn is more concerned about is using the device Tamak gave her, and now that she's aware that I know—apparently she'd been keeping it secret only to prevent more embarrassment for Tamak—her mixed feelings on the matter erupt.

"I know we haven't known each other long, but he's my best friend," she says. "Does that sound crazy?"

"Not to me," I say. "I didn't love your brother at first sight like stories sometimes go, but I did know before we'd even spoken to each other that I could trust him. Your intuition is strong."

Elowyn lets out a breath, and her shoulders droop, like tension has run out of them. Yorani scrambles briefly for purchase and Elowyn soothes her as she confesses, "I don't want to lose Tamak as a friend, and I'm not sure if this is helping or making it worse."

"Even after he made a point of giving you something you can choose to leave behind?"

She shrugs—with one shoulder only, since Yorani is staring at her pointedly from the other. "But it makes me feel like if I leave it behind, it's a rejection of him. Because if I ever leave it, he'll take it as a sign that I can't deal with him after all. Does that make sense?"

I glance down at my wrists thoughtfully, then hold them up. "Did you know Deniel gave these to me?"

She blinks, then stares at them more closely. "Really?"

I'm not sure if that's a comment on what she thinks of her brother's taste, so I let it pass. "Yes. And if you think back, you may realize I never take them off?"

She glances up at me. "Why not?"

"At first out of habit," I admit. "I grew up wearing security bracers, and the familiar weight on my wrists was so comfortable it didn't even occur to me to take them off. But Deniel was worried I felt like I *had* to wear them, not that I wanted to. So I decided I would keep wearing them on purpose as a visible reminder for *him* that I have no doubts about him or my choices on this front."

Elowyn is quiet, thinking that through.

"But," I say, "I can take them off. Part of trusting what we have together means that if I ever have cause to, I can trust that Deniel won't panic or assume the worst, that I've discarded this symbol of my commitment to making space in my daily life for him without a discussion. Obviously this is not exactly the same as your situation, but—if he *did* take it that way, if he had so little faith in me, all that would mean is that he couldn't deal with *me*, not the other way around. If the occasion arises, I would not hesitate to explain that to Tamak, either. He has to be able to let you out of his sight *and* trust you."

"I know," Elowyn says again, and this time she sounds a little sad. This must have really shaken her trust in Tamak's regard of her. "But he's not there yet. He still feels guilty, even though I was never mad at him, which is the only thing making *me* feel pressure about this!"

"Elowyn," I say, "you also have to trust that he will trust you, and respect your choice to leave the device behind without reacting badly when you decide to. It does go both ways."

Elowyn purses her lips. "Okay. I guess I'm not there yet either, then. But in my defense, he did almost panic and sever a rare and powerful magic over guilt."

"But he didn't, and he had also accidentally saddled you with a rare and powerful magic without telling you, so some guilt was warranted," I say. "Freezing the bond means you have all the time you need to decide if you can trust each other that deeply. I don't think anyone has ever said trust has to only deepen and can never struggle or else it's worthless. That's certainly never been the case in any of my relationships, whether it's with Saiyana or Lorwyn."

"Even with my brother?"

"Even then," I say gently. "We have argued, and we've misunderstood each other. Talking matters."

Elowyn's brow furrows but she only nods, keeping the rest of her thoughts to herself. Well enough: this is hers to think through and decide how she feels.

I am glad to hear her explicitly framing this as an issue of trust and boundaries, and not romantic love or partnerships. Given how they've begun, I think it's an important framework for them to build first, regardless of whether they have feelings in a romantic direction as I suspect at least Tamak does. It's at least not their only focus: mature though Elowyn is, I'd be much more alarmed by this prospect if she were thinking of it only as a sign of magical love and not how to manage both their expectations and hopes.

I take advantage of Elowyn's silence to fill her in on the basics of what I've learned about the arcanists. She is my apprentice, and more than that, since she'll be in a position to covertly observe the Nakrabi, she needs to know what to listen for.

While I do wish to know what Thiano makes of the Te Muraka device Elowyn now wears, I also want to see what *he* will tell me about the arcanists and their relation to the Cataclysm.

My lecture is interrupted by Yorani's ears flicking back as she hunches on Elowyn's shoulder and hisses. It startles us both into silence, and as my heart rate increases searching for the danger, we look ahead toward Thiano's stall.

Thiano is there, unharmed.

So is Lady Kireva, her brows arched in challenge.

Spirits. Quietly I murmur to Elowyn, "Did you notice anyone following us?"

She shakes her head. "No. I would have known if we had human watchers."

"Even unmoving? You're sure?"

She nods tightly.

"Magic then," I surmise as I start walking again. "That must be convenient for her. Change of plan: do not under any circumstances let her know what you're capable of."

"What if she already knows?" Elowyn whispers.

"Then she would have contacted you," I say. "I'm sure of it."

"Miyara," Lady Kireva greets us as we approach, and Yorani sits up on her hind legs on Elowyn's shoulder, puffing out her chest.

Making a point of defending Elowyn—or distracting Lady Kireva by giving that impression?

"My apologies, Thiano," I say. "I didn't mean to have your stall overtaken so early in the morning."

His eyes gleam. Not only have I blatantly ignored her, I've ignored her slight against me and only acknowledged hers against Thiano, thereby socially elevating him over us both.

"But later in the day you wouldn't have thought twice," he says.

"Well, by then I'd be sure you'd at least have had the opportunity for a bolstering cup of tea. To give you cause to exercise your mood at this hour seems unfair."

"Oh, I don't know about that," he drawls, looking archly at Kireva, who absolutely deserves his mood.

Lady Kireva sighs. "I thought we were past this, dear."

"My title is tea master, Lady Kireva," I say coolly. "I'm certain you remember."

"And I'm certain you remember our previous discussion," she says, "and yet, here we are."

I look at Thiano and say, "She believes you're untrustworthy and that I shouldn't rely on you as a source of information."

"Quite right," Thiano says. "Sounds unobjectionable to me."

Ha. "I object to the assumption that I needed to be told, and that, having been told, I'm apparently too stupid to understand or make informed judgments."

Thiano grins at the old woman. "Dear lady, if you had but asked I'd have given you the advice for free to not piss off Miyara."

"Such advice would be worth as much to me," Lady Kireva says. "We're not going to be discussing state secrets with a foreign asset, no matter what she thinks."

"Certainly not with you, at the rate you're assuring any trust in you is unwarranted," I agree easily. "Fortunately the number of things in my life that have nothing to do with you is quite high, and my visit today is among them. Thiano, I wanted to introduce to you my apprentice, Elowyn."

Elowyn bows, the perfect picture of nervousness. "It's an honor to make your acquaintance, grace. Thank you also for your part in the tea pet Miyara gave me."

"I'm always happy to help procure anything you can dream of." Thiano winks.

"Elowyn is going to be helping with some of the tea shop operations while I'm busy with the summit," I say. "Given how you've assisted in the past, I thought she should know where to find you."

"An apprentice, did you say," Lady Kireva muses.

In an instant, Yorani has launched off Elowyn's shoulder straight for Lady Kireva's face. The old woman rapidly steps back, but not fast enough to keep Yorani from biting her nose.

Lady Kireva instinctively swipes at Yorani, but by now I am there, and she hits me instead as I shield the tea spirit with my body.

For a moment, it seems as though the entire market freezes.

Cradling Yorani protectively in my arms, I straighten to look coldly at Lady Kireva. Emotions flit across her expression too quickly for me to read before she contains them.

All calculations aside, I suspect she wouldn't have frozen like that if it hadn't been with the visceral knowledge that she'd just struck a princess, the granddaughter of the woman she serves. To a woman like her, that will mean something.

But it's not what she'll acknowledge, and she says, "Oh, I see. Now you mean to make me out as the villain, when it is *your* familiar that attacked *me*."

"Yorani is a spirit," I say quietly. "Attacking her is an offense on its own. But she is also, as you say, my *familiar*, with the judgment to match. I will say this only once, Lady Kireva, so listen well. My apprentice is not available to you for any reason. You will stay away from Elowyn. You will not watch her. You will not contact her. If I learn you have done otherwise, and believe that now I will make it a point to learn, I will move against you all the spirits of water, earth, and air."

Lady Kireva's expression turns sardonic. "All I noted was that she was your apprentice, Miyara. What exactly do you think I'll do?"

"I think you'll do whatever you think is best for the nation, regardless of what is best for her," I say. "Test me at your peril."

She sighs dramatically. "Yet you wonder why I don't trust you to speak to this ingrate unsupervised. Really, do you not know better than to reveal something like this to him?"

"I," Thiano says mildly, "did not need to be told."

She narrows her eyes at him. "If we are being blunt, then I'm still not leaving *you* unsupervised with *him*."

Thiano's grin widens, an expression I am all too familiar with. "Well, I gave you free advice, didn't I? I have a piece for Miyara then, too." He looks at me. "Nakrab is obsessed with deception and illusion. You'd do well to play on that."

He's as good as told me this before, which makes this advice actually worth nothing to me—except that it, too, is a piece of deception, an illusion for my and Elowyn's benefit.

Elowyn and I bow, Thiano scratches Yorani's head, and a few mild quips later we are back on our way.

After a minute Elowyn asks me, all evidence of nervousness gone because she truly is skilled at this work, "What now?"

What indeed. "We're finding out how Lady Kireva knew we were coming, and we're preventing her from ever getting in our way again."

"If we undo it, she might just set it up again," Elowyn points out.

I nod. "It'll have to be something more subtle. Illusion, presumably, given Thiano's hint. We're going to need Glynis and Entero."

"I can do the legwork without Entero," Elowyn says. "It's not using me if it's what I want to do."

I shake my head. "That's not why. Entero has been working with Lady Kireva—he may already have some insight into how her network operates. Since we still need to confirm whether Thiano can detect your device, we'll need to go about this another way. You can sneak in close, and Entero can go inside to ask pointed questions and see if Thiano has sensed anything without asking outright."

Elowyn frowns. "Will that work? I thought Thiano didn't like Entero. And Entero isn't as good at questions as you are."

"Thiano likes deception plenty well, though, and he'll know this comes from me," I say. "In fact, he's expecting something. And Entero is plenty good at interpreting Thiano's responses."

"One more plot before the plot," Elowyn says, smiling. "This is fun."

I'm not surprised she thinks so.

Part of me is reassured that enough of *my* network is in place that this is a problem I can address without any particular difficulty; it bodes well for handling surprises during the summit.

But I'm troubled that even now, I still can't tell whether Elowyn will be happier as a tea master or a spy—and what that says about me.

CHAPTER 15

IT'S THE FINAL NIGHT before the summit begins. I should go home and rest, because even if everything goes smoothly—and I am not so naïve as to believe it will, no matter how well we have planned—I will need to be at my best.

But I'm too unsettled to rest, so I'm fluttering around Talmeri's instead, straightening and adjusting and dusting. Part of me acknowledges that sitting on the couch with Deniel might relax me—or sufficiently distract me—but there is another part I am learning not to ignore.

That part is my instincts. Listening is my strength, but only if I choose to use it.

According to Karekin, it is part of my "magic" as a tea master.

This is the crux of it: I do not understand what that means for me.

I do not have my own house in order.

How can I prove my place here is worthwhile if I don't understand that worth after all?

I wince at a sudden, sharp pain in my head. Oh, spirits, that's just what I need. I've never been much prone to headaches, but it would stand to reason I would have to deal with one now of all times.

I sit, pressing my hand to the side of my head—but now the pain has moved, to my forehead. Steady pulses, like someone is knocking on my brain.

I frown, and then all at once my eyes widen.

In sitting, I turned to face the back door. It's not the headache that's moving, it's the *direction*.

I stand up and quickly cross to open the door to the back, and Yorani promptly swoops in, nipping my ear as she passes.

So my familiar can evidently alert me to her location, or at least get my attention looking the right direction, when she so chooses. That's... new.

Or perhaps Yorani has simply only decided now to make me aware of the fact. We've spent most of our time together, so it wouldn't have been necessary, but in recent days she's been going off more on her own.

This is mostly reassuring, in that respect? But also a bit troubling, because a creature of Yorani's mischief could potentially stab my brain whenever she's bored or annoyed with me.

Another stab from behind me, presumably in reaction to that thought.

I take it back. It's definitely a new trick that she wants to show off. What timing.

"Thank you, I noticed," I drawl, looking around the back. "Lorwyn finally went home?"

Yorani chirps from the table she's landed on.

"Without saying goodbye or letting you back in? She knew I was still here."

Yorani chirps again and puffs out her chest.

"You asked her not to." I frown, not only because this is unexpected behavior, but because this is the closest Yorani and I have come to direct conversation and I'm not sure what to make of it. "Why?"

Yorani flaps up and lands again with a clunk behind the tea counter. I recognize the sound of her claws on that particular material.

It's my tea kit.

She chirps insistently from where she's hidden. A nose and ears poke up over the counter briefly before she drops down again with a clunk.

"I'm coming, little one, just a moment."

It's not exactly that I don't know who we are, is it? It's that I don't know who we're becoming. We're all of us changing, and I fear I don't have a handle on how we're changing and what it means, when I'm ostensibly supposed to be driving us.

I lift the tea kit off the floor, tea spirit and all, and carry it over to the middle of the room.

All our new, small circular tables are arranged not throughout the room, but in a circle. Like a conference table, where you can see everything that happens, but where everyone also has their own designated space.

The center is open, and I kneel on the floor. Yorani finally hops off the tea kit, and at first I think she wants me to serve *her* tea—

Which, on reflection, why have I never performed the tea ceremony for my familiar at times when we've struggled to understand each other? What would even happen?

But apparently this is not what she has in mind today. She hops across the room to a different table, the curls up to watch, and wait.

I think as I prepare the kit. I need answers. For myself, and for us all. I can't afford to botch the summit: the world is quite literally at stake.

Answers. I purse my lips, glancing at Yorani and remembering the headache she gave me.

Tea mastery as a kind of magic that preceded arcanism, is it.

Well.

Let's see.

I select a light air blend—a traditional white tea using only the shoots of the tea leaf plucked in a sunny morning. And although it seems vaguely blasphemous to alter this tea in any way, I add a single pod of sunshine.

I bow, centering myself, and begin.

I perform this tea ceremony for myself, first. It is an act of centering on its own, which I need and crave.

I perform for Yorani, my tea spirit, my familiar. Not just because she is connected to me, but because she wants me to; because she asked.

I perform this tea ceremony in the spirit of welcome. From our customers to those who think they can't afford to be, from the delegates of the summit to, particularly, the old woman who gifted me the teapot.

I perform this ceremony for her especially.

How can I properly help and host people if I don't know what they understand of our shared history? How can I find out what they know when I can't be sure of what I should already know?

If I'm going to save us all, I can't neglect addressing our history.

But equally nor can I neglect who we are now, and who we are becoming—who we must, should become. The preparations are the first step, the beginning of the path, but the direction we take is still to be carved. It is still for *me* to carve.

A path of welcome, so all of us in this world can live, and strive. A welcome that acknowledges who we have been and who we can be. A welcome that includes everyone at the expense of no one.

That is the dream; the goal.

But can a dream built on a shoddy framework stand? Or:

Can it launch from those foundations and fly?

I bring the ceremony to a close, and take a breath of air.

When I open my eyes, the old woman who gifted me the arcane teapot is seated grumpily across from me.

"You've made this place downright inhospitable, haven't you?" she asks, picking up a cup.

I blink, startled by this question in a way I'm not by her appearance. Then I realize: she means the magical wards.

"It doesn't seem to have given you any particular trouble," I note wryly. I hope it's more effective against Nakrabi magic.

"And," she says, "you've learned a new trick."

Yorani chirps, fluttering over to land on the old woman's giant sack.

"Yorani is correct," I say. "She gave me the idea. In fact, I don't think you two have been introduced?"

Yorani chirps shyly.

The old woman reaches out a gnarled finger and, when Yorani doesn't react badly, gently rubs the top of her head.

"You won't get a name out of me that easily," she says.

"Nor did I intend to," I say. "Since you're here, can I get you a chair?"

"No," she says, taking a sip of the tea. She frowns down at it, then at me. "You need to have a care with boundaries, child."

It's the clearest admonishment she's ever given me, and against all reason I bristle. "Do you think I'm not *trying*?"

"Not well enough." She takes back her hand, and Yorani tenses. "Have a care or don't."

I narrow my eyes. "Now *that* is nonsense. Trying matters. Efforts aren't wasted if full success isn't achieved the first time."

Though despite everything, at this I think of my grandmother, failing witches. Is trying enough or isn't it? Is trying only enough in certain circumstances? Because I don't accept her failure.

"If you say so," the old woman says, sipping again.

"What's that supposed to mean?"

"It means I'm not going to give you all the answers," she says. "It means I have had to give up too much for too long, and I do not answer to you, child." She glances at Yorani. "Or to you."

Yorani shifts uncomfortably, looking away as if abashed. That's a difficult reaction to garner from her.

I stare down at my tea. I have resolved not to interrogate this woman, because that would make her unwelcome. I nearly came to blows with Saiyana over the matter. I have operated without answers before.

But before, the stakes weren't so high.

Except, weren't they? The matters of individuals are not less important than the world. Perhaps that's it: it's that in this, it's all of those stakes piled together.

I am confident I can do *something*. I am less confident I will do the *correct* thing. It is no one's job to reassure me, and yet that is what I want: for someone "objective" to tell me I can do it.

No one has that luxury. It doesn't exist.

But spirits, if ever a situation deserved such insight—

"Oh, child," the old woman says. "You have to solve this one. That's the point. That's all of us—you're not that special."

I sigh. "People keep telling me that not everything is about me but also that I have to do everything," I say. "I'm not sure there's any way I could *not* be struggling with boundaries."

She huffs. "All right. Let's pretend for a second that I had all the answers and could tell you exactly what you were to do. Would you really just accept that, and not believe you could do any part of it differently or better?"

I close my eyes, almost laughing, though I hold it in because I fear the hysterical edge that would erupt with it.

That's certainly one way to make me see the point.

"Quite," she says dryly. "And as it happens, I don't have the answers, or we wouldn't be in this position. So don't be looking to me to save you."

At this, Yorani abruptly lifts off, heading for the back door.

The old woman waves a hand, and the door opens—and despite its weight, stays ajar.

That's magic I've not seen before, from her or anyone.

"I'm not," I say as Yorani flies for whatever she needs in the back. "I'm not unwilling to work—or to think for myself and act accordingly. Which you believed before. But it's clear I don't understand what's going on, in more dimensions than I initially thought, and I don't want to make everything worse."

"Respectable. People generally don't. But you're the tea master—if you don't understand enough to act, that's your problem. Not mine."

"What's yours?" I ask softly.

A smile cracks her face. "See? There you are. See the people, see the patterns. Do your thing."

"Mine as in—"

"As in *you* bring people together. You wanted the freedom to forge your own path? Well, go on and forge it, then."

I sigh. "I suppose it's still freedom if I don't know how to make good decisions."

"Oh, child. That's just life. And that's not a subject I can *ever* help you with."

She finishes her cup and stands. I rush to my feet to help her, but she waves me off.

So instead, I bow, forehead to the floor. "Thank you."

She pauses.

I look up at her. "For caring."

Her expression softens. "Oh, child. Thank you for the sunshine."

She reaches a hand out like she means to brush my face. But her body doesn't bend so easily, and I'm too far away, and by the time I realize she can't reach me without assistance she's aborted the gesture and left the way she came: suddenly.

Yorani flies back in just before the back door slams shut behind her, struggling to carry a slim volume in her talons, then drops it with a sad chirp as she sees the old woman is already gone.

"What's this?"

I walk over and blink in surprise. It's Talsion's favorite book, the story of a cat adventurer who solves mysteries, beginning with the tale of the vanishing fish snacks.

"You wanted to give this to her?"

I remember suddenly that Yorani left when the old woman said it wasn't her job to save us, and I understand my familiar's intention at once.

It's our job to save *her*, and she cannot help us. Perhaps especially because whatever she has worked for in her life, she doesn't know that's part of it.

I crouch down next to Yorani, brushing off a layer of dust from the book.

No, not dust—tea shavings.

How did the book even get here? I certainly didn't bring it, so it must have been Yorani—

Who is best friends with Talsion, a cat who opens doors.

"Talsu is okay parting with the book?" I ask.

Yorani chirps firmly in the affirmative.

Well, then.

Yorani perhaps could have slipped a volume this slim into my bag without my noticing. But she has also been determinedly going about on her own: she also could have flown it here herself. In stages, presumably, because even now I could see how she struggled to carry it.

"I have no idea how you managed to get this here, but I'm both impressed and worried," I finally say. "I had no idea what you were up to, and I would have had no way to know if anything had happened to you. Please promise me you'll be careful."

Yorani waddles forward and noses my bracelets.

My eyebrows lift. Can the bracelets alert me to her state? "I had not considered that could be part of their ability."

Yorani's face scrunches up, and she attempts to lift one shoulder.

A shrug. Oh my spirits.

All right. So she doesn't know for sure either. *And also she just tried to shrug at me.*

Another puzzle. There's so much I—we—don't know. How can I do it all?

Before I've even finished mentally asking the question, I reach out and pet Yorani. "Yes, I know. Together. You're right. And we'll make sure to give this to the old woman next time we see her, so before then let's go home and wrap it up nicely for her, all right? We can practice what Thiano taught me."

Yorani chirps, and this time, once I've tidied my things, we really do go.

─────

Thiano told me to get my house in order, and I've been fretting about it since.

I have been thinking a lot, about what to do and how to do it. About what I don't know, and how to find out. Acting, too, but maybe what I should be focusing on is what I have *now*.

I can always keep thinking, and keep acting. The world will keep changing, and so will the people in it, and that's where my work is, where my focus should be.

There are always going to be things I don't sufficiently understand. But how I react matters.

That's a function of who I am, which is—perhaps not a result of, but not separate from what I do.

At home, Deniel has already gone up to bed; I can hear him moving around. I leave most of the lights off as I carefully wrap the book. It takes me a few tries to tie the cloth correctly as Thiano taught me, and Yorani chirps softly in approval the final time. I stow it away in my bag and motion her with me to the altar.

I bow before approaching it. I pick up one of the matches stashed there and strike it, lighting the candle that floats in the middle. That done, I dip both hands into the pool until they rest on the rocks at the bottom, breathing in the warm air before the candle.

I bow again and begin to withdraw, but Yorani lands on my shoulder and nuzzles my neck.

I glance at her, and our eyes meet.

In all the maneuvering I have done since Thiano's advice, I have not considered my relationship with my familiar.

Getting my house in order means Yorani, too.

No: *especially*.

Gently, I lift her from my shoulder two-handed and set her back legs in the water until her feet hit the rocks. She breathes in the candle and then puffs—a tiny whorl of flame more air than fire, and the candle goes out.

She begins to scramble, and I soothe her. "Shh. You're fine. Want to try again?"

Yorani settles down and spreads her wings for balance. She blows again, carefully, and this time the candle re-lights.

I bow again. After a moment Yorani lowers her wings, and I lift her back out of the pool, cradling her.

"I've been underestimating what we can do together," I say, "haven't I?"

Oh, I took on the task of the summit knowing Yorani was with me, but I didn't really understand what that meant. Perhaps I never will. But even though I've known Yorani wanted to help, I haven't been thinking about how. Not just what she can do, but what *we* can do, given who we are *together*.

I settle us on the floor and hold out my wrists. "Want to see what we can figure out with these?"

Yorani chirps at me in query.

"I don't know either, but we'll only find out by trying."

She curls up abruptly as if asleep, and I wonder if she's bored by my suggestion.

Then she stands up quickly and chirps again in query.

Ah! "Yes, we should definitely get some sleep, but we can work on this for at least a few minutes first. Maybe it will give us ideas."

On who we are, and who we're becoming, and who we should strive to be, and do.

Tonight is for us.

Tomorrow, the world.

CHAPTER 16

YORANI AND I EXPERIMENT, but no matter how I focus I can't locate her without her input. If she were unconscious, I couldn't find her. Not as we are now.

I wonder if I need the tea ceremony to activate the bracelets somehow, but in attempting to sense Yorani I see something unexpected: a glimpse into the world I think Yorani—and Talsu—sees every day.

A world full of spirits.

It's like the vision of flying through the Cataclysm, but... calmer, somehow. Less chaotic. Flashes of colors, textures, and shapes, floating through space.

I glimpse it all for just a moment before the shadowy impression fades, and I sit back, somewhat stunned.

My faith in the elemental spirits is hardly knew, and between Yorani's birth and my experiences performing the tea ceremony recently, the notion that minor spirits can exist has been provably true. And it makes sense that they would exist here, in this home where I've performed tea ceremony countless times.

It's still somehow different to recognize that even when we can't perceive them, they are here in a physical way, in possession of forms. And it's a sobering reminder to take with me into opening the summit.

I am responsible for them, too.

I created them without knowing how. Being able to see them at all implies possibilities I can scarcely comprehend.

It's a revelation that perhaps ought to leave me daunted beyond imagining, but instead, here with Yorani, I am instead inspired: by what I can do, when I exercise care; by what can be, if we dare to imagine.

So that is what I take with me into the start of the next phase of saving our world.

The day begins early. Saiyana, with logistical powers that border on the uncanny, has managed to ensure that each delegate has arrived in Sayorsen no earlier than today.

(I do not ask if mysterious accidents befell them on the road to make this happen. I'm not certain I wish to know the answer.)

This means that the morning is spent greeting the delegates and their parties, making sure all known accommodations are appropriate and adjusting for any new information, then arranging for them to settle in.

The Taresal delegation is the first to arrive. Ambassador Perjoun is a woman in her forties, olive-skinned and tall even for a Taresal, with her thick, wavy hair gathered in a gentle tail. Her manner is serious and deliberate, but not overly upright.

We understand each other immediately. This is a woman comfortable in who she is, and she will deal with me in kind.

This is a relief, and also a reminder to myself to be judicious in how I manipulate these proceedings. She will respond well to honesty, but if she senses underhanded tactics directed her way I have no doubt she will respond accordingly.

The Velasari delegation is next. They had a carriage drawn unsafely through the streets in order to arrive earlier than Saiyana asked, so as a slight and warning masquerading as an honor, I send Reyata to meet their ambassador first while I finish up with the delegation from Taresan.

Unlike Ambassador Perjoun, Ambassador Ridac will be a problem. I had hoped for a younger delegate less mired in old prejudices in charge but hadn't expected one; not for a summit of this import. But Ridac is as extreme as they come in Velasar. He's nearly my grandmother's age, stocky and jowly, and there was a time in her reign when he was banned from Istalam entirely due to his inflammatory rhetoric against the Istal government. Ridac thrives on political games, and he hates Istalam with a passion.

I have had his measure for years of watching him and my mother verbally circling each other at official functions, even with my father's presence working against her. I must be on my guard with him always, but I know well what sort of bile and vile tactics to expect.

Ambassador Perjoun is clearly here to find a resolution, and Ambassador Ridac to establish Velasari supremacy. Neither choice is a surprise.

The Isle of Nakrab's ambassador, on the other hand, is entirely outside my knowledge.

We had arranged at Istalam's expense for the Nakrabi delegation's transportation upon disembarking after the Isle of Nakrab had proposed bringing their own. While I was as curious as anyone what it would have entailed, we aren't about to allow Nakrabi technology that large and obvious on our shores without greater understanding of what it literally means.

Diplomatically, of course, I knew. Traveling in a showy piece of technology through Istal cities and across the countryside would have demonstrated Nakrab's technological superiority and reputation well before their arrival. More, it was a ploy to see how far we could be pushed, because we all know perfectly well Nakrab doesn't need Istal money.

So when the Nakrabi delegation arrives at the city hall in an ostentatious carriage that I know Saiyana did *not* arrange, that means something, too.

Two attendants with shaved heads precede the ambassador out. Yorani and I watch impassively, my familiar perched on my shoulder as if nothing of moment has happened—just as I am behaving.

Then the ambassador alights, and it's time.

"Greetings, Ambassador Cherato," I say, inclining my head in acknowledgement rather than bowing.

The ambassador smiles without showing any teeth as he looks around. He's far younger than I expected, which may be a sign they're not taking this seriously; not too surprising.

Nakrabi tend to be lighter-skinned than Istals and Velasari, though with a slightly different undertone than the Gaellani, and so it proves with Ambassador Cherato. I have no understanding of how his dark hair is styled or what it means, but such elaborate twists must require either extreme chemicals or magic to defy gravity thus.

But when the ambassador pauses, it's his face that sets my heart beating faster.

It's not the vibrant color painted on his eyelids and lips, nor the perfect symmetry of his features.

It's that there are images of the negotiations that took place after the Cataclysm. With a memory as trained as mine, I know I am not mistaken.

This face was there, also using the name Cherato. *Exactly* as it appears now.

Could the effect be produced with makeup? Or is this a relative of that previous Cherato, and the name is a family one?

"Tea Master Miyara," Cherato replies in accented Istal, not returning my nod. "I am glad to put such an arduous journey behind me."

Pretending to be ignorant, as if he can't be bothered with our customs, while still exuding superiority. This is too predictable.

"I hope you will enjoy exploring Sayorsen during your stay," I say, just as blatantly not apologizing.

Ambassador Cherato looks me in the eye, and my breath catches.

Faced with his gaze, I am certain. This is no young man.

This is the same man who accompanied the delegation to Istalam decades ago, and he looks as though he hasn't aged a day.

Illusion and deception. Thiano's warning echoes in my mind. It's possible the ambassador has not aged physically, due to some application of magic; it is equally possible he has, and this is a public mask.

I do not believe I was meant to identify him, though, which means I have learned something.

Nakrab has a strange fascination with youth, *and* they are in fact taking this summit seriously enough to send an expert.

All this passes in an instant, and in response to my expressed hope, the ambassador says only, "Do you really?"

As if he couldn't possibly find any enjoyment in Sayorsen.

Or as if I won't enjoy the kind of exploration he'd prefer.

"If you have to ask, then we have much to learn about each other in the coming days," I say. "Allow me to introduce you to my familiar, Yorani. She is a young spirit given form, and she will accompany me throughout the negotiations."

"What a quaint way to make decisions," Ambassador Cherato says.

I smile mysteriously. "Stranger than you know."

A blink is the only change in his expression, and I make a mental note to thank Tea Master Karekin for the advice to not be shy about cultivating an air of mystery.

"I'm sure we will all be duly fascinated," Ambassador Cherato says, sounding uncommonly bored, and I contain a grin. Always nice to have confirmation that a tactic has worked. "But who is this?"

Another carriage has pulled up, somehow *more* ostentatious than the Nakrabi delegation's, and Karisa flutters toward us in a yellow and orange confection that is both perfectly in fashion and makes her look even younger than she is.

I bend my expression into a faint scowl while turning back to the Nakrabi ambassador—in time to catch the naked hunger in his expression at the sight of her.

Before, I might have thought her appearance perfect for her role; now, I have a growing concern.

As she approaches, the ambassador masks the hunger but not the blatant interest.

"You must be the ambassador from the Isle of Nakrab!" Karisa exclaims, bowing gracefully—if only barely, belying her own apparent arrogance—before him. "I just couldn't wait to greet you. It's so exciting for someone like you to be here."

In an annoyed tone, I introduce, "Her Highness, Princess Karisa of Istalam."

Ambassador Cherato ignores me entirely. "Someone like me?" he asks.

Karisa grins impishly. "Here to stir things up," she says slyly.

"Your Highness, that's enough," I say.

"What a delightful child," the ambassador says. "Though you misread me, of course. We certainly aren't here to, as you say, 'make trouble', despite what certain parties have implied."

"How extremely disappointing," Karisa says. "Perhaps you can make it up to me." She turns to me. "I've been trapped here and am bored to tears. You don't need him for the rest of the afternoon, do you?"

I keep my expression neutral. "The official negotiations begin tomorrow."

"Then," Karisa says, deftly insinuating herself and linking her arm with the ambassador's with a wink, "*I* will see about making sure the ambassador feels welcome. What could be more appropriate for a princess?"

"Not setting herself up as a personal attendant to a foreign emissary," I say dryly.

Karisa waves a hand. "That's what *he's* for, isn't it? I will be the ambassador's... cultural advisor."

The ambassador tears his amused gaze away from Karisa, following the "he" she gestured toward.

"My assistant, Taseino," I say. "He will be your liaison during your stay, as I will not always be available to you. If there is anything you require, communicate it to him."

The ambassador considers Taseino for a long moment and apparently finds him adequate or at least inoffensive—he is young, too—and says, "I will be happy to do so."

I wonder what that means. But the boundary is set: I will arrange for his needs but will not be at his disposal.

"Then we're all set! I'll take it from here, tea master," Karisa says.

I bow. "I leave it to your wisdom, your Highness."

The ambassador doesn't smirk as he takes his leave; he doesn't need to. I have played my hand as though my sister is harmless and annoying yet situated such that she is privy to information like an ambassador's arrival schedule. We can act as though I will make allowances for a princess that the ambassador will expect to be able to exploit to work around me, as she's made it plain she enjoys tweaking me.

That went as well as it possibly could have, but there is a thread of unease in my triumph.

"Find a way to make sure Karisa knows he has an odd relationship to youth," I murmur to Taseino.

"She's aware," Taseino tells me. "She's sure it isn't a sexual thing. She says it seems to be a philosophical one, and she'll let you know more later."

A cultural obsession with youth? How does she know already? And how does *he* know what she knows?

There's no time to say more, but I trust her to be able to read people, and to draw the same conclusions about the ambassador from our education.

Taseino catches up with them, making himself unassuming without difficulty.

Not just youth, then, but perhaps the trappings of it: Taseino is accepted because he's young and thus can be safely disregarded. But he's not interesting to the ambassador because he isn't flaunting the aesthetic of youth the same way Karisa is in her manner; likewise the staff attending the ambassador, whom he neglected to introduce.

So Taseino is perfectly suited, too: established from the start to coordinate between Karisa and Elowyn's team and me, as well as to serve as a scout and potentially plant things for their use if needed. A person the ambassador will treat as a meaningless functionary, too young to be worth targeting or watching himself around, so he will let him observe while being unobserved.

At least, that is the hope.

Ambassador Cherato's measure I do not have in full yet, but one thing is certain:

He is *absolutely* here to make trouble, and he's well capable of it.

And it's my job to stop him.

⁂

Deniel and I have finished eating and are cleaning up the kitchen when he asks, "That reminds me—have you seen Talsion's book?"

Dinner tonight was soup made from paste, assorted pickles his mother made up a jar of, rice, and fish with a thick, sweet sauce. The discounted fish is a treat, and the rest cost next to nothing—the paste purchased in bulk apparently keeps for many months—so Deniel thought this would be both a good meal for me to learn to cook as well as an easy one when we're both too tired for more serious experimentation. And it still gave us something to do together.

I assume it is the fish that has made him think of Talsion's book. "Yorani took it. She wants to give it as a gift to the old woman who gifted me the arcane teapot. She claims Talsu said it was okay."

Yorani hops up on the table in the living room long enough to shoot me a look.

I raise my hands. "Peace. I'm not accusing you of anything."

The baby dragon hops back onto the floor.

"I have... several questions," Deniel says. "Though the first is what they're doing right now."

Yorani and Talsion have both been lounging on the floor for some time now, just... looking around. And occasionally focusing abruptly in the same direction.

"Perhaps the notion of playing is too exhausting to contemplate," I say.

"They have naps for that," Deniel says. "In my experience cats have a never-ending supply."

"They're taking a break, then."

"Cats do behave inexplicably," he acknowledges. "I suppose there's no reason Yorani can't too. Especially as she's *your* familiar."

"As if you can't easily predict me. I'm fairly sure they're watching spirits, though."

"See, you call yourself predictable, and then you just casually drop that into conversation," Deniel says. "Do I want to know?"

I shrug. "There's not much more to tell, honestly. At least on that front. I think spirits are somewhat more concentrated here simply because of how many times I've practiced tea ceremony here, but it's not materially relevant as far as I know."

"But you can see spirits now."

"Sometimes. Yorani and I are experimenting."

"And you two are... talking, now?"

I dry my hands and go to my bag. "I'm somewhat less certain how well we're doing there. Let me check with Talsion and make sure I didn't misunderstand Yorani."

I pull out the wrapped book and begin untying it.

"Miyara," Deniel says patiently, "just because you can communicate with *your familiar*, who is a *spirit*, does not mean you can talk with a cat."

"You don't know that."

Deniel makes a strangled noise. "Miyara—"

"Which of us reads him books?"

"I don't expect *answers*."

"Does Talsu prefer tales of cat detectives to law tomes or doesn't he?" I ask with mock-severity.

Deniel throws up his hands. "I give up."

I show Talsion the book, setting it down in front of him in case he wants to sit on it to demonstrate his claim.

Talsu sniffs it.

He glances at Yorani.

Then he stands up, turns around, and settles down again with his butt facing the book.

Yorani chirps shortly at me as if to say 'I told you so'.

"There you have it," I say, setting the book on the low table so I can re-wrap it.

"Very scientific," Deniel teases me.

"If we accept that Yorani can communicate with Talsion, and I can communicate with Yorani—"

"I'm taking the night off lawyering," Deniel says, throwing up his hands. "Do what you will."

No sooner has he said this than a paw darts up to attack the corner of the cloth I'm attempting to re-tie.

I look down at Talsion. "Do you protest after all?"

Talsu stares at me.

I start moving the cloth again and his eyes follow the motion, gleaming.

"Oh, I see," I say. "*Now* it's time for cat games."

I look around for Yorani and find her flapping next to me with a ribbon in her mouth.

"My mistake, it is a dragon and cat game," I say dryly, looking back at Deniel who has doubled over laughing. "Can I get some help, here?"

"What do you think giving her a ribbon qualifies as?"

I huff, and the next few minutes are spent playing and ultimately distracting our furry and scaly friends with a different cloth and a twig so I can re-wrap the book.

Eventually, they chase each other upstairs, and Deniel and I end up settled together on the couch with me nestled in his arms.

"This was good," I say. "Well planned, past-Miyara."

"I agree," Deniel says, dropping a kiss on the top of my head. "Though since you scheduled a night for us knowing the coming days would be too busy, I hope you also did so for yourself? You-time and us-time are different."

"And I need both," I say simply. "I have spent plenty of time with my own thoughts, believe me."

"Knowing you, that doesn't sound like taking a break," Deniel says dryly.

"It has been what I needed," I say. "But time with you is... relaxing in a different way. Being with you reminds me of who I am and wish to be, so in some ways it also counts as both."

Deniel takes my face between his palms and kisses me deeply.

He pulls back, and we just watch each other for a long moment. Then Deniel's expression flickers.

"What is it?" I ask softly.

"It just occurred to me," he says, "it must have been very difficult for your mother. Of course I knew that before, but—"

"She doesn't have a partner she is safe being herself with."

"But also no one else, right? She must not trust *her* mother, who put her in this position. And then she couldn't attempt to create such a relationship with her children, either."

I sigh, burrowing into him more deeply. "I am not sure whether to hope that she wished to, because it would mean she loved me after all and denied our relationship because she felt she had to, but—"

"But." Deniel's arms tighten around me. "But then it means she's suffered greatly all this time."

"Yes." I close my eyes, breathing in his scent. "Perhaps someday I can try to help her find more happiness. My father, too. For now my sisters are enough of a challenge." I huff. "Well. And me, of course."

"You're doing just fine in my estimation," Deniel says, taking one of my hands and squeezing it, "for whatever that's worth."

"Quite a lot," I say. "But once Iryasa learns—no, Reyata's reaction will probably be worse—"

"You're fretting about the teens again."

We already covered this while we cooked: Karisa, Elowyn, and Taseino have all been safely home for hours now, and their first experience with the Nakrabi delegation was entirely uneventful.

Though noteworthy, both in that—unless it turns out they are humoring us—our strategy appears to work, and also that Karisa has sussed out what is going on with the ambassador's strange reaction to youth.

It's not just philosophical, but magical: youth is indicative of vigor and strength, and a display like the ambassador's appearance demonstrates the resources and political clout to bring magical fortitude to bear.

She thinks it is probably an illusion rather than a transformation, but isn't convinced it's only skin-deep, which might be why he wears it even in Istalam. Too soon to say on that count. But my estimation was correct in that youth is not respected for its own sake; quite the opposite. Nakrabi respect the *symbol* of youth, but otherwise consider it delightful but lacking in teeth—or perhaps staying power.

I admit I am less worried about the precise form of the ambassador's particular magic—though I am curious how it will fare with the wards on the tea shop—as I am about why the appearance of vigor implied by magic is so noteworthy on the Isle of Nakrab.

Is there a problem with their magic? Or is there another problem they're using magic to compensate for?

"Now you're thinking again," Deniel says. "Every one of them is prepared for their tasks. Do you believe in them?"

"You know I do."

He kisses me.

While I'm still savoring that, he murmurs, "And you've done all you could to prepare them. Are you going to change your mind now?"

"I—"

He kisses me again, and since he's made his point I let him distract me.

More specifically, I decide I will distract *him*.

I pull out of his arms only to twist him underneath me, and this time I kiss him, with more urgency than before.

Somewhat later we separate, breathing more heavily. "Wait," Deniel whispers. "I don't want to rush."

We have so little time together already that I don't want to slow down, but I nod.

Deniel takes both my hands in his, holding them still. "My boundaries this time," he says, and his crooked smile is going to kill me. "Rushing like we'll never have more time is different than enjoying the moment, at least for me. The latter is what I want."

I consider and, despite everything I'm feeling right now—or perhaps because of it—decide that I agree.

Deniel laughs softly at my look of grave contemplation and adds, "There are still plenty of things we can do. We're not in a hurry."

"What if I am?" I challenge, smiling down at him with raised eyebrows.

"Then I hope you'll be patient with me," he says, and I wonder if perhaps it is his voice rather than his smile that will be the death of me. Or the look in his eyes as he gazes at me.

Then I decide, for just a little while, to do somewhat less thinking, and the rest of the evening passes with me in Deniel's arms.

CHAPTER 17

SIMPLY BEGINNING A NEGOTIATION like this is a complicated process in its own right. It is not enough to set a start time for a meeting, expect all invited parties to arrive, and set to work.

It takes most of the morning for all the ambassadors and their attendants to make their appearance at all, and each behaves differently: an early, intentional indication of the kind of behavior I can expect from them as they represent their governments.

There have been few surprises, except where their reactions to the tea shop's wards are concerned.

As she crosses the threshold, Taresan's Ambassador Perjoun's head tilts, just for a moment, and I make out curiosity swiftly followed by satisfaction and determination before she continues on. She's pleased by the security measures and keen to know what exactly we did so Taresan can replicate it. I expected Taresan to be cautious in these negotiations, but I am increasingly optimistic.

It does surprise me that Ambassador Cherato and the contingent from the Isle of Nakrab are next. His is the reaction I am most concerned with, and I am not disappointed.

His entire body freezes for an instant, and I glimpse the old, canny predator in his focused stillness.

It is enough to tell me we have done *something* that will challenge Nakrabi magic, if not precisely what or how effective it will be. It's a start.

The ambassador enters the room and then, despite the favorable implication of his timely arrival, proceeds to blatantly demonstrate no interest in interacting with anyone else present. He ignores most overtures and responds to others absently—though this does serve to let me know who he wants me to think he considers important enough to bother with.

I keep an eye on his explorations of the tea shop, cataloging his actions, but my other hosting duties and the arrival of Velasar's Ambassador Ridac keep me occupied enough I don't feel obligated to intervene.

Ambassador Ridac also notices the wards immediately, and his reaction turns to mottled anger as he glares his way through the door. If he's at all intrigued by how we've managed to counter Velasar's magecraft rather than entirely incensed that we have, and that we've accomplished it through incorporating "heretical" or "low"—by which I mean, not traditional magecraft—forms of magic, I can't tell it yet.

I wish I could feel smugger about our clear success in this experiment, but despite the fact that no one brings them up explicitly, the unique magical security costs us an additional layer of diplomatic complexity to navigate.

The Velasari ambassador is going to be a problem, and one I'll have to solve quickly to make any inroads on our actual purpose—and to get at Nakrab.

But even the preliminary mingling can only extend so long.

"I didn't come here for parlor games," Ambassador Ridac of Velasar says.

My sisters have seated themselves, as has Ambassador Perjoun of Taresan. Ambassador Cherato of the Isle of Nakrab stands, but at least he does so quietly.

Yorani has deposited herself in a glass teapot on a high shelf and glares down at each ambassador in turn.

Now—

Now I can begin in truth.

"I am a tea master, and I do not play at tea," I answer.

Ridac sneers. "Insulting enough to think that all the blood on Istalam's hands could be settled in a court room. This is a travesty."

"You may choose to indulge me, or you may choose to leave. And then Velasar will have no voice in any agreements between Istalam and Nakrab or Taresan." I glance away from him, unconcerned. "Taseino, please serve the tea. Ambassador Cherato, I invite you to sit for the proceedings."

He does so without a fuss, making me reevaluate what all the standing around was for—he may also be obfuscating his intentions toward Ambassador Ridac.

"And what assurances do you offer that we can know you're not feeding us witched tea?" Ridac demands.

He knows what the store is about, then. "Either I'm dangerous or I'm not worth wasting your time on, ambassador, but you cannot have it both ways."

"I would not have thought," Reyata observes, "Velasar would forget its reverence for tea masters. Curious."

Ridac settles into his chair with ill grace. "You've always been a brat, your Highness."

Reyata's amused smile and the mocking bow she returns preclude my having to stand up for her honor; all is well.

I was always hiding in the palace, but I'm still mildly surprised Ridac hasn't recognized me along with my sisters, even with us all arrayed together.

This start isn't worrisome, though. Ridac is posturing, as though we'll be so distracted soothing him that we won't notice when the real sallies start coming.

"That's enough of that," I say. "Let us to business, then. As we are in Istal lands to discover the root of attacks on Istal sovreignty, we will be using Istal as the language to conduct this summit. Ambassador Cherato, as you have had fewer dealings with this language, please signal if at any point our meaning is unclear."

"There will be no need," the ambassador replies. "Your tongue is quite simple for us."

His accent falls away with the claim of superiority, though I suspect it will return soon enough. Istalam's former empire made our language the most ubiquitous language on the continent before the Cataclysm and therefore the most useful for trade. If Nakrab has been as involved in dealings on the continent as I suspect, the ambassador is likely as fluent as Ridac.

Taseino finishes distributing tea and falls back, ignored and listening. I am endlessly grateful for his presence here.

"Then let me begin by making sure we all understand the business at hand," I say. "Ambassadors, within the last few weeks, the Cataclysm, whose boundaries have held steady for generations, have suddenly begun expanding."

This abrupt claim is met by silence all around, as everyone attempts to surreptitiously or openly study each other's reactions.

That is, until Yorani shifts in her teapot, and our collective attention turns momentarily to the figure of a spirit—if a presently ridiculous one—looking down on us and listening to our words for posterity. Even Ambassador Perjoun appears mildly discomfited by the tea spirit's regard.

"I trust I don't need to explain that if this continues, there will be no escape," I continue after a pause. "Not for any of us."

Taresan knows this well; they lost territory to the Cataclysm, too, if not as much as Istalam. So I focus on Ridac and Cherato.

"Your land's peculiarities are no concern of the Isle of Nakrab's," Ambassador Cherato says in a bored tone.

Predictably. This will be an attempt to sound out how I will respond to Nakrab's customary isolationist stance, and the control that has allowed them to leverage in the past.

"I would be deeply grateful to learn why you are certain the Cataclysm cannot expand past our borders," I say with a bow. "It would relieve me greatly to know there is a natural boundary to the Cataclysm, since our mages have determined the edges extend into the sea."

The ambassador tilts his head inscrutably and doesn't deign to elaborate.

Ridac is not so circumspect.

"You summoned us out here for this, when you've willfully allowed taint to grow and spread here rather than rooting it out, despite what happened before?" Ridac demands. "The Cataclysm has always been the fault of witches. Clean the poison out of your house before it affects the rest of ours, or stay out of the way of those who will not shy away."

This makes my anger burgeon. Ridac is old enough to have been a player during the post-Cataclysm negotiations. "No trustworthy evidence supports that claim."

"Oh, will you now cast aspersions on Velasar's academic institutions, then?"

I cannot let him control the field. "The development of Velasar's policies is not the matter for this summit. What is relevant is that witches have lived peacefully near the Cataclysm with no ill effects."

Ridac pounds his fist on the table in front of him, the tea sloshing in its cup. "The effect is cumulative. You let them live—"

"I will do more than that before I'm through," I say coldly.

I persuaded Iryasa to let me lead this my own way, but I can see the tension in her shoulders and Reyata watching her closely, sure she will move.

I have to get this under control, and I must do it my own way.

"Witches are not what has changed, before the Cataclysm or after. We are here to determine what, precisely, has, and why. To that end, I have the backing of the tea masters' guild, and the spirits are with me," I say formally. "We are here to work, not for games, ambassador. Unless your prejudice is to blame for the expansion and is thus relevant, then I will ask you attempt to overcome it for the duration of these talks."

"You dare—"

"I'm not finished," I say in the mildest of tones. "You may, as I said, walk out if you wish. But let me make one thing perfectly clear from the outset. Understand that anyone who chooses to abandon the quest for answers now, knowing the world is at stake, I will rule in my capacity as negotiator in this summit to be an enemy of the state of Istalam. Istalam will respond to your nations accordingly. So think very carefully."

"You can't make that stick," Ridac says, his eyes gleaming.

Offended, certainly, but more than anything I think I have finally managed to intrigue him by offering a variety of opponent he did not anticipate.

"Test me at your discretion," I tell him coolly. "But understand I will not offer you second chances."

"What a delightfully barbaric custom," Cherato remarks. "So we must agree with you or be made war on? Fascinating."

"Agree with me? Hardly," I say. "You must agree to engage earnestly. You must understand we do not have time for the usual fictions. We have a job to do, and I mean to do it. Decide quickly, ambassadors."

My heart races. This is a risk; they could all walk out now, and we will see what consequences I can muster.

An audible sip answers.

Everyone turns toward Ambassador Perjoun as she sets down the cup she has drained. "The embassy from Taresan has no objection to these terms," she says. "Though I would speak to you about a few of my own."

I bow. "I would be happy to discuss them with you, though I have one final term you may wish to hear first."

The ambassador inclines her head curiously, gesturing me on.

"Be they members of ambassadorial staff or a princess, understand I will tolerate no harm coming to anyone in this room."

I can practically feel Saiyana's ire at this statement, at the behind-the-scenes bureaucracy it implies to not make a liar of me. But Iryasa only quirks a brow, merely finding this interesting.

Which means she doesn't realize this is a measure designed to protect Karisa specifically.

"Are your princesses so fragile?" Ridac's disdain is palpable. "Perhaps you should not risk them all at once, then."

I smile. "Unprecedented, isn't it? Indeed, as I am conducting this summit on behalf of Istalam, I would be remiss if I did not make clear that any harm befalling a princess during these talks must necessarily result in both censure by the tea masters' guild and reparations to be settled by war." I bow. "Under such a circumstance I will muster an army of witches to send to your borders myself."

That gets Ridac and Cherato's attentions. Velasar considers witches tainted; and now I am sure Nakrab has at least suspicions that its magic is not effective against witchcraft. Another mystery, but not today's.

Today, we will see how very far I can push my power.

"This is why I extend the same guarantee of protection to all your staff," I say. "Let no one fear, be it favoritism or for their safety. The Cataclysm expands, and we must be bold.

"It will be my honor to hear any further thoughts each of you have on the matter. But first, please," I say, "do try the tea."

I wait, meeting their gazes in turn, and breathing easily as if I am absolutely confident I can do everything I have just claimed.

I let them see in my eyes that I am.

After a long silence, representatives from each delegation sip their tea, and I smile.

The work is upon us, and I will meet it.

We break shortly thereafter, and when only my team and my sisters remain, Reyata begins, "I about had heart failure when you talked about mustering an army of witches."

"That would prove difficult, given the history of our relations," I admit. "I hope it doesn't come to that. I'd like to be able to sleep again someday."

"Forget the witches; let's talk about guaranteeing security for that many people," Saiyana growls. "When were you going to run that past me?"

Karisa sighs. "Witches were the only interesting part. I'm bored now."

Our sisters all simultaneously shoot her a look of disdain as Karisa wanders over to tease Yorani, pretending she isn't listening. I would laugh at how effective she is in this role if it wasn't so sad that it works on us this well.

I refrain from spoiling the maneuver, instead answering Saiyana. "I wasn't going to run it past you, because you've already taken security precautions, and Entero is handling our information."

"So it's a deterrent," Iryasa says. "Making explicit that there will be repercussions in the event of violence."

"That's the idea, yes."

Saiyana throws herself into a seat to stare at me intently. "I'm surprised you decided to start on the offensive. That's not your usual style, even now."

"Except with you, you mean?"

She grins at that. "Yes."

"I don't want them thinking they can get away with their usual tricks," I explain.

"Miyara. That just means they'll have to make moves you wouldn't predict."

"But that they're not practiced with, which means they will slip more easily."

"Only if they come back at all," Iryasa points out. "I didn't know you were going to alienate them like this."

"I haven't, though." I glance at Reyata. "Tell me you've ever seen Ridac that intrigued."

Reyata smiles faintly. "I'm more amused by how he clearly doesn't recognize you. You spent all those years learning how the court thought without the players having any idea they were being watched. Ridac's canny, but Cherato's the one you'll need to be careful of."

"But also the one least likely to be put off by this approach. Nakrab knew what we had in mind when they sent a delegation." I look at Iryasa. "I'm sorry. I know you like to plan. But I'm at my best adapting situationally. I can be your agent in setting the parameters. My taking this stance allows you to take a step back, be inscrutable, and take your time."

I don't just need to set my own boundaries. Like with Tamak and Elowyn, this summit is also an opportunity for me to help my sisters—Iryasa and Karisa in particular, but perhaps in a way Saiyana and Reyata, too—learn to set boundaries.

Let them see me model how to shift burdens off a leader's shoulders without abdicating responsibility, so none of us need ever follow our mother into the trap made of her life.

Let them see me model how to set an aggressive boundary that doesn't backfire.

No pressure, Miyara.

For once, though, I don't in fact feel worried in the slightest. After all the fretting, it should have occurred to me that adapting situationally *is* my strength. I can listen, and I can act.

For once, I'm sure I am exactly where I should be, and I know my course.

I just have to have the courage to live it.

I withdraw with Taseino into the back to consult, since excepting Karisa my sisters aren't aware of the extent of his involvement.

We've long since covered the basics, though I suppose it's not considered basic to people without my education. Taseino learns quickly enough it can be easy to forget.

Istalam and Taresan are the two remaining continental nations, to the best of our knowledge, who share borders with the Cataclysm and were most directly impacted by it. Taresan had trouble taking in refugees because it wasn't as wealthy as Istalam had been by comparison, but given its smaller size it also wasn't damaged to the same degree. Ambassador Perjoun will wish for a solution that stops the Cataclysm's expansion but that also leaves it with good relationships with both its neighbors. Taresan relies on Velasar to the west for trade just as Istalam now does, but to their south they also rely on Istalam's stability to prevent undue strain on their own resources.

So Taresan will be willing to back any measure that I can persuade Velasar to agree to, and that is quite a different challenge.

That Istalam's growth pressed against Velasar for generations, even though Velasar's borders have largely remained unchanged for the last hundred years, created a point of cultural contention. Velasar pits its identity in opposition to Istalam, so Ridac cannot be easily swayed and expect Velasar to honor his word. He will require concessions, and I will have to find acceptable terms.

They cannot include ceding land once held by Velasar, and with it people, to a nation that will execute witches.

Fortunately, Istalam's current struggles are an irresistible political opportunity, and Ridac won't squander it. Velasar dreams of one day ruling an empire like Istalam did, with Taresan and Istalam under Velasari jurisdiction, and his demands will be designed to undermine the royal family's grip.

This is fortunate, because Velasar has never understood that it is not our family in particular that our people value: it is our dedication to service. Istalam has mis-stepped throughout its history, but in this its rulers have been steadfast, or they have not remained rulers long.

The Isle of Nakrab is the unknown quantity. We know they're proud and isolationist: visitors from the continent are allowed to dock in their ports but not permitted any further onto the island. We know Velasar would very much like their excellent naval technology to change the nature of its battles with Istalam but has not managed to entice

Nakrab into sharing. We know the islanders maintain the fiction that the continent has nothing of interest to them, but we also know it's false by the way they do not cut relations entirely.

Increasingly I am convinced the reason is to do with the Cataclysm, and that is why they are here at all now.

And why Thiano has been here for so long.

"There are a few new items to focus on beyond Nakrab's opinions on or approach to magic," I tell Taseino.

"What they know about witchcraft and how it interacts with their tech, the state of their relations with Velasar, any devices in their quarters notably missing since our last interaction, and after your second declaration I'm thinking some closer observation of how Cherato treats his aides," Taseino rattles off. "I'll make sure Karisa and Elowyn are on the lookout. Anything else?"

I blink, then smile ruefully. Of course he already understands what needs to be done. "I should have expected that, shouldn't I?"

"I've been watching you for a long time now," Taseino says.

It hasn't been that long. But perhaps we're both young and flexible enough to change rapidly enough—and events have pushed us to—that the literal length doesn't matter.

I think about Yorani again, who as I brought Taseino back here stopped staring and curled up to sleep, though her tail keeps swishing ominously; plotting without me. She's changed so much in this timeframe, too, to be putting her own plans into motion. How could I ever expect less from Taseino?

"In my defense, not with this kind of politics," I say.

"It's all politics, isn't it? Negotiating what people want and what they need, listening to what they do and don't say. It's what you do every day, but with more context and a different goal in mind."

Oh dear. I run a hand through my hair. "I feel as though I should apologize for getting you involved in this."

Taseino actually *rolls his eyes* at me, which is how I know I'm in for it. "Yes, you should apologize for teaching me how to leverage skills I already had that no one else cared about. You should definitely apologize for believing I could handle higher-level tasks, whether it was managing at the store or personally training the leader of the dragons. I will never be a... a flashy person, and everyone else in my life has written me off as having no value because of it, and you helped me learn how I can make a difference in the world as myself. So keep your apologies, and let me."

I will horrify him completely if I cry, but it takes all my copious training as a princess to hold it in.

"As you will, Grace Taseino." I bow.

Taseino blushes as he scowls. "Stop that. Anything else?"

I smile, and based on his suspicious reaction I think it must come off as a more beatific version of Lorwyn's shark-smile.

"No," I say. "The summit is officially afoot, and we have everyone we need in position but one. So this is what we're going to do."

CHAPTER 18

GLYNIS CAN CLAIM ALL she wants that her ability to locate a spy like Entero at any time is just part and parcel of being a messenger, but I and her colleagues at the guild know better. But eventually they are able to find *her*, and she in turn delivers a message to Entero that our career spy is evidently all too pleased to receive.

Entero arranges a distraction for Lady Kireva and her agents, while Taseino follows up with Ambassador Cherato to ensure he too is occupied.

And Yorani and I hie ourselves to Thiano's shop.

Thiano is already holding the door to his shop open when we arrive, and as soon as we enter he locks it behind us and flips the 'open' sign to 'closed'.

"It should probably concern me more that despite all the measures we just took you knew exactly when Yorani and I were going to be here," I say as she flies around his head in greeting.

"Fortunately you're not sensible enough to worry about that," Thiano says. "Even though you understand all your compatriots may end up embroiled with me, too."

I roll my eyes. "You couldn't wait even one sentence to poke at my feelings about the spy team, could you?"

Thiano pauses.

Looks back at me through a curtain of flapping wings.

"The *spy team*?" he echoes. "That's what you're calling them?"

"I assure you it was not my idea," I say. "To answer the question you didn't ask, no, I'm not worried about you corrupting them any more than I would worry about Yorani unsupervised with you. And my tea spirit has never missed an occasion to visit with you."

Yorani chirps and boops Thiano on the nose.

Thiano sighs, snagging her out of the air to pet the scales on her nose as she makes a different noise in the back of her throat—attempting to mimic Talsion's purr.

"Little one, you are a tremendous interference," Thiano mock-scolds.

By this I think he means in his attempt to project an unsavory image of himself, but it occurs to me to ask, "Has Yorani ever visited you without me?"

"Does it matter?" Thiano asks without looking back at me.

"Only in that I'm trying to figure out what has been going on with her."

Thiano laughs at that. "Then the answer is meaningless, as you never will, and I won't tell."

Yorani bumps her head further into Thiano's hand.

"So, she hasn't yet, but you're inviting her to and promising to keep her secrets," I say.

Thiano smirks at me. "And you only said that out loud to make sure she understood."

Yorani glances between us curiously and then launches off to a nearby surface full of clutter to start nosing around, apparently unconcerned.

Thiano leads me to one of the back aisles in the shop, which is a disaster further down the scale than what the warehouse at Talmeri's used to look like. "Since I've closed my shop to accommodate you, you can do some work while we talk," he tells me.

"Have you just been waiting for an opportunity to take advantage of my labor for free?" I mentally calculate whether I should go ahead and order food now before we even begin—but no, that's an opportunity for Lady Kireva to interfere and possibly undermine Entero's efforts. My sleeves are long and loose today, so I tie them up as I consider.

It hasn't been so long since our inventory overhaul at Talmeri's that I've forgotten certain grim lessons.

"I've been saving this for you specially," Thiano drawls, cutting into my preemptive logistical planning. "There aren't many people who can organize a store inventory and who I can trust with my store's particular contents."

"I'm honored," I say in my driest tone, since Thiano clearly wants to disguise the emotion in this.

He could not have said any more clearly that he trusts me in a way he trusts no one else, and I am both immensely proud and unbearably sad.

He may be angling for something in the telling, of course, but that doesn't change its truth. And that he has arranged a task in his life particularly for me so I might 'earn' information from him when needed and we may maintain the fiction that we are not hopelessly in each other's debt... that's food for later thought, too.

We get started sorting first. There are piles for 'expired' and 'no longer in fashion' and 'needs to be cleaned before anyone would consider purchasing'. There are piles for 'probably trash but let Thiano check in case it's actually magic'. Occasionally Yorani hops into this pile and decides the matter for me.

Once we've fallen into a rhythm, I ask Thiano, "What can you tell me about Ambassador Cherato?"

Thiano doesn't even pause. Either he already knew who the ambassador was or else he had no doubts who would be sent.

"He is one of the few who knows part of why I deserve to be here," he answers.

I, on the other hand, stop entirely.

I've understood that Thiano believes he's done something he cannot atone for. But this is confirmation not only that someone else knows what he's done, but that it ties in some way into international politics. That his long tenure in Istalam is likely an official punishment rather than a self-imposed exile.

Yet, that he says 'part'—that tells me there is more to his presence here than his government knows.

And he wishes to keep it that way.

"He's also the same Cherato who was present during the negotiations in the immediate aftermath of the Cataclysm, isn't he?" I finally say. "He wears the same face."

Thiano inclines his head as he hands me another stack cleared at random from a shelf. "He wasn't young then either, if that's what you mean to ask."

Interesting, though that he offers that detail freely confirms it's likely unimportant. Cherato would have been experienced then, and he'll only be more so now.

"I don't suppose whatever magic he's using will have kept him from solidifying mental habits?"

"It will not, but don't assume decreased mental flexibility—which *is* applicable in his particular case—makes him careless. And don't assume he cares about what you or I might."

People.

He means the ambassador doesn't care about *people*.

I shiver. That will be important for me to remember; to try to make myself believe. Even Ridac's pride is connected to people, but there's only one thing I know for sure Nakrab cares about.

Magic.

"You mean my usual methods won't work, because I can't reach him the same way," I muse.

"No," Thiano says. "I mean you can't reach him at all."

I frown at him.

"Yes, I know I'm a cynical old crotchet, but I assure you I'm correct," Thiano snaps. "You wanted my take on the ambassador? That's it. Don't treat him as a person, because he won't treat you as one—at least not in the way you understand."

The only person I've known Thiano's judgment to be fundamentally wrong about is himself. So I nod slowly, fairly sure I don't fully understand what he's trying to tell me, and make a mental note to ask the spy team to pay special attention to Cherato's treatment and consideration of the staff accompanying him.

"Will he pretend to care?" I ask.

Thiano considers. "Likely. But it's not an illusion he's committed to, so it will wane as his interest does."

Like his interest in maintaining accented Istal faltered when presented with an opportunity to showcase Nakrabi superiority. His tactics will change fluidly with no attempt at consistency outside his core priorities.

Yorani breaks the silence that's fallen between us as I consider that by swiping sand with her tail out of a bowl she's dived into.

"Stop that," Thiano says.

Yorani immediately freezes, then ducks her head like she's embarrassed. Then she carefully flaps out of the bowl and lands on a pile of glittering rocks to inspect instead.

Thiano's expression betrays his surprise that Yorani actually listened to him.

"I hope you realize you have just moved to the top of my dragon-sitter list," I tell him.

Thiano flashes a grin at me, but his eyes are sad. "You may not wish to rush on that. There are other political entities who could have come to Istalam for this. That it's Cherato means they're being careful."

"To protect their future interests on the mainland by sending someone who knows Istalam."

"Who believes he does," Thiano corrects, his gaze intent on mine.

My breath catches.

I haven't changed Istalam's character fundamentally. But maybe I've already shifted enough of its heart—the ugliness and the beauty—into the light that the ambassador's previous experience won't help him as much as he expects.

"You need to ask the right questions, Miyara," Thiano tells me. "Now more than ever."

As if I don't know. It's too bad no one will ever tell me the correct questions to ask, but the mysterious old woman's argument is well taken—the whole problem is that no one else will ask questions the same way I will.

But today I don't know enough to press Thiano. I still need more information before I can understand the pattern I'm operating in, and I'm not going to lose this opportunity when he's in a mood to answer.

"What can you tell me about Nakrab's relationship to magic?" I ask.

Thiano snorts. "Too much and too little. Saying Nakrab has a relationship with magic is like saying you have a relationship with the idea of service."

I blink. "Foundational and ubiquitous, then?"

"To put it mildly," Thiano says. "But you knew that."

"I'm wondering more about how they feel about witchcraft," I say. "I know they look down on magecraft for its reliance on physical structures, but Nakrabi magic somehow powers physical structures, yes? Like the weapon that was deployed in the Cataclysm. Witchcraft also doesn't require structures but can alter reality."

Thiano eyes me thoughtfully before returning to his own piles, focusing on them so he doesn't have to look at me while he figures out what to say.

"Nakrabi magic works by infusing objects with magic," he finally says. "Naturally I am no expert in witchcraft—"

The very fact that he says this makes me unaccountably suspicious.

"—but my understanding is that a witch can change the nature of an object, perhaps to have a magical purpose, but not to *hold* magic. You see the difference?"

So Nakrabi magic makes ordinary objects into objects of power.

I carefully do not look at the bracelets on my wrists.

"Similar, but not the same," I muse. "If I assume that Ambassador Cherato may have ways of learning that Lorwyn deployed witchcraft to directly counter Nakrabi magic where magecraft cannot be so utilized—"

"Then you may correctly infer Nakrab's likely interest in witchcraft, yes," Thiano says. "And you should guard against it."

Yes. I suspect the ambassador's distraction at our first meeting at Talmeri's may be mostly explained by his preoccupation studying Lorwyn's contribution to the wards.

What he can do about them is another question—as is what he *will* do.

"Are physical repercussions a possibility?" I ask.

Thiano thinks about that for a moment. "I would not say 'never'," he says slowly. "Because anything is always possible. But for a Nakrabi politician of Cherato's resources to resort to physical violence, that would be... noteworthy."

That ought to be encouraging, if physical violence is profoundly unlikely. But the way Thiano phrases this tells me he fears it may not be as unlikely as it ought to be.

And the fact that he is willing to tell me this, even in confidence, is distressing in its own right.

"Will you meet with the ambassadorial team?" I ask.

"I cannot avoid some contact, given my role," Thiano says wryly. "But I will avoid all interactions with him it is possible to."

Which means he expects nothing good to come from them, but there is a purpose he cannot ignore.

With sudden insight I understand Thiano's boundaries between who and what he is have collapsed: he sees himself now as a role, not a person, and it's in this spirit—not as the role the Isle of Nakrab sent him to fulfill, but as what he's chosen to make of it—that defines all his choices.

It's a cold realization for me on two counts.

The first, that I can never let this happen to me, no matter what. I cannot let being a tea master become everything, or I will lose what makes me effective as a tea master.

I can't lose myself in a role and still be a person for Deniel. Or Yorani, or my sisters, or any of the people in my life for whom personal connections make all the difference—which is all of them.

The second is that Thiano, despite valuing *me* as a person, and my commitment to seeing people for who they are, nevertheless considers himself expendable in the face of whatever role he's assigned himself.

I wonder at what the old woman who gifted me the arcane teapot had to sacrifice to be who she is, and I wonder *why* Thiano has had to sacrifice himself, and how long they have both been existing for duty rather than living.

"Can I help?" I ask him.

Thiano gently takes the cloth I've been gripping too tightly out of my hands. "No. This is mine."

His duty, his burden, his task, his penance, his fault, his fate.

Yorani flaps up suddenly and squawks, fluttering urgently.

"You should go," Thiano tells me, standing.

My palms tingle with sudden awareness. "What do you know?"

His smile is pained. "Your tea spirit will guide you."

Thiano disappears into the bowels of his magical store, and I clamber out of the mess we've sorted and run.

It doesn't take me long to realize where Yorani is leading me. My chest grows tighter, and not just because I'm out of breath.

Something is wrong in the Cataclysm.

The barrier is awash with color as we approach at top speed, a coruscating rainbow bubble. It might have been beautiful, were it at all standard behavior for the barrier.

As it isn't, I grit my teeth and dive in after Yorani.

Once we cross the threshold, Yorani hangs back so I can hold onto the end of her foot gently, letting her guide me through.

I don't know what she does. I don't sense anything at all.

But it's impossible not to notice that the Cataclysm parts around us.

Roots that should snare my ankles withdraw. Swarms hold back rather than attacking. Even arcane streams angle away from us.

So it isn't long at all before we get to wherever it is we're going.

I hear the sound of voices before I can identify them. But I recognize a familiar whirring, exactly like the Nakrabi machine the Velasari spies deployed in the Cataclysm.

Hot rage lends me a burst of speed.

"Will you attack us, then?" Ambassador Cherato's voice is curious. "A witch, a dragon, a noble of a treasonous House, and an officer of the law? I do wonder how that would look."

Lorwyn, Sa Nikuran, Risteri, and Entero are frozen surrounding him, and the machine continues to whirr.

Yorani tugs where I have a hold on her.

Our gazes lock for a long instant.

I can't see him, but I clearly hear Ambassador Ridac add, "We have diplomatic immunity, and you have no authority to interfere in our affairs."

I let my tea spirit fly.

She darts through the wall my friends have formed, and my heart about stops in its chest as I break through in time to see her fly straight into the machine.

The sight of weapons raised; the exclamations raised.

Then the unmistakable, relieving sound of it powering down. *Perhaps we were in time.*

Ambassador Cherato makes a cutting gesture, and his two attendants step forward. "Deal with the obstacle however necessary," he says.

My rage turns cold in an instant, and I ignore the twisting in my gut.

"Tea spirits are sacred, and if you do anything that might constitute *possible* harm toward her, it will be an act of war," I say in a voice that could freeze a leaping flame. "I am confident the royal family and indeed every citizen of this continent will agree."

Cherato pauses, for the first time registering my presence as I stride forward and eyeing me with a darkly glittering gaze.

I pass the line my friends have formed, heading right for the center of this debacle and placing myself as a clear obstacle between both sides. My heart pounds as I wait to see how seriously the Nakrabi ambassador will take me—and whether this is a threat he cares about to risk pushing. I can practically see him weighing options.

Ridac places a hand on the Nakrabi ambassador's hand and gives one shake of his head.

Ambassador Cherato's lips twist, and for a moment I think the offense he'll take at being touched will outweigh his caution.

Then Yorani zooms back out of the machine seconds before it crumples to the ground.

She alights back on my shoulder—substantially heavier than before, like she's eaten all the magic the machine contained.

She's fine.

And for the moment, the Cataclysm is fine, too.

A distant rumble echoes, and I do not move even a flinch.

Nor do they.

I let my silence hang in the air, let the ambassadors and their people look upon a vision of me fully righteous in my anger, confident in my power, and not bothering to hide my extreme displeasure.

"*I* have every authority to interfere with your activities," I say, slowly and deliberately. "So ambassadors, you will attempt to explain the gross misconduct I've just witnessed immediately, and if I am not satisfied with your answer, a cell awaits. You may begin."

CHAPTER 19

MY ULTIMATUM HANGS IN the air.

It's another test, for both the ambassadors and myself: do I truly have the authority to make such a judgment, and the power to back it up?

There are different parts to power. There is what I can do on my own, which depends on me: my will, my abilities, my limitations.

But there is not just what I choose to do, because once my actions interact with the world, there is also perception. There is whether others believe I have power, or are willing to act as though I do; there is, indeed, little effective difference between the two.

I have the will to enact vengeance upon anyone who attacks the Cataclysm. In this moment, full of fury, I am certain I can summon the means, though later I may doubt.

But will the ambassadors believe, or will they decide to try me?

And if they do...

"You are quick to throw threats around, tea master," Ambassador Ridac says, his eyes narrowed.

"You are quick to challenge the very core reason we are all gathered in this place, which I made plain not hours past," I say.

"Challenge? No one here has exacted the violence you cautioned us against. No one has abandoned your talks of peace—except, it seems, yourself."

"Ambassador, you have misunderstood me greatly, and for that I accept responsibility," I say. "We are not here to talk of peace. We are here to *survive*. And as for violence, how should I take it when your first act, it seems, is to attack the very barrier that protects us all from the Cataclysm?"

"We have done no such thing."

"You have, and whether it was done in ignorance or full knowledge I care not at all," I say. "Let me be perfectly plain. Until this matter is resolved, no member of an ambassadorial team may enter the Cataclysm without an escort I have approved."

"Except the Istals," Ambassador Cherato remarks.

"Princess Saiyana is responsible for stabilizing the Cataclysm to the extent such an undertaking may be possible," I say. "I will hold all others not directly involved in its safe-keeping to the same standard."

"Will you?" he asks. "I question your objectivity, tea master."

"Do you? I question your motives, ambassador. I question whether you are unaware of the consequences the last time such technology was deployed within this sphere. I question whether you invited the Velasari ambassador here to be Nakrab's shield. I question whether you truly did not understand what a grave offense you have given, and ambassadors, I still await your justifications."

The Nakrabi ambassador spreads his hands. "Then you will wait, tea master. You are already prepared to believe the worst of me, it seems. If I am to be guilty whether I provide an explanation or don't, I will keep my counsel."

Here it is, then.

"You are partially correct," I say. "I will not believe your presence here to be entirely innocent, as I will not do you the disservice of believing you to be stupid."

Our gazes lock.

Then his gaze drifts to Yorani at my shoulder, and I tense as he considers her lazily.

Yorani has done more than thwart him this day. She's demonstrated that she can and will get in his way, which means she's made herself a direct threat.

I lift a hand, letting the gesture draw attention away from the tea spirit. "Ambassadors. With, as you say, a witch, a dragon, a noble of a treasonous house, and an officer of the law, I surely have sufficient ability to detain you until I am satisfied."

It doesn't work: Ambassador Cherato's next words are, "Not with a tea spirit, then?"

I let my gaze narrow. "No spirit is for *use*, ambassador, be it personal or worldly."

Ambassador Cherato tilts his head to one side, as if this is a curious notion and not a foundational principle.

"Enough of this," Ridac says abruptly. "I was interested in seeing the Cataclysm for myself, and Ambassador Cherato invited me to view a demonstration of the Isle of Nakrab's technological ingenuity. Rare opportunities, I'm sure you'll understand. To provoke a reaction like this from you, my curiosity about its power is certainly satisfied. You of course have Velasar's apology for any unintended consequences, tea master, but I think any further discussion should occur in official negotiations."

No apology for the intended consequences, at least not explicitly.

But he has taken a more important step: he has answered my demand for them both, tacitly accepting my authority.

And in doing so, he has complicated whatever understanding existed between Velasar and the Nakrabi ambassador.

"I concur, Ambassador Ridac," I say. "Ambassador Cherato, do you have anything to add?"

He smiles, close-lipped, and shakes his head.

"Then understand it is only Ambassador Ridac's words and my desire to find a real solution that spare you today from a cell," I tell him. "And understand that if I learn you have employed Nakrabi technology again inside Sayorsen or the Cataclysm, I will not be willing to extend you further opportunities of any kind."

That's as much as I can do for Ambassador Ridac, for the huge risk he has just taken, making it appear that he has just saved the Nakrabi ambassador rather than betrayed him. Ridac is canny enough not to react.

But Cherato, experienced as he is, does not bother with a non-reaction.

He turns to leave the Cataclysm, and we are obliged to follow in order to escort the ambassadors outside, leaving the awful technology abandoned behind us.

Where the Cataclysm ignored me before, it takes the opposite approach in this case.

When I glance back, the machinery's structure is disintegrating into the air.

Outside the Cataclysm, the ambassadors go their separate ways, and I can only watch. I have no force prepared to detain or escort them.

Clearly this was an extreme oversight in my preparation.

My stomach twists, and even though the ambassadorial staff is not quite out of sight, Lorwyn says, "We can speak freely now."

I let out a breath, prying Yorani off my shoulder so I can take a closer look at her.

The tea spirit is definitely fatter, but as far as I can tell she's unharmed. She chirps at me drowsily, and I settle her back on my shoulder. She curls herself around the back of my neck and falls asleep directly.

"I forget sometimes what you can be like when you're really furious," Risteri observes, not sounding particularly concerned about it. "Have I mentioned recently that you're kind of terrifying, Miyara?"

Next to her, Sa Nikuran snorts. "Foolish. The tea master is more dangerous than any of us."

"Really?" Lorwyn asks. "Because we were all helpfully quiet there and you still didn't manage to put the Nakrabi ambassador in his place."

"No," Entero says, "but she did the first important work with Velasar."

Lorwyn frowns. "What?"

"Velasar believes their interests are more aligned with Nakrab than Istalam," I explain. "I've just driven a wedge in that relationship. Ridac doesn't have to like me, but if he respects me and believes Nakrab is willing and able to sacrifice Velasar in its machinations, I may yet turn him."

Lorwyn blinks, then scowls as she sees Risteri nodding along, having also understood the undercurrents of what just happened. "I hate politics."

"My life is going to be nothing but for the next while," I say grimly. "I may have gotten them to leave, but nothing prevents them from entering the Cataclysm somewhere else and starting over right away."

"Not right away anyway," Lorwyn says. "I made sure the device couldn't be salvaged. They didn't have anything else on them big enough to channel that kind of power."

I stare at her, remembering how my gut had twisted earlier in the middle of my ultimatum and I hadn't thought anything of it.

Lorwyn misinterprets my stare and glares at me. "I didn't disable any of his other tech for him to inspect later, did I? And I made sure to do it at a moment when my witchcraft could be mistaken for Yorani's power. Worth it to confirm Glynis' hypothesis from before, anyway—looks like I can un-work Nakrabi tech easily enough. We'll just have to keep them from recovering it to study and try to counter my witchcraft to fix."

"The Cataclysm took care of that," I say.

I can't help wonder if this is why Cherato abandoned it without a thought: perhaps because he knew it couldn't be used anymore. There's no way to be sure if he knew why.

"What do you think they were doing, anyway?" Risteri asks.

Entero answers her. "At a guess, Ambassador Cherato was demonstrating the technology in exchange for whatever the Velasari agents learned in order to continue the work."

Risteri looks stricken. "Do you think they finished before we interrupted?"

"What were you doing there, anyway?" I ask.

She shrugs. "Honestly, it was luck. Lorwyn and I were going to explore, since we haven't done that in... well, years, and we needed get out of the apartment for a bit."

"It really isn't big enough for three." Lorwyn shrugs.

"You shared a room with a whole passel of sisters until weeks ago," Risteri reminds her.

"They're smaller and easy to shove in corners when they annoy me."

"Not if you expect them to stay there, unless adolescence has somehow made them less impossible," Risteri says. "Then Sa Nikuran wanted to come, and then she decided to invite 'Lorwyn's Entero'—"

"I will enchant your underclothes to stay on when you next need to pee," Lorwyn threatens easily. Entero looks faintly amused.

Risteri rolls her eyes. "Anyway, we picked up the trail and followed."

I ignore the pang of feeling left out of this excursion. Exploring the Cataclysm together is a perfect thing for them to do together now that they're friends again, and there's no reason to invite me, especially since

I couldn't have joined anyway. Instead I ask, "It didn't occur to you to send for help?"

"What help?" It's Sa Nikuran who asks. "If it hadn't been ambassadors, we would have been sufficient for any navigational, magical, physical, or bureaucratic problem. Since it was, who else but you could have helped, and how could we have reached you in time?"

I take a breath. Sa Nikuran has been the Te Muraka's right hand, and that means more than just as an enforcer. With one question, she has focused me on the immediate problem.

"We have a small window before Cherato can conceivably retrieve any additional machines he may have brought and return to the Cataclysm," I say. "We need some sort of system in place to prevent that entrance or at least notify me that he has attempted it. Any ideas?"

"Not sure magical prevention is a good idea," Lorwyn says. "It would be tricky to specify anything enough to limit it to just ambassadorial staff, let alone for the exemptions you mentioned. Honestly I'm not sure it's a good idea to rely on any magical working near the barrier of the Cataclysm in its current state."

"You need physical guards," Sa Nikuran says bluntly. "There is no reason the Te Muraka cannot fill this role. This is not so different from your princess' own idea."

"Princess Iryasa also noted that there is a problem," I say, "which is that we don't want the perception of the Te Muraka to be that you're only valuable when fulfilling a function, and we don't want Te Muraka to *have* to do this to be perceived as valuable."

"Perception is irrelevant given the current stakes," Sa Nikuran says implacably. "I can have a team of volunteers to patrol the border in less than an hour."

"Perception is unfortunately the opposite of irrelevant," I say. "Please believe me when I say that the summit will fail entirely if I lose control of the narrative."

"Then let it be not just a Te Muraka thing," Lorwyn says. "You still need a way to be notified, right? I can work on that."

I hesitate. "I don't want to force you into this either."

Lorwyn's brow wrinkles, and then her eyes widen. She snaps, "Are you kidding? I hesitated to help you *once*, and that was *ages* ago now, and now you're never going to count on me for anything ever again? Are you trying to be an ass?"

I bristle. "I am *trying* not to manipulate you into something you don't want to do!"

"I volunteered!"

"Yes, but would you have if I hadn't messed up, and then started having this conversation like—"

"Are you really kidding right now."

"You're the one who reminded me to make sure not to put you on a pedestal," I snap.

Risteri steps between us. "You're not. The Te Muraka will help, and Lorwyn will help, and so will the guides. Since it won't look good if the Te Muraka start apprehending people, we can track them inside the Cataclysm until help arrives."

"And I," Entero says, "will handle what comes next."

My gaze flicks to him, and he crosses his arms, daring me to tell him I'm not willing to involve him in this either, to let him do the job he's chosen after the consequences of my last usage of him.

When I keep my mouth shut, having the ability to read a figurative room even if I feel conflicted about it, Entero continues, "Furthermore, I'm going to organize this so you don't have to. You have a different role."

I close my eyes and take a breath. He's right; they all are, even if I don't like involving my friends in my problems.

In this case it's clear they're going to insist on involving themselves, and a part of me can't help being glad for it.

I knew we were going to have to prepare to change our plans on the fly, and here we are, with the people and capacity to do so. Now I have to do my part.

"What exactly does Miyara have to do now?" Lorwyn asks suspiciously.

Risteri puts a hand on her shoulder, restraining her. "Liaise with the official royal authority."

"Oh," Lorwyn says. "Yeah, you're definitely on your own for that part."

Iryasa is already in the library of House Taresim waiting for me when I arrive without my having to summon her.

"Why am I hearing from Lady Kireva that you've had an altercation with two ambassadors outside official negotiations?" my sister asks without preamble.

"Because Lady Kireva's a meddling old woman who wants to drive a wedge between us and is trying to prove that you need her and can't trust anyone else," I say. "I have literally not stopped anywhere else since I exited the Cataclysm following said event."

Iryasa considers that for a moment. "I suppose it's not impossible she was trying to save time by making sure I was ready to receive you."

"I suppose it's not," I say an equally bland tone.

"I take it whatever altercation she's referring to occurred in the Cataclysm? That explains why she didn't have details for me, but I can't say I'm pleased by this explanation."

"I wish I could be happier about this discovery of a certain way to keep happenings secret from her, but under the circumstances I have little to smile about."

I carefully lift Yorani from where she's slumbering around my neck and settle her in my lap. She curls up a little tighter but otherwise doesn't wake.

"She's grown," Iryasa observes.

"In one direction," I agree, trying not to focus on why exactly it is she's so exhausted she's fallen into such a deep sleep in the middle of the day, and launch into a detailed recounting of what has just occurred.

Iryasa is just as angry as I am—and, also as I am, with both ourselves and the ambassadors. We should have been prepared for them to push in such a way, but I hadn't thought they would try something so blatant so soon.

When we come to the matter of guarding the barrier, though, her unease is clear.

"You're relying too much on physical threats," the crown princess cautions me. "We can't scare them into agreeing to terms if we want them to hold."

"I'll use whatever tactics work," I tell her. "Ambassador Perjoun hasn't been put off. What I need is to pressure them to be willing to get to the point."

"Not luring them in? I was under the impression that defeat by graciousness was your primary mode of operating."

"It is," I admit. "I planned to transition into that tomorrow, when we start in on the meat of thing and work toward getting answers. But I won't get anywhere if the ambassadors don't believe I'm worth taking seriously."

"Posturing is not worth the risk of our entire framework of international relations, Miyara," Iryasa tells me. "We got them to come to this summit at all, but now we have to give them a reason to *stay*, not give them reasons to not go. Do you see the difference?"

I tilt my head to one side, considering. "What is your best-case scenario for this, exactly? What are you hoping for?"

"An answer to what's caused the barrier to expand, and a solution we all agree on," she says in the tone of someone admitting something radical. "I know the latter will be nearly impossible, but I want for all of us to leave with a shared goal."

"Is that all?"

Iryasa mimics my gesture. "What do you mean?"

"I want to know what caused the Cataclysm in the first place," I say. "I want us to not have just a common goal to prevent its expansion, but to have common cause in preventing whatever systems allowed it to come to pass in the first place. I want all of us—Te Muraka and Nakrabi, Velasari mages and Gaellani witches, princesses and refugees—to find understanding and common cause together."

Her eyes widen, her breath hitching, and I know why.

I've dared to state intentions out loud what she's never dared to think.

"You're not talking about plugging a hole," she says. "You're talking about unraveling a whole system and rebuilding its foundations."

"We have to," I tell her seriously. "It's the only way we stop this for good. Or else power will change hands and the Cataclysm will be caught in games for political leverage once more, and we'll lose this continent span by span."

Her gaze catches mine, piercing to the core. "*Can* you change a culture? Can you change *several*, all at once?"

"We're going to find out," I say. "I have bigger dreams, Iryasa, and I'm going to get them. I think that's what you want too, but if you're still not prepared to admit it and what it means, then my work starts with you."

Iryasa huffs out a breath, leaning back. "You never give, do you?"

"I do," I disagree. "But usually only if it furthers my ultimate cause."

She laughs at that, shaking her head. "All right. You think I'm being too passive and letting the ambassadors set the pace, don't you? Give me a moment to think."

I do. Someday she won't have these moments, but someday, I hope, she'll have trained herself out of such mental patterns of habitual nonconfrontation.

"How's this," my sister finally says, and I keep my expression blank rather than react to the fact that my elder sister the crown princess is seeking my approval. "There needs to be some kind of repercussion for their blatant disregard for both the proceedings and the barrier's integrity, yes? I'll also need to specifically make clear my support of witches and the Te Muraka in particular, as representatives of each were involved in forestalling the ambassadors' scheme. We will use the barrier defense for both, framing the new service as a reward for those involved and an indication of my trust in them, while it will also function as a formal slight and a preventative force against the ambassadors."

"Perfect," I say. "You'll need to frame it in such a way—"

"—that the service does not become obligatory for those groups indefinitely, and that they're not only valuable for being able to provide this service, yes, I know," Iryasa finishes. "I can lay the foundations for wider recruitment among all Istalam following their lead, and we'll adjust the parameters once the summit has concluded." She smiles at me. "Favorably."

I bow. My worry for my friends and my fear for Yorani and my anger have not yet faded, but this, at least, is good work I have done this day, if Iryasa is willing to believe we can succeed.

"I'll start working with Sa Rangim on this right away, unless there's anything else?" Iryasa says, standing.

"You'll want to speak to Saiyana too—"

"She'll be busy with the barrier now, I assume."

"—so I'll stop by to update her in person so she's prepared later," I finish dryly.

Iryasa's lips quirk.

Finally, we are in tune.

"There is one more thing," I say. "Now that I've begun working on Ridac, I think you will be better suited to continue."

Iryasa looks startled for a moment—that I'm asking her to take a more active hand, and that I believe she can.

But as she nods decisively, I know the timing is right. I can model what making space and a role for myself looks like, but Iryasa will have to figure out hers for herself.

"But in the meantime," I say in a danger-sweet voice I know my eldest sister will understand, "let's set some spirits-blighted boundaries and make them stick."

CHAPTER 20

THERE IS NOTHING QUITE like righteous anger to impel me to move pieces into play at speed.

That the anger is at myself—for setting events up in a way that allowed what occurred in the Cataclysm yesterday—is an additional motivator, and I am addressing my errors with prejudice.

If I don't actively curate and enforce boundaries, I can't expect them to hold.

In the early hours before negotiations for the day begin, I send Glynis to summon Entero, Elowyn, and Taseino to a meeting at House Taresim. With Entero as an adjunct to the local police, and Taseino and Elowyn—not that she'll be seen—as my assistants, it's the easiest place to make sure no one remarks on their attendance.

And that no one, including my sisters, takes note of Karisa's.

"Is Yorani well?" Entero asks immediately as we gather in the library, for once absent a tea spirit.

I love him for asking this first. "She seems to be, but she's in a deep sleep. I don't want to bring her anywhere contentious until she's well enough to be aware. Glynis assured me the protections on our home are almost as thorough as the ones at Talmeri's."

Entero nods, looking thoughtful. "You didn't hesitate."

I blink. "I did consider keeping her with me, since as my familiar she heals faster in my presence—"

He shakes his head. "I mean when you called it 'our home'."

Oh.

I think about for a moment, and then startle into a smile. "So I didn't."

"When do I get to see it, then?" Karisa asks, closing the door behind her.

This honestly hadn't occurred to me. "Would you like to?"

"Everyone else has," she replies, which is its own answer.

She would, in part because she feels left out, but our new relationship is still tenuous enough she's not confident asking earnestly.

"I haven't," Taseino points out. "Or do non-princesses not count, your Highness?"

Caught, Karisa tosses her hair airily. "Certainly not."

"I haven't been over since Miyara moved in either, and my brother lives there," Elowyn adds, emerging from a corner of the room where she really shouldn't have been so invisible.

What's really curious though is that no one currently in the room reacts when she makes herself noticeable: all of us could tell she was there, Taseino and Karisa included.

Interesting.

"We'll set something up, then," I say. "Let me think on it. Today I have a new wrinkle to add to our plot, and I think it will take all of you. In short, I want intel on Velasar and Nakrab's activities outside the negotiations: specifically what they're working on together, and what they're not."

"We're taking Ambassador Perjoun at face value, then?" Taseino clarifies.

"Some people are who they appear to be," Karisa says. "Saiyana confirmed that ambassador's gotten where she is through consistency, hard work, and building connections rather than the usual intrigue."

Karisa's even spying on our sisters. I suppose I can't be surprised—if anything, she's *always* been spying on her sisters, myself included.

It makes me feel better about Taresan to hear this, though—that they would choose to send Perjoun for this summit. I hope the ambassador and I can learn from each other.

"That is my read as well, so no, we're not going to devote resources on her at this time," I say. "The further complication is this: I want to get a hold of Nakrabi technology that Lorwyn and Glynis can experiment with. Saiyana or Ostario too, if we can steal them. But I need a better understanding of what we face so I know what to maneuver around or against."

"No problem," Karisa says. "I'll talk them into giving me something." She shrugs. "Or I can always steal."

"I think we should avoid that," Taseino says.

"You don't think I could?" Karisa challenges, her smile sharp.

"No, I think they might let you," he says. "Either to gain leverage over Istalam or just to see what you'd do with it, which would then blow your cover. If a piece of tech goes missing and you've been at their base, you're going to be the logical suspect, not me."

"Yes, because I'm the entitled one." Karisa rolls her eyes. "Annoying but predictable I suppose."

I try not to stare. I have never seen anyone get agreement out of Karisa this quickly in my life, and I'm not sure how much of this is Karisa's willingness to work with us rather than against, and how much is Taseino's hidden talents coming to light. He didn't even call her ego into question.

"Do you have a suggestion?" I ask him.

He nods, turning to Elowyn. "Tamak made that tracking device for you, right? It looks entirely normal on the outside."

"A swap?" Elowyn surmises, nodding slowly. "That could work."

"Nakrabi tech requires a steady stream of magic, though," Karisa points out. "Can Tamak make a decoy fast enough?"

"Yes," Elowyn says, which makes me wonder how much more she understands about Te Muraka magic than I do. "The bigger question is whether the decoy will last long enough before it's discovered as fake. I don't think that will work permanently, so we'll have to place it and *re*place it."

Taseino looks at me. "We'll work out the details on our own. Anything else?"

"You've learned more about Nakrabi magic already, it sounds like," I say.

"Still working on it," Karisa says, "but it's clear their tech is entirely magic-dependent. And it's a status symbol: Cherato's attendants don't use the tech at all except in service of the ambassador. I'm not sure yet how much of that is resource scarcity as opposed to cultural hierarchy. I assume you haven't missed that their makeup is designed to hide how exhausted they are, though, which begs more questions. Oh, speaking of makeup—Nakrab loves deceptions, right?"

"Right," I say, trying to process all the implications here and keep up.

"Interesting side effect of our ruse here: they have a higher opinion of me than I anticipated not because of the age weirdness, but because Cherato's realized I'm not entirely stupid."

"*What?*"

"Not like that," Taseino clarifies. "He's not onto her. It's more that he's treating her like an entitled noble who's been constrained by her minders and is trying to stretch her wings for the first time but isn't as experienced as she is clever."

"Which has the advantage of being close to the truth," Karisa says smugly. "But he's amused I'm smart enough to deceive our sisters and is hoping he can use my own ruse against them. But you should be aware I think he's also figured out you know what I'm up to and are allowing it, which also makes him think more highly of *your* skills at deception. It's all delightfully circuitous."

"I'm glad you're having fun," I say, my mind still racing. He's as sharp as I feared. "I don't think we need to adjust our overall strategy for that yet—Entero?"

He nods shortly. "Agreed. I don't have much more to add on the Nakrabi magic side, though I'll make sure we're aware of their movements. Let me focus on the Velasari—my contacts will be more use there."

"Police or unofficial?" I ask.

He shakes his head. "My business, not yours."

That's fair. I didn't want to go into the spy business; I owe it to him to manage without interfering.

"Then we're settled," I say. "Let's get ready for today's challenges."

⁂

The day's negotiations are grueling. We don't make any progress on the main issue.

But by the end of the day, everyone has conceded to the new restrictions. It's a victory, and I will take it.

It's forward movement, but at the same time it sets my immediate goals for the negotiations back several steps. I'd intended to start with clear boundaries and then lighten my touch. Instead I've cemented an impression that I am immoveable, which is not entirely to my advantage.

It will be harder for me to see what they're up to, if everyone feels they must commit to underhanded tactics. They may not try to take advantage in the same way, but there are others that can be more troublesome. Saiyana's warning from the day before haunts me, but I can't regret it now.

I have demonstrated thoroughly that I mean business, and that isn't nothing: a long-term strength even if the short-term is more complicated.

And my covert preparations are well in hand.

Still, when Tea Master Karekin comes through the tea shop door, I can practically feel myself droop.

"Oh dear," he says sympathetically. "One of those?"

"Long day, yes," I say. "I was looking forward to getting home. Can whatever this is wait?"

"Perhaps, but I can't guarantee it."

I sigh. "Let's take tea in the ceremony room, then."

"Allow me," he says once again, waving me away. "Take your time finishing up; I know you weren't expecting me."

Thoughtful of him, considering there was no way he could have alerted me during the negotiations without distracting me. I take a few minutes to check in with those who remain at the shop preparing it for its afternoon opening to the public—Taseino and Meristo, not even Lorwyn since she's rushing back to the Cataclysm to work with Sa Nikuran—and ushering the rest away.

"Busy, even outside the negotiations," Karekin notes when I finally enter the ceremony room, closing the sliding door behind me.

"Always," I agree.

He nods. "The work doesn't stop just because the scheduled times for action do. The surrounding preparation is just as important."

"I know," I say. "I fear my preparations are inadequate across the board, however."

"Always," he agrees wryly, and I manage a tired laugh. "You don't mean the summit itself, though."

"Right at the moment I mean the tea shop. We established a system for the shop to run in my absence, but it may not be sustainable after all.

Everyone involved besides Meristo, our most experienced tea specialist, has taken on too much outside the shop responsibilities, and skilled as he is, Meristo is only one person."

I don't count Iskielo and Talmeri, who are as likely to help as hurt.

Karekin pours hot water over the cups and tea pet, then adds it to the pot. "Perhaps you might make use of my assistance, then."

My brain screeches to a halt.

Then the dratted thing starts moving again, in a different direction.

Karekin brought up the busyness of the shop in the first place—was he angling for this? Of course he was, but—

"Why?" I ask.

"Because I'm here to assist you," Karekin says. "I can't run the summit for you, nor would I try. That requires your particular touch. But while you are saving the world, I should think I might manage the serving of tea."

It would do more than that—for our trust in and understanding of each other, and the tea guild, and external perceptions of both.

And yet.

"I will take you up on that," I say, "but you are here today to tell me something you don't think I'm going to have an easy time hearing, and you're trying to alleviate my burden in another way. What is it?"

Karekin smiles briefly as he pours the tea. "I heard Yorani had an adventure yesterday and wanted to check in."

I frown. "I'm going to see her as soon as I'm done here."

"No, I don't mean her health—not precisely. I assume you would not have left her if you'd had any sign she was unwell."

"You think there might be signs I would miss?"

"Only perhaps due to lack of education, and that is what I hope to rectify," Karekin says. "Though lest you worry, I have no reason to believe Yorani is in any present danger. Events merely inspired me not to wait for that time to talk to you about the nature of tea spirits. The guild was too late to help you last time, and I would not have a repeat occurrence."

I sip my tea.

He's going to change all the rules on me again, just when I felt like I was beginning to get a handle on things—after discovering I'd already made critical errors with what I thought I understood.

I change my mind and tip the entire cup back, then set it down. Karekin wordlessly pours again.

"You're aware that Yorani is the first tea spirit seen in centuries," he says. "You may not be aware the last known appearance of a tea spirit was created by an arcanist turned tea master."

I had not. "I'm not an arcanist."

"I'm aware," Karekin says. "But it is relevant to you to understand what we know of the magic involved in tea spirits. What do you know?"

"Tea is a sacred practice because of its ties to the spirits," I say. "Tea spirits are made from earth—in this case, leaves—steeped in water, and released into the air. And whenever I perform the tea ceremony, I give spirits shape, though they are not typically visible."

"Ah," Karekin says, "good. I assumed you must have made that connection, given what you did at the tournament. Yes. May I ask how you knew?"

I swirl my current teacup. "I'm not at liberty to discuss the particulars, but I was gifted an object that allows me to see them briefly when they form."

The bracelets, the teapot. It begins to seem like my surprising success at creating a tea spirit was less accident than design—someone else's.

"Interesting," Karekin says.

I tilt back this cup, too.

"There is a theory," he says, "that the increasing demand on the world's magic over the years—with the rise of other forms like magecraft and witchcraft, especially as they diverged and grew—have left less ambient magic to form familiars. Perhaps still for spirits, though that too had been much in doubt before your recent experience."

What? "I've never heard there might be a limit on available magic."

He shakes his head. "Spirits are not just any magic, though. They are a form of wild magic given shape. Chaos rendered to purpose. Consider what you accomplished with the barrier during the tea tournament."

I stare down at our empty cups, pondering as Karekin dutifully pours again.

"I shaped them into form and purpose," I say, "which created a patch—the barrier is the line between chaos and stability, then? Is that it?"

"That is my essential assumption," Karekin says, "though of course this is conjecture, not studied lore, and I am no mage. But there *are* stories of a lost application, or possibly origin, of the art of tea, as a kind of defense. Consider that you are also taking magic and creating a degree of consciousness in each spirit."

I do not in fact wish to consider that very seriously, or I would be forced to come to some troubling conclusions about the potential for disaster in my own home, particularly with a cat able to see spirits and willing to get into trouble.

"No two spirits are identical," Karekin continues. "They change depending on the tea master performing the ceremony and the recipient, and because people change, a ceremony between the same two people at a later date would not produce a twin. They're unique, and that prevents their magic from being available to any purpose. A conscious spirit cannot be harnessed for magecraft, for instance—unless they wish to be."

"But wild magic can be," I say slowly.

"That is the theory. I see you've had a thought, but before you chase it, let me explain where I'm going with this. A tea spirit, a familiar, has a purpose, and it's one we know: to reflect *you*."

My burgeoning thoughts of the Cataclysm derail. "I'm sorry? Yorani has her own personality. We may bear some similarities, but she isn't me in dragon form."

"No, she's not a copy. But she learns from you."

Sa Rangim had said something very similar, but Karekin is making me think I didn't fully understand. "By living with me, she learns my values, doesn't she?"

"As well as your role in the tea ceremony of her creation, and what that means for her," Karekin says. "Yorani's near-death experience during the tournament caused her to shrink, so you may not have yet noticed that she's growing."

"You make that sound much more ominous than I typically understand growth in a child to be."

"Yorani eats both physical food and magic, does she not?"

"I wasn't sure the magic actually had any... nutritional value for her," I admit. "But yes."

"Oh, yes. Either will sustain her, but while she's not big enough to eat much physical food now, she'll grow. And at some point, how much physical food will it take to fill her?"

My eyes widen. "How big do you expect her to get, exactly?"

"When we're talking about legends, it can be difficult to be clear on specifics," Karekin says. "But Miyara, I would be shocked if she stops growing once she's the size of your house."

Oh, spirits.

I point at the teapot, and Karekin obligingly fills it with water as I knock back another cup and pours me another.

"What you're very carefully not telling me," I say, "is that there's no internal limiting factor on her growth."

"Breathe," Karekin says. "I'm not finished. Eventually as she grows bigger, and stronger, she'll eat more magic than food, and the more magic she eats, the more she will become magic only. Her physical form will eventually disperse. *This* is why tea spirits are considered sacred: we believe they eventually become guardians of the spirits themselves. It will take far longer than your lifetime, but how she lives once you're gone will be a reflection of what she learned during your life."

My eyes fill with tears. Spirits, I have so much to teach her. About change and growth, roots and friendship, and flying free. I don't want her to be sad and alone.

I take a breath. She made friends with one cat very much without my help; I'm sure there will be more cats for her to make friends with. And Yorani is too curious to ever be bored for long. She will be fine, and I will do whatever I can for her to make sure of it.

"You're not worried about her breathing fire or stomping on cities," I manage. "Why are we talking about this now?"

"Because while she does eat magic, she's not strong enough to handle all that much at once at her current size," Karekin says. "It won't make her grow faster; it will make her sick. For better or worse, be careful that what she learns from you isn't to endlessly push herself too hard—even, and perhaps especially, if the cause is just."

The breath rushes out of me. *There's* an indictment, and perspective.

I'm already working on boundaries. But while Yorani has grown quite a lot, if not physically, I have to remember that for a tea spirit, she is still very small. I can rely on her to do what she can, but I don't know what her limits are: and if she does, I need to make sure she attends to them.

I can't rely on her to tell me 'no' when I am in need, not unless I model that for her.

Karekin sets his cup down, and I look up.

"As I said, I have no reason to believe Yorani is currently in jeopardy," Karekin says. "And allow me to add one point further. You are the only person who has created a tea spirit in centuries, and I don't think that's an accident. Whatever magical circumstances of that ceremony contributed, it's not an accident that you, who actively a chose a path of greater connection to the world, succeeded where no one else has.

"No one since an arcanist who made the choice to become a tea master, going from, in a sense, greater power to greater understanding. So I have every confidence in both you and Yorani, Miyara."

To that, I find I have nothing to say. My throat is tight with tears.

It somehow matters more to have faith from someone who I know clearly sees exactly what my weaknesses are.

I struggle to take a breath. "The tea guild should hire you out as a career coach," I joke.

"I doubt many would be well disposed toward my particular brand of encouragement," Karekin notes wryly, "given what it comes with."

Constant, directed challenge. No, perhaps not.

"Well, then it's my turn to pose you some challenge," I say. "Let me show you Lorwyn's station in the back, and the ingredients we use to make tea."

Karekin bows over the tea tray. "Lead on, tea master."

I intend to.

CHAPTER 21

WITH TEA MASTER KAREKIN'S assistance, the rest of my time at the tea shop is less grueling than I feared. It takes time to teach systems to another person, but there is so much he knows already that working with him is still a relief.

When I finally leave the tea shop, Sa Rangim is waiting for me outside.

"Glynis," I surmise as I turn to lock the door.

Sa Rangim's lips quirk, though his eyes remain solemn. "No need for such extremes, when I have some understanding of the work you've taken on and your commitment to it."

I sigh. "You think I'm modeling over-work too, then."

Sa Rangim tilts his head to one side. "Only if you allow this to become your regular way of operating. Our current situation is, it must be said, unique in its acute nature. But I gather you don't need to hear this caution from me."

"I've just had it from Tea Master Karekin, not that it was especially a surprise. Though the implications for Yorani are somewhat more complicated." I blink at him. "How are you again the first person I see after he's upended my understanding of the world?"

"I thought catching you here would be the most efficient way to get your thoughts on the proposed border guard before I meet with Princess Iryasa later this evening," Sa Rangim says. "Under other circumstances I might table such a discussion for another time, but—"

"No, let's walk and talk," I agree. "What I've just learned may affect your people more directly, and you should have all available information when planning the Te Muraka's future. I need to stop by the market on my way home—will that do?"

"Beautifully," Sa Rangim says. "I will have more questions for you once we arrive there."

I look at him quizzically, but he gestures for me to go first.

So I do. I tell him what Tea Master Karekin has explained about a tea spirit's fundamental nature: her lifespan, her consumption of magic, all of it.

"Ah," Sa Rangim says. "This is why you're worrying about the Te Muraka. You don't know how much magic Yorani will need to eat, nor how much there is available, and whether there will still be enough for *us*."

"And yet you don't sound worried at all," I say with some confusion.

Sa Rangim laughs. "I may have a better understanding of how much magic there truly is in the world than you," he tells me. "I certainly know precisely how much it takes us to survive, even with *our* lifespans. But while I'm pleased your consideration jumped to us so naturally, I believe you may have missed the fundamental point your tea master attempted to convey."

"Did I? Because being aware of and managing my—in this case literally—outsized impact on the future seemed to be the core of his point."

"Then perhaps he missed it," Sa Rangim says. "You focus on what you can control, Miyara."

I scowl. I am too tired for more puzzles of this nature. "I don't know what I can control."

"You know some," Sa Rangim tells me. "You can't control the future, but you can gather the kindling you, or generations beyond you, may need to burn. You set in place what you can, and you trust in the future. You're not the only one working toward the future, and you're not the one who has to solve every problem—yes, even if you were involved in Yorani's creation. You set goals within your power to attain and focus *there*."

I mull that over. I may not be able to control how much magic will be available in the Te Muraka's futures—yet—but perhaps I can lay out processes for future generations to manage distribution.

I think perhaps Tea Master Karekin and Sa Rangim have related but different points, though. Really what I can control isn't what people—or spirits—will need from me when I'm gone: it's what they need from me now.

"Do you think Yorani needs another tea spirit to be her friend?" I blurt. "I don't want her to be lonely."

Sa Rangim's expression looks soft in the light as we approach the Gaellani market closest to my house. "I think she will be content to be unique, like you."

"But I need people," I say, and startle myself at the simple truth of the statement.

Fundamentally, connections are what I was missing back at the palace. A purpose, too, but since my life's work is in building bridges, the one necessitates the other.

"So does she," Sa Rangim says, "but they need not be scaled and fire-breathing. She may not ever be as close to another human as she is to you, but she communicates easily with Deniel's cat, does she not? I suspect she will always be partial to cats as her first friends. They see spirits too, you know."

I roll my eyes. "I've gathered. With all that pouncing, I knew the two of them were up to something."

"But then, so are you," Sa Rangim teases.

I smile back. "Well, I definitely don't control cats, so let's talk about something simpler, like multifaceted international politics."

To my surprise, Sa Rangim doesn't hesitate to outline what he and Iryasa will be discussing in front of the Gaellani hesitantly listening in. After a moment, I understand why: it's an effort at normalizing, and also of trust, one with minimal consequences since no official documents have been signed yet.

Our assessments largely match. As we move through the market, I point out some particular legal phrases for him to ask Iryasa about that she might be so familiar with she'd forget to explain their particular connotations, while Sa Rangim asks my opinion as an expert Istal taster on various foods we come across.

As he selects one delicate broth over a heartier bean sauce, I ask, "Is determining what is least offensive to an Istal palate your goal here?"

Sa Rangim eyes me. "You know who I'm cooking for."

"Yes, and I know *why*, which is why I'm asking."

"I want to be able to share myself with her," he says simply.

Which is sweet, but. "It's important that you not misrepresent who you are, too. You have to trust that you can share what you like and she'll still like you and want to fit with you even if you don't fit neatly or easily into her preconceptions."

Sa Rangim eyes me thoughtfully. "You have a suggestion."

I hand him the second starter sauce; close his hands around both bottles. "Let her choose what she likes and tell you her honest opinion. She doesn't get to, much."

Sa Rangim blinks at me, a deliberate movement as the color of his eyes flash with something deeper. He bows without a word.

<hr />

At home, Yorani is awake, though still lethargic. Talsion is carrying a string around her in circles, trying to tempt her into a game, but Yorani only rolls on her back and bats at it lazily. It's clear who she learned *that* from.

I wonder if future generations will curse me for not interfering with her befriending a cat in her impressionable years.

She appears well, though one thing I have learned is her health benefits from close contact with me. So I set her on my lap as Deniel and I eat, and try not to think about how she'll heal when close proximity with me is no longer an option. I'll have to hope by then she'll have grown enough to be able to recover fully without me. It's an odd contradiction, wishing to both be present and to make myself redundant.

Deniel continues working on council arrangements after dinner, and I lean against him with Yorani settled in my lap. My brain is too exhausted for any real work of my own now, so I content myself with answering his legal questions by rote and petting my baby dragon.

Eventually, Deniel says with amusement, "It might help if I could move my arm more freely."

I don't move. "Are you quite certain?"

"Content though I am, I would dare to risk a test."

I sigh in a long-suffering way and slide slowly down the side of his body until my head is resting in has lap and I'm looking up at him. "There. How's that?"

He shakes with laughter.

Talsion chooses that moment to pounce from the ground, startling Yorani into flight. Then a chase is on, and it's just Deniel and I left on the couch.

"I guess she's feeling better," Deniel says. "Being close to you really does help."

"I can get closer," I suggest, burrowing in a little further.

As he laughs, I dare bring one hand to his stomach, and begin to stroke upward.

Deniel's laugh stops abruptly, his breath hitching.

"Miyara," he says, and it's half-groan.

Perhaps I have a bit of energy after all.

I pull myself up, wrap my arms around his shoulders, and lock my gaze on his for a weighted moment.

I lean forward slowly, letting the anticipation build for both of us, and—

A knock on the door shatters the moment.

Deniel frowns. "Do you think—?"

"It can wait," I say firmly, palming his face, trying to bring back the focus we just had.

"She might not be home." Taseino's voice is quiet outside but nevertheless audible.

"Someone is home," Elowyn answers. "I can see light from the main room. I don't know about Miyara, but Deniel wouldn't leave the lights on if he were out."

"With everything that's happening, Miyara could be at another meeting elsewhere."

"I told you we should have asked Glynis. She could find her for sure," Karisa says, and then after a pause adds, "Or open the door so we could wait for her."

I bang my head against Deniel's shoulder. He laughs at me again, but helps shift me to sitting up.

"Come on. You don't want them to risk deciding you don't actually need to know something that badly, when all three of them thought whatever this is merited coming over."

He's probably right, but I also remember Karisa felt left out of seeing the house and wonder how much that has to do with the sudden visit.

I throw open the front door, but the mock-scowl I'd prepared for my sister dies swiftly once I take a look at them.

They're all holding together, but I'm a tea master, and I can't miss that they're also shaken.

Something happened.

"I applaud your timing," I say.

Karisa narrows her eyes reflexively. "Oh, are we interrupting?"

"Not compared to if you'd been a few minutes later," I say.

The distraction is immediately effective. Karisa's eyes sharpen with curiosity, Taseino winces and laughs ruefully, and to my delighted surprise Elowyn, rather than being embarrassed, smiles like the idea of her brother and I making out is the best thing she's heard all day.

The tension snapped, I usher them all inside and start the kettle while Deniel carries the dining chairs closer to the sofa and large chair, so we can sit together in a circle.

"You bake, don't you?" Karisa asks me.

"When did *that* come up?"

She shrugs. "I must have overheard it somewhere."

"You consummate eavesdropper," I say. "Another time. If you want homemade baked goods I need warning so I can host you properly."

She sighs. "I know. But if I wait for you to feel like you have time to host me properly I wouldn't get to see your house until next year."

I hope it won't be *that* long, but she does have a point. "So this is a plotted visit, then?"

"Only recently," Elowyn says, setting a bag on the middle table and beginning to unload small packages from inside. "Just long enough for us to pick up some snacks so Deniel wouldn't worry about not being able to feed me."

"I'd still be able to feed you," Deniel says, somewhere between amused and offended.

"But this way you don't wear yourself out more doing it from scratch."

Spirits, both our younger sisters have us pegged. I exchange a look with Deniel, wondering for an entirely different reason if I should ever have facilitated their getting along.

Taseino walks up to the kitchen counter at just the precise moment to dispose of the trash and then casually take the tea tray from my hands and carry it over himself. "It's a little bit worrying how quickly Elowyn was able to buy all that with my money and no one ever seeing her."

"Show-off," Karisa remarks. "Next time let me try, and I'll see if I can get *everyone's* attention at the same time."

"Okay, that's enough," I say, throwing up my hands. "Taseino, go sit down in the comfortable chair and let me serve the tea."

"I—"

I cast him a thoroughly unimpressed look. He shuts his mouth and passes me back the tray.

Karisa frowns after him, as if I'd needed confirmation that this part of their plot.

"Karisa, Elowyn, the couch," I instruct.

Elowyn moves off her careful perch on the dining chair without otherwise reacting, though Karisa rolls her eyes like I'm being tiresome in my insistence that they be comfortable.

Deniel sits in one of the dining chairs, and I follow suit. I exchange another glance with him; he lifts his eyebrows and gestures for me to take the lead, presumably since whatever they're up to clearly has something to do with me and is therefore my problem first. I manage not to roll my eyes.

"Now," I say, "who wants to tell me why you're preemptively making up to me?"

There's a moment of silence.

Then Elowyn and Taseino say in sync, "Told you."

Deniel casts me an amused look while Karisa crosses her arms.

"You're going to be mad," my sister warns me.

"You don't get to decide that for me," I tell her.

She lifts her chin. "I told Cherato you're one of us."

It takes me a moment to process what on earth she means by that, and then it hits me all at once.

She told him I was a princess.

What she just told *me* is that she still thinks of me as one.

I'm apparently silent a beat too long, because Taseino steps in. "She's leaving out the context."

"Because it doesn't change what I did," Karisa says matter-of-factly.

"It's still *relevant*," Taseino snaps. "If you're so desperate to prove your sister should hate you at least let it be for the right thing."

That shuts Karisa up.

Now I'm speechless for an entirely different reason.

Taseino audibly angry? And not just seeing Karisa for who she truly is, but managing her?

Exactly what foundation for the future did I lay here?!

"Karisa was working on drawing information out of the ambassador about Nakrabi tech, to see what she could get about what Velasar and Nakrab are actually working together on," Elowyn finally supplies.

Karisa says flatly, "I let the old man talk me into a corner where I had to give something, and that's what I chose."

"She had to give him something or none of us were getting out of there without... considerable difficulty," Taseino says.

"All of you stop," I say. "Karisa, if you're waiting for me to get mad and hold this against you, I won't. You improvised and got the job done and kept yourself safe. That's all that ever matters."

Karisa shook her head sharply, her shoulders hunching. "*Taseino* got us out of there safely, too. Not me."

"Which means the team is working as *intended*," I tell her. "That's the point of a team: so you don't have to do everything alone. And before you even start, it's not because you're not capable, it's because *no one* can do everything alone. If that were a lesson I'd learned better I wouldn't have had to rely on the accidental grace of my friends being in the Cataclysm yesterday to prevent a magical disaster. You know how many people have berated me for that oversight?"

Karisa looks at me mutely.

"Zero," I say. "You want to guess how many people have rightly yelled at me for not relying on them sufficiently?"

Deniel coughs.

Karisa almost smiles. "Is it all of them?"

I sigh. "Very nearly. Do you think you could manage to make different mistakes than me? I really do have this one solidly locked down."

"I'm sure I can come up with something," Karisa says. "You'll be very impressed."

I shoot her the look that deserves, since making an adverse impression on people is a well-worn skill in her arsenal, and she finally laughs.

"So now who's going to tell me what it means that you were trapped and in danger of not being able to make it out?" I ask.

"None of us," Elowyn says softly.

I stare at her.

Taseino says, "This isn't your job for a reason, Miyara. And we're a team for a reason. We handled it. You don't need to worry any more than you're already going to."

"You don't think wondering about the specifics isn't going to make me worry?" I ask. "And don't you dare say 'not as much as knowing them'."

Elowyn speaks up again. "What do you think you'll notice that we collectively wouldn't?"

I swear, standing abruptly from my chair so I can pace into the kitchen and back.

She's right, drat everything. Alone I might notice something one of them would miss, but all together? No. They've been proving for days that collectively they can stay a step ahead of me. They may be shaken now, but they're together enough to still be analyzing and plotting as a team.

I hate not knowing, especially when I can't not feel responsible for putting them in harm's way. But I also can't smother their freedom without shifting into what Saiyana tried to become for me: an oppressive force under the guise of support I learned not to trust.

How does anyone ever judge when to hold the ones in their care tight, and when to let them fly?

I drop back down into the chair again and glare around at them, Elowyn last.

"If I ever hear you doubt again whether you have the ability to become a tea master, I may throttle you," I growl at her.

Elowyn ducks her head shyly, smiling.

"And you would all tell me," I press, "if there were something I needed to know or could help with."

Emphatic nods all around.

Taseino adds, "And we do also know that you can help with more than most people expect, and that you can do a lot with a little information, which is why we're working on this in the first place. We're okay, Miyara."

Deniel reaches out and grasps my hand. "Okay?" he asks.

I take a breath. "I am tentatively willing to be mollified by hearing what was worth such a near miss," I say with poor grace.

Karisa smirks. "I got the tech is what."

I raise my eyebrows. "Nakrabi tech for us to experiment on?"

"Glynis took charge of it; she's going to show Tamak first so he can make a duplicate, then Lorwyn, since Saiyana, Ostario, and Sa Rangim were apparently busy," Karisa explains. "Do you know how she always knows? It's like magic."

I blink. Maybe the abilities that make Glynis an astounding messenger are related to why she grasps principles of magecraft and witchcraft so easily.

"Maybe it is," I say, filing that thought away for a time when my brain has borne fewer assaults. "You compared notes with her on what you've observed, I assume?"

To my surprise, Karisa reports all her findings and conclusions methodically, with only occasional interjections from Taseino or Elowyn and with an organized discipline I hadn't known to expect from her.

Some we knew, or had surmised: Nakrabi are dismissive of magecraft because its structures are observable, and they value illusion and deception, because it's important to appear to have access to more power than they do.

What limits that access is not yet clear, but what is evident is that their tech requires a steady stream of magic they exhaust faster than they can replenish. After Karisa saw Cherato activate magic in correlation with one of the ambassador's attendants slumping into exhaustion, she echoes my fear that Nakrab makes some citizens effectively an underclass to be harvested from for magic, with others like Cherato above them and given their magic to use for their tech.

We don't know enough about what this means for them on a societal level or a magical one. I don't understand how Nakrab's harvesting of magic differs from continental forms, but I can't ignore the dead spots that appeared around the barrier before the first breach or the vast swaths of similar areas Ari told us about in Taresan.

It's not so surprising Ambassador Perjoun is willing to treat with us, but perhaps I need to message Ari for a professional opinion on the tech sooner than later.

"We—Glynis and I—think Nakrabi magic works by infusing objects with magic," Karisa is saying, and somehow I manage to not compulsively touch the bracelets Thiano made for me. "So it's similar to witchcraft but not the same, right? Because like Thiano told you, a witch can change the nature of an object to have a magical purpose, but not to actually hold magic. Whereas Nakrabi magic makes things into objects of power."

She must have talked with Glynis more than I realized, to have this casual depth of understanding of witchcraft.

"It seems obvious at this point that Nakrab is harvesting the magic of the barrier to use to power its tech," Karisa concludes, as if this isn't a revelatory accusation that would send corps of diplomats into apoplexy. "I haven't figured out why they think it won't be a problem though. Whatever else Cherato is, he isn't stupid, and he doesn't seem even remotely worried. That bothers me."

"Either there's something he doesn't understand, or there's something we don't," I agree.

"Probably both," we say together.

And now we're back to my role in this business.

"I think it's time to bring Ari in after all," I muse. "Ostario can communicate with them remotely."

"Isn't Ostario a little busy halting the expansion?" Karisa asks, a note in her voice I recognize and ignore, since she's clearly trying *not* to feel slighted.

"All the more reason to get them here directly. Ari's the only other mage who's already an expert on those dead spots around the barrier. They'll be able to take some of the burden off Ostario and Saiyana."

Deniel's hand tightens on mine, and I look at him.

His expression is pointed, and he nods.

I take a breath. "Everything else can wait. Eat, and I'll make a new pot of tea."

Somehow making tea morphs into my giving Karisa and Taseino a tour of the house, where to my surprise Karisa isn't shy about asking practical questions about what it's like to live here. I wonder how much of this is for Taseino's benefit, to hear his dry reactions to particular juxtapositions she reveals about our way of life in the palace.

We carry a once-again drowsy Yorani and nap-ready Talsion back downstairs to settle in. I look around at all of us—me and Deniel, our sisters and apprentices, the creatures in our care—and am struck by how surreal this moment is for me. For who I've become, and where I'm going.

"What is it?" Deniel murmurs to me.

This isn't a subject we've talked about, and it's awkward to broach it now but would be perhaps a worse idea, given all the underlying expectation I sense in the room, to lie.

This particular group of people is perhaps the only one that I think would always be able to tell a lie from me. I don't think that's what it means to be family in general, but given how I'm capable of manipulating people as a tea master, perhaps it's part of what it means to be mine.

"I'm wondering what it would be like for us to have children," I say, waving a hand to encompass the room. "A house with children. Us as parents. It's like a strange glimpse into a possible future."

Deniel smiles crookedly. "Miyara, do I need to break it to you that that's already becoming our present, at least in a figurative sense?"

Karisa answers before I can. "She's worried about what kind of mother she's going to be, given our background."

"Thank you, your Highness," Deniel says, rolling his eyes. "Having met Miyara before, it certainly would never have occurred to me that she would have doubts about her own abilities that are patently obvious to anyone who chooses to look."

Karisa blushes in surprise at this takedown, and she looks between Deniel and me in sudden understanding.

I sigh. "Why is your ability to peg me like that without hesitation what convinces my sisters our relationship has substance?"

"I'm not sure you actually want me to answer that," Deniel says, amused.

I close my eyes. "Surely this is a perfectly normal thing to have concerns about."

"Miyara," Elowyn says tentatively, "if you and my brother decide to have children, you're going to be a wonderful mother. I don't know if it helps to hear from someone else, but I think all of us can agree on that?"

Emphatic nods again from all around, which is sweet and obscurely embarrassing in a way I can't quite pinpoint.

"Will I?" I ask. "I certainly can't model balance. I keep trying to solve problems for people instead of—"

Taseino cuts in, "You listen and learn and change and act. What else do you think you need?"

Deniel leans back, pulling me with him in a hug. "There, you see, next time you're worried about something, we'll just call all the teens you know. They have all the answers."

This teasing chastisement causes all available teens to find simultaneous interest in drinking tea and snacking, and the near uniform response surprises them and makes me laugh.

"I will remember this tactic and turn it against you," I tell Deniel.

He kisses my cheek. "I have met you," he murmurs.

I smile at him fondly, but this close I can't miss the weary lines on his face.

I sit up. "As educational as this has been, I think it's time we all get to bed. Do all of you have a plan for getting home?"

"Yes," Taseino answers me, beginning to tidy up, but I wave him off. "We'll take care of that," I say. "Thank you for thinking ahead."

He ducks his head, hearing the underlying meaning in my words without my having to embarrass him acutely with praise and gratitude.

Elowyn and Taseino get up readily, but Karisa lingers.

I raise my eyebrows at her.

She purses her lips, looking speculatively from me and Deniel, to where her compatriots are still listening. Finally she asks, "It's the norm outside the nobility to try out sex before formalizing anything, right, so you know if you're compatible?"

"That is my understanding," I say slowly. "Though I'm sure you're aware plenty of nobles have tried the same with varying levels of success and discretion."

"Right, obviously. But why did you and Deniel decide to move in together without that? Forget worrying about motherhood, what if you're not compatible in that way?"

Taseino and Elowyn are frozen, and I'm not much better.

"I have so many questions for you right now," I finally manage.

Deniel clasps my shoulder. "I have an answer. It's that we already know we're attracted to each other, and the rest we can learn together. Norms aren't requirements, and this is what works for us."

Karisa considers that, and then gets up decisively. "Okay."

"Okay?" I echo.

She grins at me. "Good night, sister."

And more suddenly than they arrived, the teens are gone.

I sink back against Deniel. "I am extremely confused about what just happened."

He snickers. "I am possibly more used to being surprised by a sister than you are."

That's... fair. I've always known my sisters so well—or at least what to expect from them—that they couldn't surprise me easily. Oddly, removing myself from the family legally has changed all that; deepened our connections in a way I never could have imagined.

But Deniel removed himself physically from his family longer ago, and perhaps that had a similar effect on his relationship with Elowyn, who is always a surprise.

"I am not even a little bit equipped to talk to any of my sisters about navigating societal expectations of sexual engagement," I say. "Where did that even come from?"

"It came from her trusting you not to lie to her about what matters," Deniel says. "If you model anything, Miyara, it's certainly that."

I sigh. "That's something. Though it's also certainly something that I of all people am trying to teach all my sisters about boundaries and balance in work and life when I have yet to figure it out."

Deniel rests his chin on my shoulder from behind. "I think the secret is there's no such thing as perfect balance," he says. "Too much overlaps, doesn't it? You're doing what you can to make a world that anyone, whether it's children or dragons on your sisters, can be safe in. How can it not overlap when your work is part of who you are?"

I pull out of his embrace so I can turn to look at him. "If you put it like that, how can I ever expect to set reasonable boundaries?"

"Goals," Deniel says promptly.

I stare. "Now *you* have all the pat answers. Did the teens rub off on you?"

He laughs. "Maybe. But this one is from being an artist—and also still trying to do other things with my life, but mainly art. I can't control what someone will think of my work, can I? There are things I can do to help sell pieces, but some of it always depends on other people.

"So a successful work day for me isn't whether I've sold a piece; it's whether I've done *my* work. Whether I showed up and put in time. Whether I did my best crafting a piece of pottery. Whether I presented it to customers as well as I could have. That's what I can control, so those are the results I focus on. There's enough art to tea mastery that I think there must be some overlap there."

It's a curious echo of my conversation with Sa Rangim, and I look over to meet Yorani's drowsily watchful gaze.

Part of tea mastery is shaping perceptions, but ultimately I don't control them. I can't control what people—or scaly spirits—will do, now or in the future.

But I can control what I do.

I can do my best as myself, and by extension for them.

Maybe that will be my legacy.

CHAPTER 22

I DON'T KNOW WHAT Nakrab will do with the information that I was once a princess, but Cherato is experienced enough that he will try to use that secret against me: even if it is only by holding the knowledge that he can over my head. Until he tips his hand and I know how he means to play it, I need to be cautious.

"It might be best if I find you a dragon-sitter for today," I tell Yorani.

Yorani flicks her tail into my face.

"I'm not saying you couldn't deal with it, but it's only been a day since you ate enough magic to make you sick. You shouldn't be in the way of a surprise like that again so soon."

Yorani sits back on her haunches, head tilted to once side as she considers that.

She's mimicking my gestures again. Spirits.

With no further attempt to communicate, Yorani flies to the door and lets herself out.

I run after her, staring as she rises into the sky. When did she get to be such a good flier? Probably all the games she plays with Talsion.

Ultimately, I don't call her back. I told her my concerns, and she's abiding by them. I have to trust she knows what she's doing.

It's one burden off my shoulders, that I won't have to watch out for her in the coming meeting. But I've grown used to having her at my back.

Now I go back into negotiations alone, because no one else can do all the things I'm attempting.

Figure out how to restore the barrier. Somehow.

Prevent future interference by establishing systems and holding relevant parties accountable.

And sort out my sisters' lives—and my own.

All at the same time, all of which has somehow become my job.

I've demonstrated my resolve, but that's not the only part of being a tea master.

It's time to show the ambassadors, and my sisters, another side.

Ambassador Ridac flops down in his chair. "Well, what useless point did we leave off with, then?"

"Clearly not one worth continuing to discuss, if it has figured so little in your memory," I answer. "Perhaps we can approach today's negotiations in a different way, if the ambassadors will indulge me."

I say this with a smile directed at Cherato, who smiles close-lipped at me in return.

Oh, he's excited to play this game with me.

Good.

"Ambassador Cherato, Ambassador Ridac had the unique privilege of witnessing some of your technology in action," I say.

"Not mine," he demurs.

Really, this? I manage not to roll my eyes and match his level of subtlety to head this off. "Oh, I didn't think you made it, but I was under the impression as a representative of Nakrab you had the ability to understand how it works."

"What a vulgarly blatant sally, tea master," Cherato says. "One wonders about your education. Of course I understand, but as a representative of Nakrab it is not my duty to explain it to you."

"Ah, you're aware my tea master training has been somewhat unconventional? Excellent, that will save us time. One of the joys has been learning the history of the discipline, and how it overlaps with the development of other magical practices." This gets the attention of everyone at the table, but I brush past it. "But since you are so certain your tech, created with your magic, can't possibly be damaging to the Cataclysm, I wonder if there is some critical difference between continental and island magic after all, and if it might be something we could apply to our current difficulty."

"I'm afraid that's not possible," Cherato says.

"How can you be certain?" I ask, knowing full well that's not what he meant.

He smiles. "You misunderstand me."

I smile too. "I don't think I do."

We keep smiling at each other in silence for a full minute while the rest of the room waits, still and silent and crackling with tension.

When it's clear he sees no reason to elaborate or counter me, I continue, "We are here in part to better understand a unique magical occurrence that affects all of our lives. Surely we might all benefit from an exchange of magical understandings."

"The Isle of Nakrab understands all it needs to of your magic," Cherato says. "And Nakrab has noted that you are unwilling to accept our assurances on this matter."

"If you were unaware you were damaging the barrier of the Cataclysm as you claim, then that cannot be so," I say gently.

Cherato's face tightens minutely.

Finally, *finally*, I have landed a hit.

"Let me rephrase," Cherato says. "Nakrab cannot benefit from such an exchange."

"The continent has plenty to offer in an exchange," Ridac rumbles idly, though his eyes are sharp on the Nakrabi ambassador.

"Not that we can use," Cherato says, and something about the way he says it—the lack of ego for once—catches *my* attention.

"Can exchange with the continent damage *your* magic?" I ask. "I would not have thought so, given your ease around magecraft."

"Certainly not," Cherato says. "Your magic cannot touch ours."

This is not actually an argument against what I'd said, and perhaps Cherato realizes I've noticed he answered regarding magic when I didn't specify it because for once he continues.

"Nakrab works as one," he explains. "Strength of common purpose is at the core of our power. With the quantity of long, sustained focus our magic requires, your efforts cannot hope to match it."

This, it turns out, is better than an answer, because now I do understand after all: the exchange that threatens them is of ideas.

It's not an accident that only a limited number of Nakrabi ever visit the continent, and that ships from the continent are never allowed past the port. We knew that, but we never knew why. It's not our magic that's the concern: it's the disruption of different ideas in a system that requires common purpose. Apparently literally, for the sake of the tech at the base of their entire society's infrastructure.

But that begs the question why they risk contact with us at all. To prove they can, perhaps.

No; there's something else.

"You are not at risk from us, then," I say. "I'm relieved to hear it. But I'm afraid I don't understand how you can be certain we are not at risk from you."

Cherato's eyes darken as he gazes at me. Of course, we *are* at risk, and he knows this too.

"Are you not confident in the protections of this place?" he asks, gesturing around. "Are you not confident in your guarantee that you can keep us all safe from each other? Is this the limit of the service you promise?"

Well, this is a trap. Not an unexpected turnabout, given what information I've just extracted from him.

"I trust my people," I say, which is *an* answer, if not an ideal one to this particular question.

"But not me," Ambassador Cherato says, his eyes glinting in a way I don't like. "With such protections in place, I would be delighted to show you a demonstration of Nakrabi technology, like I showed the ambassador from Velasar."

Panic stabs me, a violent gut reaction of *no*.

"I think not," I say evenly.

"I disagree," Ambassador Perjoun pipes up. "I seem to be the only one who has not yet been privy to a demonstration. I'm sure the mages from Istalam would appreciate such an opportunity in controlled conditions away from the barrier as well."

"Indeed, how can you object, tea master?" Ambassador Cherato asks. "Is this not what you wanted?"

Given how eager he is, definitely not.

"First answer me this," I say. "When you deploy your technology, what happens to our spirits?"

"The technology I would show you would not act on your bodies at all," Cherato answers easily.

And then pauses as he senses the sudden but unmistakable shift in tension in the room.

He frowns, realizing he's misstepped in some fashion but not understanding how. "Your tea spirit is not here today either."

I have taken Thiano's understanding of our people for granted. Despite his brilliance and experience as a political operator in Islatam, Ambassador Cherato does not share it.

"You misunderstand me," I say this time. "I assume, as you are an ambassador for your people, it is not a problem for me to give you information about us?"

His eyes flicker with annoyance. "Of course not."

"I am speaking of the spirits we cannot see but that are nevertheless always around us," I say.

"Yes, I'm aware of your quaint notions—"

"As a tea master who has created a corporeal spirit, I assure you unique spirits abound, in this place especially."

There's a pause while Cherato considers that, and the reactions of the others in the room: they may be surprised, but no one laughs or treats my claim with any kind of skepticism, as he clearly expects us to.

"Perhaps it is you who should give a demonstration," he says, amused. "This sounds like the fanciful story a sheltered child would believe."

I withhold a sigh at his new favorite tactic. He's just going to keep on with the princess digs, then, and I'm going to keep ignoring them.

"Spirits on the continent cannot be hurt by our magic," I say. "This is part of tea master lore. But I wonder how that works with your magic, ambassador."

"Our understanding of the world is somewhat more, hmm, evolved, than yours," he says, gauging the room.

I'm not surprised Perjoun is keeping quiet; she prefers to gather information before acting. I *am* surprised Ridac is letting me run things, but by the purple tinge in his skin I think he may recognize he's too furious by this turn to act carefully.

My sisters are all eerily still and silent. It's possible they're attempting to present a united front in support of me, but I admit to wondering if Saiyana has deployed a spell to keep them from interfering. Either way, I'm grateful.

Their watchfulness doesn't deter Cherato; if anything he grows bolder. "It's a very... primitive? Let us say *animistic* way of looking at things. In Nakrab, we know magic to be a force flowing through the world. But our different perspectives on this point don't change reality, do they? I wonder, if you do in fact wish to bring us together in common purpose as you claim, why you will not cease emphasizing our differences. Why you *assume* and imply Nakrab's magic must be dangerous when yours is not. Do we not all use the same magic, tea master? Are we not all people of this world?"

Oh, he is good.

But he is not good enough.

And to my surprise, I think it may be related to a fundamental misunderstanding after all.

"Because I watched Nakrabi technology latch onto the barrier of the Cataclysm just before it breached," I say.

"Correlation does not equal causation," Cherato says. "This is another truth we in Nakrab understand—"

"And I repaired the barrier with spirits," I interrupt him, and his eyes narrow. I'm not certain if he knew that, or knew what we believed about it. "So you can see why I might be interested in honing in on exactly what that correlation signifies. That you do not consider spirits at all does not reassure me that you can in fact be sure how they are affected by your technology, ambassador."

"Then let me show you," he says. "You challenge my understanding but allow me no way to prove my case."

"You've offered no assurances I can take except on faith, which you disdain to give me reason to extend," I say.

"Nakrab does not dance for your whims, tea master."

"Will you consider answering one question?" I ask.

He pauses, noting my phrasing. "I will consider. Ask."

"Please forgive my *primitive* understanding of your expertise," I begin.

"Always," he murmurs.

His ego is truly a thig to behold.

"I understand your technology functions by infusing objects with magic," I say, and by his utter stillness know I've surprised him: he didn't think we'd worked this out. "So hypothetically, if you turned out to be wrong, and the magic powering your tech turned out to be spirits. Are you confident you could release our spirits?"

I am watching intently enough to catch it: the flicker of confusion before his amused disdain settles on his face.

"I have indulged your fanciful notions, but I do not abide by them," the ambassador says. "If we are to negotiate based on imaginary creatures, this summit is a greater waste of time than you had led me to believe. You refuse Nakrab's generous offer for a private demonstration of our magical capabilities, then?"

"Without representatives of all magical expertise on the continent present, it would be a waste of an extraordinary opportunity," I say smoothly. "I would be honored by such a demonstration with Te Muraka and witchcraft practitioners present, if you would consider—"

"I would not," Cherato says with finality.

I'm not sorry. My suspicions that Nakrab may be involved in driving anti-witch sentiment for their own ends grow. "Then let's adjourn—"

"Quite," Cherato says. "Let's leave the princesses to collude some more. Do you think we don't notice how they let you speak for them?"

Is this it, then?

"I am explicitly their representative," I say. "Or are you accusing me of something else?"

He smiles, letting the moment hang.

"Bias," he says. "The same thing as before."

Not now, then, just a reminder for me. Letting me know he doesn't believe my façade of not caring if he knows. He has no doubt that I'm aware he knows I was a princess.

If the only leverage he leaves this meeting with is what he thinks he walked in with, I'll consider this conversation a success.

"Very well, your fellow ambassadors have noted your concern," I say, looking to both. "Have you not?"

"We have," Perjoun says, "and I for one do not consent to be made into a bargaining chip in your personal or political frustrations."

She sweeps out without another word, following Ridac, who's blatantly ignored us both.

Bless them. It's the best response I could have hoped for. Because if they're not obviously on my side, Cherato may still expend diplomatic capital with them.

But if they realize what I've realized, they *must* be or become on my, and Istalam's, side.

I have been worrying about what the Isle of Nakrab was doing on purpose. Never did I think they might be attacking our spirits on accident—or willful ignorance.

That doesn't change the fact that they don't care what happens to our spirits, and that their actions within the Cataclysm nevertheless constitute an attack even if they don't consider it one.

They bind their magic to objects and never release it. What must that do to their island?

Magecraft lasts only as long as structures do. Witchcraft is limited by an individual witch's power. But magical workings of the enormity the ambassador implied, given the extreme concentration—with that much magic, if there's no way to release it—

It explains the dead patches of land, an occurrence we have no records of prior to the Cataclysm.

Nakrab's obsession with who has power, and who appears to have it, and how much, makes a great deal more sense. Their unwillingness to give up access to the continent despite their clear disdain, even more so.

Thiano was right. I can't predict what Nakrab will do, because they're desperate.

If I'm right, they're killing their own island.

And now they've come for us.

CHAPTER 23

AS SOON AS THE room clears, Iryasa stands and begins to pace. "Miyara, you are going to make Cherato do something rash."

"Yes, I'm going to push him into a mistake, and then I'm going to trap him with it," I return evenly. "Don't pretend this isn't a tactic you've employed to great effect."

"Not when there was this much at stake!"

Saiyana cuts in, "Which is exactly why we need to hurry things along. Your spy has been waiting in the back, Miyara—can I tell him he can come in?"

I blink, my mind racing. "You mean Entero, I assume."

Saiyana's gaze whips to me, eyes narrowing. "Obviously."

Spirits. That was a mistake.

"I didn't realize you two had a way to communicate remotely," I attempt to redirect.

It doesn't work: her gaze changes not at all, though she says, "We don't. Ostario has a method worked out with his apprentice, who is also in the back."

"We need to talk about this," Iryasa insists.

"As you like, but Entero wouldn't be waiting if there weren't some urgency," I say. "I'm not keeping parts of our strategy secret from him in any case."

"I will decide who hears my thoughts," Iryasa says firmly.

I incline my head. "As you like," I say again. "Nevertheless, your opinions of my tactical failings, while important, are likely less time sensitive. So if you please, let us take this first."

"You fall back on formality when you're uncomfortable," Iryasa tells me.

"I'm aware," I say. "It gives me no pleasure to be at odds with you."

Saiyana cuts in again. "That is Miyara's way of saying she is not going to poke back at you despite that provocation. Can we move on?"

"I can hear as well as you can, Saiyana, and I do not please. But yes, by all means, ignore me."

Oh dear.

I carefully do not exchange looks with any of my sisters as Saiyana opens the door for Entero.

"Finally," Entero says without preamble. "We don't have much time; you need to listen."

I don't see how Iryasa reacts; I only sense the mood in the room ratchet up in tension higher than before.

Entero's no fool, and he bows to Iryasa immediately. "Please forgive my lack of etiquette, your Highness; we haven't the time."

"I understand, there never is time for the crown princess' opinion on anything," Iryasa says. "Please, do continue."

Perhaps my mental blessing on Saiyana for keeping Iryasa quiet was ill-placed.

Entero bows once more but takes her at her word, which is how I know it's serious.

"Something is blocking Ostario from communicating with Ari directly," Entero tells me. "He can't break through it without alerting whoever's responsible."

My eyebrows shoot up. "And indirectly?"

"Too dangerous to attempt," Saiyana interrupts, frowning. "Anyone who knows enough to target Ari and can block Ostario may have laid traps for indirect methods. Ostario could reach another mage with a message only for Ari to be attacked, or subverted."

"Why is this time critical?" Iryasa asks.

"Because Ari is the only other mage expert on dealing with the barrier, and we were summoning them as backup because Ostario and I are going to burn out," Saiyana says matter-of-factly.

"Also because our communications network is now forced to adjust," Entero says. "We've been relying on Glynis. I sent her to smuggle Ari out."

My eyes widen, and I exchange a quick glance with Saiyana. "He's landed on the best way immediately," I say. "Everyone knows she's been working as your messenger. She'll have access. And—"

"And she's clever enough to figure out whatever needs to be figured out, magically or otherwise, even if she's never been to Miteran, yes, I know," Saiyana says, passing a weary hand in front of her eyes. "I'll figure out a magical alert system. I assume our need to factor this change into our plans affects whatever else you're here about?"

None of my sisters are stupid. Entero nods and continues, "I have information for you on Velasar's situation you'll need before he approaches you. My sources indicate it will be soon."

I glance at Iryasa. "You're up."

Iryasa closes her eyes and opens them again. "I'm ready."

I take a breath, relieved she's willing to work with me for a little longer without addressing this. I keep looking at her, so Entero will know to wait for her signal to begin rather than mine.

I am running this operation, but this will directly impact her. And any deference toward her authority right at this moment will help smooth matters between us later.

Entero's report is at once troubling and less surprising than it should be.

"Ostario suspects what's blocking him from reaching Ari is magecraft, which likely means the faction of magecraft supremacists is involved. We're working with Aleixo—"

"Who?" Iryasa interrupts.

"A Velasari operative Miyara convinced to cooperate with us," Entero says. Iryasa's face tightens, but he continues, "The faction is operated by Velasar but does include Istals. But the fact that it feels like magecraft to Ostario may not be definitive given Nakrab's contempt for that form of magic."

"They may have crafted an illusion together," I murmur. Velasar and Nakrab with Istal sympathizers. We're not just working against external forces here: we have to root out the bigotry in our own home, too. In ourselves.

"We can't rule it out," Entero agrees. "We have determined that Nakrab is funding the faction, but Velasar is more invested in the Cataclysm operations than we'd previously thought."

Saiyana interrupts with a quick explanation for Iryasa. "The assumption being Velasar was willing to do Nakrab's dirty work deploying their tech in the Cataclysm in exchange for the island tech they've always been angling for—seafaring and so on. You know. What they want to give them leverage on Istalam to overthrow us."

"Which isn't wrong," Entero says, "but they're more interested than we'd thought in studying the tech and its applications themselves, given how reticent Nakrab has been to share. Apparently the idea is that if Velasar can leverage the tech for magecraft, they can demonstrate their fundamental superiority and not only be rid of witches—and now the Te Muraka too—for good, but also use that advantage to overthrow the Istal government."

"And the cost to the continent?" I ask.

"As far as I can tell they don't consider it a problem," Entero says. "The faction is focused narrowly on short-term goals; if they recognize the potential for catastrophe at all, they're deferring responsibility for dealing with it to future generations."

"Meanwhile," Iryasa says, "Nakrab doesn't care about the cost to the continent at all."

"Though they probably do understand what it means, at least in one sense," Saiyana says. "I bet they're also fully aware of Velasar's intentions."

"Velasar is the perfect partner for Nakrab," I agree. "The Nakrabi don't think there's any chance Velasar will actually be able to use their tech, but destabilizing Istalam will make it easier for them to access the Cataclysm. So they can fund the supremacist faction without fear of repercussions." I look at Entero. "We keep equating this faction with Velasar—are they dominant there, or is this shorthand forming inaccurate framing habits?"

"In terms of political power, they're fairly dominant, though the active agents are operating in the shadows rather than with popular support," Entero says. "Wanting to overthrow Istalam is pretty standard, as is fearmongering against witches, but allying with Nakrab to gain an advantage doesn't match the common rhetoric. Velasar can't be seen to need help or outside intervention."

They really are the perfect partner for Nakrab.

But I think of the arcanists and their separation, and I wonder if perhaps that's the flaw that will allow me to bring them down.

"Is Ambassador Ridac with the faction?" I ask.

"In theory," Entero says. "In spirit, I can't say."

"Good," Iryasa says. "Then he can be moved."

Because if his position isn't known, deviating from it won't cause him embarrassment. "Ridac is a loyal hardliner, but he isn't stupid," I agree. "If we put pressure on that—"

"I don't need you to spell my work out for me, Miyara," Iryasa says.

Right, still not happy with me. I turn back to Entero. "Is there more?"

"That's the overview," Entero says. "The details can wait. But there's some indication your pressure may already be changing the wind in his camp. He's gotten very careful to appear uncareful, which means he'll likely use a distraction to make a move soon. Expect him to spring a meeting on you any time now."

Which explains Entero's rush to get me this before we go back into negotiations. "That's far more concrete information than you were able to get on your own during the tournament," I note. "Your relationships in the city are bearing fruit?"

Entero's face doesn't twitch. "Not in the way you mean. My police contacts have not been as useful as I'd hoped, and I'm reevaluating my approach with them. But between the groundwork I laid during the tournament, Aleixo's knowledge, and Lady Kireva's assistance—"

"What kind?" I ask sharply.

"Resources and practical experience," he says. "Most of my life has been spent executing missions, not coordinating intelligence. She's training me, as we specified. Yes, I'm watching her, and yes, I have measures in place to handle her interference. Anything else?"

I wince. "Sorry."

"So you take criticism from some people," Iryasa remarks. The implied, Just not me, your eldest sister the crown princess goes unsaid.

I take a breath. "Entero, would you step outside please?"

"He can stay," Iryasa says. "It's fine for him to overhear everything, isn't it?"

"I choose not to, your Highness," Entero says, and is so fast out the door Iryasa doesn't have a change to respond.

Iryasa and I watch each other for a minute.

"Would you like some tea?" I finally ask.

"Thank you. No." She doesn't look away.

Here we go.

"One of the benefits of being a tea master is I am free to weigh all criticism with the weight I determine it deserves rather than skewing it depending on the provider," I say. "I don't have to favor those with greater political power over anyone else. You came here explicitly so I could run things my way. I am not going to apologize for doing so."

Reyata speaks for the first time. (Karisa, I notice, stays silent and subtly watchful, observing how I handle our sisters.) "Consider that part of the reason she chose you is due to your assumed understanding of how to deal with royalty."

"Consider that I have," I reply. "Excessive deference is no more useful to any of you than excessive obedience."

"Excessive deference?" Reyata repeats.

By which she means: I haven't shown any.

"I am your sister by birth but not by law," I say. "I am a tea master. None of you outranks me. Which means I am in the unique position of being able to be a friend or coworker to you."

"You don't outrank us either," Reyata points out, and I notice now it's Saiyana who's being quiet, not trying to help and just letting me work.

By my count that's two sisters currently on my side and two against. Spirits, that shifted fast.

"But I am leading this project," I say, looking Iryasa in the eye. "I told you I would be doing this my way. I told you I would not clear every decision by you."

"You are not making us aware of any decisions," Reyata says.

Iryasa puts a hand on her arm to stop her from going further, but I reply anyway.

"We literally just listened to an intelligence report together," I say. "But I do have information you don't, and that you don't need, which is informing my decisions. Whereas I am not, for instance, pressing any of you for details on Iryasa's security, or the magical solutions to containing the barrier, or the coming border guard, because while that all ultimately affects me, the details are under your charge and I trust you to see to them. Managing the summit is my work."

"That is true," Iryasa says, her voice deceptively mild. "But part of the reason I came to you, Miyara, was to be involved. Not just silent behind the scenes."

I nod. "You're right, you should play a more active part in the actual negotiation meetings. Why don't we all actually take our break now, and then we can meet early tomorrow to plan how best we can work together in sessions tomorrow?"

"Am I expected to sit silently for the rest of the morning, then?" Iryasa asks.

"No, as I trust you to not thwart me outwardly even if you don't know all my reasons," I say, which is not entirely true but perhaps speaking it will make it so.

"Or if I don't agree with them," Iryasa says.

"Just so. By which I don't mean I expect you not to disagree with me in public—"

"But to endeavor not to subvert the core of your strategy at the same time. That will do for today, and we will coordinate our strategy for tomorrow, yes?"

Thank the spirits. "Yes, I think that will be best."

Just when I think I can take a breath, the front door opens.

"I do hope I'm interrupting," Ambassador Ridac says.

Thank the spirits for Entero.

"Ambassador, what a pleasant surprise," Iryasa says, going straight to work. "I was just thinking I can't recall of a time in all your visits to Istalam when we've had a chance to connect privately. Perhaps now might be the time to address that missed opportunity."

He closes the door and locks it behind him. "I'd be happy to entertain the possibility, your Highness, if for no other reason than the number of people whose heads would explode," Ridac says. "But right now, I need to have a word with the tea master."

I am torn between triumph that he's chosen to seek me out and despair, because after the conversation I just had this is possibly the worst thing he could have said.

As all of us are frozen in existential social horror, Ridac clarifies firmly, "Alone."

I stand corrected: this is the actual worst.

"Tea Master Miyara is here at the request of Istalam," Iryasa says.

"She may be working for you, but she doesn't answer to you, and if you think there aren't things she's keeping from you you're deluding yourself, your Highness," Ridac says congenially. "She wouldn't be doing her job otherwise. So if I may cut in?"

I have to stop this before Iryasa can either dig in too far or feel like the ambassador has outmaneuvered her. Because unfortunately, if Velasar is willing to deal with me, I can't afford not to take the opportunity. Iryasa will understand that, even if she doesn't like it.

Making sure the interrogative inflection is clear, I ask, "Your Highness, it would be remiss of me not to offer the ambassador tea—but although you have already graciously scheduled me for tomorrow morning, perhaps we might move my initial report to this afternoon?"

Let the implications all go unsaid: that we are as she suggested working together, that she is a priority for me to report to, and that I will likely share my findings with her promptly.

Iryasa's expression is placid like flint. "Let us see how the afternoon progresses, tea master," she says, then turns and walks out the back. Reyata's face is carefully neutral as she follows her.

Everything I thought I had a handle on is spiraling. In the space of one morning all my foundations are coming apart, and it occurs to me that this is it. I am going to have to hold them together by force of will.

All of a sudden, between one meeting and another, the final stretch is upon me.

I bow to my remaining sisters, silently thanking them for remaining rather than leaving me with an obviously shaky foundation as Ridac watches. "With my apologies, princesses, I will take my leave now. Ambassador, let's adjourn to the tea ceremony room."

He inclines his head and follows me. "I don't have time for a proper ceremony, but I'll take the additional wall."

I smile as I slide the door shut behind us. "I admit I'm unsurprised to hear that. May I bring you a cup while we speak, regardless?"

He looks amused. "As you like. It'll take more than drinking your tea to win me over, though."

I wonder if he's witnessed the tactic I employed with Aleixo to convince him to cooperate with us. Surely Saiyana would have mentioned if he'd been permitted to visit. He may have also seen another tea master at work—but there is also the fact that Ridac hasn't maintained his power without craftiness on his side.

"I gather I just caused some problems for you." Ridac gets himself comfortable as I busy my hands with the kettle. "Princess stretching her wings at last, is she?"

How many young, ambitious politicians has he watched try to rise? And has he helped them, or hindered them?

"She is different than her mother or grandmother," I say. "I look forward to the world finding out what that means. But I am grateful for how you handled that interaction." At least after the explosive start.

He shrugs. "Easy for someone like me to voice uncomfortable truths to Istals in a position of power. Especially when I've just put my foot in it. I hope you're right about her difference from Queen Ilmari."

I smile faintly again as I pour. "I don't mean that Princess Iryasa will be any easier for you to maneuver around."

Ridac shakes his head. "Don't think I don't appreciate Ilmari's mastery over being an immovable stone in politics. She's painstakingly kept anything from changing. But while that may have prevented changes that would be negative to Istalam, not being willing to work with anyone is also keeping beneficial changes at bay. Or don't you agree?"

There it is. "In principle, you know I do," I answer, pouring the tea. "Though you will forgive me for observing that willingness to work with others is not an approach I characteristically associate with Velasar."

Ridac sips his tea. "Superb as expected. Thank you. Now, if I may be blunt, tea master, since I know you can be?"

"When the situation requires," I murmur, sipping my own cup.

"Ha. You're playing a dangerous game, and I want to make sure you're clear on how dangerous."

Which game? I'm playing dozens. "Oh?"

"We both live on this continent and are invested in its future, yes? The Isle of Nakrab isn't, but you can't fight them," he says bluntly. "At least not and win. I'm speaking in the literal sense, not the existential. You are aware that magecraft is completely useless against their magic?"

I consider for a moment and then follow my instinct. "We have been operating under that assumption for some time, yes. Are you aware that both witchcraft and the Te Muraka's magic do work against Nakrabi magic?"

His eyes widen, then narrow. Velasar may have had suspicions, just as Ostario, Saiyana, and Glynis have regarding magecraft's interaction with Nakrabi magic, but we have both just confirmed this to each other freely.

My intelligence is the rarer: it would be far more difficult for him to conclusively arrive at that information than it would be for me to learn about Nakrab, even with Velasar's better relations with the island. So this is an offering, and I wait to see how he takes it.

"That is very interesting, isn't it?" Ambassador Ridac muses. "So are you proposing we send all the witches and Te Muraka on the continent to the island to ensure our sovereignty? It's tricky, but I believe that's a proposal I can get Velasar's government behind."

Is he testing me, or is he serious?

I sip again, giving myself a moment before I say, "No, ambassador. I am proposing we work together against a common threat you yourself have identified."

"Ah," Ridac says, lifting his cup as if to clink it against mine, "but you are the real threat, aren't you? You and your unwillingness to eradicate witches."

For the first time, I am convinced he honestly believes this.

But I also believe this is not a conviction that's inviolable for him if it does not remain politically useful. Perhaps I'm to be his imaginary foe, to test out how he might play this to his people.

"Witches are not responsible for the Cataclysm," I say firmly.

"So what?" He swirls his tea. "They're still abominations. And you're helpfully setting Istalam up against the Isle of Nakrab, who can crush you. Oh, your witches and Te Muraka may be worthwhile someday, but against Nakrab's organization today? I think not. So why would Velasar throw in its lot with you?"

I set my cup down and give him a severely unimpressed look.

Ridac raises his eyebrows, smirking. "What, going to try some tea ceremony magic on me?"

I wonder if "tea ceremony magic" is a deliberate phrasing or a Velasari idiom—it at least doesn't carry the overtones of blasphemy with which they treat any allusion to witchcraft. But now is not the time to pursue that line of inquiry.

"I have never once said that I expect Velasar and Istalam to become best of friends over the signing of a single treaty," I say. "I hope you do not think me so naïve. There are deep rifts between Velasar and Istalam, and they will take more than one conversation to heal."

"A marriage, then?" His gaze is keen.

"Is that what you think Ilmari and Cordán have? When they are both actively working toward their own ends and not only not each other's, but against each other's, that is not a true partnership."

Ridac sets his cup down and sighs. "You are naïve."

"Really? Because if this specious notion is what you have in mind to broach with Princess Iryasa, I recommend, in my capacity as negotiator, you reconsider. She has many reasons to not favor such a suit, and she'll think less of you for proffering it at this time."

"Will she be able to refuse what I'm offering, though?" Ridac asks, staring at me intently. "That's the real question."

I smile with my lips closed. "I would not presume to speak to what Iryasa will or will not choose. Though I do wonder who asked that question of Queen Ilmari and Cordán the Consort, and if they're quite satisfied with how that turned out." I set my cup down. "I will speak to you, bluntly, of mine, however. Which is this: I am going to get what I require. You may stand with me when the time comes, or you may consider yourself my next problem to solve. And if I do say so myself, I am becoming quite accomplished, ambassador, at solving problems satisfactorily."

I get to my feet, signaling the end of this meeting, and Ridac follows suit.

"You're not an empire anymore," he tells me.

"As you yourself reminded, I'm not foremost a representative of Istalam, ambassador," I say. "I serve the spirits."

As we part ways, I find myself with the uncomfortable understanding that while I may have facilitated our communication, I'm not sure I actually improved our relationship.

As with Iryasa.

And Cherato.

I close my eyes, imaging all the pieces of this game swirling around, circling closer and away at different rates.

Occasionally we'll collide. That's life.

But I can't help wondering what patterns an arcanist would see in this situation that I am not.

CHAPTER 24

IRYASA DOES NOT RETURN for the next session of negotiations, but rather than participating—undermining me or not—she is coolly, aloofly silent. Although I am inclined to think this is a bad sign, it is not impossible she's decided to hold herself in reserve until she's had time to process and choose a plan of attack with more deliberation.

When she is the first one out the door before any of the ambassadors, that is a snub of me specifically. Given that we discussed in front of Ambassador Ridac meeting afterwards, it is a pointed rejection of considering my expertise valuable enough to politely decline, let alone to make time for.

Saiyana comes up to stand next to me, presenting at least the façade of a united Istal strategy as the other delegations take their leave. "She'll come around," she murmurs.

"Only if she takes a more active hand and it matters," I say.

"Obviously, but you were already planning for that, weren't you?"

I sigh. "Apparently not well enough."

Saiyana huffs. "It'll be fine. Iryasa is cool-headed, and so are you."

We are also both hot-blooded, so I'm not certain that will help. But I accept her faith in me and nod as she too goes to depart.

Then Karisa appears at my shoulder. "I'm thinking I should lay off Cherato for a bit."

"I agree," I say. "But placing the duplicate—"

She rolls her eyes. "Already done. Give us some credit."

I blink. Karisa has been with us during the entirety of negotiations, which is when we can be sure the ambassador is not in the Nakrabi lodgings. Either Elowyn placed it alone, which I like not at all, or they went another time when the ambassador could have been there, which is possibly worse.

Karisa watches me placidly, waiting for the objections that will demonstrate I don't have faith in their ability to handle this and think through these obvious factors without me.

"You've had word?" I finally ask.

"I'm sure, if that's what you're asking."

She's not going to give me specifics, and I am going to tear out my hair if I think about this any further.

But her answer also comes out... practiced. I can't help wondering if there's something about their communication Karisa doesn't want me to know.

So all I say is, "It's probably not a good time to work on Velasar either. He'll be expecting it, and any reactive move will undermine the conversation I just had with him."

Karisa nods, relaxing a fraction after I let it go. But then she responds, "Want me to watch Iryasa instead?"

Spirits. "*Please* do not spy on her on my account."

"Fine. But if I happened to hear anything relevant, would you want to know?"

I close my eyes. "I will trust your judgment on whether you should report any actions that are taken with the understanding that I won't find out about them."

Karisa rolls her eyes. "Wow. Way to undercut all the fun. Well, some of the fun."

"One more thing," I say. "Could you let Elowyn know I'd like her to come to the back, please? And that I'd like her to take care to keep out of sight."

At this point, I am at least confident the teens can all get in touch with each other and share information far faster and more effectively than I can with anyone, even without Glynis' presence.

"As if she needs to take care," Karisa says.

"I did not misspeak."

She pauses; her eyes sharpen. "Do I get to know what this is about?"

"Elowyn can share anything she learns in this case with anyone she chooses," I say. "That's in fact the point."

We'll see if her judgment matches mine, and if she comes to the same conclusion about what should done about it.

"Karisa!" Saiyana calls. "Stop bothering Miyara. Let's go."

Karisa rolls her eyes dramatically and flounces after her.

I wonder if Saiyana will still be on my side when she realizes I've participated in Karisa misleading them all.

But for now, I have someone else to, hopefully harmlessly, mislead.

※

To the best of my knowledge, Tea Master Karekin and I have the back to ourselves. If Elowyn is here, even I can't tell, which is at once encouraging and alarming.

If she's here, I hope she'll understand why I wanted her to listen in and will act accordingly.

If I understood the tea guild's rules better, I might have insisted on her presence as my apprentice or relayed this knowledge anyway. But I need Karekin's information right now more than I need to win that particular fight. I hope, if he finds out, he will understand, too.

"You want me to teach you about arcanism," Karekin says. "May I ask why the urgency?"

"Not yet, if you don't mind," I answer. "I'd prefer not to bias you. My intuition here may be off base, but that's why I need more information."

He regards me for a moment, not entirely satisfied by that answer, but he doesn't push me.

"A moment, then. Hmm. Will you clear that tray, there? Yes, that one. I'll be right back."

I lift my eyebrows but do as instructed, carefully following Lorwyn's protocol for handling the Cataclysm ingredients resting on it.

Tea Master Karekin returns from the stacks—I am both pleased and oddly challenged that he has completely learned my inventory system so quickly—with a bag of sand, which he proceeds to pour into the tray.

Then he takes one of Lorwyn's magecraft practice sticks and begins to draw.

"Watch the patterns, and how they shift," he tells me. "See what you can see."

His words have the weight of ritual behind them. "Don't tell me you're a master of Taresal sand art, too?" I ask. "How in the world do you have time?"

Karekin laughs. "My skills in this arena are hardly adequate, actually. But many tea masters pick up hobbies to help keep us grounded. Have you truly none?"

I consider. Tea had been my hobby at the palace.

Then I remember how much satisfaction I was taking in learning to bake, and wonder if I should meet Deniel's mother for a lesson after all or keep exploring. Perhaps I can do both.

Someday. Once I've ensured I have a future to play in.

Now, I watch.

I see why he is teaching me this way, though I hope Elowyn has a good view. Arcanism is about patterns, and much of what the tea guild knows of arcanism must, by virtue of the lack of arcanists today, be recorded. So he can sketch the records for me and let me draw my own conclusions, rather than rely on his interpretation.

I wonder if this is how arcanists taught their apprentices, too: by training their perception.

I fall into an almost ceremony-like trance as Karekin traces and erases different patterns, converting them into different shapes.

The first thing I understand from this is that arcane magic is, in a way, like witchcraft: the power is internal. Or at least: they're able to use internal spirit.

All I am perfectly clear on, watching the flow of the patterns, is that arcanists could handle magic directly, without shaping it in any way.

Yorani is the only being I've known with that ability, and she is made of magic.

As if that weren't world-shattering enough, what I realize next is that it is also like magecraft—which stands to reason, as both witchcraft and magecraft are supposedly derived from arcanism—in that theoretically anyone can learn it. Where magecraft is about discipline, though, what rewards arcanist power is increased perception of the world.

"The arcanists must have all ended up very eccentric," I murmur, with a new appreciation for some of the more ridiculous legends I've heard. "Each with their own processes for seeing hidden patterns and truths."

Karekin nods, his hands still moving. "I understand that matching apprentices was always particularly important and difficult, to help people learn compatible patterns. I don't quite remember the exact progression for this section from our lore, so I'm afraid I'll just relay this one directly: arcanists tried to learn multiple approaches, because the greater their capacity for perception in that way, too, the greater their power."

"But they also believed in separating from people to gain perspective," I say.

Karekin brings his drawing to a close, sensing that I've gleaned whatever I was going to. "Traditionally, yes. They tended to be hermits, many losing time in projects no one else could understand, others attempting to negate their selves using various harsh meditative practices. Since they could, we believe, manipulate their internal magic—or life force, or spirit, it's not entirely clear—this is what made them immortal. So they could remove themselves for not just decades, but centuries."

Humans as immortals. This, I can scarcely credit.

But unfortunately it supports a suspicion that has been growing in me.

"You're not surprised by this revelation," Karekin notes.

He's not wrong. "More distressed, perhaps. Please, in the interest of training my perception, may I review what I believe I've learned here?"

He gestures for me to go ahead, and I do, filling in with context from previous conversations in case Elowyn is listening and wishes to check *her* perception.

"I can confirm your reading matches mine," the tea master says. "Whether we are correct in our assessment, I cannot say. So?"

"So I'm wondering," I say, "if it was arcanism that produced the barrier."

"You would not be the first," Karekin says. "But it is not something we can prove."

"Because all the arcanists have been gone since the Cataclysm, which is a noteworthy correlation. Did they sacrifice themselves to create it?"

"It's not impossible. But arcane works are... impossible for those of us who aren't arcanists to aspire to."

"I assure you I am impossibly impressed by a barrier capable of halting the advance of the Cataclysm," I say.

He shakes his head. "Consider your teapot. *That* is clearly arcane work: almost terrifyingly untouchable."

An arcane teapot, from an arcane bag, carried by an old woman I can't explain.

But I leave that aside to point out, "I've only managed to affect the barrier with actual spirits."

But as soon as this is out of my mouth I realize what he's getting at.

"Yet the barrier was breached," he says. "I've never known arcane work to be vulnerable to attack. It is difficult to imagine that, if the magic of the Isle of Nakrab is vulnerable to witchcraft, which is a derivative of arcanism, that an arcane work of that scale could be affected by their technology."

"Magecraft is also a derivative of arcanism, though, which is entirely useless against Nakrabi magic," I say. "But I actually have a more troubling question."

Karekin looks at me, not asking. But waiting.

"You said the arcanists had removed themselves from the world," I say. "There was already a magical disturbance in the east before a tea master went to summon them. We don't know what caused it, though I'm beginning to guess. We don't know how powerful the Cataclysm, or whatever led up to it, was by the time they were summoned."

"You're suggesting the arcanists may have caused the Cataclysm," Karekin says. "This, too, has been suggested before."

"No, that's not what I mean," I say.

"What, then?"

"I mean that for all their power of perception, the arcanists had been unusually removed, even by their standards, for some time, to the point they had to be summoned.

"I mean they were used to being wise and powerful—immortal, even!—to the point that their understanding might have suffered from lack of awareness or empathy or both.

"I mean the arcanists were human, and different, and pressed for time."

I take a breath. Karekin's expression has gone politically blank, but I voice my question nevertheless.

"What if the arcanists did make the barrier, but they made a mistake?"

When Tea Master Karekin leaves, Yorani arrives. I don't see her fly in—I am staring, lost in thought, at the sand box Karekin drew in.

Until my baby dragon starts kicking up sand from the tray.

I startle, then sigh. "Are you trying to get my attention, or are you just enjoying making a mess?"

Yorani pauses long enough to meet my gaze.

Without breaking eye contact, she deliberately kicks a clump of sand out of the tray, spraying it across the room and the floor.

Burying my face in my hands, I laugh ruefully. "So, both."

I set the tray on the floor so at least Yorani's continued fun won't spread more over Lorwyn's workstation and leave her to it as I go for cleaning supplies.

"So," I say, starting on Lorwyn's desk with a damp cloth. "Where have you been today?"

Yorani turns her back on me, shaking her tail and then lashing it into the sand to swipe greater quantities all at once.

"I don't *need* an explanation, but is it so wrong that I'm curious? I know perfectly well that you're devious."

Yorani turns to me to preen dramatically.

Then resumes her sand spree.

I take it that's all the answer I'm going to get from her, and I'm oddly unbothered. (Growing sand mess excepted.) I don't know what Yorani's up to, but I nevertheless feel like we're... in alignment, perhaps. We may not be pursuing a goal in the same way, but we're still working as a team toward a common purpose.

I wish I were more confident that were true with the rest of my allies.

Then again, perhaps this is the problem: I always needed to be in alignment with myself, first.

The foundation is built; maybe now I'm in a position to mend the cracks in it. In this, it's like air: the shape is indefinable, and it can be everything or nothing.

The foundation is what I make of it; I direct its shape. Unlike the tides, air can blow in different directions. I have shown different faces of myself to different people.

I'm still too used to hiding. It's a useful skill, but tactically, I need to change.

It's time to show everyone who I am without apology, and see how they meet me.

But speaking of hiding.

I scan the room for my apprentice, but as far as I can tell she isn't here. "Do you know if Elowyn *was* here recently?"

Yorani looks at me and, very deliberately, nods her head.

Oh my spirits, she can answer yes and no questions now.

Am I supposed to make anything of that? Will she wished to be praised? I think not, though I can't say why.

"And was she?" I ask.

Another nod.

Well. That's something that's gone right, then, though it does mean she is capable of hiding from me when she really wants to. Elowyn has enough of the gift for tea mastery already I have faith she'll know what to do with this information—or at least, what I expect her to do. In the grand scheme... that I haven't decided. Maybe she will.

"Thank you," I tell Yorani, running a hand over her scales.

She croons back at me.

With her supervision, I clean our tea house. It's the calmest and most assured I've felt in days.

Events will always transpire too quickly. This is the core I have to remember, the center I have to hold as the world swirls around me, so I can choose my path through it all.

When a knock sounds at the back door, I am almost resentful of the interruption.

But I have also never been more ready.

Or that is what I think before I open it and find Iryasa on the other side—without Reyata.

Iryasa's eyes narrow just a fraction at the sight of me, and we regard each other in silence for a moment.

"You were here for Lorwyn," I realize, though I can't guess why. "She's out. Would you like to talk to me instead?"

"Not particularly," Iryasa says. Her tone isn't nasty, but the fact that she says this at all, from her, is nastiness nonetheless. Before I can continue, she adds, "I suppose you can help me, however. Can you direct me to the abode of Risteri of House Taresim?"

I have even less idea what's going on. So much for my confident serenity.

"I can guide you there myself," I say.

"I would prefer directions."

"I'm not offering them."

We stare at each other.

Her jaw firms. "I don't want to talk about earlier with you yet."

Has she still not decided how to deal with me, or has something happened? "Very well. We can speak of other things or not speak at all. Would you like to tell me about the Te Muraka food Sa Rangim introduced you to?"

Her skin tightens so imperceptibly if I were anyone else, I wouldn't have noticed. If *she* were anyone else, I wouldn't have cared.

But we are who we are, and this is akin to a full-body cringe.

Something *is* amiss. Iryasa would not have left—perhaps *could* not have, lacking such provocation—Reyata behind.

"No, then," I say smoothly. "Yorani, I'll finish cleaning up the sand later. Let's go."

The tea spirit alights promptly on my shoulder, then does a full body shake that spatters sand on Iryasa and me both. The sudden need to shield her eyes distracts my sister from whatever she might have said, and I lock the door behind me.

"That's it?" Iryasa asks suspiciously.

"That's it," I confirm. "You don't wish to talk with me, and so we won't."

"For now."

"All things considered, I am not promising I will never speak to you again ever, no," I say dryly. "Nor is that what you asked. Shall we?"

Still, she hesitates. "I truly can go on my own."

Have I betrayed her trust in me so deeply?

Or is it that she knows I can see too deeply, and she's feeling a need for privacy?

I raise my eyebrows. "Then do you want to tell me what's wrong? Because it's one or the other. I'm certainly in favor of respecting personal boundaries, but they don't obviate basic safety precautions. Your choice."

She doesn't have to consider. "Let's go."

CHAPTER 25

I LEAD IRYASA TO my old apartment, and we don't speak.

Except for one moment.

Yorani hides in my bag, remarkably still—I think she's amused by the stealth operation of our trying to pass through the streets without being recognized. If Iryasa is noticeable, Yorani is even more so.

I take us on a shortcut through a Gaellani market, because if Iryasa's hood falls she's still less likely to be recognized here than by Istals. At one point, she lifts a hand to part a curtain, and as her sleeve falls I see her security bracelet.

She hadn't been focused on me, but she still notices how I minutely relax. Suddenly suspicious, she asks, "What?"

"You're still wearing your bracelet," I say. "I wasn't sure if you'd taken it off."

Iryasa frowns at me, but she falls into step as I start moving again, tentatively reassured I'm not leading her into a trap. "I'm not stupid, Miyara."

"I've never thought you were." I lift my own wrists, which, though in possession of bracelets, are distinctly different than the ones I used to wear. She startles minutely—I'm sure she knew I didn't have them anymore, but I haven't made a point of bringing it up, either. "It's not as though they don't come off, though, and you clearly didn't want to be found."

Iryasa's jaw tightens. "I'm the crown princess, Miyara. I don't have the luxury of taking off my duty when I don't care for it."

I consider my response to this. On one hand, she's already angry at me, but on the other? I *just* resolved to show people who I am, and I am not backing off right at the beginning.

"I have only ever dedicated myself to one duty," I finally say, "and I answered the door when you knocked. Will Reyata track you?"

Iryasa's lips purse in anger, but she lets me redirect back to the original topic. "Not unless there's an emergency. She'll respect what it means that I've gone to the trouble of leaving her behind and will respect my wish for space."

And it has become abundantly clear that Iryasa isn't convinced anymore that I respect her wishes or boundaries.

"The closest you can get to privacy," I murmur.

"Yes," she agrees. "*Some* of my sisters trust me."

I make a point of rolling my eyes so she can't miss it. "Are we talking now, or are we still not talking?"

My sister looks away for a moment, and then turns back quickly and asks, "Why the bracelets?"

Mine, she means. "They're a gift from Deniel," I say, leaving out Thiano's role in their procurement. For the purposes of her question, it's not relevant, and I'm not currently filled with confidence on how spiteful she feels toward me. "He noticed I was uncomfortable without the security bracelets—I'd grown too used to their weight. Even though these don't serve the same function, wearing these helps me feel at ease."

I don't mention the reminder they are for me about Deniel, our feelings and relationship and commitment, either. She may infer that on her own.

"So we both have our illusions, then," Iryasa finally says.

Which is how I am absolutely certain something has gone badly wrong with Sa Rangim. My heart races: if there is bitterness between them, everything I am trying to hold in balance is at risk.

But her words were a deliberate challenge, and I meet it the way I absolutely must.

I respect her boundaries.

I don't ask.

The rest is silence.

Risteri isn't the only one in the apartment. Lorwyn's presence isn't a surprise, at least to me; nor is Sa Nikuran's. But it's immediately clear Sa Nikuran is low on the list of people Iryasa wants to see right now.

I see my sister mentally calculating her position—whether it's worth trying to do this another way, whether she'll be able to get away at another time—and deciding the same way she did when I pressed her.

She's moving forward.

Once the immediate pleasantries are taken care of, Iryasa says to Risteri, "I understand you're the best guide to the Cataclysm in Sayorsen."

I had been selfishly hoping she wanted to talk to Risteri about a House Taresim matter. But in that case, she wouldn't have needed to leave Reyata behind.

So I'm not surprised, exactly, though I may be the only one.

"I am," Risteri agrees slowly—not arrogantly, but cautious of what she's getting herself into. "Was there something particular you wanted to know about the Cataclysm, or—"

"I think it's past time I see it for myself," Iryasa says. "I was hoping you might favor me with a private tour."

From a crown princess to a scion of an out-of-favor house among her subjects, this is not a request.

Risteri glances at me, and Iryasa snaps, "Miyara is not in charge here."

Risteri blinks, startled by this vehemence.

But however much she's rejected her upbringing with her father, it doesn't change the fact that she was raised as aristocracy. It only takes a moment for her expression to even out, and she says, "No, your Highness, if we're talking about a trip to the Cataclysm, then *I* am in charge."

Iryasa narrows her eyes.

"Is there anything I should know about this trip?" Risteri continues. "If there are to be clandestine meetings, for instance, I will take different precautionary measures."

Iryasa relaxes minutely. "You will take me, then?"

Risteri thankfully does *not* look at me this time. She's clever enough to understand my silence means I'm not going to intervene, and if I were opposed to this I would have to precisely because Risteri isn't in a position to.

Guiding is what she does best, so I let her lead.

"It would be my pleasure, your Highness," Risteri says. "But any trip into the Cataclysm requires planning, so—"

"I have nothing specific in mind," Iryasa interrupts her. "I just want to see it for myself, this focal point on which so much turns."

It's a good idea. I wonder about the reasons for it.

"Very well," Risteri says. "Let me get you both some more suitable clothing for traipsing through the Cataclysm, then, and we'll get started."

Iryasa's eyes narrow. "Perhaps I was unclear. Miyara will not be joining us."

Risteri takes a deep breath. "Perhaps *I* was unclear, your Highness? I am in charge. And this is exactly why Miyara has to come."

"Explain," Iryasa says, because she can't twist a narrative she doesn't understand.

"On a trip to the Cataclysm, a guide's word is absolute," Risteri says. "If I give you a direction, I can't afford for you to argue about it or decide whether it's worth following. The Cataclysm is life and death."

"I can abide by your directions."

"With all due respect, your Highness, I think you are not accustomed to abiding by *anyone's* directions except her Majesty's, and I can't risk that you will slip out of habit," Risteri says. "Miyara will be accompanying us because she has demonstrated she *will* abide by my directions. And, to be frank, your Highness? She is one of the only people who, if the situation arises, can tackle you to the ground without putting her precarious household at risk of your further displeasure."

Iryasa absorbs that, expression souring. She won't have missed Risteri's usage of the word 'further'—Risteri caught on to the tension between us. But given how she started this conversation, Iryasa won't be able to reasonably persuade Risteri that she can follow orders.

"So that's why I need traipsing clothes," I observe. "They're to be emergency tackling clothes."

Lorwyn says, "You have prevailed on me for emergency clothes-salvaging witchcraft more than once."

"Not from visiting the Cataclysm, though," I point out. "When your explosions at the tea shop are the cause, I don't feel bad asking you to clean up the consequences."

Lorwyn looks at Iryasa. "I've always wondered this. Is the whole 'remaining pristine even when running through a magical monstrosity' ability a princess thing?"

Iryasa stares at her. "You are remarkably confident in addressing me so casually," she says in a chilly voice.

Lorwyn shrugs. "You have more gravitas than Saiyana, but if one princess has to treat me like a person I don't see why any of the rest of you should be exempt."

"Miyara's not a princess."

"And I was talking about Saiyana," Lorwyn says blandly.

The words hang in the air.

Iryasa scowls at me. "Your doing, I take it?"

"No, Lorwyn is just like this," I say as blandly as Lorwyn, knowing full well Iryasa was referring to Saiyana's behavior.

My sister shakes her head; takes a moment. Then she looks at Lorwyn and says, "Yes, it's a princess thing."

My chest tightens, and I breathe.

We're not okay yet, but I think maybe we will be after all.

"I would also like to accompany you," Sa Nikuran says, and the moment shatters.

"No," Iryasa says flatly.

Risteri glances from Sa Nikuran to Iryasa, clearly not understanding the undercurrent there. "It would be irresponsible to bring the crown princess to a place as dangerous as the Cataclysm without a protector familiar with the Cataclysm's ways. If Sa Nikuran is willing—"

"No," Iryasa says again, more softly.

More icily.

Sa Nikuran bows low. "Please, your Highness. Sa Rangim—"

"Sa Rangim does not rule here," Iryasa says, her voice ringing with finality. She stares a challenge at Risteri. "Are you only the best guide under Te Muraka oversight?"

Risteri's expression evens. "Of course not, your Highness. But I gather time is of the essence in the interest of stealth. Lorwyn, can you come?"

"Sure, I do like nothing better than to serve at the crown's pleasure," Lorwyn drawls.

I can practically see Iryasa consider a scathing response, remember Lorwyn is a witch and that the crown she will one day hold has allowed witches to be persecuted for decades, and keep her mouth well shut.

"Risteri—" Sa Nikuran begins uncomfortably.

"My love, under the circumstances there is absolutely no way I am getting in the middle of a fight between Sa Rangim and the crown princess of Istalam," Risteri says.

Circumstances could mean her House's position, but I know Risteri better than that: she means without knowing what went wrong between them. Given her firsthand knowledge of Te Muraka bonds, I wonder what she's guessed.

More to the point, Iryasa's attention sharpens at her words. She must have known Risteri and Sa Nikuran were keeping company, but to bring love into it?

I admit mine sharpens at that as well. To throw a word like 'love' out there so casually—

"Then I will take my leave," Sa Nikuran says, bowing formally.

"Wait," Iryasa says, and I tense.

So does Sa Nikuran.

"Do not allow any Te Muraka to interfere," Iryasa commands. "If Sa Rangim requires an explanation, you may remind him that I make my own choices and don't need his protection."

My eyes widen.

Ohhh dear.

Sa Nikuran's expression remains impassive, but her eyes flash. "I will communicate this to him, your Highness."

The directive itself, or that Iryasa directly commanded a Te Muraka? Which she legally is allowed to do, and yet—

It occurs to me that Sa Nikuran was insisting on accompanying us because she knew Sa Rangim would have wanted her to.

And in that case, if what Iryasa needs is perspective after an altercation with Sa Rangim, and she is choosing to *take herself to the Cataclysm with minimal protection*—

I can't give any sign I am not entirely behind my sister right now, even to give Sa Nikuran a hint that I will do what I can on the Te Muraka's behalf. Not if I wish to be *able* to do anything for them *or* my sister.

As I have asked Iryasa to trust me publicly in negotiations, so too do I now keep my mouth absolutely shut on her behalf as Sa Nikuran takes her leave with a final inscrutable glance at my tea spirit, whose reaction I can't see from her perch.

But once Sa Nikuran's gone, I turn to my sister and say, "I hope you understand the statute on my not talking is going to run out the moment we cross into the Cataclysm."

I thought this might make her angry, but instead it's like a weight has lifted off her shoulders.

"Yes," she says, and there's the ghost of a smile as she adds wryly, "but until then, keep your mouth shut."

Lorwyn makes us all invisible—which makes Yorani sneeze and then chirp in delight at however that feels to her—as we head to the Cataclysm. To avoid accidentally bumping into people Risteri takes us on a roundabout route. Our invisibility means we all have to keep quiet or else ruin the point, though that doesn't stop Lorwyn from casting pointed looks my way.

I ignore them, as does Risteri, who is at least noble enough to understand the façade of discretion where royalty is concerned.

As does Yorani, who flies around Iryasa's head in an attempt to get her to laugh.

And I have at least enough awareness for how lonely I have felt witnessing Lorwyn and Risteri's exchanges that even were Iryasa not a princess, I would endeavor to refrain from weighted glances right now. Iryasa can't have intended her adventure to go exactly like this, but she is nevertheless stuck with three people (and one tea spirit) who are all close friends with each other and not her. Yorani, at least, is in more of a position to address this by virtue of not existing in a firm category in Iryasa's mind.

The barrier to the Cataclysm is placid, swirling lazily as if such currents visible under the surface are entirely expected, and not a reflection of us. My sister does not appear to note anything amiss—and why should she? This is what she knows.

But for her taking one deeper breath as if to gird herself for what her life means, we pass through without any pause or acknowledgment. My stomach twists, and Lorwyn announces, "We're visible again. I don't want to maintain that while being ready for anything else."

"Can't people see us through the barrier?" I ask.

"So what if they can?" Lorwyn asks. "No one's looking, and no one innocent is going to follow if they were. If they're not innocent, I'd like nothing better than to deal with them first and get it over with so we can continue."

Iryasa murmurs, "I'm glad you assume this journey would continue after an altercation."

"Of course, your Highness," Lorwyn says. "I'm glad my eagerness to get into fights doesn't bother you."

"How could I be at risk, with one such as you to defend me?"

Lorwyn lets out a crack of laughter. "Always pleased to be appreciated. So? Are you ready to move on, or do you want to take a minute?"

I've been watching Iryasa gaze around while she bantered, a lifeline to hold onto something human when the landscape around her is decidedly not. Yorani, who moments ago had been entertaining her with antics, has now slipped in among the chaos like she belongs here, and Iryasa notes it. She takes one more moment, and then she inclines her head to Risteri. "I am ready when you are, guide."

Risteri regards her thoughtfully. "Your goal is to get a fuller impression of what the Cataclysm is, correct?"

Iryasa inclines her head again, not answering with words.

Risteri nods sharply, apparently confirming a decision. "Then I will take us on a more... nuanced tour than where I typically bring tourists. Follow me."

She shoots a glance at Lorwyn, whose eyebrows lift but she nods.

All at once I realize what she has in mind. It's risky, but—maybe she's right. She is the guide, and if anyone knows the Cataclysm's heart, it's Risteri.

"Well?" Iryasa asks, and I startle, realizing she's addressing me.

Expecting me to start in on demands.

"I can wait," I say.

Her eyes narrow. "If you're trying to give me a break—"

Lorwyn comments, "That is really not Miyara's way of handling anything."

I roll my eyes. "You wanted to get an impression of the Cataclysm, and my input will only interfere in that."

"So you can at least understand your input isn't always helpful."

I incline my head, glancing ruefully at Lorwyn. "I'm at least capable of learning. And biding my time."

Lorwyn snorts but happily does not disagree with either sentiment outright—I wish I were more confident that's because she actually agrees and not just that she's choosing not to undermine me in this situation.

Iryasa considers me for another moment and then decides to take me at my word, gesturing for Risteri to begin.

If she is willing to take my word at all, things between us are not as broken as I feared.

That means I will be able to do what I do best.

※

This tour begins like my first visit did, and I keep quiet as promised.

Risteri gauges Iryasa's response to seeing a site where the Nakrabi tech was deployed: my sister is calculating and watchful. No tenser than she was, but no lessening of her anger, either.

Risteri exchanges another glance with Lorwyn, who nods.

After that, everything is different.

What follows isn't an exact path I've taken before. At least not as far as I recognize—I'm no guide, so for all I know it could be.

What is clear, though, is that Risteri is leading us deeper into the Cataclysm.

Very, very much deeper.

If I'd had any doubt, given the roiling landscape and ethereal shrieking, the rapid shifts in temperature and scent and color, it would have been clear by the time the ground vanished from underneath us.

Risteri takes Iryasa's hand from the front; I have been down a path enough like this I instinctively reach for my sister on one side and my best friend on the other while Yorani alights on my shoulder to stay connected to our path of human magic. Lorwyn catches us all as we freefall and holds us aloft with witchcraft I barely feel given the tumult.

No one says a word. No one needs to.

Thus connected, we continue, led by Risteri's knowledge, carried by Lorwyn's power, and Iryasa and I holding the center together as Yorani rides along.

Until Risteri pauses, drawing us up in a line so we can all see.

Iryasa immediately freezes at the sight. She isn't stupid.

A static, dead vision below, caught in the shifting winds of chaos, is the bleak, empty expanse of the Te Muraka's desert.

Iryasa attempts to snatch her hands back, but we hold fast.

She whirls to face me. "You told her to bring us here."

"No, I did not," I say. "My friends aren't any stupider than I am."

"Then you must all be stupid indeed, to have thought that at this moment, when you have clearly realized I don't want anything to do with even *thinking* about the Te Muraka, this would be a site I wished to see."

Risteri answers her. "I think it's a site you need to see, if you want to understand where the Te Muraka's protective impulses are coming from. I don't know what Sa Rangim could have said during negotiations to anger you this badly, but as a person who is dating, sleeping with, and maybe forming a mate bond with another Te Muraka, I can promise you there's no way to have any kind of functional relationship with them if you're not prepared to deal with this part of them."

Iryasa is vibrating with anger. She bites out, "Your choices are your own, but *I* will not be controlled. I will not curb my own behavior to make allowances for another's need to wrap me in a protective cocoon."

"Nor should you," Risteri says evenly, and Iryasa's eyes narrow. "Well, I guess I have no place with 'should' where you're concerned, but what I mean is that's not at all the point."

"And what," Iryasa's words are measured with violent calm, "in your vast expertise, is the point?"

"If I may cut in," I say softly as Iryasa's gaze snaps back to me, "the point is his story, and where it overlaps with yours. If you wish to shape the narrative, you have to understand both. If you are part of the story—which in this case you cannot deny—it's even more important to understand how it might shape you."

"I don't wish to be shaped."

So little emotion in that statement I recognize how vast it has to be underneath: a cry, a plea, a shout.

And oh, do I understand it. I can't give her the freedom I felt realizing I did not have to contort myself into the person everyone expected me to be.

But maybe, if I really am the tea master I claim to be, I can help her find it for herself.

"Shaping art shapes the artist in the doing," I say. "People aren't different. I of all people know you are here to change."

"I am here to change *myself*."

"So am I, and if it could happen in a vacuum you'd already be how you wish," I tell her. "Risteri, can you find us somewhere calm? Or at least flat, where it's safe to sit down?"

"Uh." She jerks her head in the direction of the Te Muraka's prior residence.

"No," Iryasa says.

"No," I agree. "If anyone brings her there, it should be Sa Rangim. Not us."

Risteri frowns. "Then not nearby, no. It's like the existence of an ordered chunk makes the surrounding chaos even less stable than elsewhere in the Cataclysm. Do you want to turn around?"

"Yes," Iryasa says.

"No," I disagree this time, and my sister glares at me. I turn away from her and look to Lorwyn. "As long as you can hold us."

Lorwyn narrows her eyes. Then with her free hand she reaches into her pocket and pulls out a bunch of sticks, then casually tosses them into the air.

Not truly casually, of course: each of them moves, directed remotely, to a specific point around us. They hang their midair, a mage structure suspended by her witchcraft.

Glowing lines appear connecting each stick, and then it's as if each stick is the point connecting facets of a cloudy jewel that flares with opaque light.

When it clears, Lorwyn looks a question at me for permission; I nod. She lets go of my hand.

We all drop onto a solid, invisible, nonexistent surface. Lorwyn winces with the impact but waves a hand as if to banish the distraction.

"Risteri, I'm going to have to focus on this," Lorwyn says. "Yell if you need me. Better yet, yell at Yorani."

My tea spirit lifts off my shoulder to gently brush Lorwyn's face with her wing; an acknowledgment. Risteri also nods, turning her back to watch around us, confident in herself and in us.

It's incredible to stand here between them and recognize this clear demonstration of how far we've all come.

"And what will we be doing?" Iryasa asks archly.

I sit down on a transparent floor, the gleam of the magecraft nodes in the corner of my vision, the expanse of the Te Muraka's drifting prison below—for now—and the whirling currents of Cataclysm all around.

I unstrap my tea kit and begin to unpack it to Iryasa's frank look of astonishment.

"You once asked me to perform the tea ceremony for you," I say. "The time for it is now."

CHAPTER 26

"YOU WANT TO PERFORM a tea ceremony for me now," Iryasa echoes flatly. "Here."

"Here and now," I agree.

I use water from a bottle to fill the teapot.

Yorani breathes magical fire inside to heat the water.

I look up at Iryasa: ready; waiting. She holds my gaze for a long moment.

Then, at last, she sits before me.

With that act, we are committed, and I begin.

Here and now, suspended in the sky, I can only choose the traditional white air blend.

Fitting, as we sit above the former home of people with dragon forms.

Fitting, for a princess making a path out of nothing.

For Iryasa, I float more than flutter through the movements of the tea ceremony. Because my eldest sister can only be deliberate, even when flying for freedom: this is what it means to be crown princess.

It also means, despite what most people think, that there is very little able to be controlled concretely. Nothing tangible can ever be grasped: always, everything is a matter of nebulous connections and the gaps between them.

As a former princess, I know this well.

As a tea master, I know it better.

How do you control a future—yours or the world's?

You can't: it's that simple. Yet it's also infinitely more complicated, because you can shape yourself with your actions, and in so doing shape the world.

Incrementally. A shift in the breeze, perhaps. But a breeze can gather wind and become a gale, building into an unstoppable storm.

With deliberation; with care. Actions defined by the choice of which winds can combine, and how, to work together, because no single person can shape a future for the world alone.

We can choose who to add to our lives, but once combined we cannot then prevent changes in their wake; the act itself is a change. As it should be: connections are not static.

We choose as best we can those who will lift us up and support the people we wish to be, not the ones who smother who we would become.

This, I think, is the core of what Iryasa needs from me today: the understanding that relationships are not about giving up or sharing control of ourselves.

It's about finding people whose visions of who we are and can be are in line with ours. It's about people who want to help us grow into ourselves.

Not by stealing the work for themselves, clouding our selves out: by being a tangible port in an otherwise indefinable storm.

Not *taking over* the weights we carry but lightening them; or adding the clarity of their vision to ours.

Not taking over our selves, but helping us become more ourselves.

We sit here literally in the midst of chaos; it is an unsubtle metaphor for life.

The air itself is a torrent, this bubble of stillness only guided and extant by the power of others we chose to do just this: to guide us, and support us, so that we could do the work we came here for. It's not a *giving up* of control, but a shaping.

We choose our connections; we use them to shape our paths. And by our actions, anything can be possible.

Connections are how we make ourselves, and the future.

They can be a bottle containing us or a tether holding us back, it's true. Thus care, and deliberation: paying attention not just to the existence of feelings, but their strength, and what they are in specific.

Passion is not the problem. Passion working towards the same, or compatible, ends, is the key: passion that makes us feel like more, and more ourselves, not less.

Some people make us feel stifled and small. Some people can also make us feel vast and powerful.

We can't control people, exactly; this is, fundamentally, their power. Because people can always be an opportunity.

They can be the wind that gives us wings to fly.

If we're willing to trust, to risk enough of ourselves that they can know the shape of our wings, that they can be the air beneath us.

This is my strength as a tea master: to see who people wish to be, and to create a connection that will help them generate that lift. It's how I've brought my friends together, and my partner, and a terrifying team of teens, and witches and Te Muraka out of Istalam's shadow, and every one lifts me up: there is more yet to come.

I have not reached my limit yet.

A tea master's every act does not have the same scale of effect as a princess', but we have more freedom to choose our connections. That's why the choices a princess *can* make carry so much weight: the narratives a princess takes into her heart will ripple throughout her realm.

I can't decide for Iryasa who those people will be for her. She does not have to trust me, or any of our sisters; she is free to decide that Sa Rangim's vision for them is not one she can embrace.

Protectiveness, fierceness, and the channeling of passion are part of where he comes from; his life has shaped him, and he shouldn't have to make himself smaller, either. But wouldn't it be a marvel for Iryasa to have a person in her life support her as fiercely as the leader of the Te Muraka can; what a marvel for her, to have a person at her side whom she can count on to be both passionate and to know how to not inflict the dangerous sides of themselves on others.

Still. Iryasa can decide the shapes of specific narratives cannot affect each other in a way she will be happy with: that is her choice. But she will not become anyone she wishes to be without acting in the world, and acting in the world means people. It just doesn't have to mean giving up ourselves.

It can mean seizing our insubstantial dreams and never, never letting go.

That is how we shape the future: for ourselves, and the world.

When I pour, an amorphous shape rises out of the spout.

It doesn't solidify—perhaps Lorwyn's magic bubble prevents the requisite codification of spirit. But while I can't see any meaning its shape, Iryasa clearly can: her yearning expression, turned toward the sky, almost hurts to see.

When I present the tea to Iryasa, I don't look away. She can choose whether to engage with me on this stage.

She drinks. Shudders.

And meets my gaze head-on, her eyes glassy with unshed tears.

"You are an absolute monster as a tea master, and I love you," she whispers.

I choke out a shaky laugh, tears leaking out of my eyes. "I love you too."

⁂

We're all fairly quiet on the trek back. Outward expression of true feelings is still fairly new for all of us. But our silence this time is a peaceful kind, rather than with an edge: the feeling of thoughts settling into place.

As we pass some indefinable point after which the landscape returns—not to stability, but to an environment not actively anathema to human existence without application of magic—Risteri begins, "Your Highness?"

Iryasa looks at her inquiringly.

Risteri takes a deep breath. "One thing I have been learning is that to get what I want, I have to be unafraid and open and clear."

My sister doesn't blink. "An interesting strategy, but not one a princess has the luxury of testing."

"No, I realize that," Risteri says. "Which is why I'm saying—if you have any questions about... personal relationships with the Te Muraka that you can't ask them yourself—namely the, uh, experience of being in a relationship with a Te Muraka as someone who is *not* a Te Muraka—please feel free to ask me? I promise I am discreet."

Throughout this monologue Iryasa's expression has grown increasingly keen, and now she appears to be weighing whether Risteri can in fact keep her mouth shut and to what extent.

"...Did you just offer to give sex advice to the crown princess?" Lorwyn asks.

Risteri says, "I also promise not to be like Lorwyn."

"What does that mean?"

I answer first. "A person who always deliberately tries to either start a fight or make everyone around them maximally uncomfortable."

Lorwyn gives me a look.

I shrug. "I don't know why you would ask something like that in front of me of all people if you didn't want an answer."

"Oh yes," Lorwyn says dryly, "of the two of us I am definitely the one who starts the most fights and makes people most uncomfortable."

I nod serenely.

Lorwyn makes a strangled sound.

"Thank you for the offer, Risteri," Iryasa says gravely. "Perhaps we can share our stories in the future."

Lorwyn's eyes widen momentarily before she starts choking.

Iryasa's expression is placid, but amusement shines in her eyes.

And another light, too.

We're interrupted by Risteri's sudden halt, and as we all turn toward her the reason is plain.

We're nearly to the barrier, and it's flickering.

No, flickering is the wrong word. It's as though the barrier is made of lightning contained in a layer the shape of a dome, but now tendrils zap outwards like lightning.

I look a question at Yorani, wondering if she'll try to take a bite out of this strange magic. But she hunkers down on my shoulder, eyes narrowed and tail swishing. She's ready, but whatever she senses from this magic, she doesn't like it.

Lorwyn steps forward, and she and Risteri share a quick, low-voiced conversation—the kind full of half-statements the other fills in automatically and interrupts so it's entirely opaque to the rest of us. After a minute, they nod at each other, some consensus reached.

Risteri motions Iryasa and I closer as Lorwyn frowns and my stomach twists. Lorwyn carefully ensconces us in a silvery sphere, like we're standing in a spotlight of glowing witchcraft.

"Stay close," Lorwyn says in a tight voice, her face pale. She's used a great deal of magic in a short period of time. "This isn't solid, which means it's possible to step outside of its area of protection. Don't."

"Not a bubble this time?" Iryasa asks.

Lorwyn shakes her head. "I don't want to experiment with how that would pass through the barrier right now. This should negate any magic that tries to act on us."

"Not a sure thing then," Iryasa murmurs. Before Lorwyn can take that as criticism, my sister continues, "I suppose it couldn't be. Shall we?"

One choice, made.

We walk forward, a tight unit.

As we approach the barrier, bits of lightning from it flicker in our direction, only to dissipate like fire doused in water.

The spotlight grows warmer, and Lorwyn breathes heavily, but evenly.

Risteri looks a question at her when we reach the barrier itself, and Lorwyn takes a deep breath and nods sharply.

We pass through.

It is unlike every time I've passed through the barrier before. It's the sensation of static electricity just before a shock, that crackling in the air when you know it's coming.

But it never lands. We come out the other side, and Risteri keeps us walking until we're some distance from the edge but can still see it.

Then all at once Lorwyn lets the magic go, doubling over with her hands on her knees as she gasps for air.

I pull out her bottle of water and shove it in front of her face, helping her drink when her hands shake. She practically chokes it down.

"Try not to antagonize anyone until backup arrives," she chokes out.

"Never fear," Risteri says in an odd voice. "I think it's here."

I turn in time to watch Sa Nikuran drop from the sky, landing lightly on two feet in front of the barrier. She's followed by three more Te Muraka, who arrange themselves at her sides and behind her like they're in formation.

"Ready?" I murmur to Iryasa.

"Absolutely not," she whispers back without moving her lips. "I will cope."

I take one of her hands, squeeze gently, and bow over it.

That's how it is for all of us.

She squeezes my hand in turn, and I rise, meeting her gaze.

Then we turn as one to face the Te Muraka together.

"Your Highness," Sa Nikuran begins, and all four Te Muraka bow in sync, disciplined.

Controlled.

"Sa Nikuran," Iryasa acknowledges with a shallower but respectful bow of her own. "Can you explain what occurs with the barrier?"

"Not what, but why, yes," Sa Nikuran says. "As we could not accompany you into the Cataclysm, Sa Rangim arranged for us to protect your privacy."

"Did he," Iryasa says neutrally, and I hold my breath and hope Sa Rangim knows what he's doing.

Carefully but unflinchingly, Sa Nikuran says, "Sa Rangim will not interfere with what you deem important but wishes you to understand he will likewise act of his own accord. He thought you might appreciate a demonstration of usefulness."

Iryasa's eyes widen.

From her, it's like she's been slapped in the face.

Spirits, what did *she* say to *him*?

I close my eyes briefly. From everything I've witnessed, I can guess: she felt like he was trying to control her and lashed out, treating him like someone who needed to learn his place with her; not as an equal.

I can't help noticing that Sa Rangim himself is not here waiting for Iryasa to deliver this information himself, which can only be on purpose. Respecting her space, but also not begging for her attention.

"I do not require usefulness from him to understand every Te Muraka is valuable, and as worthy of my respect as every Istal," Iryasa says softly. "Yet unless I miss my guess, you have nevertheless served me in some capacity since we last spoke."

Sa Nikuran's eyes gleam, but none of her cohort relaxes. "Your Highness, we intercepted agents deploying technology in the fashion of the Isle of Nakrab against the barrier."

Iryasa stills. "Here?"

Sa Nikuran shakes her head. "No. The exterior changes you see occur with greater intensity where we intercepted them. We believe smaller ones like these appear everywhere a recent cross into or out of the Cataclysm has occurred. Cataclysm guides accompanied by Te Muraka for protection are evacuating anyone currently inside the Cataclysm and making sure no one enters until the barrier's stability is restored."

Not a long-term solution, but a stop-gap measure deployed competently until Iryasa could return and take her own action.

"And the agents?" Iryasa asks.

"Entero is tracing their origins. He suspects they will be revealed to be Nakrabi masquerading as Velasari operatives, rather than Velasari in truth."

That's extremely interesting. And while I'm glad to hear that Entero is already part of this situation, I don't think that's what Iryasa meant by her question.

Yet there are few ways for her to ask for clarification without causing offense, so I put in, "Is Entero in possession of the agents?"

Sa Nikuran's eyes flicker again as she takes my meaning. "He is not. We stopped them but prioritized protecting the barrier."

"You let them go," I confirm explicitly. Because Te Muraka are capable of letting go: they are disciplined enough to do so, guided but not ruled by their passions. Without demonstrated control, Sa Rangim would never trust a Te Muraka outside his direct oversight.

Sa Nikuran once again takes my meaning and echoes me for Iryasa's benefit. "We let them go. They were able to get as far as they did because they appeared invisible. Magecraft defenses did not deter them."

"Thank you both." Iryasa's tone is final; she's heard enough.

Sa Nikuran, her cohort, and I all bow to her. She takes a breath.

Outwardly, she looks just as calm. But I recognize the weight of silence in preparing to take a step that cannot be walked back.

To Sa Nikuran, Iryasa says, "Please convey my appreciation to Sa Rangim for his foresight and let him know I would be honored to set up a time to discuss the implications of this situation and our response at his earliest convenience."

Our. She doesn't specify who that means: her and the Istal government alone; her and Sa Rangim. But she wishes to discuss it with *him*, and that matters.

Sa Nikuran bows her head again, and her shoulders droop a fraction too; when she straightens, she is visibly relieved.

"In that case," Sa Nikuran says, "Sa Rangim has asked me to convey that he can be at your disposal immediately, your Highness."

Iryasa glances at me, a wry look on her face I can decipher easily: relieved that he's willing to work this—whatever this is—out with her, and at the same time recognizing that of course she will have no time to collect herself or process anything before taking her next enormous step.

"Shall I accompany you?" I offer. "We could stop by the shrine on the way."

She considers, then shakes her head. "No. Visiting the shrine is a good idea, but I will proceed on my own. This is between us." Iryasa turns back to Sa Nikuran. "Are you available to escort me?"

The cohort snaps upright, bows again, and rises, all in tandem. "It would be our pleasure, your Highness," Sa Nikuran says.

Iryasa inclines her head, then turns to face we who escorted her on her journey through the Cataclysm.

"My thanks to all of you," she says. "You can handle the immediate particulars from here?"

She knows we can; the question itself is a peace offering. All three of us bow.

When I straighten, Iryasa tells me, "There will have to be consequences for this."

I nod. "We will need to discuss our strategy before tomorrow's negotiations. Message me when you're ready to meet?"

This time, she clasps my hand, and we both squeeze.

Finally in sync.

When Iryasa and the Te Muraka have departed, Risteri says, "I need to check in with the guides."

"Can you take Lorwyn home first?" I ask.

"Second," Lorwyn says. "I'll go with her."

I look at her.

"I'm tired, not stupid," Lorwyn says. "I may notice something—or learn something that will help later."

Risteri adds, "She's right. You can tell she's not stupid because she didn't say I shouldn't help her get home later."

Lorwyn rolls her eyes but doesn't dispute the point.

"We've got this," Risteri tells me. "I gather you have something else you need to attend to."

"This can't stand," I say seriously. "We're going to have to make a storm. While Iryasa's busy, I would be stupid not to consult the biggest expert in spiritstorms—be they literal or political—I know."

Yorani leads me to where Saiyana and Ostario are working on the barrier. We take a detour first, so we arrive with food in hand.

They're both so intent on what they're doing they don't take note of us immediately. It takes me a moment to locate the hasty—which is the only reason I can find it at all—spell to alert them to an emergency. The rest of what they're doing is more complicated than I can follow.

We watch them for a minute.

Then another.

Yorani's tail twitches with impatience.

"Do you think they can be interrupted?" I ask her.

She nods.

What does a spirit know about magecraft? I'm not certain I want an answer to that question.

"Would you like to go poke Ostario?" I ask.

She tilts her head curiously.

"Saiyana has a more volatile temper," I explain. "She's more likely to lash out and ask questions later."

Yorani's tail twitches again, accepting that, before she flies off.

This is not an entirely fair description of Saiyana. Set on a task under normal circumstances, she is focused to a fault, and will ignore any provocation right up until she doesn't.

These are not, however, normal circumstances. Or a normal task—or what I have come to believe is my sister's normal ability to cope.

Ostario is certainly under incredible pressure as well, if not precisely the same as Saiyana's purview. However, he has never had the luxury of being able to lash out. While I'm sure he could be provoked, an unexpected dragon nose isn't going to do it.

Yorani blithely passes into their circle to do just that. Ostario sees me first, and then somehow Saiyana follows his gaze.

I heft the bag of dumplings in one arm, then the sack of sugary beverages in the other.

They communicate silently, in quirked eyebrows and scowls and nods.

I'm not quite close enough to hear the words, but I can read Ostario's lips as he very deliberately holds Saiyana's gaze and says, "I will hold for you."

My sister's expression tightens, but moments later she's extracted herself from their combined magework to leave the circle.

"You really like those Gaellani cloths," Saiyana says, dropping on the ground next to me.

Yorani is evidently going to keep Ostario company. I settle down next to her.

Two princesses, eating food off the street out of a sack without even a chair. I wonder what our mother would think.

"They're handy," I say, passing her dumplings and containers of dipping sauce. "I can make a sling now so I can carry two beverages by a single handle."

"You should learn how to do these at your store too," Saiyana says, hefting the drink. It's green, frothy, composed mostly of sugar, and entirely delicious.

"No relevant Cataclysm ingredients," I say regretfully. "I could make them at home, perhaps."

"So there's still tea outside even the tea master's capacity," she says, her gaze still fixed not on me, or even Ostario, but past us all to the Cataclysm.

"I'm a master, not an actual spirit," I say. "We can't ever know everything there is to know. That's part of what makes life worth living."

Her jaw tightens. "Is it? There was no warning tonight before our emergency flares went from nothing to the barrier is on spirits-cursed fire. We've been in crisis mode for hours, and it's just starting to settle."

"I'm not surprised." Saiyana looks at me sharply. "Please actually put that dumpling in your mouth while I explain."

Scowling, she does, and I do. She eats and drinks grimly, her motions stilted like she's following a proscribed rhythm and not tasting a single flavor she's swallowing. When I'm finished, Saiyana swears—not so much angrily as wearily.

This is how I know I have a problem.

"Miyara, this has to stop," my sister tells me seriously.

"I know."

"No, you don't. If I had an entire platoon of mages at my and Ostario's level—"

"Geniuses, then. Or at least expert practitioners." She does have a platoon of mages under her command her, but that isn't the same.

"—that could expend power constantly, we could keep the Cataclysm from growing. *We still can't stop whatever's making it expand.* Or at least, we can't figure out how to stop it while holding it."

I watch her stare down at the drink in front of her like she has no idea what joy looks like. She doesn't need to say anything more, not to me.

I now know what desperation from my sister looks like, and it's Saiyana admitting limitations to me without my provocation.

"If you see a site where the tech was deployed," I say after a moment, "do you think you could prove cause and effect?"

She blinks; her eyes narrow.

My sister looks up and stares bleakly at Ostario, maintaining whatever magework they were doing for the barrier not so she could talk with me, but so she would, if not rest, then at least eat.

"Ostario will do it," Saiyana finally says, still looking at him. "I'll hold here for him."

This, finally, surprises me, that she's recommending him rather than doing it herself. It shouldn't, but a part of my chest I thought might finally loosen now that Iryasa and I are working in the same direction has tightened again, like a shard of ice pointed at my heart.

This could be growth. This could also be Saiyana cracking.

"Thank you for having my back earlier," I say softly.

"You know I always will."

"I do. I just want you to know that I appreciate what it means."

Saiyana's head bows. "Miyara. Please don't have feelings at me right now. I am too tired for feelings."

But not so tired she couldn't manage to say that, rather than snapping at me. Oh, sister.

She's been carrying us all this far; it's time for us to carry her for a while.

"I'll take it from here," I say, still quietly, but a note of steel in my voice that makes her look up. "And Iryasa will help."

"Be careful—"

"We have it in hand."

I have the beginning of an idea, and with Iryasa's input it will become a plan. My eldest sister is probably still occupied, but so much the better. I have more to do first, and consulting with Entero is at the top of the list.

It's going to be a long night.

Saiyana is still studying me—blankly and bleakly. I rise and help her to her feet.

"If you need time and an army of expert magic users at your disposal," I say, "then I will get them for you."

CHAPTER 27

AT TALMERI'S TEAS AND TISANES, the ambassadors wait for me to begin. They all clearly know something has occurred; what's more, they expect me to take action on account of it.

In that respect, at least, I have succeeded. They know I will not stand idly by.

They also know I will not act in a way they can predict, and so they are watching me.

I'm glad I finally have their attention.

I'm also confident they're not going to predict what we have planned, even if they think they know the corner it's coming from:

That being the delegation from Istalam, the one section of our circle that remains empty and waiting.

Taseino is here as my assistant, with Elowyn keeping out of sight behind the tea counter but close enough to observe in person, rather than through Lorwyn's witchcraft in the back. I can't have Cherato associating Elowyn with me, given her role with Karisa, and since Elowyn and I haven't had much opportunity to work on appropriate etiquette for such a situation this is hardly the time for an education rite by fire.

Still, if she is ever to be a tea master, she will need more experience of negotiations than her life has hitherto been preparing her for, and now that she has some context for what to expect—well, there will be very few as high stakes as this.

Yorani watches from a shelf, so anything of notice from that quarter will be attributable to her, though I don't expect there to be. Karisa sits alone in the Istal camp, affecting obliviousness and occasionally sipping her tea. Not loudly, exactly, but with just enough irregular volume to grate on nerves in an otherwise silent room.

Until the front door opens, and Iryasa enters.

Followed directly not by Reyata or even Saiyana, but by Sa Rangim. Ridac sucks in a breath.

My eldest sister pauses inside the threshold for Sa Rangim to reach her side, and then they continue walking together. Only then does Reyata enter the tea shop, following afterwards.

Ambassador Ridac's reaction is entirely what I expect, as the canny old operator's expression moves rapidly through shock to outrage and then naked calculation as he thinks through the implications of this power move.

Iryasa is not only expressing her support by bringing Sa Rangim with her; he is expressing his support of her. The arrangement of their positioning indicates mutual respect, and moreover that there is an understanding between them. Ridac's plans of pushing a new Istal-Velasari ruling marriage have been greatly complicated. His eyes narrow on me as he realizes I must have known this was in the works during our last conversation.

Ambassador Perjoun of Taresan smiles faintly, inclining her head to me as if in recognition of what I've done. When I don't acknowledge her, her eyes narrow, her whole body shifting in readiness. She takes my hint for what it is: that this is not *my* doing, which means that what *is* my response is yet to come.

Ambassador Cherato's response is the most interesting of all, in that, for once from him, it's visible, in the tightening of his entire expression when Sa Rangim passes through the door.

Sa Rangim: a Te Muraka who, unlike the rest of us, can nullify—or perhaps consume—Nakrabi magic.

"This summit purports to be a meeting of equals," the Nakrabi ambassador says. "The Isle of Nakrab has allowed this fiction in deference to local custom, but this passes permissible propriety."

Ridac had also been opening his mouth to object, but at that he clenches his jaw in annoyance at such an offensive argument—now sharing a position with Nakrab will put his own point in a less optimal light—and waits for me to respond instead.

I don't.

Instead, I look to the crown princess of Istalam, who is taking her time settling into her seat and making a point of ensuring Sa Rangim is oriented.

After a minute has passed, she meets Ambassador Cherato's gaze directly and says, "Istalam is honored to serve the Te Muraka as our own citizens, and we value their counsel just as highly. Where we are welcome, so are they."

Ridac lets out a breath, shaking his head. "Tea Master Miyara, are we to understand that his presence here is with your permission, and you support the Te Muraka's sudden intrusion into our talks?"

"Say rather 'belated welcome'," I say blandly.

Ridac snorts and leans back in his seat, lacing his fingers behind his head. He, at least, recognizes, this isn't the end of the excitement I have planned.

I ask, "Are there any further objections to Sa Rangim joining our discussions?"

"You have yet," Ambassador Cherato says, standing, "to answer mine."

I smile. "So I have." I look inquiringly over at Ridac and Perjoun, both of whom motion me onward.

Cherato's eyes darken.

"Now then," I say. "Ambassador Cherato. We have business."

"You would insult us so?" he cuts in. "You begin with this affront, deliberately ignoring the concerns of a respectable ambassador, and now you will hurl accusations—"

"Say rather I will lay them out calmly," I say. "Taseino, if you would distribute the report in front of Princess Reyata to each of the ambassadors, please."

"Honored ambassadors," Reyata says in her cool voice, "in this document you will find a copy of reports, first from Istalam's Cataclysm Defense, of an attack against the barrier that contains the Cataclysm by Nakrabi persons using Nakrabi technology. Second, from Istalam's magical research division, who have laid out clearly the connection between the knowing deployment of this technology and its direct effect on the Cataclysm—which is to say, its expansion. We have clearly found the immediate cause of our current difficulties."

"Despite," I add softly, "very, very clear instructions to each *respectable ambassador* about what interactions with the Cataclysm are under no circumstances permissible."

"These are lies," Cherato says flatly. "You cannot prove this so-called attack—which we have only your word for its occurrence, I must add—happened at all, or that Nakrab had any part in it."

Sa Rangim speaks for the first time. "I understand, ambassador," he says calmly, "that you are inclined toward magical demonstrations. Shall I demonstrate for you, how a Te Muraka reveals what is beneath Nakrabi masks?"

The room stills.

Cherato points a single, deliberate finger. "You threaten me, and thus the Isle of Nakrab."

"Was it a threat, then," I say, "when you, and thus the Isle of Nakrab, insisted on demonstrating Nakrabi magic to *me*?"

"From the beginning, you have decided against me," Ambassador Cherato says. "The Isle of Nakrab sent a delegate in good faith, as the continent seeks to address a problem that affects us not at all, and you have slandered us at every turn."

"For the record," Iryasa puts in mildly, "that is not at all why the Isle of Nakrab sent a delegate."

Ridac casts her a shrewd look, and Perjoun's expression is considering as she takes the crown princess' measure anew—and mine.

"When the ambassador from Velasar was found inside the Cataclysm with unsanctioned magical technology, you both can recall that I confronted him as well," I say. "If you are uniquely the subject of my censure, Ambassador Cherato, it is because you uniquely disregard the boundaries I have clearly, in deference to potential for cultural differences, set. By participating in this summit you have consented to abide by my judgment, and I have promised consequences. So we come to it, Ambassador:

"On behalf of the continental nations, I, Tea Master Miyara, demand reparations from the Isle of Nakrab, to be tithed in the form of magical service."

The entire table stares at me in shock.

"Reparations?" Ridac finally asks, as if he cannot quite believe what he is hearing.

Reparations have not historically been a tactic with much success on the continent; he'll be shocked that I would bother deploying it. But if Iryasa and I can make this work, if we can teach the world and ourselves to shoulder responsibility for our actions, we can change a great deal.

All the way to the Te Muraka, and Gaellani, and witches.

Ambassador Cherato's entire demeanor has shifted now. He openly displays a façade of amusement, inviting the other ambassadors to join him, because he believes this to be impossible.

Impossible is my specialty.

So first, we start here: that this is not a sally to slip in what I actually want; that I am, in fact, completely, utterly serious. Let them believe that when I show my aim, it is because I am entirely confident in its inevitability.

"Reparations," I repeat firmly. "We cannot move forward equally together on this matter when one party is allowed to disadvantage the others. The Cataclysm's growth disproportionately affects Taresan and Istalam, whose lands and citizens have been lost, even as they have taken in an influx of refugees into ever smaller areas. Velasar has not been immune to consequences either, as Taresan and Istalam have leaned on Velasari resources for support when theirs were drastically altered and strained.

"The Isle of Nakrab has had no care for this continent's greatest treasure: their spirits. So to make amends, the continent will have use of the Isle of Nakrab's treasure. And we are all aware of how Nakrab values its magical expertise."

Ambassador Cherato's expression goes sardonic. "Of *course* you demand our magic. It's what you've wanted all along."

"What I want—"

"Is to serve as a proxy for your family, Istalam's rulers. Tea Master *Miyara*."

Ridac startles and swears.

Ah.

My body runs cold, like I've been doused with freezing water from within.

After all this time, there it is.

I'd known this move would provoke Cherato, of course, but I had expected him to hold this play in reserve for a while longer. That he has not means I have struck closer than he would like to admit, which is good.

Ultimately, dealing with this may also be good. But right now, it is... not optimal. I cannot afford to falter.

Karisa, spirits bless her, doesn't miss a beat: she affects shock and betrayal and shame in quick succession, that Cherato would reveal what she had told him in confidence, then dramatic obliviousness.

Ridac snarls, "Of course you're the spirits-cursed fourth princess."

"It brings me great joy to merit such recognition," I say dryly.

Because of course, until this moment he *didn't* recognize me or even suspect. He, who has spent more time than any of these ambassadors at the palace where I lived, did not note undue familiarity between me and the princesses.

His face mottles as he slams his hands down on the table in front of him. "You didn't think that merited disclosing? The integrity of this entire summit is now in question. We have all wasted our time."

To my surprise, Ambassador Perjoun speaks up. "The tea tournament."

It's all she says, but it's all that's needed.

The tea tournament is the highest profile event on the continent. Ridac throws himself back in his seat, remembering: the unusual addition of a tea master, the tournament's clear attempts to disfavor me, and my victory without the tea guild's support. At the time, that lack raised eyebrows: now it is notable that I likewise triumphed without support from the crown.

I still disagree with the guild's actions, but right now they're about to serve me well.

"You are not the first to voice such concerns, Ambassador Ridac," I say. "I have been called to prove my position before, and I'm sure I will again. The Istal crown as well as the tea master's guild have separately accepted my position as an independent operator from both of them. That is not the issue of this summit."

"Are you kidding? You can't expect this information to change nothing," Ambassador Ridac says.

"I'm no stupider than the last time you spoke to me, no," I say dryly.

I can read a room. Ambassador Perjoun is more firmly on my side than before: Entero's intel indicated her respect for established order—which in this case, for better or worse, means lineage—runs deep. She likewise respects work, and both I individually and the Istal royal family's special commitment to service play well there.

On the matter of reparations, I might have been able to convince Ambassador Ridac to vote in favor of such an idea by my and Iryasa's choice to position Velasar as a beneficiary of Nakrabi magic. But the revelation about my heritage, and the fact that he wasn't aware of it, has made him feel manipulated by Istalam, which will speak to a long history of perceived slights—some of which I'm sure I could not fault his interpretation of.

Ambassador Cherato, of course, I have lost entirely; but then, he was lost before this meeting began, and it is not worth my time to invest precious energy in someone who will always possess no regard for my life or the lives of those I care about.

That makes him my enemy, and I will not pretend otherwise. I will triumph.

And that means today's strategy needs to change.

One more day, Saiyana. I will have to trust she can hold that long.

"It seems this day has been a surprise to many of us," I say. "I invite you to take the afternoon to review all of the information made available to you today, foremost the packet in front of you, and we will reconvene tomorrow. If you have any questions about it, or me, or the shape of reparations, I am happy to answer your questions."

"A question then, before we adjourn, regarding your position on reparations," Ridac says smoothly.

Spirits. If he wants to do this publicly, it won't go as smoothly for me.

"I am happy to clarify," I say.

His eyes gleam; he has outmaneuvered me at last. I wait.

"Istalam," Ridac says, "has historically resisted punishing the witches for their part in creating the Cataclysm."

"Witches were not responsible for the Cataclysm."

He waves this off. "Let us pretend we agree, for the sake of argument, that they did," Ridac says. "You claim to be in favor of reparations regarding the Cataclysm. My question is, would you impose that same judgment on the architects of that disaster?"

Ambassador Perjoun steps in to equivocate. "If I may be so bold, I believe that is outside the scope of this summit."

A solid effort, but Ridac judges me correctly as he says, "I want to know if Tea Master Miyara is willing to push that scope and go all the way."

Have I considered all the implications, is what he means. Will I see this to its natural end.

I look at my eldest sister; she nods.

Without breaking eye contact, I say, "If in the course of this summit I discover that Istal mages are responsible for the creation of the Cataclysm due to permitted bigotry among the mage council of the university of Istalam, I will hold that council to account."

I turn to regard each person in the room in turn as I continue.

"If overseers of Taresan's department of the interior are aware of and abetting the weakening of the barrier, I will hold them to account." Ambassador Perjoun's expression reveals nothing, and Ridac's is hostile as I say, "And if I discover that a Velasari intelligence division backed by the Velasari government is responsible, the Velasari government may expect to hear from me. Does that answer your question in full, Ambassador?"

"No, as you've avoided it entirely," he says. "Your biases cloud your judgment after all."

"*My* biases?" I shake my head. "Your hypothetical is a false equivalence, and as it is already demonstrated false I will not engage in it. I do not allow it for the sake of argument, because the argument is moot at best and discriminatory at worst. Shall I be clearer, ambassador? If witches are involved in communal reparations, it will be as the recipients."

To my vast relief, Iryasa, who could trip me here and now, does not balk at this. Instead she calmly nods, as if this is entirely obvious and she has no objection to holding such an unequivocal stance on a subject Istalam's royal family has been forced to back down on in the past.

As I am backed into a corner, she takes a stand there with me.

Thank the spirits.

"Istalam," Ridac sneers, "always looking for those they consider smaller."

He harkens back to Istalm's imperial history as a smear against us and is thus surprised when I don't dispute him.

"Exactly so," I say. "I will not stand for any measure that attempts to extract service from witches, or Te Muraka, or Gaellani. They have been wronged, and it is our duty to serve *them*."

"Will you answer for your wrongs to the Isle of Nakrab?" Cherato cuts in softly.

The one major player in this room I have not yet named, which I'm sure no one missed.

I meet the ambassador's gaze and don't entertain *his* false equivalence, either. "If I learn the Isle of Nakrab engineered the immense destruction brought on by the Cataclysm for its own selfish benefit, then you may rest assured that I will demand satisfaction, and I will not rest until I receive it. Am I perfectly clear, Ambassador?"

Tension crackles between us.

He meant to trap me into accidentally admitting bias he can use to take me down.

Whereas I am entirely confident in intentionally showing him the shape of the snare that he is poised to step into.

If he steps into it, I will see that it snaps shut.

"Perfectly, Tea Master *Miyara*. I believe we all now know where we stand."

I've drawn the battle lines.

Now we will see who steps over them, and how.

The truth is out, and my past a princess has been revealed.

Now everyone will know.

Word travels quickly now that Cherato is actively using my identity to discredit me, so I spend the rest of the afternoon at the tea shop to prove to Sayorsen nothing has changed: I am still their tea master, the same I was before.

It's as much an effort to prove it to myself, that there is still a place for me here, that people will still look at me the same way.

The last is not true. Maybe someday it will be, but not today, not with the news so exciting and fresh—or raw.

The full employee roster of Talmeri's Teas and Tisanes comes in to help—not including Entero, who's officially resigned, but for once including Talmeri herself, as she can't miss a chance to tell the tale to anyone who will listen.

This is a gift: the more people listening to her, the fewer demanding royal stories of me.

The shop is as busy as it was during the height of the tea tournament; I am both grateful and ill at ease that no ambassadors seek me out.

The tea boys rotate line management. Talmeri remarks that the queue is likely to increase as those who are overawed at first realize they can in fact still ask a princess to serve them. Meristo cracks jokes constantly, mostly at his own expense, as a continual prick every time tension considers rising. Iskielo endears himself to the customers by visibly sharing their astonishment at the whole thing.

Yorani emerges from the back to be charming and adorable, while Elowyn and Tamak remain there working companionably as if nothing was ever amiss between them. On the occasions I retreat there this is balm to my spirit.

Not that they have found each other, but that honesty and good intentions turned to action can overcome strife and bring people together. Or at least, the possibility of that.

Because there have been people today who feel betrayed by this secrecy from their tea master, too; or let down upon learning, or deciding that I'm not one of 'them' after all.

If ever there were a gauntlet to convince me I cannot be everything to every person, this would be it.

I can only do my best, and it can never be enough for everyone.

I hope Saiyana is holding on.

Weeks ago, this announcement would have meant the end of my freedom, forever. Today it means... more work. Difficult work, to be sure, and more to come, but the life I have built has not been blown away in the emotional whirlwind.

I am afraid to believe it. When the doors finally close, I'm so wrung out it takes me a moment to process that while everyone who came to support me today is exhausted, they're also, to my surprise, largely in good humor.

Lorwyn takes the towel out of my hands while I stand there numbly. "You thickskull. You're one of us, and we're not abandoning you. That's how this works, remember?"

I stare at her, tears springing to my eyes.

It's exactly what I always hoped she would expect of *me*—I never dreamed of the reverse. From Lorwyn most of all.

Her eyes widen as she seems to realize the meaning of what she's just said, and now she's almost as surprised at herself as I am, because she believes it, too.

A coat drapes over my shoulders, and Taseino comes into view, holding my tea kit. "You've done enough. I'm taking you home."

You've done enough. That isn't true. In a very real way, this shop is my home—

And apparently it still will be tomorrow. With some fuss, to be sure, but—no dramatic arguments, or contests of my place here. No challenges I—*we*—couldn't handle without too much trouble.

A strong foundation, ready to support when an unexpected wind blows in.

Meristo promises to handle everything, and Talmeri herself shoos me out the door with Yorani at my shoulder and Taseino escorting us.

"I can walk myself," I say. "You don't have to go out of your way."

"I'm aware of that," Taseino says. "But we will all feel better knowing you weren't accosted on the way home with no one to defend you."

I let it go, too tired to push and selfishly not wishing to. Yorani is quiet, just being present—not asking anything of me or giving otherwise. I wonder how she learned that.

But Taseino, it turns out, isn't done.

"You know I've learned a lot watching you," he says after a few minutes.

I smile wearily. "I sometimes fear how much."

"You never just rescue people," he says. "You make them part of their own solutions."

I stare.

He chooses his words with care. "You're so used to standing as a lone pillar. But I think sometimes it's important for *us* to actually see you lean on us, so we all remember that we're in this world together. We should know that we can hold you up, and you should know that we will—especially when you need to lie down for a while."

Which is, at this moment, *exactly* what I need. For so many reasons.

I'm not on my own here. That's an enormous part of the point.

We're going to win this for everyone, and we're going to win it together.

I did my best today, and I will do my best tomorrow, and so will we all, and it will be enough.

We will *make* it be.

Tomorrow.

CHAPTER 28

THE GREENERY AROUND OUR house is thoroughly trampled, though no strangers are loitering outside. The door is, for once, properly shut and locked, not just defended with magic.

Inside, the pottery shop at the front looks like a strong wind blew through. The shelves are nearly barren, and what's left is in utter disarray.

The lights are on in the living room, but Deniel isn't moving around. After a moment I locate him on the couch, a cat on his lap and an open book covering his face. I set my tea kit down gently and go to the kitchen as quietly as I can.

Nevertheless, Deniel stirs. The book slips off his face, landing with a thud on the ground that jolts him to consciousness. He blinks a few times before his gaze fixes on me. "Miyara?"

"I just got home," I say. "I didn't mean to wake you."

He blinks again, then glances down at his legs. "I didn't mean to sleep, but Talsu ambushed me. He knows an easy mark when he sees one. I don't suppose Yorani would consent to distract him?"

"No, she left with Taseino," I say, coming over to the couch. "I'm not sure what she's planning, but I am very nearly too tired to care."

Deniel levers himself up to make space for me on the couch and carefully rotates, keeping his legs together until his feet hit the floor so his lap is still stable for Talsion. The cat flicks an ear suspiciously, but once Deniel's movement ceases he curls into a tighter ball. I slip in next to Deniel, and it is the easiest thing in the world to lean my head on his shoulder at the same time he slips an arm around me.

"Maybe," Deniel says, "Yorani is also learning about boundaries."

"From me? That seems unlikely, don't you think?"

Deniel smiles, wearily amused. "You're perfectly fine at establishing them for people other than yourself, and just because you haven't learned it all at once doesn't mean you don't do it at all. But let's call it giving people space, then."

I'm quiet for a minute.

"I didn't do a good job of making sure you had space today," I finally say.

"Not exactly your fault," Deniel says. "You sent warning as soon as you could."

"That was Meristo's idea," I admit. "I'd like to think I would have thought of it on my own, but—"

"Miyara, that's literally why you have a support team." Deniel's tone is exasperated.

"Did you, though?"

It's his turn to be quiet for a beat, because of course this is one of the things we had in common when we both met: no one knew who we were, not really; we hadn't trusted anyone with our full selves.

Then he says, "Actually, yes. One of the Gaellani construction groups I won work for with the summit sent people to manage the crowd. Some of the food workers set up mobile carts out front and did a brisk business, and the hospitality staff sent extra supplies for the nearest businesses with bathrooms so I didn't have to let anyone into the house to gawk at how a former princess lives with an artist."

I wouldn't have thought of any of that. Karisa's reaction to the tour of our home had been cute, but the idea of the judgment of strangers looking to consider me as a princess rather than as myself, and Deniel as a quirky accessory, makes my skin crawl.

I'd expected the reveal of my past to affect his day, but I hadn't fully appreciated the disruption to him would be on par with what I'd been dealing with.

I should have, though. Even before his position on the council, Deniel was a recognized figure in the public, by some metrics the most successful sole Gaellani artisan in Istalam. He's been known in Sayorsen for years.

He has also advocated for the Gaellani community for years, and now, even though he's stood apart from them and alone for so long, it is a relief to know they see his work and appreciate him, at least now.

Still. "I'm glad people took it upon themselves to manage the logistics, but I think the most draining thing for me today was all the talking," I confess.

"Oh, I wasn't finished," Deniel says. "A couple Istal council members showed up, too. One was clearly attempting to make nice now that he knows who you were and the kinds of connections he's suddenly hoping to be able to access through me. But one of the others apparently experienced a scandal earlier in her career and guessed I wouldn't be prepared for all the attention, so she brought one of her aides to run interference while she stayed near me to deflect some of the worse comments. I'd have been... much more at sea before you set me up with Saiyana for political lessons. I'm trying to think of today as a field assignment supervised by a teaching assistant. Not that I've had those, so maybe they don't work that way, but—anyway, thank you."

"You're thanking me?" I lift my head to stare at him incredulously. "After all this?"

He tilts his head. "Yes? A year ago I don't know that anyone would have come to my defense even if I'd asked. Certainly not voluntarily. That change is because of you."

"You wouldn't have needed anyone to come to your defense if not for me," I point out.

Deniel rolls his eyes. "First of all, sooner or later everyone needs help. Second of all—Miyara, it's not like I didn't know you were a princess and that people might find out someday. You've never lied to me."

I sigh, settling back down on his shoulder. "I know. I just didn't want who I was to destroy your life."

He hugs me a little tighter. "It's hardly destroyed. Remade, maybe. But from the moment I first let you into my home, I knew my life would never be the same."

I glance up at him. "Is that why you repaired the tea pet for Lorwyn that time? A marker of change?"

Deniel smiles. "No. And I'm still not telling."

"Strict," I murmur, draping myself over his lap to hug the cat instead.

He laughs, running a hand over my hair. "I'm more than I was, and we are more together," he says simply, as if it's the easiest thing in the world. "We'll get through this."

And it is, and we will.

I wrap my arms around him, and he hugs me back, and we stay there. That we can find comfort in each other with no more expectation than this, this easy confidence between us is why—though we have taken things so slow in part by preference and in part by necessity—I am sure I am ready to move our relationship forward physically.

But truly, it will have to wait for another time. I sigh.

"Hmm?" Deniel murmurs quizzically.

"I really am too tired for any other kind of fun right now," I say, "but the next time we're both capable of more than collapsing in a boneless heap..."

Deniel huffs a quiet laugh. "Agreed. On all counts. I know we're both trying to find balance, but—"

"We've gotten to the busy stage of this undertaking," I say wryly. "Which is to say, the stage where I can't even pretend I will be able to make any kind of balance work until I see it finished."

"And then?"

I turn my head to look at him. We're close enough to kiss, but Deniel's gaze is distant.

"Perhaps sleeping," I say, "though I don't want to set my hopes too high."

He grins fleetingly, glancing back long enough to take note of my proximity and take advantage of it to drop a kiss on my mouth. But then he says, "I meant farther ahead than that. What do you want your future to look like?"

I blink. Several times.

I've gotten so caught up in what I need for everyone else's immediate future—my sisters, Sayorsen, Istalam, the continent—I haven't given this much thought.

What's even sillier, I was trying to plan for Yorani's long-term future past my death without considering my role up to that point: my most important role for my familiar isn't to shape her on purpose, it's to live the model I wish for her to have in me.

I drop my head down and bonk it against Deniel's shoulder.

He laughs again and squeezes me tighter. "Let me start. I want more nights just like this, with you and me together. Though I'd angle for some where we're not too tired to move, too."

"Me too," I whisper.

"Your turn," he says.

I consider, looking across to the room to the shrine to the spirits we set up in our home—that we had separate and, working together, combined. Imagination, the intangible, is also the stuff of air: to reach what I want, it matters to be able to dream it.

I want to dream that future with Deniel.

"I want to have demonstrated publicly that the path I've chosen for myself is worthwhile," I say. "As you've pointed out, I may never be able to settle entirely, but I need this in order to be semi-settled, so I don't have to... fight quite so hard for my reality to be allowed to exist. There are other problems I want to attend to."

Deniel returns, "And I want to not be such a unique example of Gaellani business success for people to point to as an exception, so I can be a person to my community and less of a figure on a pedestal."

I cup his face in my hands. "We're working on that."

"On yours too," he says, and adds with amusement, "Now try one on a little smaller of a scale."

I frown, at first pretending to think hard and then actually trying hard to think of something else.

"Miyara."

Oh, fine. "I want to be able to bake with your mother without embarrassing myself. I consider this a long-term goal."

He shakes with laughter. "She's not going to judge you for not having years of experience."

"Perhaps not, but I'll judge myself for not possessing at least enough competence to not get in her way, let alone appreciate all she has to teach."

"Well. In that case, I want to feel confident in my position as a councilor. Not to know what I'm doing in ever circumstance, exactly—I know I will always have more to learn. But to feel confident that I am capable of serving in this position."

"You'll be more comfortable once you have more experience," I say.

"Which I am getting, with this project, and Saiyana's help, and with some of the councilors and their various intentions," Deniel agrees. "But I will be glad once some of that experience is behind me rather than all in front."

"And," I nudge him, "you'll have a law degree."

His whole face lights up, and, shyly, he nods. It's been such a dream of his for so long that no one ever considered a plausible reality, I think he forgets sometimes he can be openly excited about it without the same consequences now.

At least he can with me, and having someone at all is already a world different than no one.

I say, "I want to eat noodles with you at a Gaellani market and also at an Istal restaurant."

Deniel blinks. "We haven't eaten out together much, have we? Easy to fix. Although, ah—"

"I would also like to be able to do so without getting swarmed or goggled at, yes," I say. "I'd like to be able to explore and experience Sayorsen with you without it being a cause for remark."

"Do you think it will ever be?" Deniel asks. "Even if people get used to us in our positions, we will never really be... unknown, here."

"That's possible," I admit. "How about this: I'd like people to be able to notice us without considering our presence behaving just like anyone else as cause for note. They can identify us as the master potter councilor and the ex-princess tea master without thinking it strange that we, say, buy groceries." I look at him, smiling. "Or release lanterns into the sky. Which I also want to do with you again. Every year."

His gaze is serious as he meets mine. "I also want us to light lanterns for our children together. If that's something you also want."

My heart thumps, and for a moment I am breathless. It's a thrilling sort of pause, the kind where imagination runs wild with the possibilities, packed into the space of an instant.

This requires more of a response from me, and I lean up to kiss him. "It is," I whisper. "But... not quite yet."

His crooked grin is light. "We have years and years. I suppose that's also one of my hopes: I want to have you to myself for a little while."

I grin, but it's a fleeting one, and when I next speak it's more pensively. "I do want for us to be able to do our work without worrying quite so much about the people in our lives."

Deniel's forehead creases. "I can't imagine you not worrying about your people."

I shake my head. "I don't mean not worrying at all. More like not worrying that each of them is teetering on the edge of a precipice, and which way they fall materially depends on my intervention? I want to matter, and I don't want to not do the work I've committed to, but this is... a lot, very personally, all at once."

"How do you mean?"

I sigh. "Risteri is... probably fine, now, though between House Taresim and her relationship with Sa Nikuran her life isn't exactly not fraught. I believe Lorwyn and Entero will figure things out together, but until Entero's position is stable and witches are at the very least legally welcome in Istalam I can't exactly rest, as I've had a hand in all that. Then between the spy teens—"

"They seem to be doing well, but they are teenagers so I suppose our work there isn't done."

That 'our' warms me, but— "and my sisters—"

Deniel purses his lips and says, "Well, Reyata isn't on a precipice."

"Reyata's future happiness depends on my ability to keep Iryasa out of a situation where she has to marry a Velasari for political reasons so that Reyata can freely pursue a relationship with General Braisa."

Deniel's head falls back. "I forgot about that. And Iryasa and Karisa aren't clear of their own difficulties yet, and Saiyana is... struggling."

"Perhaps it's naïve, but I really think I won't continue to accumulate dire circumstances requiring existential systemic solutions at quite such a pace once all these are... at least confidently progressing in a hopeful direction that doesn't consistently require my effort to maintain!"

"That is certainly a hope for future Miyara and not your present," Deniel agrees wryly.

There is a glaring hole in that list of worries and responsibilities, and my eyes narrow as I consider.

"You know who's always been playing the long game, before any of us?" I ask. "Thiano. He's a step ahead of every player, every single time. Even when I personally surprise him, it's like he's thought of all the ways a situation he's interested in could possibly go and made plans for every contingency."

"Or it means he has a very specific focus," Deniel says, "combined with a long timescale to plan for. You can seed a lot that way."

I nod slowly. "Yes. Yes, precisely."

"I forgot to mention before," Deniel says, "but the reason the Gaellani contractors got the news that the Nakrabi ambassador had revealed you as the former princess quickly enough to help was because of him. Thiano's how they knew to come."

That makes me sit up.

"What's wrong?"

I'd thought I was too tired for anything, and I suppose this isn't 'fun', but nevertheless I will have to find the energy.

"They told you the Nakrabi ambassador revealed me? And they got that from Thiano?"

"Yes. Is it not true?"

"No, I'm sure it is true," I say, thinking rapidly. "But it probably means the Nakrabi ambassador enlisted Thiano to spread the rumor, and that Thiano hates him but isn't willing to entirely burn that bridge. Which means he needs something from the Isle of Nakrab, and, as you said, Thiano must have been very focused on something very particular for a very long time."

I pry myself out of Deniel's embrace and stand. It feels impossible that I should still have to move, and yet.

Deniel asks, "You're worried you put him in a difficult position with your demands today and should have warned him?"

"I—no, but it didn't really occur to me I should warn him, I admit. I just assumed he'd know, because he knows everything."

"What, then?"

"I have a theory," I say. "It's a ridiculous theory, because it would require a person to have both a massively overdeveloped sense of ethical responsibility as well as the ability to lie in wait for years, acting only in the shadows, and to never let either slip."

Deniel stills. Most people know Thiano only as a crotchety, crafty foreign merchant, but I have had the opportunity to see deeper, and Deniel knows it. "And?"

"And if I'm right, there are only two reasons Thiano wouldn't be willing to burn that bridge with Nakrab," I say. "One possibility is he doesn't know everything Nakrab has done and is planning."

"Which would be terrifying, as it would imply levels of craftiness beyond even Thiano's staggering ability," Deniel says. "Which is also why it's unlikely, if they're at all related to his purpose in Istalam, as seems to be the case. And the second option?"

"The second option," I say, "is that there's something far worse on the horizon that I don't know about. And what I do know is that we're facing the risk of the Cataclysm expanding endlessly. Either way, it's past time for Thiano and I to change our understanding."

Deniel resettles Talsion in the warm spot on the couch where I'd been sitting and stands himself, crossing over to kiss me. "I'll get some food ready for you to eat quickly while you prepare your tea kit."

I love this man.

Maybe one day it will be possible for me to show him how much—endlessly, every day, living it.

CHAPTER 29

AS I MAKE MY way toward Thiano's shop, I think about what I know, and what I can do that will matter, to Thiano. Tea mastery is my tool and my weapon, but arguably I haven't been using my whole arsenal.

Because I haven't been planning with Yorani in mind.

I draw to a stop and close my eyes, focusing on her, on my *concept* of her, as if through our connection I will be able to reach out across a spiritual thread and know where she is and how to reach her.

I hold that thought for a long minute, waiting for a sense of change, or really any sense at all.

There's nothing.

Perhaps I will be able to sense Yorani in that way someday, but not today. That's not among our skills yet; I can only focus on what we can do *now*.

For one thing, Yorani is the one being in this world Thiano loves without reservation, who can put him at ease reliably and without provoking him by reminding him of his humanity, and the connections we all share.

For a second thing, Yorani is enormously more advanced at responding to my inner state than I am at knowing hers: perhaps a consequence of her being my familiar, rather than the other way around.

So I close my eyes again and focus on my familiar once more.

Yorani. I need you. I think the words as hard as I can.

When I open my eyes... she's not there.

A disappointment, but not exactly a surprise. Imagine if she'd just spontaneously appeared in front of me! I hardly expected that.

I leave it alone and resume walking. She either got my request, or she didn't.

But I believe in the strength of our connection, even if I don't understand how to manipulate it.

So I'm also not surprised when, by the time I'm in view of Thiano's shop, Yorani swoops in from above and lands on my shoulder.

"Thank you," I whisper.

She nuzzles the side of my face gently. Not even an inquiring chirp: she knows she's here for Thiano's support.

Together we face forward and approach his door.

I knock. There's no answer.

I wait, and try again: still nothing.

I glance at Yorani. Her eyes narrow, and her tiny ears flick, ending pointed toward the shop.

Thiano is definitely inside, then.

"I don't technically have any authority to break into your place of business," I begin casually. "However, the strictures on what I can and cannot get away with in my capacity as Sayorsen's tea master remain rather nebulous. I'm confident I can successfully make the case to anyone who might ask that your uncharacteristic lack of response made me fear for your health and I felt obligated to investigate. As ward-breaking isn't among my skillset, I would naturally turn to my familiar, forlorn at no longer being welcome at your hearth, so I cannot guarantee the state your door would be in once Yorani—"

The lock clicks; the door swings open, and Thiano glares at me.

"Why, Thiano," I say evenly. "I'm so delighted to find you home and well."

"You're a menace." He points at Yorani. "You are *also* a menace."

Yorani chirps and hops off my shoulder, fluttering until she lands on his.

Thiano sighs. "You know I know what you're here for."

"It had certainly occurred to me you might have some reasonable guesses."

"Then you know I'm not going to talk to you."

I step closer. "There are many people's actions I can confidently predict, but in this case I would not dream of presuming to know your future course."

"Convenient for you, you can take me at my word," he snaps. "Or is that not good enough for you, princess?"

I tilt my head to one side, studying him. "Am I no longer a tea princess in your eyes?" A change after today's news, or something else?

Thiano's eyes narrow. "Does it matter?"

"To me personally, rather a lot," I say seriously. "I value your estimation highly."

"A curious choice for someone who hitherto has not seemed unduly fond of disappointment." It's not quite a sneer, but it's close.

If he really wants me to go away, he should know perfectly well that his standard cantankerousness isn't going to cut it.

I heft my tea kit. "Also I don't actually expect you to talk, but if you think I can't make you an adequate cup of tea I would ask if you might consent to allow me the opportunity to challenge your understanding."

Thiano frowns at me. "A tea ceremony is not going to help, Miyara."

"All to the better. Then you won't be disappointed when I don't try to help. But surely no one can reasonably object to a cup of tea freely offered from a master?"

By 'no one', I mean Ambassador Cherato, and Thiano knows it. His glare intensifies.

Yorani butts her head into his ear.

"Yes, I know I'm going to let you both in, you menace of a spirit. It's past time you learned about dramatic timing. Observe."

Thiano gives Yorani a look to make sure she's paying attention; glares at me; flings the door wide; gestures grandly with great implicit sarcasm for me to enter; and sweeps off into the shadows of his shop.

"There," he mutters to Yorani, a disembodied voice in the darkness. "*That's* how these things are done."

"You're spiteful," I call after him, closing the door behind us, "teaching her things that she will certainly use against me."

"It's no less than you deserve!" he growls back. "Now hurry it up while I find the space to accommodate your demand. Anyone ever tell you a forced gift isn't, tea princess?"

The 'tea' is back now; interesting, and a relief.

"No need," I say. "I know perfectly well we both fit kneeling in the aisles of your clutter. I have everything else I require."

"Hmph." Thiano emerges bearing a chair before he passes behind the shelves, and I follow him as he slams it down in between two over-stuffed rows, causing some of the items to rattle.

Yorani looks up at the movement with interest, and without taking his eyes off mine Thiano casually yanks her back down to his shoulder before she can get into trouble.

"My knees aren't what they used to be," Thiano says, a cruel smile that makes me wonder what real emotion he's covering for there. "I'll sit."

"And I am happy to kneel." I do so on the ground before him, and look back up. "I am at your service."

Something flickers across his face before his expression closes into its sardonic default. "Then proceed, tea princess."

※

Once again, I extract a water bottle I've added to my kit—possibly a better addition even than the emergency snacks. But to get to it I have to pass Yorani's emergency socks, and she promptly flies over to plop on her back in my lap, feet pointing up imploringly.

"My apologies, it appears I must pay a tithe before she will heat the water," I say dryly. "A moment, please."

I unfold the baby socks and slip the first one over her foot, carefully slotting her claws into previously poked holes. Once Glynis returns to Sayorsen with Ari, perhaps I can ask her to adjust the holes properly so they don't continue unraveling.

"You bought Yorani cat socks?" Thiano asks, faintly incredulous.

I'm surprised he can make that out in the dim lighting here. "It was her idea. Talsion is her friend, and she has no concept of moderate behavior where her friends are concerned."

Thiano's expression flickers. "You're one to talk."

"Certainly not." I know it's not what he means, but I lift my skirts enough so Thiano can see my own socks: a matching pair.

Thiano buries his face in his hands. I'd like to think he's amused despite himself, but something tells me that's not it; or at least not all of it.

There's something there about friendship, and equals; moderation and protection. And clarity in this, for me: the tea ceremony is the journey, but as though Yorani's wings cleared a path, I see where we begin to take flight.

As I finish with Yorani's second sock, Thiano shakes his head, dropping his hands. "That would be quite some moderation for a princess."

"Ah, so now I've lost even that moniker from you," I note. "Weren't you not going to talk to me?"

Thiano scowls, caught out. He's so used to deploying barbed words with veiled meanings he's out of practice at how to use silence.

Yorani flutters back to Thiano, pausing right in front of his face for him to admire her socks. His scowl deepens.

"You're perfect, little one," he says gruffly, his words at odds with the severity of his expression, with the line of tension in his shoulders, as if Yorani and I together present an enemy of the highest caliber.

Yorani chirps happily, flies around his head once, and settles on his shoulder.

I meet Thiano's gaze: there's a challenge in his expression as if to ask, *Am I truly a match for my familiar?*

She breathes a glowing stream of magical fire toward me that stops just at the teapot to heat it.

We'll find out.

I begin.

I am once again using a traditional air blend, but this one is a dark tea: not light, but sharp.

Despite its history, it's not commonly used for tea ceremony. Tea ceremonies are typically thought of as a soothing comfort, and this is not a tea for soothing—or rather, not for calming.

This is a tea for the clarity of anger.

This is not a tea that makes a person feel as though everything will be well: this is a tea for fighting. For acknowledging that the fight is necessary, and matters.

There is comfort in easing pain. But sometimes, the real comfort to be had is not by trying to lessen it, but by acknowledging it.

Perhaps I cannot help Thiano. But I can *see* him.

I can see into this man who has operated from the shadows longer than I've been alive.

I can see a man who has intentionally isolated himself—from the people he came from, as well as the people he traveled to—and I can see his understanding that this distance is fundamentally necessary to the course he's committed himself to.

And never, never strayed.

I would admire that dedication alone, but it matters too that I see that Thiano works in the service of others, not himself.

He's not habitually sarcastic because he believes he's better than anyone: it's a distancing mechanism. He's not isolated because he prefers it that way, but because of lack of trust.

From our first meeting, he has tested me: my mettle, my resolve. His pressure has honed me like whetting a blade, and at every turn he has tested the currents in the air to predict how my ideals and actions will interact, taking their place into account in his grand scheme.

I would have to be stupid not to see the pattern, that every time I demonstrate to him that I care about others more than myself, that I will use whatever skills and strength I have to fight for those who cannot, he has chosen to aid me—in ways that far surpass how any spy should behave.

I flick my fingers like a flicker of flame. A strong wind can snuff out a candle.

Thiano is so wary of me, and I imagine will be for many years to come, if not forever. A deep betrayal from a power you should have been able to count on leaves scars. I personally couldn't have had any role in whatever happened in his past—the timelines can't match—but I don't begrudge him his tests: I will simply be sure to pass.

Every one. As many as it takes.

Let him see that his dedication is a model for my own. I will not abandon my path, or minimize it, or betray it.

Whether he can ever consider me a friend is moot: I consider him one of *mine*. So he can choose to look away from me, but I will never stop looking for him, to him; after him, if he allows it.

He will never be invisible to me. I will never forget what he's done for me, from the small gestures to the large, from the scathing moments to the tender ones.

He will never be negligible to me. Not just because of what he's done or who he is—though those, too; somehow he teaches me even when he's actively not trying to—but because he is a person. He matters.

I truly believe everyone's existence matters to the world. Even if I didn't, though, I would believe Thiano mattered to the world.

I can be absolutely certain he matters to me.

I don't know how many people's lives have been affected by his choices and actions. Air can smother flames, but it can also fan them: how many plots has Thiano quietly managed with no one being the wiser? And:

What flames could he fan if he chose not to be quiet?

Whatever he chooses, I will still consider Thiano a friend: I believe in him, even if he does not believe in himself.

But I am not above adding some pressure of my own to the air.

Thiano may dream for the world, but not himself; never himself, unless it is to be enough to see his course through.

So I will dare to dream for him.

I don't know what cause has driven him all this time, what it is that he safeguards. But it is clear to me that he is currently on the defensive, moderating himself, and I can't help but wonder:

What could Thiano, on an aggressive offense, do?

What could he risk, if he believed anyone would have his back, and that it would matter?

What if he believed, not that I can help him by performing a tea ceremony that magically transforms him into a happy person, but that I can help him by taking him—his anger and his silences—as he is, and believing in him not despite it all, but because of it?

What could Thiano be, if anyone dared to see him, and believe in him, for who he is—in *my* perception, not how he thinks people perceive him, or how he thinks they ought to?

I do; I am.

The rest, we'll find out.

I pour the tea into Thiano's cup and offer it to him with both hands. Looking directly at him.

He does not meet my gaze.

But he does deliberately reach out to me and takes the cup.

Thiano holds it for a long breath, considering. Even Yorani is still: this moment is for him.

Finally he says, "You give me too much credit."

"If anything," I say, "I suspect I may not give you enough."

His face is like stone, but I see the twitch around his eyes that another time might have been a visible cringe.

At last, like a man who believes the cup is poison, his hand shaking, Thiano chooses.

He sips my tea.

He closes his eyes and bows his head.

Without opening them he says, "I will give you one chance to speak your piece."

That is what my tea ceremony has won me: a chance; a chance to allow myself to be tested.

This is who he is, and what he needs, and I will always do my best to be a person who can pass tests in his eyes without fail.

I do not hesitate.

"I'm sure you're aware that yesterday there was an attack on the Cataclysm, deploying Nakrabi technology against the barrier to weaken it. I do not know if you're aware that the assailants were not Velasari agents, but Nakrabi under illusion magic. Nor did they use magic themselves. While I believe Entero is still tracking them down, I will be shocked if they do not appear just as Cherato's attendants do, drained of vitality.

"But I also have no evidence that these Nakrabi had any understanding of what they were doing, Thiano. They are sacrifices, because Ambassador Cherato, on behalf of the government of the Isle of Nakrab, does not care about the lives of anyone lesser. *We* are sacrifices, because he, on behalf of the Nakrabi elite, considers us lesser and thus expendable. Those elite do not allow themselves to be changed or influenced away from who they are: people who will sacrifice the entire world for their own short-term self-interest.

"Cherato is not a person who can be changed. This is not a person you can reason with and expect to hold to promises, but he is also not a person who can be made to care when, not if, he does not. You can undermine him from the shadows, but you cannot stop him alone, because you have limits and he does not.

"So I am asking you to tell me what I need to know so I can apply systemic power to force limits upon him. Because while you may emerge from this round still standing, someday you will die, and the Nakrabi government will live on. Whatever you are protecting will never be safe unless we make it impossible for them to succeed. *Please.*"

Thiano's knuckles around the tiny teacup are so white I almost expect it to explode in his hand, and he is breathing hard, like my words alone have exhausted him.

But steadily now, he lifts the teacup once more and knocks the rest back at once.

Then he looks at me, and his gaze is clear.

There's anger there, but also a tremendous sadness I don't know how to compass.

"The Cataclysm," Thiano says, "was caused by a series of mistakes there were many opportunities to prevent, or correct."

My heartrate kicks up.

At last, this is it.

CHAPTER 30

MY HEART POUNDS. I suspected whatever Thiano has been about all this time had to do with the Cataclysm, of course I did, but that he's had knowledge all this time of what no one else seems to? Cherato truly does not believe Nakrab is responsible for the Cataclysm, so I assumed it had not been deliberate, but—

"How did they begin?" I ask softly.

"You need more context." Thiano sets the teacup down and gazes past me, like he can see the past in the shadows of his shop. "Nakrabi magic is strongest at the monasteries: that's where all of us, the 'elites' as you call them, train."

I hadn't even known Nakrab had monasteries.

"We imbue objects with power through ritual chanting," he continues. "With exceptional focus, a sustained effort over time, and multiple people of one mind, we can channel tremendous power. Monks train to deny their bodies, clearing their minds of distraction, in order to make themselves optimal conduits. That is, in a very simplified way, how our magic works."

"But it stopped working," I surmise.

"Oh, not entirely," Thiano says. "Not all at once. But gradually, yes. No matter how strong the monks' chants, no matter what measures they took to ensure focus and shared thought, the magic in the objects was not as strong as it was in our history. For a long time, as you might expect, our politicians blamed the supposed laxity and degeneracy of younger crops of monks. However, time has more than demonstrated that either our monks, under the same time-tested training or more rigorous versions of it, are growing weaker—"

"—or there is less magic for them to access."

"Just so. You have seen what is happening to spots of land on this continent. Now imagine vast stretches of that as far as you can see."

Oh, spirits.

"Just," Thiano says softly, "so. For generations, magic came from all around us. We have no tradition of what to do when that's not the case. So our leaders pushed, and our monks trained harder, going to dangerous lengths I am confident would horrify you. Some of us learned to pull magic from further and further away, which takes even greater strength. And pull we did."

We. Perhaps I should be surprised to learn Thiano was once a monk. I am not at all surprised to learn he was one of a select group with uncommon strength of will and focus.

"I wish I could tell you," Thiano continues, "that realizing the effect of our magic was enough to make us stop. It was not. But once upon a time, I had a friend."

This would be bad.

Silently, I refill Thiano's cup. Yorani butts her head against Thiano's face, and he pets her not absently, but frowning. Like he doesn't believe he can be trusted to.

"My best friend in the world," Thiano says. "Shegano. Ah, but I haven't voiced his name in years."

I press the cup into his hand.

"We were the top of our class, as you would say. We drove each other to new heights—of intensity in our training, of vision—and we were evenly matched in our ability to channel power.

"We had a... group of followers. You need a group for any substantial work on Nakrab, now. I didn't understand at first that they were with us for him, not us. Where Shegano and I differed is that I have never been one to inspire others. And ultimately it turned out I had limits, and he did not."

Thiano knocks back another cup of tea and continues without pause, like he cannot trust himself not to stop now that the tale is coming out.

"I'll never finish at this rate. Allow me to summarize. Shegano always claimed it was his idea, but I have my doubts. One way or another, the idea arose that if we couldn't pull magic from our own land, we could pull it from another. Once the thought kindled, it spread. He spread it.

"At first, I didn't think much of it. Well, that's not true. I thought of the idea quite a lot, just not that it was possible. Even the two of us combined could only pull from the edges of our island: how could we pull from farther? But then once, I mentioned it would only be possible if we could travel and take the magic ourselves."

Thiano takes a breath. "It was a comment made in full sarcasm. I wasn't the same then as I am today, but sarcasm and adolescence go hand in hand. Still, that idea was mine, and Shegano took to it and would not let it go.

"We fought. To make a long story short, I broke my vows and left the monastery over it."

I have so many questions about how much is contained in those two sentences, but I can't imagine interrupting Thiano now. Not in the middle of a story I suspect he has never, ever told.

"In Nakrab, I was seen as a failure and a traitor and useless besides, so of course it will not surprise you to learn that no one told me when Shegano, and the monks he'd drawn to him, set out for the continent."

Thiano did not know in time then, and he has made it his mission to never not know anything of import since.

"I did learn of it eventually. Some factions were behind the endeavor in principle, if not necessarily all the specifics, and others weren't. Eventually, one of those came to condemn me for leaving, because perhaps, if I had stayed, I could have eventually prevailed and prevented him. We'll never know."

But he'll never forgive himself nevertheless for what might have been; that much is plain. Oh, Thiano.

"Even then, I decided it was too late for me to do anything to stop it, even though I knew Shegano better than anyone and knew what his plan would be. So it is not difficult for me to understand what happened:

"Shegano would have led the monks to the place most teeming with life he could find. There was once a massive rainforest well to the east with few visitors; a limited chance for anyone to stop them. They would have attempted to channel, through sustained chanting over weeks, all the magic they could into a single object they could easily carry back with them—something as common as a rock no bigger than your hand, say. They would have focused all their effort toward imbuing the object with one purpose: to continue absorbing magic until they decided to stop."

I suck in a breath, the pieces falling into place. Not just the purpose of the Nakrabi machines now, but what went so badly wrong all those years ago.

"You think someone found them out and tried to stop them," I say.

"Yes. Specifically, I think they were killed. Frankly, it could have been anyone on the continent, and they would have been justified. The Nakrabi government has always assumed the continent was trying to protect is resources; they can't understand people here would believe they were stealing spirits. Of course continentals killed the monks."

"And then there was no one to stop the object they'd created," I say.

"Specifically, there was no one to manage the channeling of power," Thiano says. "Any object will crack if you slam it with enough power fast enough. Trained monks can manage that flow. But without them, the object—which already held several weeks' worth of power from the most skilled monks of our generation, and I don't know how to fully express how tremendous that would be—would have continued to absorb magic until it cracked. And then it would have exploded."

Not witchcraft. Not a magical battle or even a deliberate attack of any kind.

A series of mistakes from everyone involved.

Part of me wants to rage that if only people had known the truth, so much suffering could have been avoided. The Gaellani, the witches—

But of course this is what cuts me short: the people in charge did know it couldn't be witches. It didn't matter.

Prejudice doesn't need a reason, because people who are insecure will seize any "reason": being open to difference and change is harder.

And yet also the easiest thing in the world. Hatred is learned.

I have so many different questions for Thiano now. "And the barrier?"

Thiano shakes his head. "That I don't know. I surmise it had to do with the arcanists, or the Cataclysm likely would have expanded throughout the world, but that's only an educated guess."

As opposed to everything else he's said, which, even without firsthand knowledge, he's confident is truth. But of course he did have firsthand knowledge of exactly who his friend was; what his people cared about.

And he believes they almost destroyed the entire world on accident.

"Do you think the Nakrabi government was behind the monks'..." What to even call this? "Quest?"

"Explicitly? No." His tone of voice is not reassuring. "I think they were entirely in favor of it but wanted no connection in case it failed. Not just to save face with their people—the reason a land as isolationist as Nakrab has a powerful naval fleet was the beginnings of admitting to its magic resources problem and exploring options of what to do about it."

Trade, conquest, resettlement. The ability to send their people elsewhere created opportunities.

"So they knew what the monks were trying," I say, realizing Thiano also termed them 'they', "and at the very least approved enough to let it happen."

"Yes. Now they're trying it again, on their terms. The Cataclysm is known as a great trial to the continent; Nakrab won't imagine that anyone could object to draining it of its wild magic."

"But of course they also can't imagine asking permission, and what they're actually doing is draining the barrier that protects us all. Spirits." I shoot back my own tea and look at him. "You're here because you're in exile, aren't you? Because you know the truth, and they can't risk the response of their people if they were known to be responsible."

The perfect spy for them: someone who knows enough to monitor the Cataclysm's activity.

And someone they can feel superior about, forcing him to be useful to them after he tried to refuse to be, placing him in the place that must cause him the most pain in the reminders.

In confirmation, Thiano lifts his cup as if to clink it against mine. "I was already in disgrace for breaking my vows. No one would protest my execution. Working for them stays their hand—and... lets me try."

I don't have to ask, now.

Thiano will never stop wondering if he could have stopped Shegano—and the mission, the monks' deaths, the explosion—if he hadn't broken his vows and left; or if he'd tried once he learned. So now he can never leave, he can never stop trying, and he can never free himself from this vow:

To see that it never, never happens again.

This is the hold Nakrab has on him.

But if they're going to charge forward anyway with their plot—despite everything he's done, everything I've told them—then they always will. No amount of cooperation or undermining from Thiano will keep Cherato from killing more people.

"Will they know you've talked to me?" I ask. Between Nakrabi spycraft and magic, it would be foolish to underestimate their information network. "Will you be in danger here?"

"Sooner or later," Thiano says, not specifying which question that's an answer to. That's telling on its own.

"Can you set up protections against them with your magic?"

"No doubt, but I will not. Think it through."

"Nakrab wouldn't want you to be able to continue to use skills you wouldn't allow them to profit from as they saw fit," I say slowly. "But if they could prevent you—but wouldn't they have wanted a steady stream of infused objects from the continent if you could make them?"

"I'm sure they would," Thiano says.

"If you would make them." I realize all at once. "But you won't, now that you the consequences. I can't imagine Nakrab just accepting that, though."

"No, they believe I'm unable to summon magic as part of their punishment for breaking my vows," Thiano says. "But I worked out how to get around that bit of magic long before I left Nakrab. I had precious little else to occupy me."

Not to mention he's a magical genius.

"I still don't think I understand," I say.

"Don't you?"

"No, not that part. My—" I pause. "Can you tell me about the bracelets now?"

Thiano blinks, then shrugs. "I suppose there's no reason not to now." He pulls a small metallic ball out of his pocket—an object no bigger than my hand—I realize it's one I've seen him holding before, but not since...

The first time he tested me in truth. When in exchange for his services he demanded I stay out of the situation with Kustio, and I refused.

Thiano holds it up so it catches what light there is to be caught, gazing at it contemplatively. "This was the first object Shegano and I infused together, as children. Shegano never understood why I kept it. It was always a reminder of... limits, which I found an important perspective and he disdained. So I suppose there was always that difference between us."

"What did it do?" I ask.

His smile is heart-breaking. "All it did was hold magic. It didn't accomplish any other purpose."

"You didn't summon magic for the bracelets," I breathe, "you... transferred it?"

He inclines his head. "I am not able to transfer magic out of objects without instilling a new purpose, which is to say, I cannot simply free it—or the spirits, as it were. But this I can do." When Thiano looks up at me, his gaze is as piercing as ever. "You should know the magic in the ball appeared to be dwindling slowly, but when I transferred it into the bracelets, the magic felt stronger. Curious indeed." He shakes his head. "I cannot help but think the spirits, too, believe in you and wish to help."

I stare at him aghast. Yorani chirps, and I transfer my incredulity to her.

That is officially more than I can process tonight. "And the bracelets' purpose?" I manage.

"Focus," he says simply. "That's all."

"That's all? But that—that can encompass so much."

Thiano nods. "The simplest directives require the most magic for that reason."

Hold. Focus.

Theoretically simple; practically, in the world? Impossibly huge undertakings.

"There you have it," Thiano says, leaning back. "Now you know the whole sordid tale and my role in all this. So. What will you do now?"

He's utterly collected: none of cynical Thiano here, nor does he appear vulnerable. Like relieving the burden of this story has left him at emotional equanimity, and he will take whatever comes.

I can do better than that.

We can do better than that.

"I don't think I do know the whole of it," I disagree. "Kustio tried to go through you, didn't he? With his smuggling of Te Muraka magic?"

"Early on," Thiano allows. "It was a natural assumption for Kustio that Nakrab and Velasar would both want what he had and that I would have the contacts to arrange that."

"Of course, he couldn't know you personally would therefore want the exact opposite."

"It didn't take him long to realize my interests must diverge. There was no pattern to the difficulties he experienced working with me except that I did whatever I could to obstruct his sales. Eventually I had to report his activities to my government and was instructed to secure whatever tech I could without the Istal authorities discovering me and charging me with obstruction, which forced me to become substantially cleverer about blocking him so they didn't get their hands on Te Muraka magic either. So I do indeed know a great deal about his operation, if that's what you're asking."

"And you couldn't turn that information over to the Istal authorities without your role working against Nakrabi interests coming to light—"

"—which would prevent my ability to thwart their efforts to interfere with the Cataclysm in the future, yes. But make no mistake, Miyara, I knew what Kustio was doing and that the Te Muraka existed, and I allowed it to continue."

I take a breath.

I hadn't thought that far ahead, but yes, obviously he must have known the Te Muraka were trapped and not moved to help them. Part of me is angry, of course, but knowing what I do now it's hard to direct that anger at him in a way I can feel righteous about. There is too much sadness here, too many people trying their best and it never appearing to matter.

That's what I've dedicated myself to changing. Somehow.

"I'm a tea master, not a priestess," I tell Thiano. "It isn't my job to absolve you."

"Isn't it?" His voice is mocking. "To hold people to account? To uplift us all to be better?"

I roll my eyes. "You know I don't believe in sacrificing the few for the sake of the many, but I'm also not stupid enough to not realize you were doing your best to prevent the destruction of the entire world and potentially billions of lives along with it. I'm not saying I condone your choice, or that I wouldn't have tried to find another way, just that I understand the stakes you were weighing: if your role had come to light and you were no longer able to block all the machinations you've devoted your life to undermining, there might never have been an outside for the Te Muraka to escape to. We can debate what if forever, but ultimately that choice is in the past and not one I can change. I'm here about what you, and we, can do now."

Thiano's eyes narrow, and abruptly he lets out a huff of air—like a disbelieving laugh directed at himself. "You've seen through me again, haven't you? Even before I have."

"I'm not going to absolve you of responsibility or lay out punishment, no," I say. "That's not my place in this."

"I suppose that would be too easy for me," Thiano says, and that bitterness is back.

"Nothing about this has been easy for you," I say. "But to focus on the particulars, here, you know Nakrab's operations—more even than they probably realize. Moreover, you know intimately how their magic works, also better than the vast majority of their practitioners. You know what they're trying to do, and you know how they're doing it."

Thiano watches me; waits.

"You asked what I was going to do," I say. "The very first thing is to make sure you're safe from the Nakrabi delegation and their agents."

His eyebrows shoot up into his forehead.

"Yorani, will you go to the Te Muraka?" I ask. "If Sa Rangim agrees to shelter Thiano temporarily until I've handled this, they can send an escort to bring Thiano to their compound."

I think I manage to mention 'handling this' with remarkable aplomb, given that translates to 'saving the world', but Thiano doesn't even tease me about it.

He erupts, "After what I did to them? You're neither mad nor cruel, Miyara."

"Am I forcing you to torture yourself some more by telling them your part in this right this instant when you're at risk? No, I am not."

"What, shall I lie to them for my own comfort while they put their lives at risk to defend me?"

I level a deeply unimpressed look at him. "Thiano, you're whining."

He scowls. "You are behaving as though I don't deserve to take responsibility for my actions. Do you think they will take the news that I knew of their plight and did nothing better once I'm in a secure position, then? That they won't resent having protected me without knowing?"

"I think you should behave as your conscience dictates," I snap, "and I notice you're not even wondering whether to tell them at all, only how. I think you're a spirits-cursed martyr. I think Sa Rangim will understand what it's like to have no good options. And I think I will leave resolving how unpleasant you make these revelations for everyone involved to you. Yorani is going to ask the Te Muraka for their help, but one way or another, you will be protected, Thiano: that is not optional. What I will allow, if you're going to insist on making everything as hard for absolutely everyone as you can, is for you to refuse my petitioning on your behalf to Iryasa for asylum."

Thiano's expression cycles through several emotions very quickly, but my attitude seems to snap him out of catastrophizing and all he asks, finally, is, "Why?"

"If Nakrab comes for you, we will defend you."

"Yes, thank you, the stupid part of this plan was immediately obvious—"

"We will defend you with the truth. We will send witches and Te Muraka to Nakrab's shores not to wage war with magic, but to spread the word that their government is so desperate they have engaged in a grand deception—which I imagine the Nakrabi people will have no trouble believing—attempting to commit genocide, and botching it, sacrificing ever more Nakrabri resources—your magic and your people—in the doing. I am no Iryasa, but how do you think that narrative will go over?"

Thiano nods, very slowly, his back straightening. It's like I can actually watch his thinking realigning in real time. He's impossibly crafty, so he's not slow on the uptake, just breaking out of the trap of his own self-image:

It never occurred to him he could be an advantageous pawn to leverage against his enemies.

It never occurred to him that he might be able to be part of a group again; that anyone would want him ever again.

"I think I will accept after all," he says, sounding vaguely surprised at himself. "And then?"

And then.

I meet his gaze, and then Yorani's: her, waiting patiently for my word, her eyes as steely as I know mine must be.

"And then we make it so they never hurt anyone ever again," I say. "Themselves included. Then we extract reparations so someday, we will all have the option of being able to move on, informed by our past mistakes but not trapped by them. And then we end this, once and for all."

Yorani brushes her wing against Thiano's face, and his expression is full of a kind of raw hope he can't quite hide as he watches her take flight from him.

CHAPTER 31

THIANO DOESN'T INVITE ME into his living area to help him pack whatever necessities he will need.

"Seeing how I live will make you sad," Thiano says gruffly. "I don't want that from you."

My pity, he means. But I leave the matter alone. It turns out he already has a small pack ready in case of such an event, and this makes me sad enough as it is: that he has lived his entire adult life always believing that everything could be taken from him without warning. Not allowing himself to grow attached more than absolutely necessary; always not just preparing for the worst, but expecting it.

While we await Yorani and the Te Muraka envoy's return, I help Thiano prepare the shop for what I hope will be a temporary leave of absence, unless he wishes to make it permanent. In my case, that means putting the shop to order: making a sign to place in the window for customers, paying off outstanding bills, preparing arrangements for expected deliveries.

For Thiano, it means magic.

He still won't create any magical objects of his own for fear of trapping more spirits into them indefinitely. I assumed that meant he couldn't work magic beyond what he'd done for my bracelets at all, but I'm proven wrong. The details are more nuanced than I can follow with my non-expert understanding of magical theory, but Thiano can use Nakrabi magical techniques to change the magecraft wards on his shop.

"Could Ambassador Cherato have altered the protections we have on the shop like you just did?" I ask him.

"And on your house? No," Thiano says, amused. "Firstly, he'd have to contend with the Te Muraka and witchcraft magic layers. Secondly, he has neither the imagination nor the skill."

I cock my head to one side. "I was under the impression he was a talented magic worker."

"Oh, he's plenty competent. But he's old—much older than me, even—and very set in his ways of thinking about magic. It could never occur to him that such a thing is even possible. And not to put too fine a point on it, but even if it did, there's a difference between competence and genius."

"Even after you haven't been permitted to exercise your skills for years?" I ask.

His smile is sardonic. "Even then. A tremendous part of our training is theoretical exercises. I am more sensible than I was as an adolescent, but I have not lost my edge."

Thiano lowers the defenses for me to affix a sign to his outermost door, and as he begins to resettle them, a voice calls, "Wait!"

I startle, which for me means freezing completely while my brain processes the sound. Thiano's reaction is rather more interesting: his gaze goes distant, only for an instant, and I realize he has all at once thought of and prepared a chant to defend us with magic if the situation requires it.

Not lost his edge, indeed. It makes me sorrier that he's not been able to practice this path he's devoted so much of himself to.

But after a moment Thiano's gaze relaxes as he recognizes who's approaching us. It's not the Te Muraka we were expecting, and I barely have time to marvel before they're upon us.

"Sorry," Glynis says, Ari breathing heavily behind her. "Seemed like a lot of effort to undo that all the way again if you didn't have to. Can we come in?"

Thiano pulls a gorgeous tea set of Deniel's craft off his shelf without apparent concern, evidently bemused that somehow association with me has led to his hosting exhausted adolescents.

Ari is practically asleep on their feet, while Glynis' gaze is overbright: she's passed the point of tired when her body should have shut down and is running on momentum alone.

I'm close enough to that point myself to recognize it in another.

But for now, I serve them tea as Glynis fills us in on the basics.

"I assume it's fine if he hears this," Glynis says, nodding toward Thiano.

"Oh, so *he's* fine?" Ari mutters.

I gather I've been dropped into an ongoing argument.

Glynis rattles off, "Thiano was demonstrating magic I've never seen before, which probably means it was forbidden, and to Miyara, which means he trusts her, which means—"

"Yes, it's fine," I interrupt. "I trust Thiano without reservation."

Glynis blinks; that qualification is apparently further than she expected me to go. She looks over at Thiano, who gestures sardonically, leaving her to make of that what she will. He may be willing to be vulnerable with me, but that's a specific exception Glynis isn't party to.

She looks back at me and nods decisively and begins.

If we had two Enteros, one of them clearly should have gone with Glynis on this rescue mission—and it would have been eased by a Te Muraka as well. But for ability to navigate any kind of magic and do so with stealth and speed, I could not have chosen better than Glynis.

She gotten herself into the palace with only an expected amount of trouble—expected for her, that is; I wouldn't have known to do half the preparation she had, between disguising herself and arming herself with political information through her messengers' guild experience and literally getting to Ari—but getting back out with Ari was more of an adventure.

Politically *and* magically.

"Istals are definitely part of it," Glynis says.

"Shocked?" Ari asks me, their expression a challenge—spoiled by a yawn that makes them scowl.

"I am not," I say seriously. If Istalam had no problems of its own, my grandmother would never have allowed—forced or not—witches to be treated as they have; my mother would never have been trapped into a marriage that caused her to neglect her daughters; Ostario's skill would never have been disdained due to his origins—

I cut that train of thought off before I can really get going. Clearly, I have a growing list of injustices I intend to correct.

I'll stop the world from ending first, and then it'll be time to look toward addressing the root causes here at home that allowed it to come to this.

In case I ever thought I'd run out of work.

"Istalam's reckoning will come at my hand," I tell Ari. Their eyes narrow, studying me, and I meet their gaze until finally they appear to accept my conviction, at least for now.

They will see me make this promise a reality. I promised the ambassadors I would hold anyone and everyone accountable, and I will.

I imagine all my sisters will relish the opportunity to clean our house, too.

Glynis resumes her explanation. Apparently the Istal agents in question are primarily concerned with returning everything to how they imagine it once was: an idyllic Istalam with unchallenged power. They'd rather side with Velasar, a historically known quantity, than a world with Gaellani, and Te Muraka, and change that might upset their comfortable power in the slightest even if it would serve others. The same people who would rather see witches persecuted than accept any upset to the status quo uncertainty would bring.

"Probably some of the same people involved with Kustio," I murmur, glancing sidelong at Thiano.

"No doubt," he replies dryly, which is as good as a confirmation.

So Glynis and Ari had to avoid the traps set by those Istals working in concert with Velasari interests against their own government, and then to make matters more complicated, Glynis recognized agents of Istalam—which is to say agents of Istalam's dowager queen and spymaster, my grandmother.

"You're sure they were Istalam's?" I ask.

Glynis rolls her eyes. "After learning to recognize Elowyn's presence in a dark room, trust me, no one else is hard to identify. They were Lady Kireva's."

"We should talk about your apprentice, by the by," Thiano says idly.

I'm sure he has plenty of thoughts about my maybe-tea master, maybe-spy apprentice. "Not now. Glynis, were Lady Kireva's spies part of the problem?"

"Not the way you mean," she says. "At least, I have no idea. I just didn't know if we could trust them, so we had to hide from them too."

This explains Ari's earlier ire. "A wise judgment," I say. "I do not, in fact, know if they can be trusted."

Glynis tilts her head. "Really? Even though Lady Kireva works for your family?"

My fingers clench on my bracelets.

After a moment, I remember to breathe.

Of course. I should assume everyone knows, now, Glynis first of all. It will take getting used to.

I look at Ari, whose face is impassive for once. They must know now, too, and I can't imagine they've taken this news lightly.

"I'm not sure I trust even my grandmother," I say evenly. "I'm certain she means well. I'm less certain our ideas of the best course align."

Glynis' eyes widen, as she understands what I've just told her.

Not just that I don't fully trust my birth family, though that would be revelation enough. But Glynis only mentioned that Lady Kireva worked for my family: the crown.

Not my grandmother in specific. Glynis will understand what that means of my grandmother's current role in Istalam.

Ari, I suspect, is too tired to have made the connection. I'm not certain if Glynis will tell them. I look at them with a challenging expression of my own. "Nothing to say about this?"

"Oh, plenty," Ari says. "Don't worry on that count. I'm just saving up to take you on when I'm not so tired."

That gets a surprised laugh out of me, if a hysterically weary one. "Too bad. I'm tired enough myself that you might have caught me off guard."

Ari and Glynis both snort at that, which is sweet, but Thiano at least understands I'm not wrong.

"Elowyn passed on a message to me," Glynis said, "about how arcanism works."

So Elowyn concurred with my assessment after all, and Glynis has already been in touch with the spy teens.

Good.

"I assume you have thoughts," I say.

"Always," Glynis says, and Ari snorts again. She shoves them lightly with her short arm.

"I'm afraid your revelations will have to wait," Thiano says, the barest hint of strain in his voice.

Thiano has locked and covered all the windows, but nevertheless I know this means the Te Muraka have arrived. Out of curiosity, I try to focus on the bracelets to see if I can at least identify *Yorani* through our connection.

An actual laugh bursts out of Thiano. "Miyara, no. That's not how anything works."

I should probably feel proud of myself for getting a laugh out of him, except it wasn't intentional, or be glad he can laugh at all, though I'd prefer it weren't at my expense. Instead I throw up my hands.

"Well, how does it work, then?" I ask. "Neither the bracelets nor my familiar came with instructions!"

Thiano shakes his head, shoulders still shaking a little with his amusement, so at least my incompetence on this front isn't urgent or fatal.

But his smile fades as he lifts the wards and opens the door once more to welcome back Yorani.

And with her comes Sa Rangim himself.

Thiano opens the door wordlessly and steps back to allow Sa Rangim to enter.

Sa Rangim bows to me as he enters, and I return the gesture. But it's immediately clear this is not the same Sa Rangim I have become accustomed to dealing with.

This is like the Sa Rangim I faced that first time in the Cataclysm.

The door shuts; Thiano settles the wards back into place, and turns.

Sa Rangim turns, putting his back to me, Glynis, and Ari—

Or rather, putting us behind him, and Thiano alone at the door.

I quash the urge to grip my bracelets, glancing at Yorani, who remains seated on Sa Rangim's shoulder. Thiano is her friend—is she fine with this setup, or does she not realize?

Yorani's gaze flicks toward mine, then back at Thiano; her tail swishes once in acknowledgement.

So this is on purpose, then.

How to support Thiano without undercutting Sa Rangim?

I turn away from them all as if entirely unconcerned. "Sa Rangim, would you care for tea?"

"That won't be necessary," he says.

Just like that, though nothing has changed, it's like everything has; like his presence in Thiano's crowded shop is the size of his dragon form.

Thiano says from the doorway, "You're aware there are debts between us, then."

"I am not a fool, Thiano of Nakrab," Sa Rangim says softly. "I have known this long before now."

Only now, I have opened a way for him to put Thiano in his power.

But I know Sa Rangim, and I know Yorani. Whatever they're about, torturing Thiano won't be it. Punishing? Perhaps, since I didn't. Wouldn't.

Glynis and Ari are both looking at me wide-eyed; neither of them is fool enough nor so tired they can't recognize something is amiss. I make a slicing gesture to indicate they should not interfere.

My hands are steady as I pour the tea he refused.

If I have to pour it down both their throats, I will.

"Out of respect for Miyara and the work she is attempting," Sa Rangim continues, "I will shelter you for now."

In theory that's what I wanted, but that sounds... ominous.

"And then?" Thiano asks.

"And then," Sa Rangim says, "it rather depends on you, Thiano of Nakrab."

"You want to know the whole story too?" Thiano demands, his most sardonic expression firmly in place. "It won't help."

"No, I don't imagine it would change anything at all," Sa Rangim says repressively. "No, what I want to know is what you would choose to do if nothing were required of you."

Spirits, I *am* tired. Too late I see what he's about.

Bless Sa Rangim.

"Pardon the interruption," I say, walking in the middle of them with a tray holding two cups of tea and one bowl. "Thiano, is 'of Nakrab' still a moniker you wish to claim?"

He crosses his arms. "I'm an exile and now a known traitor. It is not mine to claim."

"A traitor only to those who are themselves betraying the isle itself. Perhaps 'Thiano of the Isle' would suit?"

A new name; a new role; a new chance.

That's what Sa Rangim is trying to give him. He's trying to lead Thiano on a path to make meaningful amends without trapping him in an endless sentence. Thiano can't forgive himself, and he can't accept forgiveness except from someone he feels he's wronged. I can't be the one to punish him.

Thiano doesn't answer, me or Sa Rangim. I also can't force the tea on Sa Rangim before Thiano takes it.

"Yorani, the bowl is for you," I say. "You may want to warm it a bit. Thiano, I hope you won't mind. This was on your shelf and looked sturdy."

"Think nothing of it, that's only one of the most expensive pieces even your former royal Highness has ever touched in your life," Thiano says.

"I knew you wouldn't mind when it was for Yorani."

His stasis breaks; Thiano steps forward. "Do you need my answer now?" he asks Sa Rangim.

"Say rather I will under no circumstances accept it now," Sa Rangim says. "Consider well, because when you decide your position, I will call you to account for it. And you will decide before you leave my protection."

Which might mean when he chooses to rescind that protection and force Thiano into a decision, but I can't dislike the stipulation entirely. Thiano has had a series of shocks tonight, and there are likely more to come—and he'll have a better answer for what he can or should choose once he's spent more time with the Te Muraka.

Thiano steps forward and picks up one of the teacups. "I'll drink to that."

Never breaking eye contact with him, Sa Rangim carefully picks up the other cup. In tandem, they lift their cups, and down them in one gulp.

"You're allowed to taste it, you know," I say. "I assure you its flavor is palatable."

Thiano snorts. "Some moments merit a different approach."

"Are you insulting my tea, or my manners?"

"Okay, I have missed too many things," Glynis declares. "Someone better be planning to fill me in."

Sa Rangim steps aside at last so we can all face each other. "Thiano has chosen to turn his back on the Nakrabi government, who are responsible for our troubles with the Cataclysm. He will apply for asylum acknowledging information he possessed while spying, like that he was aware of the Te Muraka's situation with Kustio."

Ari looks like they're struggling to wake up and process all that while Glynis blinks rapidly. "Oh," she says, "is that all."

"There's also the bit that Thiano is a genius with Nakrabi magic," I add while Thiano rolls his eyes.

But his shoulders ease a bit. Spirits bless Sa Rangim again, for taking on the burden of deciding how to present Thiano's situation, and doing so, so Thiano isn't forced right away to choose to bare his vulnerabilities again and again, but in a way that it won't feel like a reprieve to him.

I can't speak to Sa Rangim privately right now or do anything to show my gratitude without Thiano picking up on it, so I ignore it—for now.

"Glynis, do you know where Iryasa is? I need to get her started on the narrative for Thiano's asylum proceedings."

Sa Rangim opens his mouth to answer me but shuts it at a look from me as Glynis rattles off, "Yeah, she's at Taresim. Need me to take her a message?"

Sa Rangim's keen gaze focuses on her sharply, flicking to me only briefly before resuming studying her like a puzzle. Because of course Sa Rangim might know where Iryasa is, but why should Glynis, who's only just returned to Sayorsen?

"No, I'll go myself," I answer. "I need you to go with Sa Rangim and Thiano now—"

"What? Why?"

"Indeed," Sa Rangim says. "The danger to Ari I can infer, but Glynis?"

"I don't know that she's in danger," I say. "It's possible that she will be now that she's successfully extracted Ari. But this way I can send *one* guest who may be a mitigating influence on the others, and at the very least won't try to drive your people away with sarcasm."

"Hey," Ari protests half-heartedly, interrupted by a yawn.

Amused, Thiano says, "I think even Ari may be too tired for that tonight."

Sa Rangim says dryly, "We will, of course, be happy to welcome them both."

"I should check in with my family," Glynis says, though she sounds a little glum about it.

"Will a message do for now? What I started to say is that I need you to talk to Thiano about how Nakrabi magic works. You're the best at putting together different pieces of magic, and I think it's going to take all of us together to solve this."

Glynis looks surprised. "Me?"

I take her meaning instantly—if she were less exhausted, she wouldn't have let it slip. But she's really surprised not to be an afterthought, or in the way; to be valued and specifically chosen as part of a team for contributions she can make that are unique.

But Ari snorts. "'Me?'" they mimic. "Yes, you, the person who's been learning magic for only weeks and just singlehandedly orchestrated an extraction operation while avoiding professional agents from at least two different political factions."

"I mean, I know I can do magic stuff at all," Glynis says. "But that's not the same as being the best."

Ari rolls their eyes. "You really have a complex about being the best."

"Oh, you want to talk about complexes—"

"*Children*," Thiano scorns, in just the right tone of voice to cut them both off immediately.

Before they can refocus their outrage on him, I put in quickly, "Tomorrow morning, get the magic team together to see what you can figure out."

"About what, specifically?" Glynis asks.

"Why do you think Ari is here?" I ask her. "We're going to fix the Cataclysm and the world."

"Oh," Ari says this time, completely deadpan, "is that all."

CHAPTER 32

I'M LATE TO THE meeting the next morning. After working out the basics of Thiano's asylum I'd gotten home so exhausted my brain wouldn't stop whirring through possibilities. Deniel finally suggested brewing a magic tea to put me to sleep, which worked, but it kept me sleeping longer than I have time for.

Not longer than I needed, unfortunately, and I don't feel sharp enough to save the world with my current capacity for insight. Nevertheless, the world is not waiting, and it's not as though I don't have access to more tea. I have the skills to brew a short-term solution for myself—once I've had a cup to make my brain start working.

"Glad you could join us," Lorwyn says when I arrive at the back of the shop with Yorani, the wretch, still sleeping curled around my neck.

Lorwyn, Ari, Tamak, and Glynis are all already there, gathered grouchily around Lorwyn's workspace. They look exactly as they did when we were planning for the tournament match together, and I'm not sure if that should be a relief or a cause for concern. This time the stakes are so much higher.

Without bothering trying to get a word in—and indeed, their conversation continues without me—I duck into the stacks and come back with a tea sachet from the bulk stock area.

Lorwyn raises her eyebrows at me as she waves a kettle to heat, my stomach twisting at the sensation of witchcraft. "You sure you don't need something a little more, uh, potent?"

"I'm not drugging myself with magic," I say firmly. The tea I've selected is as basic as we carry: green leaves a step down in quality from a traditional blend. "I am going to drink something that is entirely predictable—"

"Hey now, all my blends are thoroughly tested—"

"—to my body, which is going to need to hold up however long this takes to fix and could probably use something it's entirely used to." I grab a cup and dump the tea into the nearest strainer that looks dry, so it probably doesn't have any magic on it.

"By 'this'," Lorwyn says, "you mean—"

Glynis says, "Let's pretend we believe she just means the imminent end of the world. Even I'm tired thinking of anything bigger than that."

"And I," I say, pouring hot water over the leaves with great care, because right now this cup of tea is very important to me, "am going to pretend I believe once we manage that I'll get to sleep for at least a little while. What do you have?"

"Are you, uh, sure you don't want to wait until you have some tea in you?" Glynis asks me. "We're getting kind of theoretical here."

"That's an understatement," Ari puts in.

My stomach twists and Lorwyn says, "Tea's ready. You're welcome."

She takes the strainer from the cup and passes it back to me. I take one sniff and blink: she's correct. "Since when can you...?"

"Uh, always?" Lorwyn looks both amused and smug, an expression reminiscent of one I see on Talsion when he's tricked Yorani somehow. "Obviously it doesn't work for testing when I don't know what a tea is going to taste like, but this is basic. You know what, while I'm at it, now it's cool enough—go ahead and knock it back and I'll make you another."

I take her at her word and drain the cup, passing it over.

After a moment of silence, Ari finally says, "I'm not sure which of you I'm more upset by right now."

Lorwyn glances at Tamak and whispers loudly, "That's code for they missed us terribly."

Tamak grins fleetingly as Ari rolls their eyes, though his expression quickly settles back into contemplation, like he's chewing on a difficult problem.

And, well, it doesn't take much to guess what it is.

"Before we devolve into name calling, we have a couple theories," Glynis says. "Starting with Nakrabi magic."

"Spirits," Ari corrects her.

She shrugs. "Okay, sure, let's start with Nakrabi spirits, in the sense of their magic that's infused into objects, even if they don't think of them as spirits, rather than their craft and practice of making that happen. The first thing I realized is that their way of doing things must burn the spirits out."

I look at Lorwyn. "Is that tea ready yet?"

She passes me the cup. "This one's stronger, so sip it this time."

I make a face at her but oblige before turning back to Glynis. "I assume that conjecture is based on the fact that their magic has become a precious commodity, which wouldn't be so if their existing magical objects remained at full power."

Lorwyn says, "It's unnatural that you can talk like that before you're even awake."

"If my time at Miteran's fancy university taught me anything, it's that if anything Miyara's toning it down for our benefit," Ari mutters.

"Exactly," Glynis says pointedly, ignoring them both. "But Nakrabi magic must differ from magecraft, because a magecraft working can run out of power, but then it just stops working, right? Dead spots don't crop up when your house cooler goes bad."

"We can't prove that," Ari says, switching back to the topic at hand because even poking at me can't keep them from discussion of magical theory. "It's not impossible Istalam was relying on colonialism to cover the creeping effects of magecraft."

"But no mages know how to target that drain, and I don't know how you'd make sure dead spots only appear in places you don't like if you didn't even know that was an option." Glynis shrugs. "But obviously I can't ethically test that until we know how to not trap spirits with Nakrabi magic, which is why I started by calling it a theory."

"Oh," Ari says. "Fair. Theory means something different in academic circles. I've been doing a lot of research lately."

"Hold a moment," I say.

Glynis puts her hands on her hips, exasperated. "Already? I warned you—"

"Did you just imply you can perform Nakrabi magic?" I ask.

Everyone looks at her, and she purses her lips. "I think so? I can't be sure, obviously, because I can't test, but Thiano gave me enough of the basics I can extrapolate. And we have that tech we stole too, I just don't want to experiment with it until we're pretty sure, because we only have the one piece."

She can perform magecraft, incorporate it with witchcraft, and understand Nakrabi magic.

I nod as if this is not world-changing, because in truth it confirms a suspicion I've held for some time now. "So the situation may in fact somehow still be even worse than it already was, the theory being that magecraft somehow allows spirits to return to the world, but Nakrabi magic condemns them to a slow death and they are gone forever. Do I have that right?"

Ari notes, "You're much less infuriatingly optimistic when you're tired. Are you sure you need more tea?"

I intend to settle for a mild glare, but Yorani abruptly launches herself off my neck and flaps right into Ari's face. They stumble back, startled, as the tea spirit snaps her wings wide at the last moment to halt her momentum.

"What she said," I say as Yorani lazily circles Ari's head.

"Oh good, you have an attack dragon now," Lorwyn says. "That's definitely not concerning."

"I am sure she will only use her powers for good," I say. "Ari no doubt agrees."

The baby dragon in question stops teasing Ari and flutters up to sit on Glynis' head, peering down at her and anything she might look at with interest.

I envy her perspective. I wonder what it would be like to see the world as Glynis does.

Glynis reaches her arm up to pet Yorani and otherwise ignores the small scaly creature on her head. "To your point, yes—stay on track here people, the messengers' guild would have rejected all of you for reporting this scattered—and also what that means is the first thing we have to figure out is how to free the Nakrabi spirits."

"Not why they die in the first place?" I ask.

"It's sort of the same question," Glynis says. "Like, take your bracelets."

I hadn't made that connection. I look down at them askance, at where I have been unwittingly using power that will kill the spirits it belongs to.

"No, not like that," Glynis says impatiently, even though I haven't said a word. "You're not a Nakrabi mage, so you shouldn't be able to use the magic."

I let the fact that she thinks she can do so and that isn't noteworthy pass. "Is it not that the objects work without active manipulation, just with the intent of the Nakrabi magic worker?"

"I mean, maybe, but that's not what Thiano made it sound like," Glynis says. "Since the bracelets work at your intention, my guess is it's when they work it's because the spirits want to work for you."

I consider that. "It's a nice thought, but we can't prove it. And even if they're willing to help me, I still don't want to drain their... life force. Magic. Whatever it is."

"I wonder if it really does though." Lorwyn taps her fingers on her desk. "If they get to choose. Intent seems to be the one common element of all the magic we're familiar with."

"Not the only one," Glynis says without explaining.

"If the spirits can't choose to be bound up in an object, and we have no reason to expect they can, we still need a way to release them," I say firmly.

"Completely invalidating all of Nakrab's magic expertise," Ari says. "I like it."

Tamak speaks up for the first time, though his attention still doesn't seem to be on us. "I'm not sure the Te Muraka can help with this. We can create objects too, but it uses our own power, which is a loss. When we eat Nakrabi magic, we consume it like food."

"But you don't leave holes in the world either," Glynis points out.

"You haven't seen where we lived in the Cataclysm," Tamak says.

"I have," Lorwyn says, "but more importantly I've seen where you live here. Given everything going on with the barrier lately, the Te Muraka compound would be showing the evidence of dead spots if your magic worked that way."

"We don't know with any certainty how different it is, though," Tamak says. "It's one of the reasons we're so careful. Nakrab didn't know for a long time that their magic was coming out of their own land, either."

"Eh, I don't think this is the right angle to be concerned about," Ari says. "Think of magic workers less like humans for a second and more like cows."

I admit this is not a turn I expected this conversation to take. I glance at Lorwyn without a word and sip my tea as she covers a snicker.

"Provincial farm person," Glynis says fondly.

"Ignorant city girl," Ari shoots back without rancor. "I just mean, grazing cows eat grasses off the land, but doing so also improves the land."

"Is this a poop thing, farm person?"

"Partially, yes," they say. "Cow manure is great for encouraging growth. But cows also spread seeds with their hooves to expand diversity among grasses and break up crusted earth, which also stimulates grass growth. So they're not just eating a resource, they're improving the sustainability of the resource at the same time."

"Grazing means not all in one place, though," Tamak points out.

"Sure. And in the Cataclysm the Te Muraka stayed in one place, right? You were trapped. And now you're not." Ari shrugs. "Maybe your magic won't be the key to solving this one, but I just mean, let's not go borrowing trouble, okay? We don't have any definitive evidence yet that your magic is a problem."

"And Nakrab," Glynis says, "may just be doing theirs wrong. Like if they could just fix it by learning to graze, or whatever metaphorical equivalent applies, everything would work fine. What an optimistic thought, farm person."

"Don't push it," Ari snipes.

"Great, so that brings us to fixing an entire magic system no one here can practice," Lorwyn drawls. "I'm so glad we got together to talk about this."

"So my actual theory," Glynis presses on, "is that at least in the short term, we may be able to make a temporary emergency fix. Like, uh, draining the infection out of a wound before applying a, um, poultice so it heals right—"

"I think we need to stop with the metaphors," Lorwyn says.

"For once I agree completely," Ari says. "I mean, good effort Glynis, but—"

"Fine, but my point stands, and I think it's why both witchcraft works on Nakrabi magic and magecraft at least currently doesn't," Glynis says.

There it is.

"I'm listening," I say.

"Witchcraft is about changing an object's nature," Glynis says, "rather than binding magic to a purpose. It's more... efficient, I guess. So when Lorwyn destroys Nakrabi tech, what she's doing is directly undoing their magic by instantly altering what the object fundamentally is."

"That's about what it feels like, yeah," Lorwyn confirms.

I frown thoughtfully. "That's why navigating the Cataclysm is more natural for a witch too, isn't it?"

"Yes, exactly," Glynis says. "Since there's not still any specific object causing the Cataclysm to persist, Lorwyn can't just fix the whole thing, but her magic is uniquely suited to living magic because it's so immediately adaptable."

"Not as good for dealing with lesser humans who feel threatened by my natural superiority." Lorwyn sniffs.

It's a distraction, but I don't call her on it. That witches could have been part of the solution to the problems caused by the Cataclysm this whole time if people hadn't been too scared and bigoted is worth distracting me from.

Every time I think I can't get angrier about our treatment of witchcraft, somehow I do.

"So the short version of my theory, which we are still working out the specifics of," Glynis says, "is that Nakrabi magic requires an object to infuse, so we should just be able to infuse the spirits back. But from what I got from Thiano, 'land' or 'air' or 'the world' or 'back from whence you came' aren't specific enough to qualify—they're not, like. Countable, I guess?"

"Discrete," I say. "Individually separate and distinct."

"Right, exactly. So we use magecraft to establish a perimeter, because what magecraft is great at is structures. Essentially, the magecraft will define the boundary of what will become the destination for the magic. Then within that boundary, Lorwyn changes the nature of the tech.

The spirits leave the object and go into whatever magecraft has defined, and since it's not a usable object—"

"I have many questions," I say.

"Oh, you and me both," Lorwyn says. "We're assuming that when I unworked tech in the past I didn't just kill the spirits, for one—"

"I'm not assuming that at all," Glynis protests.

"Oh, that's better!"

"Thiano thought the spirits couldn't be freed directly, but they can be transferred. So—"

"So you think they can indirectly be transferred to freedom?" I ask.

"I... yes, basically. Honestly the bigger problem is that even if we can make this work, there's an awful lot of Nakrabi tech out there and only one Lorwyn. Witches aren't exactly going to be lining up to volunteer to help with a public initiative."

"Nakrab will have to learn to help themselves," I say. "One problem at a time. How sure are you that this will work?"

"Theoretically? Very. The specifics definitely need work though." Glynis sighs. "Elowyn's message about arcanism is great for thinking about stuff like this in a broader scale and how everything fits together, but there are so many ways you can combine different threads it's kind of hard to isolate which one is the right combination, you know?"

I blink; set my cup down. "Wait. Message? I thought you talked to Elowyn in person when you got back to Sayorsen."

Glynis blinks back at me. "No, we set up a different way to leave messages for each other. Does that matter?"

I turn quickly to Tamak and Lorwyn—but mainly Tamak. "When was the last time you saw Elowyn? Or Karisa, or Taseino?"

"Yesterday afternoon," Lorwyn says slowly—

—but Tamak's eyes change color completely, turning full black.

"It's the device," he says in a low voice full of dread, and my blood runs cold.

"Tamak—"

"Don't try to stop me from going after her," he snarls, rounding on me.

I step in close to him and put my hands on either side of his face, locking my gaze on his. "Stay in human form until you know what she needs from you."

His eyes flicker, an orange slit appearing in the middle, and Tamak nods sharply. "I will be what she needs."

His voice is a growl, but it's still a voice making human sounds. I release him, and Tamak surges to the door faster than an ordinary human could move: I blink and he's gone, the door slamming into the exterior wall with the force of his exit.

"Yorani, he may need help," I say. "Can you find Entero and bring him to wherever Tamak is?"

The tea spirit wastes no time with questioning chirps or goodbyes or anything else, but is gone nearly as quickly as Tamak was.

"Wait," Glynis says, apparently catching up, "I can find—"

"No," I say, "you are the only member of that team I know the current whereabouts of, not to mention the only one who has some idea of how we may be able to save the world, and I need your knowledge right here."

Glynis abruptly sits down all the way on the ground. "And I was gone, which left a hole in the team. Spirits, you don't think—"

"Ari," I interrupt, "now that you're away from Miteran can you get communications through to Ostario?"

"Yes," they say without argument, already reaching into their pockets for structural materials. "What am I telling him?"

"It's what he's telling Saiyana," I say. "They both need to be prepared for Nakrab to try something on the barrier, because whatever they're planning will be big. We'll convey more pertinent details as we have them."

"Pertinent?" Lorwyn echoes.

But Ari doesn't ask any further questions, and I meet Glynis' stricken gaze.

"What we are not telling them at this moment," I say, "is that yes, I absolutely think that Karisa has been kidnapped."

CHAPTER 33

THE QUESTION IN MY mind is not whether Karisa has been kidnapped. All things considered, that conclusion seems plain.

The question is the specific circumstances.

I don't know if her captors are treating her like a valued political hostage or are planning to make her an object lesson.

I don't know if Karisa is alone. I don't know if Taseino is with her, and I don't know if anyone has found Elowyn.

Tamak, Entero, and Yorani have the best chance of anyone at locating my nigh-invisible apprentice, and all three have already been enlisted in the search.

Ari sends more transmissions out at my direction to members of Ostario's team to convey as appropriate: one to ask Deniel to stay inside our magically fortified home temporarily, for instance, and likewise to the foreign ambassadors and their staff. I suspect these precautions will prove unnecessary, but greater vigilance is in our collective best interest until we know more.

But after that? Until I have more answers, there is little I can do. So I do what I can, and prepare for what I do know will be coming imminently, beginning with setting a large kettle on.

I'm not surprised when Iryasa bursts in.

I'm only a little surprised that she's followed by both Reyata and Saiyana—and no one else. Which means she expects this conversation to go badly for me.

Lorwyn swears under her breath, and Glynis and Ari have both gone very, very still.

All the elder daughters of Queen Ilmari of Istalam have gathered in this room like a storm, and sooner or later, lightning will strike. It's a matter of when, not if, and the crown princess wastes no time.

"Tell me how this happened, Miyara," Iryasa begins flatly. "Tell me how a foreign government has kidnapped our youngest sister on your watch, tell me why you didn't think this merited my attention, and tell me how you think you're fixing this."

And we're back to that: you, not we. Not unexpected under the circumstances, I suppose.

At least she hasn't bothered demanding Lorwyn, Glynis, or Ari leave the room. They all hold still anyway, wisely wary of being caught in the middle of a princess throwdown, but Iryasa has the wits to know that any plan of mine is likely to involve them.

I begin, "You seem to have come by some information—"

"Don't even start with that," Iryasa says coldly. "I am not sharing any information or sources with you until you have proven yourself deserving of them."

"Do you know if she's safe?" I ask anyway.

No reaction. She's mentally prepared herself for a confrontation with me, and when she's careful I can't read that masking as good news or bad.

Fine, then.

I pour the water from the kettle.

"Miyara," Saiyana growls.

"I don't actually take orders from any of you," I say coolly. "This will go far more smoothly once you remember that."

"Are you kidding me right now?" Saiyana demands. "If you try to calm us down with tea I am going to dump that pot over your spirits cursed head!"

"Try it," Lorwyn says just as coolly.

They hold each other's gaze, and the tension in the room somehow ratchets higher.

I expected Saiyana's anger. She has tacitly backed my plays to Iryasa this whole time, she's trusted me to manage while she couldn't, and now she thinks I've betrayed her faith. I can't be happy at this reaction from her, but I understand it.

"Miyara."

This time it's Reyata. Meeting her eyes is somehow harder, because until this moment, she was the one sister I'd never known to be disappointed in me.

She doesn't say any more than my name. She doesn't have to.

I was prepared for anger and disappointment from everyone, or so I thought, but somehow not quite from her.

I look away, not responding and instead focusing on breathing steadily, and pour each cup carefully.

"Ah," Iryasa says, her voice cutting, "a show of calm. Strange that you think that will in turn calm me when in fact it is quite the opposite."

My sister takes a single step forward.

That's it, and yet it's as if the whole room freezes. She's entirely commanded the atmosphere purely by choosing to wield her presence.

I'm almost envious. That skill, or rather its lack, very nearly prevented my tea mastery. I am glad to know she can produce this on command: she will need it, in the future.

But not here.

"I am calm," I say, looking at each of my sisters in turn. "The show was, indeed, for you, as remains the tea, whenever you choose to drink it. I am calm because I can finally see the shape of this whole pattern, and for once I am confident that I am handling it."

"Handling it?" Iryasa drops her own pretense of calm in outrage. "Our youngest sister is kidnapped and defenseless—"

"Are you kidding?" I demand. "Defenseless? Have you met Karisa?"

Saiyana growls, "Being a brat isn't a defense, Miyara."

"Of course it's a defense," I snap. "That's exactly what it is, and it's an offense as well, and she's so good at deploying it none of us realized for years she was managing us on purpose."

Saiyana's whole expression shutters, shutting down like mine is trained to as well as her weary mind processes the implications of that.

She isn't fast enough. Iryasa doesn't miss a beat, voice dripping sarcasm. "Oh, what a convenient justification for you to suddenly come to that understanding now when she's at risk and people are angry with you."

"No, I came to that understanding before Karisa and I hatched a plan together that has been unfolding under your nose," I say coolly.

Silence.

The tension in the room snaps.

It doesn't lessen, though—it just changes.

"You know I haven't told you everything," I say to Iryasa, "and I have made a very careful point of that for this precise reason. Karisa not only has a role in this endeavor, it relied on her being able to manipulate Cherato's impression of her. His understanding was in turn informed by how we behaved around her. The best way to make sure your actions were predictable to her was to leave your understanding of who Karisa is and what she's capable of the way it has always been. And that is not my fault."

Reyata crosses her arms. "Do you think it's our fault for believing what you claim she wished us to believe?"

"Yes," I say. "And mine as well. We should have seen who she is, and who she needed us to be for her, long ago. That being her sisters."

"Oh, that is rich, coming from you," Iryasa whispers, "when you are telling us that you have set our youngest sister to spying on the most dangerous ambassador, on her own—"

"With a team," I correct, "but otherwise, yes."

"And yet she's been kidnapped—"

"Yes, she has," I say calmly, waiting for Iryasa to understand.

It ripples across her face, realization and anger and astonishment. "From the very beginning," she says slowly, "you made that declaration that Saiyana hated immediately—what was it, about not accepting anyone getting hurt—"

Be they members of ambassadorial staff or a princess, I said, understand I will tolerate no harm coming to anyone in this room.

"So I did," I say softly.

Iryasa's gaze snaps into focus on mine. "You knew," she breathes. "You knew—"

"Knew, what, that I would during these proceedings push the Nakrabi ambassador, a person we knew would be powerful and representing a nation whose tech had clearly been deployed against the Cataclysm and that Istalam has virtually no diplomatic leverage over nor understanding of, to a point where they would feel threatened by my unwillingness to allow them to skirt responsibility and would retaliate by attempting to demonstrate their control?"

I take a breath. "Yes, Iryasa, obviously I knew their kidnapping Karisa was a possibility because it was designed to be. Karisa and I deliberately devised a strategy to make her bait, so that the pushback from this powerful, unpredictable corner would be predictable. Meanwhile she has been spying on him all along, and if she's been kidnapped it is because she has allowed herself to be, believing she will be able to learn more from it."

"And if you're wrong?" Saiyana asks. "If Cherato has known all along what she's been up to, and if Karisa is not there by her own design, but because she was caught?"

"That is why the first thing I asked you when you arrived was for information," I say. "It is why, as I imagine you have already tried to track Karisa by her security bracers and found the magecraft negated by Nakrabi magic, those most likely to be able to pick up her trail have already been dispatched to secure more information, which we will then use to adapt a plan."

"A plan," Iryasa says flatly. "A plan where you risk our sister."

"A plan where my sister chooses to risk herself, because she has her own free will," I say. "But yes, I too will risk her, as I am risking all of us, because we are facing the literal apocalypse, Iryasa. You came here wanting to take real-world risks, well, here you go. They don't get realer than this."

This time, when I look at all my sisters in turn, they are silent.

I lift the tea tray and carry it to the surface nearest to where my sisters stand—a stack of boxed ingredients—feeling a twist in my gut as Lorwyn, without a word between us, reheats it with witchcraft.

"So yes, I am calm, Iryasa." I hand a cup to each sister, one at a time. "I still believe in our people. That includes Karisa. It includes Elowyn, Taseino, Tamak, Entero, and Yorani. It includes myself, and it includes everyone in this room. So here. Have some tea, tell me where your news of the kidnapping came from, and let's begin to plan our next step in saving the world, and our sister only if she needs it."

Saiyana doesn't hesitate, knocking her teacup back like she's starved for thirst, or faith. It is just as likely wakefulness she's starved for, so I try not to think much of it.

Reyata waits until I'm watching her before drinking her own teacup, the gesture hiding her face. With a resigned sigh, Iryasa follows suit.

There.

"The thing you have to remember about Miyara," Lorwyn notes idly where she leans against her desk, "is that she has nerves of witchcraft."

My sisters stare at her in unison.

Saiyana says, "Look, I swear I'm not trying to be offensive, but I have had a long I don't even know how many days, and all I'm coming up with is that witchcraft has a reputation for being capricious and undependable."

Lorwyn grins, and there's more than a hint of shark in it. "Immutable unless she wills them differently on purpose."

"That's an exaggeration," I say.

"No, it isn't," Reyata says.

My warrior sister. I meet her gaze, and this time it's clear the coolness has morphed into approval, and something in me unclenches.

Iryasa regards cup thoughtfully. "Perhaps you should consider a marketing slogan, if you're going to keep at it like this," she says. "'Maybe tea will help'. Or 'tea fixes everything'."

"Oh good, business advice from the crown princess," Lorwyn says. "Talmeri will love it."

Iryasa actually rolls her eyes and says dryly to Glynis and Ari, "It's safe to come over now, I'm no longer preparing to bite."

Taking charge of bringing people together, and leading by example. My breath this time is a great deal easier.

"Thank you for that distressing image," Glynis says, unflappable as ever.

But as tough as she is, her mask isn't as rock-solid as those of the princesses of Istalam, and I can see the coolness is an effort. Planned or no, Karisa is at risk, Glynis' friends are missing, and all the princesses of Istalam along with Sayorsen's tea master just threw down in front of her with no attendance to propriety.

Glynis is smart and tough, but she's still a teenager, and that's a lot.

Spirits, it's a lot for me, though I suppose I'm not truly that far out of adolescence myself. Glynis has had a solid career as a messenger longer than I've had solid anything—and of course I came into her life and began upending her comfortable system with magic.

Fortunately, Glynis hasn't minded yet.

By some unspoken agreement we all stay in the back. Even though there are no customers and we have magic aplenty at our disposal to block the windows to keep us from being on display, the front is for facing the world, and the back is for us.

We stack boxes as needed so everyone has something to sit on, and only Ari looks a little wild around the eyes at being part of such a circle—the company, and the informality of it.

I think exposure to me has inured Lorwyn at last.

Tea disseminated, Iryasa's information comes out.

The first critical piece is that Ambassador Cherato sent a ransom note for Karisa directly to Iryasa.

"Yes, of course I realized he was trying to cause trouble between us to give himself more room to maneuver," Iryasa says before I've finished considering commenting on this. "I know what he's witnessed from us in negotiations. Just because I know what a narrative is doing doesn't prevent it from working. My sister was kidnapped, and you did know about it and hadn't told me—that was all true."

"Did the ambassador tell you that I knew?" I ask.

Iryasa shakes her head. "No. That much I reasoned on my own."

She casts a wry glance my way, and I return a half-grin.

My eldest sister has learned what I'm like after all.

What's more interesting is her next piece of information: that the ransom note was delivered via Nakrabi magic. As Iryasa and Reyata were visiting the Te Muraka compound when it arrived, my sister had the presence of mind to ask Thiano what he could tell her.

"Not much," Saiyana says with a scowl.

"The most important information," Reyata disagrees. "He could tell us that Karisa is safe."

"How?" Glynis asks.

"Magically, how," I clarify.

"The note," Iryasa explains. "Because it came via Nakrabi magic and the spirits were already trapped, Thiano was able to convert the object to another use. Apparently there was very little power to work with, however, which is why he was only able to gain that information."

"Do we know if a note sent like that normally would have used more power?" Ari asks.

It's a good question: that tells us whether Cherato is hoarding power.

Iryasa nods. "Apparently so. Its power was almost used up by the time I put it in Thiano's hands—he had to work quickly, so there wasn't time to debate what information he should attempt to come by."

"A location seems pretty obvious," Saiyana growls.

I shake my head. "No, Karisa's immediate safety is the most important determinant to our next step. If we didn't have that, we'd have to act more drastically without time to prepare. This way, we have time to determine her location ourselves."

Iryasa considers me. "Thiano thought you'd see it that way. He's learned a lot from you, hasn't he?"

That question is coming from her crown princess side more than her elder sister side. "I've learned as much from him."

She nods, thoughtful. "The trigger for the kidnapping is likely to have been that too, isn't it? Not just the pressure you exerted in negotiations yesterday, but also that he's aware of Thiano's defection. He needs to exert pressure on us in turn to buy himself time, but for what?"

"We may not know the specifics, but the broad shape of his intention can be inferred," I say. "He's planning to ransack the barrier and unleash the Cataclysm unless we can figure out how to stop him."

Iryasa's eyes widen. "Do we have time, then?"

"Yes," Reyata answers. "The ambassador wouldn't be bothering to expend power he'd prefer to hoard on delaying tactics if he didn't need to buy time."

"But how much?" Ari asks. "How much time does Karisa have?"

"That's it exactly," Iryasa says, her hands clenching, and she meets my gaze. "Karisa is not expendable, but neither is the world."

Ah, now I understand better her distress upon arrival. She thought I'd forced her into a position where she'd have to choose between her duty and her love.

I can't deny I'm relieved she considers neither an acceptable sacrifice and moreover is willing to admit it.

"You won't have to choose," I say steadily. "I promise."

All my sisters' eyes narrow in unison, and I burst out laughing. "No, not because I'm planning on taking on the burden of choosing for you, either!"

"Wow," Lorwyn says dryly, "you really are related. That you all knew right away why that statement from Miyara should be suspect—"

"There was a great deal of similarity in our educations," Saiyana drawls. "Also, at this point we've clearly all met our sister."

"I love you too," I say, still smiling as she rolls her eyes.

"Is Thiano still with the Te Muraka?" Glynis asks.

Reyata answers, "No, he and Sa Rangim joined Ostario at the barrier to help defend him against any attacks from the Nakrabi delegation, since Thiano knows how their magic works and the Te Muraka can eat it."

"Oh," Glynis says with a slightly dumbfounded look, like a piece of a puzzle has just slotted into place for her. "That is a good idea. And Sa Nikuran and Risteri and the rest of the Te Muraka-guide teams are patrolling, I'm guessing?"

Reyata blinks, considering her. "Yes, we can call on them there if we think of anything more they can do. Are you a tactician then, too?"

"She's good with patterns," I put in blandly before Glynis can answer.

Both of them look at me and then back at each other, as if deciding whether to accept my intervention at face value and leave it alone.

Saiyana sighs, breaking the détente.

Backing me tacitly again once more.

I make a point of breathing normally so no one will see my sigh of immense relief.

"I should get back to the barrier, too," Saiyana says.

"Since you've been gone this long already, can you spare a few more minutes?" I ask her.

"For what? We're not making a plan here."

"I suspect more pertinent information will be arriving soon," I explain.

Her eyes narrow. "How soon?"

"Oh," Glynis says, "give it about five seconds."

Saiyana frowns at her, as does Reyata, but before anyone says anything the back door flies open.

Yorani flies in first, her tail lashing. She's followed by Tamak, in human form but gaze entirely black, and Entero, expression carefully neutral, each supporting a visibly beaten Taseino.

And no sign whatsoever of Elowyn or Karisa.

CHAPTER 34

AT THE SIGHT OF Taseino's condition, Saiyana swears and lurches into motion. "So much for no one in that room being harmed," she grimly casts back at me over her shoulder.

Before I can respond, Taseino lifts his head. His face looks so awful I struggle to focus on his words as he somehow manages, "That's what they want you to think. Karisa was unharmed and in control of the situation when I last saw her, and I have no reason to believe that's changed."

"Even though you look like this?" Saiyana demands.

Taseino says wryly—spirits that expression somehow makes his face look even worse—"Whose idea do you think this was?"

It's like the whole room pauses, processing that.

Saiyana frowns. "Wait. Karisa got you beaten up?"

"To get you away from the Nakrabi delegation," I realize. "She wasn't confident they wouldn't harm you worse if you were in their power?"

Taseino tries to nod, winces, and stops. "Yeah. We're much smoother at infiltration than emergency escape plans. But it worked, and she's fine, and I'll live."

I close my eyes for a moment. It's one thing to have faith in people, and another to see people I've allowed to put themselves in danger show up at my door severely beaten.

It worked. She's fine. He'll live.

Not good enough by half. I need to do so much better.

But this isn't the time to second-guess whether I'm deploying my power correctly or could have done so differently; this is the time to do what I am here in this world to do.

"You'll only live if you start talking," Saiyana growls, but still reaches toward him while most of the rest of the room breathes a little easier at this news. But he certainly has all of our undivided attention.

Then Ari steps between Saiyana and Taseino. "Save your power and focus for the barrier."

She frowns at them. "You know what to do?"

They roll their eyes. "I'm a self-trained mage, your Highness. Trust me, I know a thing or two about healing injuries."

Saiyana snorts, but she does step back. "Hey Miyara, remember when I thought you should work with me on Istalam's behalf?"

What's this now? "Yes," I say cautiously.

"I take it back," my sister says firmly. "Everyone you spend any time with stops being intimidated by me. My entire process would collapse."

Reyata barks out a laugh.

"In that case, I told you so," I say. "Now please come sit on this nice comfortable stack of boxes with me before you keel over."

"I'm not going to keel over."

"You look like you're going to keel over, and it would be stupid to expend energy looking sturdier when you could just sit down."

"Or you could ignore how I look—" Saiyana breaks off as Iryasa takes her by the shoulders and propels her to the nearest stack of boxes.

"Sit," the crown princess orders.

Saiyana scowls. "Fine. But only under protest."

"Your lack of self-preservation is duly noted," Iryasa says coolly, and Saiyana twitches as the room quiets again.

Busted.

"Now," my eldest sister says. "If we could return to the matter of our kidnapped sister?"

"And both our missing teammates," Glynis puts in. "Tamak, Elowyn wasn't there?"

"Taseino should start," Tamak grinds out, and his voice is definitely closer to a growl than I'm entirely comfortable with.

Entero appears to share my concern; his gaze flicks to mine in acknowledgment and back. He releases his hold on Taseino but doesn't go far, ready in case he needs to intervene.

As the potential for disaster involves a prodigy who can turn into a dragon, I strongly hope he does not need to intervene.

And maybe it will in fact be fine, because Tamak stays right where he is, supporting Taseino, who doesn't look concerned at all and is certainly intelligent enough to be, even with the distraction of pain.

"Elowyn is still trailing Karisa," Taseino says, "or at least she was when I last saw her. The Nakrabi hadn't recognized her presence yet."

I take a deep breath. Thank the spirits. We're not done here yet, but I'm glad of at least some concretely positive news I can convey to Deniel. He has faith in his sister, but confirmation is still to be desired.

Iryasa glances at me. "Isn't Elowyn your apprentice in tea mastery?"

No way around this now. "Yes. She has excellent judgment and also an uncanny ability to go unnoticed in plain sight. Better even than I ever managed. It's not actually magic, but it might as well be."

Glynis' head tilts to one side, like she's considering that, but keeps her mouth shut.

"So Elowyn's role is to keep an eye on our sister and sneak messages away to you as needed?" Iryasa clarifies.

"Essentially, yes," I say. "But it's Taseino who's coordinating their operations."

Iryasa's eyes narrow back on Taseino. "Yet he is here, having been rescued after a fashion by the princess in his charge, and I gather that while Tamak expected to be able to locate Elowyn somehow he has failed."

Oh dear. "You're gathering quite a lot when you could wait for persons with knowledge to report on actuality."

"Am I wrong?" She gestures with false magnanimity at Taseino. "Do go on, then."

Taseino nods—Ari has apparently restored the relevant muscles for that sufficiently—and continues as if he's not reporting to an angry crown princess. "Last night Karisa was convinced Ambassador Cherato was up to something, and we decided to make a play. When Elowyn signaled to me that Karisa's strategy looked to be going sideways, I interrupted as planned, which has previously been effective. But it became evident that Cherato's method of operation has shifted drastically: the techniques I've used to manage him previously were not only ineffective, he moved straight to deploying a magical trap."

"Really," I say, distracted from his circumstances despite myself. "I'd thought the ambassador was hoarding magic."

"That's Karisa's doing, too," Taseino says. "It looked like the Nakrabi were going to take me hostage for Karisa's good behavior, with the strong implication that this would be accomplished through magic and I might never recover. She convinced them otherwise, to disable me physically to prevent me from interfering but not do any permanent harm to avoid what she presented as a potential overreaction from Miyara."

"So the ambassador doesn't really believe I'll be upset about anyone's fate but Karisa's," I realize.

Taseino's eyes flash with anger, and I realize something else: Karisa likely thinks the opposite. Or is trying to convince herself that the opposite isn't true.

Spirits, that makes this whole endeavor a greater act of bravery on her part.

"Yes," Taseino says tightly. "Karisa and I managed to plant enough doubt to get me beaten up, and eventually I lost consciousness. Yorani apparently did something to bring me around, though none of us know what."

We all look over at where my familiar is perched on a high stack of boxes, looking angry and not at all tired.

My familiar can focus other people's consciousness. That's... perhaps not so surprising, given both what she is and who I am, but it's certainly interesting.

"Tamak, do you want to explain this next part?" Taseino asks, looking back with a bit of a wince at the movement.

Tamak's eyes flash red before returning to all black.

And then, miraculously, back to normal human eyes.

More than one person in the room glances at me to see what I'm making of this, and I keep my expression entirely unconcerned, as if this is not at all worth a moment of worry.

The people in the room being who they all are, this also tells them that I am not, in fact, perfectly calm, but likewise that drawing attention to this development would be a mistake in the current situation.

Then Tamak looks from Iryasa to me, and I realize, for all Tamak's magical and emotional maturity, what must be even more complicated for him to reveal under these circumstances to a person embarking on a relationship with the head of the Te Muraka whom he is answerable to.

"If I may?" I ask Tamak, who clenches his jaw but nods sharply. "Tamak and Elowyn have the beginning of a unique bond," I explain delicately. "Given their youth comparative to when a Te Muraka would normally be capable of embarking on a mating bond, Tamak paused their bond and, with Sa Rangim's approval, developed a way to externalize it in the form of a device Elowyn can choose to carry. This way he and Elowyn can make sure they are practicing active consent for all the current potential effects of the bond before they decide if they will pursue further ones."

"That is a lot of very careful phrasing," Iryasa says softly.

I shrug. "The existence of their bond has become relevant to current political events, and I think it's also important for you to know that it's being handled responsibly. I have complete faith in both Elowyn and Tamak, and Sa Rangim, Deniel—that is, Elowyn's older brother; I've forgotten if you knew of their relationship—and I are aware of more particulars of exactly how. The details of their relationship, however, are not your business."

Iryasa considers me, then Tamak, and finally nods thoughtfully. "Very well. The bond is how you intended to find her, then?"

Tamak takes a breath to steady himself.

Then he reveals a bracelet he's had clutched in one hand.

My heart aches just looking at it. Bracelets are so many things in my life now.

"Yes. Elowyn took the bracelet off for the first time and left it with Taseino. Then she must have waited until she was some distance away to try to catch my attention with the bond. It... I didn't design the device to be activated remotely like that. I could tell something was strange with the bond, but not that it was with her side rather than with me." Tamak's gaze drops. "She apparently wanted to make sure I found Taseino, but not her."

"Elowyn knew you would come for her," I say, glossing this out loud in case he didn't understand. "But the situation with Nakrab has changed in a way you didn't have plans for, and she wouldn't want to risk you being caught or injured either because we don't know enough. If Cherato had realized he was being tracked, he might have done something drastic."

"More drastic than kidnapping a foreign princess, you mean," Saiyana drawls.

"Yes," I say seriously. "Because that we knew was a possibility. Tamak, this means you can't track Elowyn's whereabouts directly for the foreseeable future, correct?"

He nods tightly, like he doesn't trust himself to speak. Oh, but this must be so hard for him, but with our audience and the immediate problem this isn't the time to counsel him.

"Then we'll have to hope Elowyn managed to follow Karisa without getting caught, and she'll get word to us when it's safe to do so or when she must. Glynis, you know how she'll leave messages while Taseino is recovering?"

Taseino answers first, "Ari's got me patched up enough that I can go out again."

"Only if you don't get beaten up again," Ari warns. "The second anyone lands even a pinch on you, you are going to drop like a stone."

"Also," Taseino bulls ahead, "before the beating, we did get some information you might find useful."

Saiyana makes a strangled noise at this buried lede, but Reyata notes, "You have a good head for reporting priority."

He began with Karisa being fine, then explained the circumstances to confirm that and why we shouldn't or couldn't locate her immediately, first, with perfect consideration of his audience's concerns.

"I have been learning," Taseino says dryly, and I almost smile and cry at the same time, because I know he means here, at the tea shop, with me. "The gist is this: Cherato figured out about their missing tech—Tamak, before you ask, I don't know how they finally recognized your decoy or what took them so long—"

"What's this now?" Iryasa asks.

Lorwyn answers, "The spy teens stole a piece of Nakrabi tech for Glynis, Tamak, and I to experiment with. Now we're saving it to test a more developed version of Glynis' theory about how to release spirits trapped in Nakrabi machines."

Iryasa blinks at her slowly and finally echoes, "The spy teens."

"Yep. Self-named."

Iryasa closes her eyes for one moment, takes one breath to process everything Lorwyn's statement contained, and then looks back at Taseino. "My apologies. You were saying?"

This, finally, abashes him slightly. "Basically the Nakrabi are afraid Miyara is arranging to destroy all their tech, which they'll need for their plan. So kidnapping Karisa is intended to keep Miyara from moving against them, since they assume her being your younger sister makes her impossibly precious."

"That strange fixation on youth again," I murmur.

Taseino nods. "Also the fascination with deception. The fact that the two of you pretended so well not to be sisters convinced him you must care about her a great deal."

"Well," I allow, "he's not wrong about that."

"But he thinks having kidnapped Karisa allows them to do whatever they want, because you won't make any moves that might risk her wellbeing," Taseino says. "And he is wrong about that."

"Well," I say again into the chilly silence that has filled the room at this pronouncement, "yes. But that's because I'm both sneakier than he gives me credit for and also know my sister's worth extends beyond her youth and fantastic ability to lie."

Taseino smiles slightly. "I know. So?"

"I'm thinking," I say.

"Think faster," Iryasa says, "or I will take it out of your hands."

I ignore her and cross the room to Taseino, still supported by Tamak. I lean down and give him a very gentle hug.

"Thank you for keeping her safe," I say softly in his ear.

He blinks rapidly, shaking his head. "I didn't. She's still—"

"Exactly where she means to be," I say, pulling back. "And yes, you did. I can't make you believe it, but all the same know that I do."

Taseino looks sideways at me. "You could absolutely make me believe it."

I smile and straighten. "No. Because if I did, it would remove the meaning behind the knowing."

Then I turn to Tamak and say, "And you did well, too."

Tamak scowls. "I did even less."

I step in closer. "I don't know everything about your bond, but I have some understanding of what it is costing you to stay like this until you know what Elowyn needs from you," I say. "I see you, and I acknowledge what you're accomplishing. Thank you."

Tamak bows his head, clenching his fists around the bracelet, and I turn back to the room, positioning myself like a shield so Taseino and Tamak are both behind me.

I survey the present members of my team in saving the world.

Ari has plopped down at Taseino's feet, taking a break from their ministrations, while Glynis is looking around constantly, as if trying to take in every piece of information and fit it into a pattern. My sisters, meanwhile—Saiyana hunched, Iryasa standing with feigned calm, and Reyata looming behind her—all manage to look as menacing as Cataclysm predators.

Entero has stood down, sort of, except he is now angled specifically to shield Lorwyn if she needs it. Not that she will, but I am glad that she now has a person in her life who will absolutely do whatever he can to protect her, even if it's a matter of dragons or princesses. For too long no one would have stood for her. Now, she can afford not to look over her shoulder and focus her attention instead on what's ahead—and trusting another person, and me specifically, to come out with a plan she can participate in without qualm.

As with Thiano's tests, I will always endeavor to be worthy of her esteem.

This is the path I've dedicated myself to.

And this is why it matters:

"Before anything else, we are going to locate Karisa and Elowyn and determine their safety," I announce.

Iryasa says, "I know it isn't ideal, but I think Thiano can use his magic to find Karisa faster than anything else we can do."

I shake my head. "No. We still aren't sure what that would do to the spirits, and I trust Karisa to manage her current situation. We'll find another way."

It is a mark of how far we've all come that the crown princess of Istalam does not argue with my flat refusal, or surety, or leadership—and nor does anyone else—and instead simply asks, "How?"

"I don't think you've yet met Aleixo," I say.

"The former Velasari spy you turned? No, but I understand he's still being held in Sayorsen. What of him?"

"I want you to release him," I say.

At this Iryasa frowns. "Since it's your suggestion, I'll consider it. But tell me why—and I don't mean your assessment of his character."

"Because between Thiano's knowledge of how Nakrab works, Aleixo's inside knowledge of their operations in Istalam, and everything Entero has learned of them, I am confident they will be able to locate Karisa."

Entero speaks for the first time. "Thiano and Aleixo's knowledge would speed the process considerably. They can provide the context necessary to sort out what I already know but haven't yet determined how it fits."

"I can help too," Glynis says.

"And me," Tamak rumbles.

"I'm failing to see," Iryasa says, "why the prisoner needs to be free for you to have access to his information."

Entero frowns, trying to think how to explain. "Spies intuitively know a lot more than we typically have a reason to find words for or even awareness of. I might not know the right question to ask for Aleixo to know what information I need from him. And there's plenty that is more effectively communicated by doing. Since Miyara vouches for his character, he'd be a great asset for this."

"You were a spy for Istalam, were you not?" Iryasa asks him directly.

Entero nods. "How does Aleixo's skill compare to yours?"

"We have different specialties. As a former soldier, Aleixo has more experience with logistics and with working with a team."

"And you?"

Blandly, Entero says, "I was an assassin, your Highness."

This time it's Lorwyn who shifts in front of him—another person no one would ever have defended, once.

That 'was' in regards to his assassin career being in the past fills me with joy, too.

"I see," Iryasa says.

Entero considers that and adds, "At your grandmother's direction."

That gets a few double takes around the room, and Iryasa's eyes narrow immediately. "I'm certain you don't have permission to speak of that publicly."

"I don't consider our current crowd public," Entero says, raising an eyebrow. "I'm also certain there won't be any consequences."

He doesn't glance at me, but I grin appreciatively anyway. Entero is indeed learning how this game is played, and what his outward confidence that there won't be consequences will communicate to Iryasa, both about him, and about his relationship with the dowager queen.

"Between them," I say, bringing us back to the point, "they will find Karisa, determine her situation, and prepare to extract her if necessary. But—" I direct this specifically at Entero, and in so doing make it clear I expect him to be running this—"treat Karisa as the competent operative she is. If she signals not to extract her, then leave her be."

"Explain," Iryasa orders.

"They will have a plan to extract her by force immediately if necessary," I say. "Tamak, I am relying on you for that."

He nods shortly, color flashing in his eyes.

"But if it's not necessary, Entero and Aleixo will have time to create an extraction plan with more stealth."

"The advantage of that being?" Iryasa asks.

Reyata answers her. "Stealth is safer. In a big magical confrontation, there's always a greater risk of casualties. That's even truer in this case, since we don't know what Nakrab's magic is capable of."

"And," Saiyana puts in almost grudgingly, "if you don't have to act immediately, then you can set the scene. Choose the stage for the confrontation for maximum effect."

Iryasa frowns at me. "You want to put Karisa on display?"

"Karisa's made her life into a performance," I say. "Let her use it. And you use your skills at crafting narrative to make it matter."

My eldest sister looks at each of us in turn and at last sighs. "All right. What else?"

And in that way, together, we set the next steps of the plan to save the world in motion.

When we've finished and my sisters have taken their leave, Glynis regards me curiously.

"What is it?" I ask.

"You didn't ask us to leave," she notes. "At the beginning, when your sisters arrived ready to ream you to shreds."

"Of course I didn't. You're part of this team, and your contributions matter," I say. "You can't make them if you don't know all the pieces."

Glynis waves this off. "You could have handled the dressing down—of you and of your sisters—first, alone, and then brought us back."

"You're not luggage," I tell her. "You're not objects I will displace and summon at my whim. But you're right if you mean it was a deliberate choice."

"Why?" she asks simply.

Everyone left is waiting for my answer to this, I realize. Glynis, Ari, Taseino, and Tamak, but also Entero and Lorwyn.

"Because you needed to stay and see that you are no less relevant in this world than even royalty," I say, "and royalty are ultimately just people, too."

Ari snorts. "No, they're super not. And I don't just mean that you're all raised with astounding privilege and it makes you think about the world differently. I mean you specifically are different."

"And so are you," I say evenly. "Every one of you. Leave rooms if you choose to, but never let anyone make you believe you don't deserve to belong in them."

Being able to work in tandem with my sisters is a victory.

This is another of a different sort.

I look around the various forms of thoughtful expressions around me. This, too, I can't make them believe. But I can believe it, and I can live demonstrating that belief.

And sooner or later, I have faith they all will, too.

I can already see it—us—beginning.

CHAPTER 35

IRYASA AND REYATA ACCOMPANY me to where Aleixo is being held. They watch through a magical viewing pane, where they can see in but we cannot see out, while inside Aleixo's cell I make him tea and explain the situation.

"The trick will be navigating the Nakrabi defenses, to make sure you don't trip an alarm while finding the princess' location in stealth," the former operative for Velasar says with a frown. "I can tell you what I know to look out for and how it fits together, but I wouldn't swear they don't have more that our—that is to say, Velasar's—spy network hadn't discovered or understood yet." He pauses. "Or, frankly, that Ignasa chose not to share with me. She survived too long to have not understood where my loyalties lie."

"I understand," I say. "Though I'd actually prefer you tell Entero directly, as he's our spymaster in all this."

Aleixo's eyebrows raise. "Sure. Spy*master* now, is it? I wouldn't have thought he was suited to that skillset."

"What do you mean? I mean, I know what you mean, but—"

Aleixo waves away my floundering. "You don't get into this line of work without being able to take initiative. Entero's a problem-solver, same as me. That's how a soldier gets recruited into this life. But we both tend to be... more direct about our approach. Spymasters are different. It's more distant, more maneuvering, less physical action. He seemed like a pretty hands-on, lone operator sort. That's all."

I nod. "That's a fair characterization. I don't think I'll qualify it for you just now."

He frowns, following my implication. "But you will later?"

"Later I don't think I'll need to."

Aleixo's eyes narrow. "Entero's not here right now, is he? So you're here for something else. I can't help with the princess or anything else if you don't tell me what."

"I would like to," I say frankly, "but in this case I believe you'll still be able to help even if you don't know all the details. Perhaps even better."

He scowls. "Not my favorite approach, but fine."

I raise my eyebrows, and he rolls his eyes.

"*You* know what I mean, and it's not this." He gestures around the cell. "I prefer to know where I stand. Especially in light of how things have gone down the last couple years for me."

Lied to and betrayed by his own government into serving a cause that betrayed himself.

"But since whatever this is comes from you," Aleixo says, "it's fine. Just point me at whatever problem you need me to solve, and I'll do what I can to solve it."

The door to Aleixo's cell opens abruptly, and both my oldest sisters come in.

Aleixo's eyes widen. He glances at me and back at the princesses he clearly recognizes, going very still and clamming his mouth shut.

"I've heard what I need," Iryasa says, nodding to Reyata.

Reyata holds up a key for Aleixo's benefit before approaching him.

He scoots back into the wall. "What are you doing?"

"Releasing you to help," Iryasa says. "I admit I thought Miyara's suggestion was ludicrous at first, but unsurprisingly here we are."

Aleixo regards Reyata's approach with something akin to horror. "I'm a Velasari spy who tried to compromise—everything that matters. You can't just *release me*."

"Can't I?" Iryasa asks mildly.

Reyata nods. "Ostario and Saiyana are busy. We're not going to fix you with any tracking magecraft. Doesn't seem necessary."

My eldest sister is no tea master, but she has spent her life in a court where even—perhaps especially—her own family tries to use her. She is an excellent judge of character. Reyata has led men and women in battle and judges them her own way, but no less adroitly.

Aleixo holds very still as Reyata uses the key to undo the magecraft holding him in this cell. "Entero isn't here for you to teach because he's busy, too, so I'm just going to bring you to him," she says.

"*You?*"

"You're one of Braisa's, aren't you?"

Aleixo pales.

Then drops his head, takes a breath. Squares his shoulders and looks back at her. "Yes, your Highness. I am."

Reyata nods like this is exactly the reaction she expected; she clearly knows exactly how to handle this former soldier.

"Before that," I put in as I pick up Yorani, who at some point curled up for a nap—another sign of approval, for her to relax her guard in the presence of someone previously involved in hurting her—"I'd like you to join us for the start of a meeting with the other ambassadors. You haven't met with Ambassador Ridac since he arrived, have you?"

"No," Aleixo says, tensing again. "I think he attempted to make contact once, but whatever defenses you have up here prevented it. What do you want me to say to him?"

"Whatever you want," I tell him.

He crosses his arms. "Is this a test?"

"Yes, but not for you," I assure him. "I think your honest opinion is exactly what Ridac needs to hear right now."

Aleixo scowls. "I don't know what you expect me to say."

"I'm confident the ambassador will provoke it from you," I say dryly.

He sighs. "I said it's fine, didn't I? What are we waiting for? The princess isn't going to save herself."

I smile. "She just might, at that. But let's go."

⁂

Yorani sleeps in my arms the whole trip to the tea shop. I poke her at one point and murmur, "Everything okay?"

She flicks an ear back at me and burrows a little more deeply into my arms. I take that to mean everything is currently okay.

But Yorani is not actually a cat, and to have put herself into a nap when so much is occurring is... notable.

It makes me think she is resting up for something big. I wonder if she knows what.

When the four of us arrive at the tea shop, Ambassador Ridac, Ambassador Perjoun, and Sa Rangim are ready for us. The tension is palpable, but of a different kind than before:

This is the kind where everyone understands we are here to take action.

"Keeping us waiting, tea master?" Ridac asks as I walk in—then his expression tightens at the sight of Aleixo following after Iryasa and Reyata.

"I had an errand to run," I say blandly as Iryasa and I take our seats. Reyata and Aleixo wait by the door.

"What is this?" Ridac asks in a flat voice.

Aleixo glances my way for direction, then shrugs when I don't offer any. "I'm here at the tea master's request."

In a voice that might sound friendly if not for the words, Ridac says, "That much was plain, traitor."

Aleixo's chin lifts. "Velasar's government is on a course that will destroy her own people and many more besides," he says. "I am absolutely a traitor to that cause."

"In exchange for, what, loyalty to Istalam?" Ridac asks, his voice dripping scorn.

"I am loyal to what I believe General Braisa would respect," Aleixo says. "Not Istalam's institutions. But the individual people trying to prevent the end of the world instead of serving their own selfish gain, yes."

Ridac's eyes flick to Reyata; so her connection to Braisa isn't unknown to him, at least.

"You two should get moving," I say. For a brief moment Aleixo looks vaguely surprised that was all that was desired of him here, and then both he and Reyata make their bows and take their leave.

He's already planted the seed I needed: to make Ridac think about Braisa. Not just about the possibilities of an alliance between the general and a princess, since we've thwarted his notions of a pairing with the crown princess.

But more specifically, a reminder of General Braisa herself: what she stands for, how popular she is, and the effect that will have in Velasar when we're done here today.

Because we will be done here today.

"Events have begun moving very quickly," I say, "and we are out of time to dawdle."

Ambassador Perjoun clarifies, "Will the ambassador from Nakrab not be joining today's gathering?"

Which is to say: did I not invite him, or did he choose not to attend?

"Ambassador Cherato has kidnapped Princess Karisa and is holding her hostage," I say. "So, no."

Her eyes widen, then narrow thoughtfully. "You're not concerned. Despite your promise of safety."

It's a relief to know how serious everyone thought me. "Say that I am not surprised, and steps are being taken."

"Thus your drafting of the traitor," Ridac notes, then rolls his eyes at my look. "The term is accurate, whether or not you agree with his philosophy."

"The question isn't my philosophy, but yours," I say. "I said 'events', plural. I have learned how the Cataclysm came to be, I know what Ambassador Cherato is here for, and I am going to do something about it."

A beat.

"You have been busy," Ridac all but growls. "Are you going to tell us, then?"

"No," I say.

"*No?*"

"Ambassadors." This time I look all the way around the table, from where Iryasa and Sa Rangim sit quietly in support, and back to the ambassadors from Taresan and Velasar.

"You have a choice to make," I tell them. "And you're going to make it now."

The time has come.

This is what I've been building toward. The relationships, the careful couching of information and managing its delivery, the demonstrations of who I am and what I will do and how.

This is when I take a stand and issue a final ultimatum, or invitation, and see if takes.

This is where we learn if the power I have in the path I've chosen is enough, or if it isn't.

Another beat.

Ridac says, "You'll need to be a little more specific—"

"No," I say again. "You aren't stupid, ambassador. You know exactly what the choice is. I have plans to set in motion and don't have time to coddle you. When I leave this room, one way or another, I will have my answer. Choose."

He glares at me.

I am forcing this on him ungracefully; there are few ways he can see this but as a capitulation.

I don't particularly care.

Then Ambassador Perjoun sighs. "This is silly. Tea Master, Taresan stands with you. We'll support your demand for reparations and whatever else is required to address this situation."

"Ambassador Perjoun," Ridac says with some exasperation, "for your sake, and your government's, have a care what you promise her, and *how*—"

"I am here," Perjoun interrupts him, "for *solutions*. We're all aware I am not Taresan's most decorated diplomat, Ambassador Ridac, nor am I trying to be. I am here because I get things done without a fuss." She meets my eyes. "Taresan is in need of healing; I've seen some of the same signs here in Sayorsen, so I assume you know of what I speak. All I ask is that we speak of this before my return, and you share whatever knowledge you can."

"I'll do better than that," I promise. "Thank you."

She inclines her head. "Then we are with you."

"Say rather we are in this together," I say.

Ridac runs his hands through his hair in agitation.

I don't have to press him, though, because Sa Rangim speaks next. "It appears the tea master has things well in hand," he says as he rises. "Let it be known that she has the Te Muraka's full trust." He bows to Iryasa. "I should return to the barrier. Will you speak for the Te Muraka regarding any further developments?"

"It would be my honor," Iryasa says softly, bowing in return.

A searing glance between them, and then Sa Rangim takes his leave. With just a few sentences and a bow he's done his part representing the Te Muraka as a bloc to be reckoned with while demonstrating his support of Istalam at the same time, and now his time is better spent leading his people from the front rather than the negotiating table.

The negotiating is done, and all that's left are formalities.

Idly, Iryasa says, "Istalam, of course, has full respect for the position of tea masters."

"Oh, stop," Ridac says disgustedly. "You don't have to rub it in. Yes, of course I'm with you, curse everything. Curse Cherato, curse his cursed technology, curse anyone in my cursed government who makes an issue of this, curse *you* specifically, tea master—"

"I'm honored to know how you really feel," I say dryly.

"Are you done with us now, or do we get to know what the spirits you're planning?" he demands.

I pull a stack of papers from my tea kit. Not an ideal place, but my aides are busy, and we work with what we have and who we are.

"I've drafted an agreement, which we're all going to finish and sign right now," I say. "Before you protest, the language allows for certain specifics to be worked out later. The ones included are non-negotiable, however, because they are required to make imposing consequences on Nakrab viable."

"That's an answer to the first part of my question," Ridac says, "not the second."

I pass him a pen. "Get started. I'll explain while you sign."

✢

It worked.

My feelings are a complicated mix of relief and surprise and bold validation, as though this working was a foregone conclusion. Of course I thought I could help, or I'd never have taken this on and made the promises I have.

Still. It is one thing to believe in my path and its power, and another to see it in action.

Ultimately, it takes less than an hour for the continental nations to officially form an alliance. We will all be working together to save each other.

I look forward to a moment when I can appreciate that I managed this and what it means, but—later.

Now, there is no time for rest—especially when a pale boy arrives in the colors of House Taresim.

A pit of dread opens in my stomach. Entero has been handling Lady Kireva, but Entero has gotten busier with more actively important concerns. Meanwhile I kept behaving like she was a threat rendered benign.

A mistake, but how big of one? What has the old spy done?

"Where is she?" I ask.

"The main house," the boy gasps. "But. Under."

There's a note of anger in Iryasa's voice as she says, "I saw the underground level on the schematics. It should be closed to everyone—and she has no business in the main house while I'm in residence."

The boy quails. "I'm sorry. She said—"

"Just me," I cut him off grimly. "Don't worry, I intend to handle her alone."

I draw myself up and turn to the ambassadors. "My apologies. Can you finish up without me?"

"We can handle what remains, yes," Iryasa says.

Then Ridac asks, "Do you know what you're walking into?"

"If you mean specifically, no," I say. "If you mean do I realize that whatever this is I'm not going to like it, at least until I ensure *she* doesn't like it, and that it will be a battle, then yes, of course I know."

"Well, in that case." To my surprise, Ridac grins. "You'd better get going. I'd hate for us to monopolize all your fun."

This, I think, is the surest mark I'll ever have that the storied, cantankerous ambassador from Velasar respects me in truth: he trusts my ability to handle an unknown situation so implicitly he can joke about it.

Or so I think, before Ambassador Perjoun bows to me deeply, and Ambassador Ridac and Princess Iryasa follow suit in tandem.

My eyes sting.

Yorani is still sleeping, this entire culmination having passed her by. I gather her in my arms, and we go.

Together, to the next challenge.

To the next step in ending this once and for all.

I descend into the basement of House Taresim, Yorani curled up sleeping around my neck. It's like walking into another world: an older one, that looks much like ours, but where things are done differently.

Dimmer. Dustier, a hint of smoke.

And, critically, no windows. Not that I'd expect them underground, but nothing down here is visible to anyone outside. The walls are thick, and the stairs go down deep: no sound would penetrate either.

But there is a... sense, I suppose, not actually a scent, of old blood.

I wonder if this perception comes from Yorani: she stayed with me insistently but immediately settled back into sleep when I let her be. Which tells me both that she believes something of import is here, but also that whatever she is sleeping for is critical.

Ominous on all counts.

At last I reach the base, which opens into a cavernous chamber, and there is Lady Kireva.

Surrounded by cold stone on all sides—one of which contains a blood-red tapestry flanked by two dark-clad figures—Lady Kireva sits in the center at a large, solid stone table that seems to grow out of the floor.

It could only be here if the basement was constructed with its presence in mind.

"Shall I offer you tea?" Lady Kireva asks. "Will we bypass the game of how you choose to accept it—"

"You're wasting my time," I cut her off, making no move to sit with her. "You also should not be opening pathways to the residence of the crown princess."

Lady Kireva rolls her eyes. "Did you really think I didn't have back ways into my own House, child?"

"Contrary to your determination to think me stupid, no. But having the ways is not the same as using them, and I also won't believe you don't have back ways into other places in the city you called home for so long."

"I still do," she says softly.

"Then why *here*, Lady Kireva?" I ask. "Why now?"

"Why now?" she echoes. "Because you know as well as I do we're at the critical juncture now."

"You could have sent me a message at any point, rather than summoning me—"

"A message, as you have sent me, keeping me apprised on that which I could advise you?" she asks pointedly.

"To what end, when you've spied on me relentlessly regardless and only made me aware of your presence when working against me? Undermining my relationship with my sisters, interfering with my operations—"

"We are *here*," Lady Kireva cuts me off this time, "because this location is secure in the ways that matter. Because had you consulted me, I could have directed you appropriately. Because you didn't, I have taken the steps you should have, but could not."

My blood runs cold. At least we're coming to the point, but— "What steps, precisely?"

Lady Kireva smiles; gestures for me to sit.

I am not prone to physical violence, but the urge to smack the smirk off her face is overpowering.

Yorani lifts her head and hisses a warning flame.

"I would not sit so close to you just now," I say softly.

Her eyes narrow, but perhaps she is remembering when Yorani launched at her face because the elderly spy doesn't push it further. Instead she snaps her fingers, and one of her thugs whisks the red tapestry to the side.

Revealing the old woman who gifted me the arcane teapot.

Chained to the stone.

I am so shocked, so angry, that as rage floods me at first all I do is gape silently.

The old woman meets my gaze, hers unreadable. There is a bench for her to sit, though she does not. Her hands are manacled together, and a chain attaches them to the floor.

"You are attempting," Lady Kireva says, "to make vast changes to not just our nation's social structure, but the entire magical underpinnings of the world. Here exists a known source of information you have neglected to tap before making your plans, and you think to lecture *me* on responsible behavior?"

I tear my eyes away from the old woman. "You will release her *at once*."

"No, I won't," Lady Kireva says. "Not only would it be a mistake, you have no power here to make any demands of me."

"No power," I echo.

"So—"

"No power?" I repeat, my voice louder. "You think your thugs, your position, the magecraft baked into these walls have any ability to stop me? You think I cannot strike you where you will feel it—"

"Not now," Lady Kireva says easily. "So you might as well sit, since I'm not vulnerable to you here, whereas you have exposed your weaknesses."

I let out an abrupt, disbelieving crack of laughter and slowly cross the room. "You think you haven't? Your weakness is how you value your legacy, Lady Kireva. It is your need to feel important when you are no more so than anyone else, the same as the people who have brought us to this point."

I know what my power is. I know how to wield it, and I am *furious*. So now, for once, I deploy it like a wrecking ball: no softness, and no qualification.

"Your weakness is the look of shame your granddaughter will bestow upon you ever after, Lady Kireva, when she learns who you truly are: not a dedicated defender of the crown, but a desperate, bitter woman without morals whose ability to raise a child like Kustio grows clearer every day. You wonder how he went wrong? At whose feet, and in whose shadow, did he learn? Yet you think you are fit to restore your House?"

Her expression grows set, but I have lost my customary restraint. I am only beginning.

"Your weakness is the House whose name and traditions will be struck from the records not due to your son's folly, but *yours*, so you can never be *remembered*, now or in the future, let alone move in the circles to which you've become accustomed."

"You could never manage such a thing," Lady Kireva scoffs. "Don't get hysterical."

"Couldn't I? The tea guild, foreign ambassadors, every member of the royal family and every Istal community leader and Te Muraka and

Gaellani and genius magic worker in the city will stand by me. As they have before, and have sworn to again. It would be no trouble at all to move any of them against you, Lady Kireva, nor will I hesitate to do so. I can see already how it will be done, and the effort will hardly be notable, but I wasn't finished."

I lean forward across the table from her, and she only just catches herself from leaning back instinctively.

Yorani's eyes snap open to fix her gaze on Lady Kireva's face as I say, "Your weakness is also the magic I can bring to bear to ensure you are trapped and unable to work power of any sort: no words may you speak to work a plan of any kind, and that, truly, is your power, isn't it? The connections you can make.

"But Lady Kireva, you may have people. Relationships, magic, certainly. Still I will triumph on every count, and you will be left not just with nothing, but with your entire life and legacy destroyed long enough for you to know in your spirit the desolation has come to pass through your own fault. And I assure you, I will never, *never* let an offense this grave go."

Finally, her easy demeanor has slipped. Her expression is even, but her face has gone ashen.

"You tell me, Lady Kireva," I say. "In this room, in this moment. Do you truly think I wield no power?"

She has no response.

The silence echoes through this horrible chamber.

"I will say this once more," I tell her in a deadly voice. "Release her *now*."

"Why?"

The voice isn't the old woman before me, though; it's the one behind. I turn and regard the woman shamefully chained.

"Why?" she repeats. "Why go to such trouble for me? When we first met, you were motivated by respect for elders, but you don't extend the same to her. Why special treatment for me?"

I am almost baffled that she has to ask, but I know a test when I hear one and am too angry to answer it gracefully. "I was motivated by respect for all people regardless of affect," I snap. "And of course I will not treat you the same as anyone now. You are magic, to be respected obviously, but also to come and go as you please, to never, *never* be chained against your will. How can I possibly do otherwise?"

The old woman smiles, though it doesn't reach her eyes. "That you believe that," she says, "and treat it as self-evident, is why I will talk to you, and not her."

She stands fully upright, snapping off her manacles as if they were made of paper.

Both thugs attempt to move toward her but freeze, immobilized without a gesture or word from the old woman.

Though there is an almost familiar roil in my gut.

Lady Kireva, too, is still and wide-eyed, though I cannot tell if it is by magic or fear.

"Your small magics are nothing to one such as I," the old woman says coldly, holding out an arm for me to support. "Come, Miyara. I could go for a cup of tea."

CHAPTER 36

I ESCORT THE OLD woman to my own home. She maintains she needs no healing, and if we were to go to the tea shop—the only other place whose wards I currently trust—there will be people, and with people come explanations. She and I are both tired—not out of energy, exactly, but for all that my power comes from people, it will do me good to have a little space from so many of them. For a small while.

I still don't know the old woman's name, though she did offer a reason for that: names have power, for arcanists. Until I know how to use them, she feels more at ease if I do not know. So 'elder lady of the arcane teapot' she shall remain in my head for the sake of hospitality.

To my surprise, Yorani stays sleeping. I thought surely offering hospitality to the old woman would rouse her from her self-imposed nap, but whatever she's resting for, it's more important than her attention.

I'm also surprised to see Deniel isn't home—or at work—though fortunately he's left me a note so I won't worry: he's off to council business, liaising between Saiyana's team and the city's leaders, and he's being escorted by a Te Muraka to defend against the chance of an attack by Nakrab. Though the possibility seems minute, I'm glad someone thought of it.

So I settle the old woman at our table while I busy myself in the kitchen.

I bring a large bowl over while the kettle heats. The old woman doesn't take any note, so intent is she on studying her surroundings. I try not to be nervous about that.

When I return with the tea tray, I set it down next to the bowl between our seats.

Then I bring over the kettle, and she finally blinks.

I gently remove Yorani from where she's curled around my neck and place her in the bowl. Then I pour the hot water from the kettle over her as though she were a tea pet.

Yorani chirps sleepily and curls into the hot water as I sprinkle a few leaves in for flavor, like accessories to a bath.

The old woman begins to laugh softly. "You do have a way about you, don't you?"

I slip a quilted round cloth on the table to protect it from the kettle's heat and set it down, too, so I can top Yorani or our teapot up as needed. "How do you mean?"

She smiles slightly. "Many things."

I wave this away. "Of course."

A huff. "But particularly your skill for creating an atmosphere of ease and welcome. I wouldn't have expected a princess of your power to be able to replicate such coziness authentically, but—" She gestures around. "The signs are everywhere. It's the note on the counter, the shared bookshelves, the pottery your partner has made but you've chosen, the different pieces of your altar that make it whole."

"My power is about valuing even and perhaps especially what others consider insignificant," I say. "So that seems to be of a piece. If not of a princess."

"Yes, I see the pattern," the old woman says. "It's a pattern of love: it's all ties to people. Caring. Valuing not with markers of status or money or any of that, but with intentionality. The cups, the pieces. It is... an odd experience, to be in such a space. Thank you for inviting me."

I bow lightly, pouring the tea. "Thank you for accepting. I admit I expected it to feel odder, seeing you interact in my space and remarking on it. But to me, you do not feel out of place here. Please be welcome always."

The old woman's gaze turns piercing for a moment. "You mean that. Not as obligation."

Neither statement is a question, but I nod confirmation nevertheless.

"Nothing here is arranged magelike, either," the old woman notes. "Surprising, given your training, that you didn't absorb such habits of pattern even despite a lack of interest. You know when the patterns drew me to you, I thought it was because you had arcanist potential."

I had wondered. "But that's not it, is it?"

"No," she says ruefully, "you're a tea master through and through, and even now I still have more to learn, it seems. It's because you're the focal point to solve what's broken. No pressure."

"Thank you," I say dryly—because this is not new pressure, and finally I feel like I have caught the right winds to lift me up.

And also because I am deeply touched to know that this old woman, the last of the arcanists from before the Cataclysm, can look at the detritus of my life and conclude I am thoroughly the self I mean to be.

"It is about arcanism, though," I say. "Isn't it?"

She huffs again. "I can never decide if it's relaxing or annoying to talk with someone nothing gets past."

Intensifying the dryness of my tone I say, "Both."

That garners the chuckle I was aiming for. "Yes. You're not the arcanist—sorry—but it's someone you've lifted up."

"I'm not sorry," I say. "That's the best thing you could have told me."

"And that," she says, "is why I believe you will be able to do what we couldn't. Send the arcanist to me when you can."

I don't need to ask who: it can only be Glynis. She and Elowyn and I all know it. "How will she find you?"

"That's her problem," the old woman says. "She'll figure it out."

I nod. "I imagine it will be soon. We're close to the end, now. Will you tell me what happened?"

"If you mean with that withered old woman, she's not so gone yet that she couldn't navigate around your spymaster's measures. Couldn't thwart them to get in your way directly, but since you weren't pursuing me she had an opening. Why did you leave her one?"

Withered. It's an apt term for Lady Kireva: withered not so much in stature, but in relevance; in ethics.

I sip my tea. "Hope," I finally say. "And a trap as well. She could have chosen another way, and now we can all be clear that even with the option, she didn't. Her own actions coupled with a new understanding of them will be more constraining than any preventative measures ever could. I am sorry you were caught up in it, however—that I truly did not expect, and my imagination should have included such scope."

The old woman waves this off too, taking a sip of her own. "I allowed it, as you know. I figured that was what you were up to—leaving a fanged enemy at your back like that wouldn't fit, otherwise."

How much credit she gives me. "Then of course you also know that's not what I mean to ask about," I say gently. "Should I not?"

She stares at the ripples in her cup. "I knew I was going to talk to you. I thought it would feel more like a relief, an unburdening, sharing this with another person. I find it doesn't at all."

"Some secrets are like that," I say softly. "I can't promise it will be easier once you begin. You know I won't ask you to."

She arches her eyebrows. "Not even if it would make it easier for me?"

"No," I answer seriously. "I am learning to have a care with manipulation, even when I think I'm helping. I won't deploy it like that for you. Not for this. I'm sorry."

She nods slowly. Then decisively. "The withered one is correct about this, of course. The arcanists were indeed present when the Cataclysm was formed, and we—they—were responsible for the barrier, such as it is."

"They?"

"Well, I'm not dead, am I?" The old woman lifts the cup shakily to her lips again. "And I'm the only one. But that's not what you need to know."

She's right; it isn't. I already know enough to have had a reasonable assumption that arcanists had been involved in the barrier.

"What do I need to know, then?" I ask.

She smiles. "I like you, but I'm still mad. Ask the right questions, child."

Prove that you deserve them. My life is endless tests.

In a way, so it is for all of us. The tests of me are just more actively administered, and I'm not sure if that makes it more exhausting or less, that there are specific agents behind them.

"The question is how to proceed," I begin. "No, I don't mean for you to tell me how—but there are questions on that front it is difficult for me to answer. I would like to think the barrier did not fail to contain the Cataclysm because continental magic and Nakrabi are so disparate; that it will be possible to release the spirits in their magicked objects without harm. But I don't know this, and I have no way to experiment, and by the sound of it all the arcanists died to make the barrier at all. My goal is for no one to have to die for it again, but to live for it instead. Yet the past is filled with miscommunications and sadnesses that could have been avoided if people had known how to bridge the gaps between them. So my question is, is there a gap in need of bridging that I have missed?"

The old woman drinks deeply of her tea and then sets down the now empty glass with a sigh.

With that, the atmosphere in the room suddenly shifts: like there was a tension, an energy that has now dissipated.

And in its wake, the calm after a storm.

"That," the old woman says, "is why I can tell you. I will share with you the pieces of the pattern I know, but for this, you must decide how to assemble them."

"Why?" I ask simply.

"Because the arcanists failed," she says bluntly. "And their failure began long before the Nakrabi monks ever dreamed of capturing magic from our shores."

I refill our teacups with the second steeping. "From what I can gather, that is true of all parties. The series of mistakes that led to the Cataclysm didn't spontaneously occur outside the circumstances that gave rise to them."

"A fair point. And perhaps it is fair that since the arcanists had greater power and should have been able to prevent the Cataclysm, they bore a greater cost accordingly for the scale of their failure. Oh, don't look at me like that—yes, of course everyone is responsible for their own choices, Nakrabi and cowardly politicians and all the rest, but you don't understand the power an arcanist can wield. How could you? The arcanists themselves forgot."

"I'm listening." I add more hot water to Yorani's bowl and then settling back with my teacup.

"Well. To make an extremely long story short, in my youth, which was... longer ago than it appears, the prevailing wisdom among arcanists was that to reach greater power, you needed to separate yourself from ties to humanity for perspective. Lots of hermits, lots of methods of self-negation. You know, sitting out naked in the snow for a few days, or not eating—oh, you don't know? Hmm. Well, stands to reason I suppose, but it was all standard practice once upon a time. I assume you know enough to understand where I'm going with this."

"The arcanists were so separated from the affairs of humans that they collectively failed to understand what the Nakrabi were trying to do," I say.

"Yes, and they failed badly. It was a failure of imagination built on a failure of empathy built on a failure of humility. They were so convinced that they were unmatched as individuals, so used to being able to command more power than anyone—and understand, for many of them, this had been ingrained for centuries—"

"Your pardon," I interrupt. "Are arcanists immortal? In the sense of living forever unless killed, I mean."

"Ah. It's not an intrinsic quality of arcanism," she explains. "It's that when you learn to manipulate the essence of magic in the world, you effectively learn to manipulate life itself. So it is no particular trouble to arrange to for all intents and purposes not age, and in continuing to live arcanists continue to grow in power: there is nothing to inhibit them in deepening their understanding of the patterns of the world."

"You chose to age after the Cataclysm, though."

"So I did. And then I chose to stop. But you are jumping ahead."

"My apologies. Of course, what inhibited the arcanists in this case was themselves and a failure to appreciate mortality, correct?"

The old woman laughs. "Ah, how I wish I could have pointed you at some of the elder arcanists like an attack. You see right to the heart of things. Yes.

"I suppose at the rate we're going I'd better summarize: the forest started dying, people came to investigate, found the Nakrabi monks. The monks wouldn't stop what they were doing—of course now we know why, given what happened without anyone to manage the channeling of power, but the people only saw fanatics unwilling to abandon their enslavement of spirits. So they killed all the monks, and about that time a tea master finally managed to get an arcanist's attention: my master, who was marginally more connected to the world on account of training the newest arcanist apprentice, that of course being me. My master saw farther than most would have: she summoned a conclave of arcanists. But by then it was too late."

"To undo what the monks had done, you mean?"

The old woman inclines her head. "In part. If the arcanists had had time, I believe they could have. But removed as they were, the patterns of Nakrabi magic were unfamiliar to them. So instead they were forced into a last resort misguided in its very conception."

I suck in a breath, understanding coming suddenly. "Life."

"Life," she echoes in agreement. She swirls the tea in her cup. "A magic they manipulated but had forgotten how to appreciate; one they gave up rather than fighting for. They had time only to destroy or shield, and to their credit they at least determined that destroying the monks' focus would be catastrophic. So instead the barrier was made with the arcanists' own internal life magic, and collectively the sacrifice was powerful enough to matter. When the focus shattered and unleashed its magical shockwave, the barrier pushed outwards until the huge concentration of magic had dispersed enough that the internal waves stopped, and then it held.

"That was the best they and all their power could do, and their best cost millions of lives."

The old woman subsides, drinking her tea, her gaze fixed bitterly on the tableau before her.

I'm not sure what she needs from me. For all her bitterness toward their failure and its cost, she is still the one who survived, and the scope of that loss—losing not just the world at large, but the arcane world she had meant to enter and all its inhabitants and being left responsible with neither guide nor comrade—I can scarcely wrap my mind around the scope of it all.

While this isn't a formal tea ceremony, I know this still isn't what—or, at least all—she needs to tell me.

"You were the newest, if not the youngest, apprentice," I say, "yes? That's why you were chosen to remain. To tend the barrier?"

"That was the theory," the old woman says. "My master, lacking options and time at the end, advised me to turn to the ancient codices from the first arcanists to guide me, since in her estimation, anyone else I could learn from would be dead."

"There are recordings from the firsts arcanists?" I breathe.

She smiles appreciatively, but there's an edge to it. "Indeed. But you see, while in general arcanists believed in studying history for the patterns, the records of their predecessors were not much regarded by that time. I invite you to guess why."

I sigh, understanding at once her reaction to my excitement. "Of course. The early arcanists weren't disconnected from people, were they? So the arcanists of your time thought they had progressed beyond them."

"Just," she says, "so. As if they didn't understand systems and patterns and cycles at all, to believe in linear progress. Your teapot was made by the very person who wrote the first ancient codex I read."

I blink. "Mine?" I query.

"Yours," she says firmly. "If you weren't enough as you are, the teapot wouldn't work for you. That's as good of a character reference to me as you can get. That arcanist was in touch with physicality and learned from craftspeople—not magic users—to make teapots herself without magic first; only once she had mastered the skill did she understand enough to create this."

"And you... just happened to have it?"

Her smile this time has no mirth. She gestures, and her normally ever-present sack appears beside her on the floor—I should have guessed she'd have hidden it from Lady Kireva. "I didn't make the connection at first. In the wake of the arcanists' death, I started traveling to each of their residences I could find. Many had been lost to the Cataclysm; some remained pristinely unaffected inside. The sack is my own magic. To remember them, to honor the sacrifice of every arcanist who died trying to save the world, I selected artifacts—mementos of their work. I'd found the teapot years before I read the codex, and by then, I'd begun hunting for more writings from the ancients, preserved as keepsake trinkets if at all, an incredible amount of knowledge divided and lost.

"My master had known she'd no longer be able to teach me, but it wouldn't have occurred to her that what I would actually learn was that the arcanists of my era had all lost their way. In their quest for power—individual, separate from any effect on the greater world, or so they thought—they spelled their own doom without ever recognizing the pattern. Ironic, isn't it?"

I am quiet, almost overcome once again by sadness.

Of course she let herself age: to become in touch once again with mortality.

And then of course she halted the process: living with the physical reminders of mortality, and how the weak and elderly and poor are treated by people, so she could never forget. So she would remain to do what they had not—could not.

Ensure that this tragedy never happened again.

Never again. Too many sacrificed on this one altar, fighting alone.

We will do better.

I will do better by us all.

"So," she says heavily. "Do you think you have what you need, after all?"

Yes.

In fact, I think I've had it for some time, which is why she can speak to me openly: because I don't need her, not for this. Or not the way she means.

I have the resolve to move forward differently than my ancestors have. To fly boldly into our future working together, working toward sharing and compassion and not wavering.

As to the how—

The door bursts open.

I'm on my feet in an instant, not sure what I will do to anything able to break through the wards on my home, when in charges Glynis.

"Sorry," she says as she barrels in. "The wards are fine, I just molded them around me for a second to let me through because there's no time and I thought you should hear this directly and—oh. Hi. Arcanist lady?"

"Not exactly an orthodox way for us to meet," the old woman says, her tone dryly amused, "but it will do. You can find me again."

Glynis nods as though this were never in question, visibly gathering her many thoughts into messenger-order. "Yes. I have questions. But this is more important."

She turns back to me, and as the old woman's entire being freezes and relaxes in an instant, I decide this is in fact the best way they could have met: knowing they're each interested in abstract mysteries but not at the expense of present concerns.

"We found them. Elowyn is with Karisa—not visible, they don't know she's there, but she's trapped behind the Nakrabi wards," Glynis tells me. "She's busy making sure she stays not caught, but Karisa has evidently been busy doing that thing where she provokes reactions—she's not hurt, just, you know, annoyingly good at getting information out of people they don't actually want to share—and Elowyn was able to get some information out to us."

It's time. "And?"

"The Nakrabi have a weapon they're planning to deploy against Yorani," Glynis says.

"What?" I breathe.

"They're not planning to kill her, exactly, because they neither know nor care if their weapon has that effect," Glynis continues grimly. "It's designed to capture and hold her using some kind of magic-draining mechanism, which is why I'm guessing it'll have worse effects. After Yorani ate the magic from their harvesting tech, apparently they verified that act halted the accelerated expansion of the Cataclysm. So now they're going to try to take Yorani out of the situation so they can use their machines to drain the Cataclysm on purpose. But of course what they're actually going to do is drain the barrier, and once they have the magic they want they'll abandon the continent to the expanding Cataclysm—"

"That's it," I whisper, turning to stare at Yorani.

She opens one eye to blink at me.

The how: I know exactly what to do.

It is down to me—us—after all.

"Miyara?" Glynis asks.

"First," I say, crossing the room to a bookshelf where a small wrapped package waits, "we focus on what matters now."

I return and place it in front of the old woman, bowing.

Yorani does bestir herself for this, jumping out of the water to land—wetly—on my head, joining my bow.

And leaning further forward to nudge the old woman's nose with her own.

"This was Yorani's idea," I explain. "She wanted you to have this. I don't know what you will think of the story, but it is Yorani and Talsion's—that is to say, her best friend who is a cat who is often in residence—favorite. As you could perceive the love in my home, I hope too you will feel it in this gift."

When I straighten, the old woman is staring at me with absolute incredulity—evidently even a magical perceiver of patterns didn't see a gift from a spirit coming.

And her eyes are filling with tears.

I bow again as she reaches a shaking hand—and this time, I don't think the shaking is due to her age—for the gift.

I don't think anyone has given her a gift of love for a very, very long time, and that could not wait another moment.

"Now," I say, as Yorani settles around my neck once again and I begin gathering my kit, "let us go save the world."

CHAPTER 37

LED BY AMBASSADOR CHERATO, the Nakrabi delegation plans for their move, and so do we.

Yorani spends every available instant inside a teapot, and I continue brewing her tea *almost* absentmindedly, but always aware when she needs a new pot, as I summon our allies.

When I am ready—as ready as I can be—Yorani emerges from the teapot without a word from me, also ready.

Together, we go to make our stand.

When Ambassador Cherato arrives at the barrier to the Cataclysm with his delegation as well as with Karisa, I step through it from the Cataclysm-side to face him with Yorani on my shoulder.

Outwardly, I am careful to look characteristically calm. Inwardly, I am... mostly calm. I know what I have to do and believe that I can do it, if indeed the deed can be done. But there is always the possibility I have not seen clearly enough; that I have missed something, misunderstood something, and that will cost everything.

The thing about saving the world is it doesn't come with safety instructions, or else the thing wouldn't need doing.

My hands will not shake, but my heart is already pounding just from emerging openly onto this battleground.

As I have just placed myself and Yorani as the lone barrier between the Nakrabi and everything they want, that's not an unreasonable response; it's just not the part of this I'm uncertain of. It isn't the first time I've stepped forward, and while it's not as though it's become *easy*, it's not my first time.

In fact, I am counting on that mattering.

Cherato's eyes narrow as he attempts to work out how I knew where he would be. He believed he had gotten past the Te Muraka patrol; in actuality they intentionally created the appearance of a minor, easily overlooked hole in their pattern so there would only be one way for him to slip through, and we controlled it.

He also does not know that Elowyn exists, let alone that she has been smuggling messages regarding his activities this whole time to people who know enough of his operation to have maneuvered him to exactly the stage we chose.

It's a familiar space, this stretch of barrier.

It's where I first stepped into this world, to bring the Te Muraka home and begin making this the Gaellani's home in truth. It's the start of the path I found to find meaning.

It's where I won the tea tournament, securing my role here and defending that home for those who can't. It's where I fought to keep the place I'd made for myself and attained the right in a way no one would contest.

Today, it's where I'm going to prove once and for all that my place here, and my path, are worthwhile and unassailable. It's where I end it all.

And it's where I begin.

My voice is sure as I say, "You will not proceed any farther along this path."

Not a question or even a demand: a statement of fact, of the truth as I perceive it.

It is up to me to make it so.

"Tea Master Miyara," Ambassador Cherato greets me without concern. "You cannot hope to stop me."

"I can," I say, "and I do."

I kneel before the Cataclysm and open my tea kit.

The kit I negotiated to be able to buy, what seems like ages ago now. The tea Lorwyn has blended for me, the cups crafted by Deniel, the arcane teapot. Gifts, all of them.

"With tea?" Cherato mocks. "Come. Surely we are past such foolishness. I have no interest in your quaint rituals."

"That is your mistake," I say. "But you misunderstand. I am not brewing tea for you, world-traitor."

Ambassador Cherato gestures, and his people fan out, setting up their dread machines. "Excellent. Then I will pay you no mind."

"Another mistake," I remark. "You only see that which you wish to, that which you believe you already understand. It is a sad way to move through life, but you do not, truly, do you? You leech life instead to stay always in stasis. Today, that changes."

"Your people lack commitment, focus, experience, and, critically, numbers in this place," Cherato scorns. "You are no match for the might of Nakrab."

He nods sharply, and one of his people aims a weapon at me.

There's a faint twist in my gut, and then the weapon and the person wielding it are on the ground.

Cherato's eyes narrow on his fallen retainer.

"Perhaps," I allow, "I could not stand against you and all your magic and your plans alone."

I finish arranging my tea ceremony setup with the traditional two cups: one to be the focus; the other the path.

And I look boldly back at him. "But I am not alone. Not here."

Karisa, weapon from the fallen Nakrabi now in hand and Elowyn at her back, step away from the ambassador.

He sneers. "So. The princess thinks she has teeth, does she?"

"The princess," Karisa smiles, "has been stealing your plans from under your creepy nose for weeks."

A Nakrabi agent fires a weapon at her, but it's deflected by a shield.

Now it is Thiano who emerges into view, his invisibility falling, and he makes a tsking sound. "Ah-ah. None of that, old man."

"You," Cherato says flatly.

"Me," Thiano agrees mildly. "Princess Karisa, if I may express my admiration for the boldness of your vision and the depth of your deception?" His voice has a mocking lilt to it surely for Cherato's benefit, as these are all qualities the Nakrab claim to excel at beyond any other. The ambassador inclines his head sardonically in acknowledgment as Karisa and Elowyn arrive safely behind Thiano.

"So," the ambassador says, "this is to be an ambush, is it? You believe you have arranged things such that your might will overpower Nakrab's. You will be disappointed."

"You still miss the point," I say. "But I will make you see it yet."

Te Muraka, mages, guides and guards begin pouring out of the Cataclysm.

Ambassador Cherato barely blinks before snapping orders at his people, and the battle moves forward in earnest.

I don't wait: I move, beginning what only I can do: performing the tea ceremony. Because it is not just any tea ceremony.

This is a tea ceremony for the very air we breathe.

This is for the invisible spirits I know surround us that we never see.

This is for the magic in our world with and without form: the spirits that make our world special. The spirits of all of us that we have needed to fight for all this time.

The spirits of the Cataclysm, lost and threatened, who can't fight this fight themselves without a voice to speak for them.

I will serve as that voice—the focus, and the path—if they will have me.

Ambassador Cherato's cuts into my thoughts. "Kill the tea master," he snaps. "She is all that holds these factions together. When she breaks, so will they."

Not a terrible deduction, but nevertheless wrong.

I don't control anyone here. I may have brought them together and lifted them up, but while I am a rallying point, I'm not their glue.

That's what this work has been all about.

A shadow passes overhead even before the Nakrabi's blast fires my way. Sa Rangim in majestic dragon form eats the magic straight out of the air, his eyes glowing with fire as he regards the Nakrabi forces.

From atop his back, Iryasa gazes down imperiously. From the perspective of a dragon in flight, they will all appear as small in body as they are in spirit.

"You have attacked our spirits, our princesses, and now our tea masters," Iryasa declares. "The continent stands united as one against you, representatives of Nakrab. You will cease and depart our shores at once, or you will be made to."

Iryasa looks more powerful than she ever has, the wind in her hair, her dragon love the literal wings beneath her feet, flawlessly executing a move that will define the course of the future.

Making truth of her words, behind the Nakrabi come more forces: Velasari, Taresal, and Reyata with the ambassadors at their head.

Even with all of our people making a point of standing together, it is not such a tremendous number: Ambassador Cherato laid the groundwork for a confrontation long before we did. Some of his people may be unwilling, but he nevertheless has many people here, trained to fight and to work as one, along with their enslaving magic.

They believe they are fighting for their home and their future—but so are we.

We have the benefit of space made for many different minds and skills, and what is possible when they can thrive together. So even with smaller numbers and less preparation, we are strong.

We are enough.

Or: we will be, and we will make sure we have the opportunity to do that work, together.

Ambassador Cherato is done talking, though. He was never here to treat with those of us on the continent, only to use us, and with what between us Thiano, Karisa, and I have learned of him, we can predict how he will move.

He knows that we have done poorly by witches and Te Muraka and Thiano, whom he has successfully turned people against, and that aside from their magic there's only one being here who can actively thwart his own. If Yorani is threatened, I, he thinks, will be rendered unthreatening myself.

Taking us out together? For the thorn I have become to him, so much the better.

So Yorani and I are already watching when the biggest blast of magic I have ever seen comes toward us, and no one stands between us and it.

It's as though the world moves in slow motion, like the air is thick, a morass for it to travel through to reach us.

It's as though I have all the time in the world to conclude the tea ceremony I have performed for the Cataclysm. To lift the pot and tilt it and pour.

And pour, and pour, and pour.

An unending stream of water that fills the cup below and overflows, and as the steam rises so do the spirits.

Water, earth, and air.

The magic bracelets on my wrists glow, and so does the teapot, and Yorani, as from one cup of tea a cloud of spirits erupts.

They burst forth, roiling magic given form as my tea spirit's magic connects us, the current we draw strength from.

This is the power we, and she, have.

We *are* the line of defense.

We, all of us, share responsibility for the Cataclysm. That is how we own it: not in possession, but in our duty to serve.

The battle that had been raging before us grows still as the Nakrabi cower incredulously before an endless wall as far as the eye can see of spirits given form, massed and looming down at them.

"Do you see, finally?" I ask into the sudden silence, eerie as everyone stares in awe at the magical feat before them. "I am not alone here. *We* demand your exile, and *we* will see it happen. You cannot fight the waters, lands, and skies. Your path ends here."

"Shaken" is not an expression I have previously seen on Cherato's face. "Shattered" also describes it.

His knees give out, though he cannot tear his gaze from the vision of the spirits of our world. "How?" he whispers brokenly.

"These are our spirits," I say simply. "Ours not because they belong to us—they belong to themselves—but because we serve them. *They* reject you, and we stand with them. So drop your weapons, or learn what a storm of spirits made manifest can do to you."

The Nakrabi don't wait for Cherato's order; machinery clangs as it's thrown to the ground with abandon.

Cherato's expression twists. I see the struggle in him, as he perceives this new reality that fits none of his framework for how the world works. But he also cannot let go of who he has always been, because he does not wish to. He is not strong enough for that kind of change.

Ultimately, I don't believe his heart can change. I can only work with who people actually are willing.

But he will nevertheless lay the groundwork for his people's future, because I will make him.

"Ambassador Cherato, in your capacity as representative of the Isle of Nakrab, acknowledge for the record your nation's role in the creation of the Cataclysm," I say.

He looks at me. "That's what you want?"

"Oh, that is the beginning," I say. "When you're done with that, you will commit the Isle of Nakrab to making meaningful amends as well as receiving a delegation from the continent into your capital itself."

"No." The word is torn from him, a gut response. "Never."

The wall of spirits roils forward, and the ambassador falls backward, hunching in on himself as his body instinctually tries to take cover, despite the futility. I raise my hand, and the spirits come to a... not stop, exactly, as the mass of them is still seething, but they're no longer advancing.

Not quickly, anyway. I think they are still scooting forward through sheer momentum if nothing else—and there may be something else.

Their patience with my holding them back could snap at any moment.

"Never is a very long time," I tell him quietly. "But never is what I promise if you balk. I don't have to lift a finger to exile any one of your people, Cherato, because the spirits will do so on their own, beholden to no government or regulation or containment you can bypass. They will keep Nakrab exiled forever, and you will be left alone, to die slowly. As you would have died already if not for your pillage of our magic. If you refuse my terms, you will condemn your people to death."

"What you demand *is* death," Ambassador Cherato hisses.

Change. Humility. "Death of the ways that have brought your people and land to death's door, that have attempted to destroy us in your greed, yes. I do demand that. But it is also a chance of an actual future, which is more than you would have had had you succeeded in your plan today. So choose, Cherato, and choose now."

He turns away from me, to look at his own people. They haven't turned away from him, whether that's for habit or confusion or fear or loyalty or something else I can't say. But they are looking at the spirits with awe, or looking to him for direction—which implies they believe there is more than one course possible: that alternatives, and thus the choice at all, exist.

And if the Nakrabi elites' "pawns" believe there is more than one path, the damage to Nakrab has been dealt already. I see Cherato realize it.

He already has the death he feared, but he can still choose against the other death. He can choose to buy Nakrab time—by his faint sneer I expect he hopes Nakrab, even if *he* is done, will find a way out of reparations and delegations, these institutions of *people* who have defiantly persisted in mattering, where he cannot challenge a horde of actual spirits.

"The Isle of Nakrab consents to your terms," the ambassador says. "You have my word."

I sip from the second cup, the tea that has overflowed into it with the spirits' grace.

My hand does not shake.

"I will have your oath on the spirits," I say, "and *then* we can discuss terms."

Glynis, Lorwyn, Ari, and Tamak, with assistance from Thiano, Ostario, Saiyana, and Sa Rangim back in his human form, confirmed their theory about transferring Nakrabi spirits out of their bound objects by testing it on every piece of Nakrabi technology.

The spirits Yorani and I had summoned had silenced everyone, but this moment gave me heart, with the cheers and buzz of inspiration it inspired in everyone who witnessed this miraculous magic, combining all our ways to help each other.

And many people witnessed it, including the Nakrabi, taking out whatever air was left in Cherato's sails.

With Cherato's oath, Nakrab's offensive machinery destroyed, and everyone under the ambassador's command taken into custody by Entero's initiative, the wall of spirits dispersed, and we got right to business.

The first round of negotiations proceeds very quickly. With the vision of the magic of the world itself made manifest fresh in everyone's minds, everyone is very focused and willing to dispense with much of the usual posturing.

Thankfully. Because I am running on the energy of a successful confrontation and miraculous magical feat, but I am aware that if I stop moving for an instant I am likely to stop moving for several hours.

The representatives involved in the negotiation have expanded from the last time we were in the tea shop—Deniel, for one, as a representative of Sayorsen's city council as well as for the Gaellani. Thiano and Aleixo even attend as advisors toward their countries of origin, garnering disdain from each corner. Risteri is there as well, not as a noble but as a representative of the Cataclysm guides, and Sa Nikuran as the Te Muraka in charge of overseeing barrier defense.

Sa Rangim is there for the Te Muraka too, but given his new relationship with Iryasa, any future initiatives in Sayorsen will have to be able to be handled without his constant presence.

And of course, the full magic genius crew along with the spy team, without whom none of this could have been possible.

By these accords, we make witchcraft legal throughout the known world and establish that witches, Te Muraka, and any other magic user or refugee from the Cataclysm will be treated under the law just as any other human.

It won't solve everything, of course. Bigotry runs deep. But it's a step, and I am adamant it be the first step taken by all of us.

I win.

I don't think anyone is surprised by that, anymore—myself included, which is perhaps the strangest of all.

What's more surprising is how well all my sisters work together, including Karisa—or rather, my older sisters' behavior toward her. I should have given them more credit: if they could change their treatment of *me* so quickly, of course they will adapt to her, and all of who she really is. It's Karisa who seems more surprised by how to deal with her sisters actually taking her contributions seriously, but for once, we are all in this with each other—as sisters; as family.

The exact form reparations from Nakrab will take is to be confirmed later, once our delegation has had a chance to assess more what the isle is truly capable of providing.

I still make sure to include provisions for Saiyana to have the army of genius magic workers I promised her.

"What are we going to call this monstrosity, anyway?" Saiyana complains aloud, as if to distract me from feeling too smug that I have managed what she thought impossible.

Yorani, finally too bored of all this discussion to cope now that there's no imminent danger, takes off, flying away toward... I have no idea what.

I smile. And I'm entirely at ease with that.

"The Tea Princess Accords," Thiano suggests slyly.

"No one is going to take a Tea Princess delegation seriously," Lorwyn comments.

"They will," Ambassador Ridac rumbles, having not even commented on the presence of a witch in the room, "because I will personally shove it down their throats until they do."

A Tea Princess delegation. I can scarcely even imagine it.

But what that will look like is a problem for future-Miyara.

Today, I—we—have saved the world after all.

I push my witch-green hair over my shoulder, smiling at the sight of my magic bracelet but feeling no need for the security of touching it.

I meet Deniel's eyes across the room, and we share a nod.

Today, I'll see what I can do to minimize how much saving the world will need in the future.

EPILOGUE: PART I

MY GRANDMOTHER, THE DOWAGER queen Esmeri and spymaster of Istalam, has taken up residence in House Taresim and is holding court, summoning all manner of people to official meetings for reports. She doesn't technically have any authority over my sisters these days, but none of us is stupid—she has nearly as much power now as she ever did as queen. So we've all decided to go along with her, at least for now.

If she wants to push any of us in directions we'd prefer not to, it will be another matter entirely.

Fortunately, my grandmother isn't stupid either.

My turn for a meeting has come at last, and I'm oddly nervous about it. Not that she'll be able to push me—I feel secure on that front. But I'm not sure what my relationship with my grandmother will be like, now that I've left royal duties and found a path outside what she intended for me.

And, of course, now that I know more of who she is: not just that she's been the spymaster of Istalam for so many years, but about what she allowed to be done to witches.

I'm angry, but I still love her. So I'm not sure how this will go.

Iryasa is outside the library door when I arrive. "Your turn at last, then," she says.

"So it seems. What are you waiting here for?"

"You," she says. "Also I asked Saiyana to make me a magecraft device to eavesdrop as needed. Thiano's in there now with Yorani."

I frown. "Trouble?"

She shakes her head. "Not so far, and I don't think there will be. Yorani and I are both being cautious. But I was hoping to talk to you when you're done. I promise I won't listen in."

"No, you can," I say. "In fact, I think maybe you should."

Her eyebrows lift. "Very well. I will, then. Saiyana's certain our grandmother can't prove I can do this, but—"

"—she's canny and likely has guessed anyway. I know. See you in a few minutes?"

Iryasa nods. "I'll meet you at the back door."

A private conversation then, not a public stroll. Since Iryasa's presence here has become public knowledge, she is both more free to go where she wills and less: she doesn't have to hide, but she does travel with at least discreet bodyguards at all times she's visible.

I knock and wait for my grandmother to call, "Enter."

I make my bows to both her and Thiano—respectful, but the one I direct toward my grandmother is not as low as the last time I saw her. She smiles wryly and inclines her head, and acknowledgement of the shift, of what it means.

I blink as Yorani flies over to meet me, processing that, somewhat to my surprise, my grandmother doesn't seem intimidating to me in the slightest. It could be that she's moderating her behavior, but I think maybe it's me who has changed.

Yorani flaps around my head once before booping my nose.

"Hello, there," I say. "I was wondering where you'd gotten to. Did you think Thiano needed backup?"

Thiano rolls his eyes fondly. "That is absolutely what she thought. Most of my time in this room has been spent convincing the little one to stop posturing."

I take a seat in one of the empty chairs. "How did that work out?"

"As well as you expect. I hope you don't mind, I've made formal introductions to your grandmother in your absence."

I do so enjoy presenting Yorani and seeing people's first reactions. Ah, well. Yorani can choose who gets the pleasure herself.

"When I was told you had a familiar," my grandmother says, "I admit I expected that to mean she would be like you in personality. But even as a child, you were always so serious, and your smiles full of innocence. Nothing like the mischief evident in this one from even an instant of her delightful company."

Could I have been, had I been raised differently? There's no way to know.

"Yorani and I are alike in the ways that matter," I say, holding my grandmother's gaze.

We'll defend who we consider ours with everything in us.

"So I understand," my grandmother says, more gravely now. "You'll be glad to know Thiano and I are coming to an arrangement on what his future will look like."

"Oh?" I ask, my tone notably cooler.

Thiano snorts. "See, Yorani's version of that reaction is hissing. Entirely different."

I relax slightly, inclining my head to Yorani as she flaps with her chest puffed out. My tea spirit can be trusted to react badly to any attempts to control another's will, so as she hasn't let loose any flame, all is probably well. "And so?"

Thiano's gaze is sardonic as he meets mine. "I'm not going to be spying for her, if that's your fear, and nor did she expect me to."

That last had been my fear—that she would try to pressure him into doing what he'd been forced to do his whole life, trapping him in stasis again and preventing him from moving on. "I'm glad to hear it."

My grandmother asks mildly, "Are you always this direct with my granddaughter? Perhaps she should sit in more often."

I smile. "Only when he's trying to make me uncomfortable, which admittedly is often."

"My rate of success is so embarrassingly low, I have to take as many chances as I can," Thiano says lightly. "The first part of our terms is that I will advise any of your sisters on Nakrabi culture should they call upon me."

I look back at my grandmother; she's watching me.

My sisters, not her, or even my mother. That is more acknowledgment of her failures—or my perception of them—than I expected from her.

Perhaps it is that she is canny enough to realize how hard I will push if I decide she's crossed lines, and that for me, manipulating Thiano's freedom to choose is a very firm line.

"I will still keep my shop," Thiano continues. "Depending on how your delegation goes, I may be able to also help my countryfolk adapt to continental ideas. But for now I will offer lessons to the Te Muraka on understanding Istalam as an outsider. Sa Rangim has given his blessing."

That is the most important thing. He's found a way to leverage his knowledge—of how people interact, of different cultures, of the profession of a merchant and expertise on just about every object under the sun—to make amends to the Te Muraka first, putting his resources at their disposal to set them up for their future, and perhaps also to the people he feels he abandoned.

"And?" I ask. Because that isn't something he needs my grandmother's approval for.

"And," he says, "when you have determined the shape reparation efforts will take, I am willing to assist."

"He'll supervise things on the Nakrabi magic front," my grandmother explains. "He's clearly the best qualified to do so."

"Are you sure?" I ask him. "You've already spent so much of your life—"

"I'm sure I don't understand how it can have escaped your notice that I enjoy teaching," Thiano growls at me.

That gets a surprised laugh out of me.

He settles back, and his eyes are softer as he says, "Miyara, for most of my life the best I could hope for was to mitigate damage. If I can use my skills and knowledge to actually *improve* the world—that is a gift I won't pass up."

My throat is thicker, and I nod. "All right then."

He smiles crookedly. "Don't make me hug you in front of the spymaster of Istalam. My reputation will never recover."

But the look he sends my grandmother promises danger, and her back straightens—in an instant, they are two predators sizing each other up.

Two old, impossibly clever shadow-operators.

And Thiano is challenging her to make it clear that for him, *I* am the line she cannot cross.

"I really am going to hug you at this rate," I threaten him.

The tension drains in an instant.

"In that case, I will make my exit," Thiano says, bowing theatrically. "If I've demonstrated to your satisfaction that your grandmother and I aren't going to eat each other without your supervision?"

I laugh. "Not at all. But I think we all understand each other here."

His eyebrows lift. "So we might at that," he murmurs. "Yorani, shall we? I need to completely upend my shop to arrange things for the Te Muraka. You'll love it."

My tea spirit trills, bumps my shoulder and looks at me quizzically.

"Go have fun," I drawl. "You'll know if I need you."

She chirps and flies to Thiano's shoulder, and the two of them take their leave.

The door shuts, and my grandmother and I are both silent for a moment.

"Well," I say. "Thiano must think this conversation is going to be difficult for us, if he's volunteered to dragon-sit."

The dowager queen shakes her head, pulling her gaze away from the door where she was frowning after him. "That man has made many hard decisions in his life, but so have I."

Hmm. Perhaps we don't understand each other after all. "He's not judging you for your decisions about the Cataclysm," I say softly. "He's judging you for your decisions toward me."

"I do realize that." My grandmother sighs, leaning back. "This should have been your job. You understand service and the responsibility of Istalam's monarchy. Managing people, seeing their strengths, the backbone to make things happen without appearing to have any power at your disposal. You're perfect for it."

"Evidently not," I say. "And perhaps, if you'd ever asked, you might have known where I shine brightest is in the light. I could be good at what you do. But it would twist me, and I don't think I'd like who I'd become."

She studies me. "You do blame me. If I had told you what I had in mind and you hadn't thought there were any other options, you would have taken it. And that would have been a mistake. This is something you need to choose."

I nod. "I realize that. Unfortunately that doesn't change the fact that I grew up believing I had nothing worth offering anyone, while also believing that only my ability to serve makes me worthwhile. I *can* blame you for the position you forced my mother into, that created the conditions I grew up in. Neither of us can change the past, but I hope *you* understand that when I offer you a solution for the future, I expect you to treat it not just with care, because I do know that you care. But with *empathy*, as *family*, and not just as a mover of pieces."

"Because that, you think, is easy for me?" she demands.

"No, I think it's become habit for you, and I'm asking you to work on breaking it, for the sake of your granddaughters. All of us."

She frowns, and then her eyes snap wide as she puts the pieces of my meaning together. "*Karisa?*"

"Karisa," I say firmly. "You want a person who can see into people's hearts, is bold enough to take action, hides in plain sight and thrives on it? *That's* the sister you should be training. And openly, this time. Help prepare her for the delegation to the Isle of Nakrab. We both know it won't happen immediately: she has some time."

My grandmother visibly considers that. "You really think your wild and barely tested sister should lead the first delegation into a foreign country? Or are you thinking it should be your innocent protégé, the tea shadow?"

"Taseino," I correct.

My grandmother's face is utterly blank as she tries to place who that is, and I smile in satisfaction.

"Don't get too excited, I know who he is," she says. "One of the tea boys who works with you."

"But you almost didn't remember, even though I have been working with him since before I became a tea master, and visibly during the tournament, and then made him my official liaison to the Nakrabi delegation," I point out. "And if *you* almost didn't remember—"

"How do you think a tea boy no one notices is going to manage a team of adolescent spies through an international diplomatic disaster?"

"He will surprise you," I say. "He's also smart, level-headed, and all the people I'd recommend as critical to this mission already trust him."

My grandmother drums her fingers on the arm of her chair. "Spymasters have always been in the family, Miyara. There are reasons for that. We're all raised to understand what our service means. You're recommending Karisa in one breath and then suggesting giving power to a nobody in the next."

"There's no reason every member of our family has to be crushed under unbearable pressure," I tell her flatly. "Just as there's no reason every member of our family has to be unhappy and alone. When it comes down to who is giving orders, I'm confident they can find a way to work as partners—all of them. Karisa was able to work with Elowyn without giving her orders. Taseino already knows how to pretend to fill a seneschal role and coordinate from the background. They'll handle it."

The dowager queen's frown is different now, and I can see her thinking it through—her eyes are bright in a different way. *I have her.* "None of that team is a combat specialist," she murmurs.

"Then maybe we'll learn to solve problems other ways," I tell her. "But if you don't want to lose another granddaughter, give her a chance to fly, to learn who she is and what she's capable of. *Before* her dedication ceremony, this time?"

My grandmother meets my gaze with a steely one of her own. "Very well. We will try it—no. We will *do* it your way. But I wish to be clear that I do not consider you lost, granddaughter."

I smile, and she answers with a soft one of her own.

Words of affection are not habit between us, but maybe this is another relationship I will be able to find a way to navigate after all.

"I'm not," I agree.

※

When I leave to go meet Iryasa, an unwelcome sight greets me outside the library door:

Lady Kireva, Risteri's grandmother.

"I'm here by invitation this time," she tells me, nodding to the door where my grandmother sits behind. "We have some formalities to straighten out between us."

I regard her flatly.

I don't regret my words to her before, and I won't ask this woman for anything.

The old woman sighs. "*But* the essence is that I am formally renouncing all claim to Taresim and passing it to my daughter to do with as she sees fit—and she has some notions of making this a base of operations for the restoration of the barrier and the Cataclysm, rather than restoring our family to court. I will also be leaving your grandmother's service to remain local and advise Risteri, Entero, and you. On whatever terms you choose."

I study her. "Why? And why are you telling me?" I can't imagine she wants any more to do with me than I want to do with her. I can't say I'll be glad to have her around, but it's not impossible Entero and Risteri might benefit from it.

"Because my granddaughter asked me to," Lady Kireva says steadily. "I believe I have experience worth sharing, but we'll see if I can't learn a thing or two from the younger generation in my old age, too."

She nods one last time and walks through the door.

※

I fall into step with Iryasa as she leads me into House Taresim's gardens. Somehow in all the times I visited, I never had a chance to explore them before my eldest sister showed them to me.

"I have a knack," she said with a wry smile, "for finding places and stories no one else wants to tell. It's one of the few ways I can find privacy without having to fight for it."

Today we make our way to a bench that is made of stone but looks like black glass, jagged around all its edges but for the smooth surface on top. The previous bench, unattended by Kustio for so long, had rotted: this one was a gift from Sa Rangim.

A way he finds to support her, even at a distance, by also supporting her privacy yet reminding her that she's not alone.

"You've been doing a lot of matchmaking," Iryasa notes. "How long have you been building Karisa a team?"

"Longer than I knew she needed one," I say. "Tea mastery isn't the same as arcanists discerning patterns, but—"

"You just sort of scatter connections that help people lift each other up in your wake as you pass, I've noticed," Iryasa drawls.

I laugh. We both know there's more to it than that, but... she's not wrong, and that delights me.

"Having her lead the delegation makes sense," I say. "She got as much from Cherato as I did and spent more time with the Nakrabi. Put her in as the figurehead—"

"And, assuming they're all willing, Taseino will help steady her, Elowyn will watch her back and Tamak will watch hers. Ari's expertise in how the land is affected will be instrumental, as will Glynis' ability to put pieces together. I do see what you did there. You, Risteri, Sa Nikuran, and Thiano prepare things on this side, while they figure out what's even possible for Nakrabi magic. Will Lorwyn go with them too?

"They can handle Nakrabi magic without her now, I think."

Iryasa's eyes narrow. "You're not telling me something."

I shrug. "I don't think Lorwyn will go, anyway. Even if she's now explicitly allowed to come back."

"Ah yes," Iryasa says. "We're back to matchmaking. I don't disagree with your plan in principle, but I don't like all of them going without someone with a little more experience."

"Lorwyn would definitely object to being a babysitter," I say. "I was thinking Aleixo. He has the experience, he knows what they're capable of, he needs something to do, and it solves the concern about potential physical confrontation." I shrug. "But that's up to you."

"Neat," she approves. "Not quite as neat as what we managed with Ridac, but neat all the same."

We share a grin. The two of us together managed the ambassador so well even he was grudgingly amused.

As part of the accords, Velasar consented to dissolve our father's hold on consort duties in Istalam, though we made sure to include a provision that allows him to remain in Istalam if he chooses to *and* our mother consents.

Let them both get to determine their relationship and roles for once.

At this reminder, I hand Iryasa two letters, one for each of our parents, which she has promised to deliver. In this case, I am both tea master and princess, taking the weight for all my sisters of beginning to see if we can have a different relationship with our parents. Iryasa will have to take on most of the burden of handling how that plays out, so I can do this much at least.

Each letter is brief. To my father I wrote, "Let me give you the advice about earth, roots, and duty you should have given me when I asked for it. Ties can be a vise or a strength.

"You can choose us if you wish to. As your daughter, I have always wanted to know who my parents would choose to be if it were up to them."

My letter to my mother is briefer still. "I don't know what you need to be happy, but thank you for making the space for the rest of us to be. It's not too late for you to choose yourself. We are hoping for it, and we are ready now."

Iryasa reads the letters, her eyes misting, and nods silently, folding them back up and slipping them inside her sleeve.

We are ready.

"So," I say, "about matchmaking."

"Whose, exactly? I'm losing track." Iryasa laughs, her hand sliding over the bench, but her eyes are serious enough when they meet mine. "Are you worrying about Saiyana and Karisa now that you've gotten Reyata and me sorted?"

Part of how we managed things with Ridac was, first of all, by making it clear Istalam will also be paying reparations: to the Gaellani, and toward supporting witches. I promised to hold everyone accountable, and I am.

But we also managed by making the opening indicators of discussing a new, different alliance with Velasar. Ostensibly this is to discuss combined military efforts against the Isle of Nakrab, so we do not *actually* have to rely on summoning forth spirits to defend ourselves from their superior technology.

Since Reyata and General Braisa would clearly be leading these efforts and we all know how they feel about each other, it's understood this is the beginning of a different kind of match between us—not one that the succession rests on, yet one that already includes love, which should make it substantially more likely to be useful to all our people.

"I can get away with not making a strategic political marriage because I'm officially disowned," I say. "I know the rest of you don't have that freedom. You and Reyata happily found politically advantageous matches, but—"

"But nothing," Iryasa says firmly. "I'm not so blind I can't see where Saiyana's affections clearly lie, and if the two of them work things out, I'll make sure it's allowed to stand. Karisa too, whoever she chooses. It won't even be hard."

I lift my eyebrows. "Are you sure?"

Iryasa gazes up at the sky. "The world is changing again, but it's not like when there were dozens of nations around. We can't just marry royals anymore, because there only *are* so many royals to go around. In a way of course that makes us rarer and more special, but it also means what a person brings to an alliance is different. We only know of four surviving nations now, and maybe someday that will change again, but now we have ties between us.

"Now we can focus on more than that smallminded vision of survival and perhaps deal with the idea that this entire strategy of creating alliances based on noble power nearly *broke us*. Trying to hold onto this antiquated power structure literally threatened the very spirit of our world."

"Well, if *that's* the scope you're thinking of, it will definitely be more of a challenge," I say. "You'll have to be prepared to leverage your power to make everyone freer."

"I don't need you to tell me that," Iryasa says, but she's smiling—she's comfortable with who she is now, and with her authority. "Though I suppose you're right that our sisters' marriages, if they choose to have them, may be more complicated to arrange once the nobility realize what I'm up to. But I will make sure of them nevertheless, and I am glad you will be watching. I will also always watch for you."

Now, we see each other. We *can* see each other, as equals—and as sisters.

"And I, you," I say, taking her hand.

She squeezes my hand briefly with a smile, and keeps holding it as she continues, "I hope you realize, in all this, what else I saw, when things got serious. Ambassador Cherato targeted *you*."

I tilt my head. "If you're thinking I need protection—"

She laughs. "No, I won't saddle you with this. Even my short time here, with minimal oversight and still in hiding, was enough to make me understand how impossible it would be for you to return to the expectations of a princess after the freedom of the life you've led here.

"I mean the value of your work—the connections you build, the very notion of bringing together different people and ideas, *that's* what threatened them. That's what stood against the greatest threat to our world and saved it. I just wanted to make sure you knew I'll prioritize that, too—in my own way."

She really does see. I slump, letting my head fall against my sister's shoulder. "Thank goodness," I manage, having difficulty speaking past my relief. "I don't want to manage a demonstration like that a second time."

Iryasa huffs her amusement, wrapping her arm around behind me at the same time. "Don't worry, I had an excellent view."

From the back of a dragon in flight. "How was it?"

Iryasa knows I don't mean watching me. "Perfect," she says. Which would be enough, but because she frames the world in stories, she gives me more words: "On every level. Politically, obviously it demonstrated unity between Istalam and Te Murak. He found a way to, very literally, make sure I could be both safe and involved when it mattered. And *I* proved—to both of us—that I can in fact handle the fact that he is also a dragon. In the most spectacular fashion possible, if I may say so myself."

"So you did," I agree with a faint smile. "And also he proved his control to you, didn't he?"

She shakes her head. "No. There was no need for that. I proved that I didn't doubt his control, which I had previously made a point of contention. While we are agreed that we will make private space for our relationship, I think demonstrating all that to each other publicly—being comfortable with it, and being who we are—mattered, too." Iryasa wiggles her eyebrows at me. "Although we're negotiating our boundaries well at this point, I hope I can rely on you to negotiate the terms of *my* marriage, when the time comes. I trust you to look out for both our interests."

"It would be my absolute pleasure," I say. "In fact, you two should both come over for dinner before you leave town."

"I would love that, but it'll take a bit of coordination for all our schedules, I suspect," Iryasa says ruefully. "But I'll be here a little while longer anyway, because when I return to Miteran I want to do so *with* Sa Rangim. He has things to arrange to make ready for that."

"Then for once, his and Deniel's schedules will be the more limiting ones than yours or mine," I say. "I am on a break from the tea shop until I've caught up on my sleep."

"Oh, I *see*," my sister says, her tone inciting me to poke her. "And what about you and Deniel?"

What a world, where two princesses can speak openly to each other about our romances. "I think we want a chance to just *be* for a little while before we take our next step together," I say. "After all—we have time."

The crown princess of Istalam inhales deeply, taking the world in. "Yes. For once, finally, we do."

EPILOGUE: PART 2

I RUN INTO SAIYANA on my way to meet Karisa. It's amazing how we all lived together for years and could manage to go without seeing each other for days at a time, and suddenly now I can't walk down a hallway without a sister popping up for a conversation.

I love it.

Though in this case Saiyana doesn't slow down. "*Some* of us are still as busy as ever," my sister tells me. "What with a magical taskforce the likes of which the world has never seen to organize. Thanks for that."

"You're welcome," I say, and I'm not even joking, really. The imminent danger has passed, and my sister can sleep again—though judging from the strain around her eyes there's still a lot for her to catch up on. "I don't know why you're complaining. I've given you the gift of the greatest logistical project of our lifetimes, a rare occasion that will actually give you scope for your copious talents."

"Oh, I'm hurt," Saiyana says with mock-sincerity. "I thought you'd ask me to plan your wedding."

I roll my eyes. "If such a thing occurs—" Saiyana snorts, which I suppose is fair, given the way things between Deniel and me are going, and I'm traditional enough to want a ceremony of some kind. "—it will be a small, private affair."

My sister looks at me sidelong. "Mhmm. I'm sure once word gets out, you will definitely be able to fend off the many people in your beloved community who will be devastated if they can't contribute to your celebration of happiness."

I pause; blink. Horror begins to dawn.

Oh spirits, she's right.

Saiyana veritably cackles, claps me on the shoulder, and waves on her way out without another word.

This round goes to her.

I suppose that means she'll be okay after all, given time.

"Miyara? Everything okay?" Karisa asks from behind me.

I start to nod, then shake my head. "Yes. No. Saiyana's just terrorizing me with prospects of my future."

"Yeah, about that," Karisa says.

My lips quirk. "Well that's quick work, which doesn't exactly detract from my argument. I take it you heard what I proposed?"

"Obviously."

She leads me down the stairs where Lady Kireva had held the old arcanist; the spy teens have been remaking the space, physically and magically, into their own temporary base.

It's a mess. Shelves partially built, piles of sticks and rocks and other magecraft materials, paper and cloth arranged in patterns that I assume are Glynis' work.

The arrangement of chairs and couches, and the table in the center with the tea set, though, reminds me of Deniel's and my home. That would warm my heart already—that we have been *home* enough for all of them that it serves as their model—but I also see an altar to the spirits, and my breath catches.

"We'll have nothing to hide from them," Karisa says. "From other people, yes. But not the spirits. As you might expect, everyone's been so focused on stripping out the magic embedded in this place and redoing it that we have some work left to do, but I got them to help me set this up at least. Check it out—I'm going to make *you* tea for once."

My eyebrows lift. Karisa may not be a tea master, but she received the same formal tea training I did in the palace. "I'm honored."

Karisa claps, and my gut twists, and then I can smell the aroma of tea suddenly coming from the teapot. She winks at me, and I laugh as she pours me her magic-made tea.

"And what have you been doing, while they've all been busy with magic?" I ask.

"Arranging furniture," my sister answers blandly, making me laugh again. I don't doubt she could pick up a couch if there were a sneaky purpose to it.

"You've been thinking about what you want to do," I say.

"Oh, no, I knew I wanted to lead the delegation to Nakrab," Karisa says. "I just didn't expect to be able to convince anyone that I should. Special bonus of having a tea master in my corner, I suppose."

"No one knows quite what to do with you yet," I agree. "Which means, of course—"

"That I have a window to decide. Yes." Karisa sips her tea. "I feel like we've traded futures, in a way. I always thought *I* would be the ambassador—everyone would want to get rid of me, so I'd travel and would be so dramatic no one would be able to tell what I really thought about anything and I could keep them all on their toes. While you would be quietly maneuvering pieces from the background."

"And instead we have a peaceful ambassador sister, and you will be maneuvering loudly and yet no one will ever know what you're doing," I say. "Which is what you've always done. And you also were aware our grandmother had tapped me to serve as spymaster long before I was."

"I'm like her, I think," Karisa says. "I'm not afraid to be divisive, and I want to be involved in everything. I suppose I'll have to watch out for that, to make sure I don't become *too* like her. Especially if she does decide to train me more actively."

I nod my agreement, drinking my tea. "I do see what you mean though. In a way, despite your... flair for dramatics—"

Karisa grins.

"—I'm the one who's ended up with the more dramatic role. My victories build slowly but are decided in big, decisive moments. For you, everything you do will be ongoing and incremental. There will rarely be such blatant, public victories as a spymaster."

She shrugs. "On the other hand, I'm the one who had a long-term plan with no projected end to find ever-increasing ways to get under everyone's skin, so, we might have expected."

I laugh again. "True. If anyone can figure out how to twist absolutely everyone into behaving how she wants even if they don't like it, it's you."

"And you're the one who opened the door to make my work possible," Karisa says. "To make sure this never, ever happens again."

In so many ways. Making sure of the Cataclysm, first, but also our family.

Let us never be so stupidly divided by ourselves again.

"You really do believe we can do it, don't you?" Karisa asks suddenly, her gaze intent on mine. "You think a group of teenagers can figure out how to fix everything."

What form amends should take, whether Nakrabi magic can be fixed, how to best handle freeing their trapped spirits and restore our world, and what changes that will require from all of us.

Karisa, Taseino, Elowyn, Glynis, Ari, Tamak. All immensely gifted and capable; all who still need to decide who they want to be in our world.

"Not just any group: yours specifically," I say, meeting her gaze and letting her read the certainty there. "But yes. I know it's a huge undertaking and will be the work of years of effort. I absolutely believe you are capable of it."

Karisa glances down, her fingers tightening on her cup for just a moment with emotion.

No one believed she could do anything that mattered for too long.

When she looks back up, her emotion is contained behind a mask. "In that case, I had some thoughts I wanted to run by you."

I raise my teacup in salute. "I am here for you."

⁂

I enter Talmeri's Teas and Tisanes from the front door for once. I raise my eyebrows when I catch sight of Taseino, who didn't welcome an entrant as a matter of course.

He smiles slightly as I approach the counter. "I knew it was you."

Of course he did. "I assume you know what I've been up to today, too. Do you want to talk about it?"

He considers. Taseino, ever thoughtful. "Maybe later," he finally says, "when I've had a chance to think of better questions. But off the top of my head, no. I can do this."

I smile. "I know you can. I can't think of anyone more capable."

Taseino shrugs a demurral. "It's only because you created the space and gave me the opportunities to."

"I didn't make you watch and listen and learn," I say. "Don't think I'll stand here and let you give me credit without taking any yourself."

Taseino smiles slightly. It's always so rare on his face, I count each one as a victory. "If you insist," he says.

"I do," I say, smiling in return. "You know where to find me if you need anything. But you have everything covered now?"

Taseino surveys around us, glances back up at me. "Yep. I have everything covered. You can move on."

I smile more widely, bow, and do.

❦

In the back, Elowyn and Tamak are rolling tea leaves together, shoulder to shoulder. They both wave at me as I come in and return to their work, unconcerned by anyone seeing their companionship.

They haven't magically moved any farther forward yet, but they've stabilized with each other again. I'm not sure of this because they talked to me about it explicitly, but because they came over to Deniel's and my home for dinner.

Elowyn has learned to speak up for herself, but she's still a girl of few words. After letting us all watch and interact with each other for a few hours, Elowyn directed her piercing gaze at me as if to say, "Well? What do you think?"

It was a challenge and question at once; a request for approval, and an outside opinion to check whether she is, in fact, okay.

As if I am such an expert on relationships. But I *do* know both of them, separately and together, extremely well.

I smiled, and inclined my head, and then deposited Talsion in a startled Tamak's lap as Elowyn laughed aloud.

Joining the delegation to Nakrab will give her a chance to choose what sides of her talents she wants to pursue—the shadows or the light. She may never decide to become a tea master formally, but that doesn't change the fact that the gift is there. She knows without my having to say anything that I trust her, and them, to sort themselves out, and I will support them always.

So today all we do is wave, and I leave them to their quiet conversation as I corner Lorwyn.

"So," I say.

"So?"

"I hear you've been busy."

Lorwyn snorts. "Yeah, you could say that. Ari and I have been talking for a while, since I got my head out of my butt and realized why Ostario was so bent on helping me."

Oddly, Ari is the one I heard this from first—I suspect because I'm the one who helped them know other pronouns were possible.

As an open and powerful witch, Lorwyn has the ability to magically alter physicality—like she did with my hair so many weeks ago. Now with Ostario's training and with greater control, that means she can alter more than that as well.

Ostario, alone and primarily a mage, could never become a resource for others besides himself who need their bodies changed.

But Lorwyn, as a powerful and trained witch, can. As a publicly known witch, no less—and she can become the start of *witches*, as a group, taking this on.

"We're starting with just a couple small things," Ari told me.

I nodded. "See how those fit and how comfortable you are with them first?"

"Yeah. Lorwyn can always do more later or change things back. So I don't have to make any permanent decisions right away. I... want more time to understand what my gender is, if that makes sense."

"Yes. And if your understanding changes, that's fine too."

But with Lorwyn now, I'm not here to talk about Ari's business; that's between them. "I'm glad you found something you actually want to do with your witchcraft that no one is forcing you into," I tell her.

"There you go, ruining a perfectly comfortable moment with earnestness," Lorwyn says.

"I'm building up your tolerance."

"That's better. But it... did occur to me that to do this for more than Ari, I probably need my own space."

My eyebrows lift. That I hadn't expected. "I admit I was planning on running an idea by you of using the tea shop as a front to train potential spies, but this is even better."

"You *what?*"

"You want to set up your own business? Your own shop?"

Lorwyn points a knife at me. "Don't think I'm going to forget about *that* comment. But, yeah. I was thinking maybe just like. 'Lorwyn's Witch Services' or something? I don't know. I don't want to just help people be comfortable in their bodies. I mean, eventually I assume I'd miss not having an excuse to set weird Cataclysm ingredients on fire—"

"That's perfect," I tell her. "Talmeri's will be your first customer, paying you for your blends. I'll make sure of it. But you'd better be planning on raising your prices."

"You think so? I mean, I know I'd have other costs, but—spirits, Miyara, the main reason I got you hired was so I *didn't* have to do all the business stuff. I *want* to do this, and I think I need to, but, *you* know me. You really think I can?"

I gesture around. "I assume you don't need me to tell you that plenty of people own businesses they need help to operate."

"I mean, point, but who would do that for me?"

It's amazing she's come as far as she has—to be able to allow herself to want something, to want *more* for herself, and to actually admit it out loud.

It will take longer before she's willing to believe people will actually believe she's worthwhile—both valuable in her own right and not someone to be shunned as a witch. That they will pay her for what she's worth, or want to work with her, and take her seriously—and, Lorwyn being Lorwyn, be willing and able to deal with her. Because she will always have a cavernous chip on her shoulder.

I jerk my head back towards Elowyn and Tamak. "Someday, either or both of those two, for one. But for now, you should hire Meristo. He's ready to be done here anyway."

Lorwyn blinks, like she's stunned by the thought. Meristo is an inveterate charmer, hiding a core decency and competence beneath—and an ability to handle Lorwyn at her worst.

She shakes her head. "That won't do at all. How could I hire someone who doesn't properly respect that I can burn him to a crisp?"

"You do seem to be accumulating those in your life," I say. "It must be dreadful for you."

Lorwyn grins, shark-like. "Speaking of, maybe Entero would be willing to threaten Meristo for me."

"It won't work. Meristo worked with Entero and knows him too well."

"Exactly. The threats where I don't actually risk making him feel bad are the best kind."

Wonders never cease.

"I can't wait to see Entero's face when I tell him I'm considering hiring Meristo," Lorwyn snickers.

"You two are better, then?"

"Oh. Yeah. I think we're going to move in together."

I comedically drag her over to a chair and command, "Tell me everything."

Lorwyn winces. "I guess you'll find out anyway. Basically Entero and I were fighting at the apartment—oh, did I tell you he decided he doesn't need to cultivate relationships with the police after all, and that what he needs is better resources? So that was good, but anyway, Sa Nikuran apparently had enough of our bullshit and burst out of Risteri's room—naked, in fact, so there's images that I can never unsee—and told us that if we were both so terrified of being a danger to others maybe we should just live with other dangerous people.

"And that... derailed the argument then, but then we both kept thinking about it, and then you kept sending people over to bunk with the Te Muraka for their own good and eventually our brains started working like functional adults'. So we're going to try living in the Te Muraka compound together and see how it goes."

They'll have both privacy and a community that actually supports them in their work. It's perfect. "And Risteri and Sa Nikuran?"

"Still splitting time between the compound and the apartment. But they're probably both going to move into the compound fulltime too and keep the apartment as a... private sanctuary for now, in case any of us need time, since, you know, none of us actually has any idea how to do serious relationships. Then later if we don't need it anymore Risteri was thinking it could be like a starter apartment for Te Muraka who want to move out of the compound. But only once we're all comfortable giving it up."

"I'm glad," I tell her from the bottom of my heart.

"I am too," Lorwyn admits, "though you're going to have to wait to grill me any further."

Entero chooses that moment to enter from the back door. "That sounds like my cue. Are you ready to go?"

"You're the worst," I tell him.

He shrugs. "There are only so many ways to practically protect someone like Lorwyn. I'll take what I can get."

That makes me laugh. "You two are perfect."

Slyly, Entero bows, and I laugh harder. He is who he is—and he is coming more into himself every day.

"See, you don't always have to do everything," Lorwyn tells me. "Sometimes someone else will yell at us in your stead."

I'm still laughing when they invite me to walk with them to the Te Muraka compound, where Sa Rangim has promised to show them some open spaces. I take one last glance around to confirm everyone is working in harmony and notice Lorwyn's tea pet that Deniel repaired so long ago at my request, gleaming down from above us. I smile, and we all move on together.

EPILOGUE: PART 3

WHEN WE ARRIVE, Sa Nikuran takes over touring Lorwyn and Entero through their options on Sa Rangim's behalf. "It's no trouble at all," she says, her smile sharp.

I laugh. "I suppose you are incentivized to make sure they're happy with their accommodations."

Sa Nikuran's eyes narrow. "I will not do badly by the best friend of the one I wish to be my mate."

Lorwyn says, "Miyara's not accusing you of dishonor or whatever—she thinks you want privacy for sex."

"Ah." Sa Nikuran nods. "That is also important to Risteri."

"Risteri," Entero puts in, "would also prefer her relationship not be discussed where every Te Muraka can hear. As you know well."

"Spoilsport," Lorwyn says.

"Miyara, we'll see you later," Entero says. "Shall we?"

I blink as they walk off, momentarily confused before my brain catches up.

Little by little, I've been losing my edge the last few days. It's as though my brain knows it desperately needs to rest but can't quite believe it's allowed yet, so it slowly decreases its capacity while I'm not paying attention.

Of course, Entero would have still noticed that although Sa Rangim promised to show them around, he isn't here and didn't have Sa Nikuran excuse his absence. Entero probably noticed where Sa Rangim is, too, but after wracking my brain for a moment I can't figure out where I missed it.

Entero was a spy for a long time. He can pace himself better than I can.

I sigh and go to ask the nearest Te Muraka where I can find Sa Rangim when the man in question finds me instead.

We exchange bows, and then Sa Rangim asks, "May I show you something?"

"Always."

The room he shows me is new: or rather, I have been in here when it was empty, but it is completely changed.

There are three low stone basins: one filled with water, another with soil, and the other with burning embers. Benches sit between. The arrangement is simple and beautiful.

Sa Rangim has made a shrine in his home.

Or—his people's home.

I blink rapidly past the sudden surge of emotion in my chest. It is one thing to invite another person into your home; it is another for them to actually feel at home there.

Whatever else he may intend with this place, I know Istalam, our spirits, and our service, have touched Sa Rangim, and he has embraced us all. As those of us who were here before make space for the Te Muraka in Istalam, he makes space for us with them, too.

When I look up at him, Sa Rangim is smiling. He squeezes one of my hands, just as Iryasa did. "A priestess will come to bless this place soon, but as the one who brought me into your world in the ways that matter, I wanted you to be the first to see it."

He releases me and goes inside, and I join him. We've shared time at shrines many times now, and we go through the motions of prayer in an almost practiced way. I linger over the warmth of the fire for a moment, wondering if I have gone through the mental motions without attending as well, before smiling.

I don't need to stay there anymore. Today I have everything I need.

Sa Rangim and I sit together on a bench. "You don't need a priestess, you know," I say. "The spirits are already here."

He glances at me. "You can feel them?"

I nod. "Since the Manifest." That's what everyone is calling the shield of manifested spirits from the confrontation with the Nakrabi delegation. We'll see if it sticks. "I still can't see them when Yorani plays with them, but I can... feel them, sometimes. Swirling. They're always here. But they're *particularly* here in this place."

Sa Rangim smiles. "I'm glad. I will have this place consecrated all the same, however. I wouldn't want them to think I take their presence for granted."

I finger my bracelets. "Glynis thinks the spirits in my bracelets are happy here and don't want to go back to Nakrab. But she said she can free them if they ever change their minds. I'm not sure how she'll know."

"But you know she will." He leans back. "Why aren't you a priestess, Miyara?"

"I didn't think of it fast enough," I say, and he chuckles. "But if I had, it would have put eventually put me into a complicated position with the crown in terms of who I serve and how. This way... in a way, I may be a priestess after all. Just a different kind."

"I agree."

That warms me. Spirits, I'm grateful for this man, his wisdom and understanding. Which reminds me— "I never thanked you for Thiano."

"There's no need. We have talked about leading before, and serving. I know what it is like to have a cause. I know what it is like to need forgiveness. I know what it is like to balance freedom and service and fail. Of course I wish he had made different choices. Now we will see what he makes of the opportunity to do so."

"He won't disappoint you."

"I don't expect him to."

I smile. "You're something of a priest yourself."

"High praise indeed, from you. Thank you." Sa Rangim glances at me sidelong. "And for your machinations on my behalf."

That makes me laugh. "I am glad beyond words that your relationship with Iryasa has worked out."

"Working," he corrects, "always. I'm glad as well. It is... more than I ever expected for myself. You remind people how to dream. I imagine that's why the spirits have always been happy to be with you."

"You are going to make me cry."

"Then cry," he says simply. "Be how you are and how you need. I and your sister and all of our people will make sure you are free to. This I swear."

Spirits. I swipe my hands over my eyes before I really do lose it.

"The world is going to change," Sa Rangim says reflectively. "I doubt it can ever be put back to how it was. Magic, like life, is all about change—I suspect that's why the backlash to Nakrab's current way of doing magic is so dramatic. It keeps magic in stasis."

"Not all magic will want to go back to how it was," I muse. "We'll have to address that. Do you think it will cause problems for the Te Muraka? With needing to eat magic?"

"No. I do worry, because at this point I am trained to. But I believe all will be well. Say rather, I believe it may be possible for all to be well, and with that in mind I will do everything in my considerable power to make it so."

I have seen only flashes of his true power to date, and those were impressive enough for this to be a great comfort.

"Every time I perform the tea ceremony," I say, "I shape magic into discrete spirits. They're not physical like Yorani, they don't interact with our physical world except with her and cats, but they... have a form. An individual one."

"You're gathering wild magic into a shape that allows the magic to disperse safely back into the world," Sa Rangim says. "The magic isn't gone or trapped, yet you channel it to freedom. It's remarkable to watch."

It's my turn to ask, "You can see them?"

"Not in the way you mean. It is a kind of sense. And it will change as your tea spirit does. You and she still have far to go together."

I raise my eyebrows. "Do you know something about what Yorani is capable of?"

"Let us say I don't believe in coincidences," he says with an arch smile, and I laugh. Spirits, it feels as though it's been so long since we met. "The world has experienced the greatest magical cataclysm in known history, the first tea spirit born for centuries, and you. Knowing what I do of at least the latter, I have my suspicions."

"Sa Rangim, please, we only just finished saving the world."

I thought he would smile, but instead it fades, leaving his gaze serious on mine. "I am quite aware, and I will not forget. Rest now. It will come to you in time."

Before I can say anything else, blue scales whiz past me into Sa Rangim's face. He does laugh then, effortlessly catching the tiny dragon chirping insistently at his face.

"Oh, to have your reflexes," I say mournfully.

He grins at me. "I am always happy to dragon-sit, as you call it. You'll simply have to visit."

Yorani freezes, as if this thought has arrested her. Did she think she would lose him, the man whose tea ceremony made her possible? She turns adorably imploring eyes at me before chirping and nuzzling my neck.

"Of course we'll visit," I say. "We do not forget our friends."

Sa Rangim smiles.

Yorani's nuzzling becomes insistent pecks. "What is this about, now?"

"I believe the little one thinks you have somewhere to be," Sa Rangim says, amused.

I pause, taking stock of how much time has passed today. Oh. "Thank you, Yorani. I remember. Will you be home later tonight?"

Looking out for me from afar, and she will know where I am. Connected but distinct.

She flaps off of me and shakes her head no, then lands on Sa Rangim's shoulder.

On my own then. My heartbeat accelerates as I stand.

Sa Rangim starts to bow, but on impulse I hug him and Yorani both instead. Sa Rangim freezes in surprise for a moment, and I hear the telltale rumbling sound Yorani makes when she burrows, as if she's demonstrating to him what to do.

Sa Rangim huffs a quick laugh. "Thank you, little one," he says, his voice a rumble too, as he returns the hug.

This time I know he means me.

Deniel is waiting for me at the entrance to a Gaellani courtyard, leaning casually against the wall. It's not one I've been to except to pass through—never the closest to any of the places I've lived or worked.

It is the closest to Deniel's family, though. It's where he grew up.

He eyes me speculatively. "You look different."

He doesn't mean my attire. I'm dressed in the same formalwear I always don, my hair its now-normal green.

Deniel looks just the same too—just as calm and sure as ever. He's even wearing the same clothes he wears to craft pottery, though this is a clean set. At first he thought he should dress up to go to council meetings, but he and Saiyana apparently decided it was better to force them to deal with Deniel as he is.

That's what we're doing here too, in a way.

"Is that your way of saying you don't know what I look like when I'm not tired?" I ask.

He smiles faintly. "No. Though given the conversations you planned to have today, I did expect some weariness. But you look... not at peace, exactly, but—"

"Clarity, I think. Just without the force of anger behind it for once. Are you ready?"

Deniel pushes off the wall. "Just about."

I know what he's going to do. My blood has been singing, my heartbeat a steady thrum since I saw him.

He closes the distance between us and takes me in his arms and kisses me.

When we finally break apart, we're both breathing hard.

"On second thought," Deniel murmurs, "maybe I'm not ready after all."

I know I'm blushing, but I am learning how to play this game. I lean in and say in his ear, "Get ready, because the next time I kiss you I want everyone to see."

Deniel's arms tighten around me, and when I pull back I see that I have, *finally*, managed to make this man blush the way he so easily does to me. I laugh and tug him into motion.

We enter the courtyard holding hands. More than one person has held my hand today, but everything is different with Deniel, like the warmth of his hand is a direct line to my heart.

People in the courtyard notice us. How could they not? At this point we're the best-known residents of the city, and today we are recognizably ourselves.

But no one says anything. No whispers or furtive glances start up. We order food, and sit at a stall, and everyone treats us as if there's nothing special about us.

Which isn't true. But I would like to think that they treat us as if we're no more special than them, which is.

Deniel has taken me to a dumpling stall—he's wanted me to try these but never learned how to make the dough. After a single bite, I withhold a groan of pleasure and decide I will.

"So what did Hanuva's apprentice want?" he asks me.

It *has* been a long day of conversations. I'd met this apprentice for the first time during the events surrounding the tournament and wasn't wholly surprised to be hearing from her again now. "A job. A couple of the other apprentices took over Hanuva's business and are managing, if with some difficulty, but this one felt too guilty to stay. She still wants to practice tea, though, and she thinks if I hire her it will help her friends there too, so she won't feel like she's abandoning them."

"Publicly demonstrating that you don't hold them responsible for Hanuva's actions," Deniel murmurs. "So?"

"I agree. Talmeri's not thrilled, since the tea boy tradition was her policy, but the shop clearly isn't what it once was and she knows it's time to embrace change."

"That doesn't sound like her."

I smile. "I didn't say she liked it or is willing to admit it yet, but she does know."

He laughs. "There we go."

"We'll need someone who knows their business quickly anyway, so Hanuva's apprentice is a good fit," I say. "It's about time for Meristo to move on, and Taseino will be close behind him."

"So that conversation went well too?"

I roll my eyes. "Turned into about four conversations, but yes."

"Of course it did." Deniel's voice is amused. He knew the plan going in, and he's also learning about how many conversations politics always takes.

"Also I think Sa Rangim expects Yorani to eat the Cataclysm."

That makes his eyebrows shoot up. He takes a bite, chews slowly on it and the thought, before nodding slowly. "Okay. That's interesting. Not soon, I assume, if Sa Rangim isn't urgently worried about it."

"You are a very difficult man to surprise," I tell him.

Deniel grins. "Not at all. You've just gotten me used to the sensation. Where is Yorani, anyway?"

"I think she arranged with Talsion to give us the house to ourselves tonight. She's with Sa Rangim."

Deniel pauses then, his gaze going intent.

He doesn't even have to say anything and I start blushing.

"Excuse me," a woman says.

We look up. It's no one I know, but Deniel does this time. She needs a favor.

This is starting to happen a lot to both of us, now. It happens a couple more times as we sit there, but each time we're able to redirect them.

We'll help them, of course. Just... not right this second.

This moment is ours.

"Look at you," Deniel teases, "enforcing boundaries like it's easy."

It isn't, which he knows. I'm sure I'll be learning this for a long time, and it will change.

But I'm learning.

"Look at us," I say. "Out in the open, as ourselves. No more hiding, no more making ourselves smaller, no more being limited by anyone else's view of us."

He takes my hands, as we sit in full view of our people, the bustle of life around us that somehow feels quiet. Like in this moment, there is a bubble just for us that we've made with our own focus.

"So?" he asks me. "We have time. Tonight. Tomorrow."

"Our whole future," I murmur.

He smiles that crooked smile I love so much. "What do you want to do with it?"

"Oh, I have some ideas."

His hands tighten on mine. "So do I. Do you want to go home and talk about them together?"

Together.

Home.

Everything I wanted and didn't know how to imagine or believe. My heart is going to explode out of my chest.

"I could not have dreamed you," I whisper.

Deniel leans forward until our foreheads touch. "You don't have to," he says softly. "I'm right here."

I make good on my promise and kiss him.

I think of all the other promises I want to make, and the future is just as dazzling in my imagination as in my reality. This moment, and all the others to come.

I can't wait.

Hand in hand, we go into our future.

Together.

THANK YOU

Thank you for reading!

I started posting Tea Princess Chronicles as a web serial in 2017, Kickstarted the whole series (and funded in an hour and a half!) to transform them into books in 2021, and now here we are. Whether you've been part of this journey for a while or are just joining in, thank you for being here.

If you enjoyed reading this book of the Tea Princess Chronicles, I hope you'll tell someone about it or leave a review!

For a FREE, newsletter-exclusive Tea Princess Chronicles short story, sign up for my newsletter at caseyblair.com! Subscribing will keep you in the loop on free fiction opportunities, sales, and new books.

Happy reading!
Casey

ABOUT THE AUTHOR

Casey Blair is a bestselling author of adventurous, feel-good fantasy novels with ambitious heroines and plenty of banter, including the completed cozy fantasy series Tea Princess Chronicles , the fantasy romance novella *The Sorceress Transcendent*, and the action anime-style novella *Consider the Dust*. Her own adventures have included teaching English in rural Japan, taking a train to Tibet, rappelling down waterfalls in Costa Rica, and practicing capoeira. She now lives in the Pacific Northwest and can be found dancing spontaneously, exploring forests around the world, or trapped under a cat.

For more information visit her website caseyblair.com or follow her on Instagram @CaseyLBlair.

ALSO BY

Tea Princess Chronicles

A Coup of Tea

Tea Set and Match

Royal Tea Service

Saiyana's Challenge: A Story of the Tea Princess Chronicles (novelette)

Tales from a Magical Tea Shop: Stories of the Tea Princess Chronicles

Stand-Alone

The Sorceress Transcendent

Consider the Dust